"I want you in the bedroom," he said quietly.

"I'm not ready yet," she replied without turning.

Quint crossed to her quickly, picked her up under one arm, and carried her from the chapel. He threw her onto the bed. She jumped up, so close to him her breasts rubbed tantalizingly against him.

He tilted her head back and sought her lips. She gave no response. Suddenly Quint gripped the high neck of her dress and ripped it down to her waist. She tried to run, but his big arms held her as he tore the fine lace of her flimsy brassiere. Her full, brown-tipped nipples swung invitingly as she struggled to free herself from those powerful hands.

She battered at his chest with her fists. "Bastard! Cabrón! Sonofabitch!" she screamed. . . .

BOLD LEGEND

★ GORDON D. SHIRREFFS ★

FAWCETT GOLD MEDAL • NEW YORK

ISBN 0-449-14488-7

Printed in the United States of America

First Fawcett Gold Medal Edition: September 1982

10 9 8 7 6 5 4 3 2 1

To Brian, who knows and loves that country.

ONE

JULY 1845. CANYON OF THE RIO CIMARRON.

The piercing call of the male canyon wren, with its seven loud notes descending the scale, sounded throughout Cimarron Canyon as the dusk wind soughed among the tall pines. A lone red-tailed hawk hung with outstretched wings on the wind. The wind was beginning to shift uncertainly before flowing down the canyon as it always did with the coming of darkness. It brought faint alien sound with it. The call of the wren stopped abruptly. The hawk tilted up on one wing and shot out of sight over the canyon rim. The distant mingled noises of a large *caballada* on the move—the rattle and clatter of hoofs on the rocky ground, crackling and scraping of brush, faint brayings and neighings, and the indistinguishable shoutings of men drifted up the canyon.

Quint Kershaw loped down a transverse trail on the canyon wall and moved swiftly down the talus slope as noiselessly as a hunting cougar. He was alone. Kit Carson was somewhere up canyon working his way down its side to meet up with Quint. The four other members of the tracking party, Luke Connors, Jesus Martinez and the two Delawares Black Moccasin and Joshua, were evidently still hunting for a place to bring the party's horses down into the canyon. A crooked grin fixed Quint's features. His hunch had been right—the horse thieves would turn west into Cimarron Canyon rather than continue on to the northeast and then up the Vermejo River Valley.

Quint was a panther of a man two inches over six feet tall, weighing 190 pounds. He was hawk-eyed and hawk-nosed. He wore a greasy black elkskin jacket, Cheyenne leggings, and Ute moccasins. Dark reddish hair showed beneath the wide brim of his shapeless wool hat; into its band of rattlesnake skin a gray eagle feather had been stuck for luck. His "good medicine" was a necklace of fearsome grizzly claws. The heavy rifle he carried was a splendid .53 caliber Hawken he proudly called "Auld

Clootie," broad Scots for "Old Devil." They were one and the same, man and rifle, with a legendary reputation for deadly marksmanship.

Besides the Hawken there were two other outstanding features about this Southwestern frontiersman, this rangy *Montero Americano*, that caught attention—his eyes and the terrible cicatrix on his left cheek marking what had once been a bone-deep furrow from the corner of his eye to the corner of his mouth. The whitish scar stood out against the saddle leather hue of his weathered skin drawing skin and muscle into a slightly sardonic look, which was not truly averse to his nature. Nothing in Quint's lifetime could ever erase or darken that scar, trademark of a rending paw swipe from a giant grizzly whose claws now hung about his neck. Quint's size and powerful physique first caught the eye, and the facial scar and magnificent Hawken added to his uniqueness, but it was his eyes which caught and held attention above all else. They were gray, clear and cold like rime ice feathering the edges of a swift running mountain stream after the first heavy frost of winter. Many enemies had seen the cold killing look in those eyes; few people had come to know the great warmth and deep humanity underlying them.

A feuding raucous jay and scolding squirrel did not hear the swift passage of the tall man-creature moving down a slope. Then suddenly they saw him, stilled themselves and vanished from his sight. Shadows began to mantle the ground and ink in the hollows on the canyon wall. There was no trace of Kit.

Quint moved ahead of the approaching *caballada*. The horse thieves had struck along the Mora and Rayado killing five herders and taking several hundred horses and California mules. They had cleaned out the ranch owned in partnership by Kit Carson and Dick Owens. They had bypassed Quint's Rio Brioso ranch and supposedly headed for the Vermejo Valley on their way home to Ute country. This is, *if* they were Moache Utes. Quint was not so sure. He had met a dogged Kit riding alone after the raiders. Somewhere miles behind him were the *vaqueros* of the Mora and Rayado. Quint had joined him with his four *compañeros* and ten horses for swifter pursuit. They had cut across country to get ahead

★ 2 ★

of the thieves. Quint's hunch was a long shot. None of the others had much faith in it, but they knew their chances of catching the raiders before they reached the Vermejo were a lot less reasonable than the slim possibility that they were headed for Cimarron Canyon.

Where were his *compañeros? Qué mala suerte!* What bad luck! Now that Quint had been proven right, he seemed to be the only one available to stop the thieves. The *caballada* was nearing him. Quint took cover on a talus slope above an open area beyond which was the rushing stream. On the far side of the stream were sheer eight hundred feet high columnar formations of yellowish rock turned golden from the dying sunlight.

The lead animals of the *caballada* rounded a curve in the canyon. Foam flecked back from their mouths, their eyes were staring from fatigue, and sweat had cut rivulets through their dusty sides and flanks. They had been driven hard. The herd headed for the stream but was driven back by shouting, cursing horsemen. One of the men shouted in Spanish, "We'll hold them here for a few hours at least! We'll water them when they cool off! There will be a moon later! We can drive them up canyon by its light!"

Quint studied them through his small German telescope, a powerful instrument made by Vollmer of Jena. There were fifteen horsemen, a murderous looking lot of Indians, breeds, and Mexicans. They seemed confident. Pursuit had evidently been outdistanced. The trail to the northwest was wide open.

Fires sprang up in the dusk casting shadows against the canyon wall, posturing and writhing, changing the figures of the men into grotesque, towering giants. One big man stood beside a fire shouting orders. The sharp powerful lens picked out his features. He took off his hat to fan a fire, revealing long hair the color of dirty sand. Quint drew in a sharp breath. *Comanchero!* Seven years ago this same man, Jake Stow, had been one of four thieving animals in human form Quint had sworn to track down and kill. He had accounted for two of them, but six years had passed since he had killed the second of the pair. It would be easy this time, a two-hundred-yard downslope shot at a big man clearly silhouetted by the fire. Slowly Quint shook his head. He wanted each of them to *know* who killed them. Besides, his premier mission was to recapture the stolen herd. He'd make it a certainty that he got Jake Stow in the process.

Quint vanished into the darkness. He'd need Kit's help. An owl hooted twice. Quint moved closer to the sound. He heard it again and echoed the hooting. There was a pause and Kit repeated the cry. Quint answered it once.

Faint moonlight had penetrated the canyon. A soft whistle alerted Quint. He looked across the stream to where a short broad-shouldered man stood close to a pine with a Paterson Colt .44 caliber revolving rifle in his hands.

Quint waded across the shallow stream. "Have ye seen the others, Kit?" he whispered.

Kit shook his head. "They're likely still workin' along the rim looking for a place to bring the horses down."

"Our friends up canyon are resting the herd while waiting for moonrise. Then they'll move on and we'll never be able to catch up with them again."

"Who are they? Jicarillas? Moaches?"

Quint shook his head. "Cochetopas."

"Chico Vasquez' bunch? *This* far south?"

Quint nodded. He knew them well—a murderous, thieving bunch of mixed-blood renegades; a pack of human wolves: Utes, Jicarillas, Navajos, Comancheros, and a few bad whites. "I saw Jake Stow," he said quietly.

"That devil? What about his partner Kiowa?"

Quint shook his head. "He might be there. I didn't see him. If he's there, I'll find him, Kit."

"You've worked things out well so far, Big Red. What's our next move?"

"Get in position up canyon before full moonrise. Move in on them before they get a chance to leave."

Kit studied Quint. "You feelin' all right?" he asked dryly.

"Why?"

Kit rolled his eyes upwards. "Two men afoot moving in on at least fifteen Cochetopas and Comancheros."

Quint grinned. "Losing your nerve, Kit?"

"No, but I ain't losin' my good sense either."

Quint tapped Kit's rifle. "Ye've got eight rounds in this cannon. I've got two Paterson Colt revolving pistols

★ 4 ★

and you've got one. That's fifteen more rounds. I've got another in my Hawken. Twenty-four rounds all told. Fifteen horse thieves. That leaves nine shots in reserve."

"Providin' we don't miss."

Quint raised his eyebrows. "Ye surprise me, Christopher. Our hearts are big, our medicine is good, and we're both center shots."

"Got it all figgered out, ain't yuh?"

They grinned at each other.

"One of us better go look for your *compañeros*, Big Red," Kit suggested. "How about you?"

Quint shook his head. "Not as long as Jake Stow and maybe Kiowa are with those thieves."

Kit vanished into the underbrush. "*Vaya*," he called back softly.

Quint returned within a hundred yards of the thieves. Hoofs rattled on rock. A horseman rode into the camp from up canyon.

"Is the way clear, Kiowa?" Jake called out.

Kiowa dismounted and relieved himself against a tree while talking back over his shoulder. "I seen a couple of greaser sheepherders. I took no chances they might talk, so now they won't be able to talk to anybody." He grinned loosely.

"You figure we should push on?"

Kiowa nodded as he turned. "Someone might have heard me shooting."

The telescope lens picked out the mixed breed's features. It was the sort of face one might see in a nightmare. The skin was dark and deeply pocked, a "rough-face," with flattened nostrils and thick negroid lips. The right eye was a pale, cold blue. The left eye was askew and sightless, milky blue in hue. Both eyes were a startling eerie contrast to the dark face. Quint had destroyed the sight in the left eye one dawn in Cañon Chacuaco.

"Douse those fires!" Jake shouted.

Clouds of white smoke rose from the quenched fires. Horsemen began to round up the herd. Their shouts and the noise of the horses and mules echoed through the canyon.

There was no time for Quint to wait for his partners. He ran noiselessly through the timber to get into position up the canyon. He'd have to make a lone stand, for a time at least. He found a crescent-shaped rock formation on the talus slope that gave him a clear view of the open canyon floor. There was no way the renegades could work around behind him providing he wasn't seriously wounded. He touched his bear claw necklace for luck. He drew both Colts and placed them on the flat rock in front of him.

A horseman spurred up the canyon, a scout feeling the way for the herd. Quint let him pass.

They moved the herd out, closing up behind them. The canyon echoed with the rattling of hundreds of hoofs on the hard ground. The moon was higher, illuminating Quint's field of fire. The first throaty roar of the Hawken was lost in the din. A man flung up his arms and fell from the saddle. The horse ran on dragging the body by a foot caught in a stirrup. The second shot picked off a lead horseman. The third dropped a horse, sending its rider clear over his head.

Jake Stow spotted the flash of the rifle through the rising dust and saw the puff of powdersmoke. He pointed his rifle toward Quint and shouted for some of his men to follow him. Three of them rode after him. They urged their mounts up the sliding talus shooting as they came. There was no time to reload the Hawken. Quint rested his forearms on the flat rock and fired his Colts alternately from each hand. Jake was the lone survivor by Quint's choice. He turned his chestnut and jumped it over one of the dead men. Both Colts cracked. The chestnut was dead before it hit the ground. Jake was dropped with a foot tangled in a stirrup. He struggled to free himself while casting frightened looks up the slope. He hadn't even seen the marksman, just the flaming weapons.

The herd stampeded. The surviving thieves turned their mounts and fled down canyon to get away from the sudden death waiting for them on the slope. The herd vanished up canyon.

Quint reloaded his Hawken and jumped up on the rock searching for Kiowa. He was not to be seen.

Jake freed himself at last. He slowly drew his pistol, concealing it behind the horse.

Quint turned and looked at Jake. "Throw the pistol up the slope, Jake Stow!" he called.

Jake stared. Someplace, sometime, he had known this tall, deadly man.

"Do you want to die now?" Quint asked coldly.

"I'll not die here like a dog in his own blood, you murdering bastard!" Jake shouted.

Quint came slowly downslope. "Drop the pistol. Drop it and run. You're good at running. I'll no shoot ye in the back. I'll give ye a fighting chance which is more than you ever allowed any of your victims."

It was the faint Scots burr that finally identified Quint. "I'll not run from you, Kershaw," Jake said slowly.

"Would ye rather die where ye stand? Come! Throw down the pistol! I'll give ye a count of ten to get out of sight, then I'm coming after ye, Stow! One! Two! Three!"

Jake hesitated.

Quint counted on inexorably. "Four! Five! Run, ye murdering dog! Six!" He raised and sighted his rifle.

Jake's nerve broke. He dropped the pistol.

"Seven!" Quint barked.

Jake whirled and plunged downslope, slipping, sliding, steadying himself with his hands.

"Eight!"

Jake reached the bottom of the slope and sprinted toward the stream.

"Nine!"

Jake ran into the knee-deep water and splashed toward the far bank. He scrambled out and looked back over his shoulder. His face was taut and white, mouth agape and eyes staring fearfully.

Quint raised and sighted the Hawken. *"Ten!"* he shouted.

Jake leaped into the brush, arms and legs outspread like a great, ungainly frog. Quint's jeering laughter echoed from the towering canyon walls. He loped down the slope and across the clearing, then waded the stream and went to ground in the shadows of the timber.

It was more instinct than sensory perception that led Quint toward a pine-clad slope. He paused at the bottom of the sheer columnar rock formations. A gunbelt with empty holster and knife sheath fell at his feet. He looked up. There was an almost imperceptible movement in a cleft high above him. Then a pair of spurred boots fell through the upper branches of a tree and thudded to the ground.

Gunfire broke out down the canyon. The surviving thieves had likely run into an ambush by Quint's companions.

Quint leaned his rifle against a tree and placed his Colts on the ground. He turned his belted sheath knife around to the small of his back and began to work his way up the canyon wall, digging fingers and toes into cracks and crevices, or inching his way up faults. He was fifty feet from the rim when a rock fell from above, struck a projection, and arched outward just over his head.

A rifle flatted off from the canyon floor. Jake Stow cursed as he ducked back from the rim.

Quint worked his way into a rock chimney and looked down. Five men stood by their horses looking up at him. One of them held a smoking rifle. "Don't kill the sonofabitch!" Quint yelled. "Don't stand there! Go after the herd!"

"Don't worry, Big Red!" Luke called out. "I'll just keep him back from the rim until yuh get up there! After that he's all yours!"

Quint slowly ascended the chimney, bracing his legs on one side, pushing his back against the other. Sweat streamed down his face. At last he hooked a bleeding hand over the rim. A socked foot came down hard on it. He almost released his hold. Luke fired. Jake jumped back. Quint pulled himself over the rim and rolled up onto his feet drawing his knife as he did so. He stood on a wide semicircular rock shelf completely surrounded by sheer rock walls rising seventy feet to the true rim. Quint grinned. There was no escape for the Comanchero.

"One of us will not leave here alive," Quint said with deceptive softness of tone.

"You'll kill because of the packs of beaver plews my partners and I stole from you seven years ago? I'll pay you back! Double!" Jake cried.

Quint shook his head. "It's not because of the plews. It will be because of what ye did to the woman."

"A Shoshoni squaw? Is she worth killing for? We didn't kill her."

"You might as well have. Ye destroyed her life as it was."

"You've already killed two of my partners. Isn't that enough for the debt?"

"I want all four of ye, Comanchero."

"And now you think it's my turn?"

Quint smiled like a hunting wolf. "You're very bright."

"I've only a knife to defend myself."

"That makes us even."

Jake studied Quint. "By God," he said quietly. "I believe you mean it."

"I said I'd give ye a fighting chance."

Soft moonlight shone on the fine steel of the knife blades. They circled slowly, knives outthrust with blades protruding from between thumb and forefinger in duelist style. They closed with grunting cries. Blades flicked out, clicked and ground together and were withdrawn. They whirled, circling all the time between the sheer rock wall and the yawning chasm, a natural arena from which only one of them might leave alive.

They closed chest to chest with blades crossed and grinding together as they rose, muscles quivering and straining. Jake was a powerful man and skilled with the knife, but he had met his equal. They threw each other back. Jake charged, thrusting for Quint's groin. Quint lowered his knife to parry. Jake slashed the edge of his left hand across Quint's eyes as he met the parry, locked blades, and twisted hard as Quint staggered back half-blinded by tears. His knife was torn from his hand and clattered on the ground.

Jake shouted in victory. He closed with knife outthrust. A heel hit him in the privates. He bent forward in agony. Locked hands smashed down on the nape of his neck. He went down striking his face on the rock. Blood rushed from his forehead, nose, chin, and crushed lips. Quint stamped a foot down on Jake's right wrist. Jake released his knife. Quint kicked it out over the rim and sprang back dashing the tears from his eyes.

Jake lay still, waiting for the crush of a rock against his skull, an arm-breaking hammerlock or a merciless pounding from hard heels. Nothing happened. He got slowly to his feet and wiped the blood from his eyes. He looked at Quint's knife lying to one side.

"Try for it," Quint suggested.

Jake tried. They met with a rush in the center of the arena. Jake drove in a powerful right jab and followed through with a left cross. Quint blocked the jab, rolled away from the cross to take it on his shoulder, then smashed a right into Jake's belly following it with a stinging left uppercut as Jake bent over involuntarily. Jake staggered back fighting for balance. He struck the rock wall with his back and fell sideways. His right hand closed on a rock chunk. He leaped to his feet and hurled the rock with all his strength. Quint raised his left arm to take the numbing blow. Jake charged as Quint backed away. The blood had run down from Jake's forehead into his eyes. All he could see was the amorphous, shadowlike shape of his opponent and not the chasm just beyond.

Quint poised on the balls of his feet timing Jake's charge to a fraction of a second. He thrust out his left leg. Jake fell over it and shot out over the brink. His hoarse scream echoed through the canyon and then was cut short as he hit the bottom.

It became very quiet, the only sound the soughing of the night wind through the towering pines.

Quint worked his way slowly down the cliff face. Jake lay sprawled on his back in the stream, his pale blood-streaked face ghostlike under the swift flowing water. "Three down, one to go," Quint murmured to himself. Mountain Woman's face, dimly seen as though veiled, drifted through his memory. He had not thought of her in a long time.

Kit and Quint's *compañeros* watched Quint as he shifted his saddle to a blocky dun from Kit's Rayado stock.

"Where to, Big Red?" Luke asked casually.

"Kiowa was here," Quint said shortly.

"Yuh figger he's still around waitin' for you to kill him?"

Quint tightened the girth. He thrust his Hawken into its saddle sheath. He turned the cylinders of his revolvers, checking the loads and percussion caps.

Moccasin shook his head. "He'll be miles from here by now, Big Red."

Joshua raised his head and pointed down canyon. "Horseman coming," he warned.

They scattered into cover, all but Quint, who remained where he was, looking hopefully toward the sound of approaching hoofs.

"Yuh make a nice target out there, old hoss," Kit said.

Luke nodded. "Might be Kiowa. If so, he'll come shootin'."

Quint smiled faintly. "I hope to God he does."

The hoofbeats stopped. "*Hola* the camp!" a man called from the shadows.

Kit came out into the open. "It's Blas Galeras of the Mora."

The big Mora man led his blown horse forward. He grinned widely. "You got back the horses, I see. Good! But where are the thieves?" He looked about with a comical expression on his face.

Luke grinned. "Most of them won't come back, Blas."

Kit nodded. "If any of them did make it out of the canyon, they can't be caught by now."

"I can try," Quint said.

Luke shook his head. "Your time will come. Yuh got Stow. Let that satisfy yuh, at least for the time being. Besides, we got to get back to Rio Brioso."

Luke was right. Quint nodded. "My time *will* come."

"I'll go back and bring up my *vaqueros*," Blas said. "Kit, Dick Owens followed us partway from Rayado trying to catch up with you. His horse got blown ten miles back. He gave me a message for you. Lieutenant Fremont is at Bent's Fort getting ready for his third exploring expedition. Fremont sent an express messenger to Rayado asking you and Dick to join him."

Kit grinned widely. "By God! I been expectin' just that!"

"What about your wife in Taos and your ranch?" Quint asked.

Kit shrugged. "Josefa can stay with her sister in Taos. Blas, did Dick say he'd go along with Fremont?"

Blas nodded. "He did."

Kit headed for his horse. "Then the ranch and stock are up for sale!"

"Dick also said Fremont can use as many good moun-

tain men as he can get," Blas added. "He said Lucien
Maxwell has already signed up."

Kit turned. "Well, *compañeros?* Here's your chance!
We'll be seein' the Sierra Nevadas and likely Califorty!
The Great Salt Water! Aye. . . ." There was a nostalgic
quality to his tone. "*Califorty!* That's the ticket! You've
not lived until you've seen that land of sunshine and
señoritas."

"Quint?" Moccasin asked.

Quint shook his head. "It's not for me. But I'll not try
to hold ye back if ye want to go, Moc. That goes for
Luke and Joshua too."

Joshua grinned. "We'll come back next spring most
likely, in time for the buffalo hunt."

Quint looked at Luke. "I've no hold on ye, Luke."

Luke hesitated. *Damn!* How he wanted to go! But not
without Quint. "I'll stay, Big Red," he said quietly.

Kit leaned from the saddle and gripped Quint's hand.
He touched his horse with his heels and rode off followed
by the Delawares and Blas.

Luke shrugged. "Maybe next time, eh, Big Red?"

Quint nodded. "Aye, next time, Wandering Wolf."

Both of them knew there might never be a next time.

★ TWO ★

RIO BRIOSO.

During the seven years Quint had been *hacendado* of
Rio Brioso, had married and acquired three children, the
occasions when he might get away from his duties to his
family and the sprawling land grant had become few and
far between. There had been no need for him personally
to pursue the horse thieves. The thieves had not dared
raid Rio Brioso. They knew Quint of old. Even the vaunted Comanches left him alone. Quint could have sent some
of his men to aid Kit and nothing would have been
thought of it. But when the opportunity had suddenly
come to get away, he had grasped it instantly. Certainly
it could not bring back the old carefree trapping days.

They were gone forever. But, for a short time a man could *live* again.

Rio Brioso was the most remote defensive bastion on the northeastern frontier of the Province of New Mexico. The province extended for hundreds of miles east and north, so far indeed that not even the New Mexicans themselves knew its limits. The outer settlements had become a scant weak fringe on the edge of hostile Indian country. The New Mexicans had never been wholly successful in holding back the tribes who came and went as they pleased raiding for horses and mules, younger women and children. The Rio Brioso had once been part of the vast de Vasquez grant. Twice in thirty-five years a settlement established along the verdant Rio Brioso had been destroyed by Kotsoteka Comanches from the Canadian River country. The inhabitants had been massacred or taken into slavery, the settlement destroyed, and the livestock driven off. The de Vasquez family had been unequal to the struggle for survival.

In 1838 a new firm hand had taken control of the Rio Brioso: Quintin Kershaw, trapper and Indian fighter, known to mountain men as Big Red, respectfully by the New Mexicans as Don Quintin, more familiarly as Don Grande Rubio, "the Big Redhead." He was considered to be a fortunate man, this tall, rangy, rawhide-tough, Scots-born, Canadian-bred mountain man. Had he not come penniless to New Mexico, his only assets his determination, raw courage, and famed Hawken rifle? Had he not wooed and won Guadalupe de Vasquez, heiress to the fabulous and legendary Taos *hacienda* of El Cerrillo de Vasquez? He had become a quarter partner in the vast grant once owned by the de Vasquez family. His partners were His Excellency Don Manuel Armijo, governor of New Mexico; Gertrudis "La Tules" Barcelo, the notorious monte dealer of Santa Fe and mistress to the governor; and last but not least Doctor Tomas Byrne, Irish-born surgeon and trader of Santa Fe. Quint had taken over as managing partner, or *hacendado*, of Rio Brioso. That had been a good business decision, for he had done exceeding well.

Quint weeded out the weak, shiftless troublemakers and patently unfit colonists. Those remaining were soldier-settlers and their women. A tough, hardy survivor breed able to defend the settlement, mill their own grain, weave their own cloth, and make tools, cooking utensils, household goods, and furnishings. Such were the frontier people of Mora, Cundìyo, Cordova, Truchas, Trampas, Chamisal, Penasco, and Rio Brioso. The most remote and exposed of these was Rio Brioso. More than anything the people of the frontier needed capable leaders; in this respect Rio Brioso was most fortunate of all in having as its *patron* the legendary Don Grande Rubio.

To the north of the Rio Brioso country were the mountain haunts of the Jicarilla Apaches, Moache Utes, and renegade so-called Cochetopa Utes. To the east on the vast plains were the Faroan, or Plains Apaches called *Apaches Vaqueros* by the early Spaniards. There too were the fierce and predatory Kotsoteka or Buffalo Eater Comanches, the powerful "Lords of the Plains." New Mexicans who traded with the Comanches in slaves, buffalo hides, and robes were called Comancheros. Some of them were hated and feared by the New Mexicans.

The Rio Brioso was a good place; there was no finer land in northeastern New Mexico. The majestic Sangre de Cristo Mountains formed a gigantic backdrop to the west. Their canyon-riven flanks were shaggy with dense forests of blue spruce, yellow pine, fir, and aspen, with thickets of oak brush on the lower elevations. Sometimes, when the weather was mild and the trees and grass sunlit, one might see mountain thunderstorms raging furiously in the distance, and often while the snow beat down on the lower slopes, bright sunlight gilded the towering peaks. Rugged foothills were flung out from the mountain bases like the bony fingers of a gigantic skeletal hand or the supporting groins of a Gothic cathedral.

The Rio Brioso, the "Lively River," rushed limpid from a yawning gorge foaming and tumbling over its rocky channel, running clear, young, and free from the drag of silt. Excellent bottomland afforded fine crops. A thousand *churro* sheep grazed on the slopes. Cattle dotted the open range for miles. In the spring they were rounded up and driven up the mountain to summer grazing. No man in New Mexico had a better knowledge of horses and mules than Santiago Zaldivar, the *viejo* of Rio Brioso. In time the reputation of the Rio Brioso for mules and horses grew to be unequaled. Santiago had saved from extinction a mouse-colored breed of fuzzy, long-eared burros. These were of ancient Spanish origin, their ancestors brought to Spain from Palestine by the Moors centuries past. Their backs were strangely marked along the spine with the sign of the Holy Cross. Such burros had been bred at El Cerrillo for one hundred fifty years until hard times had overcome the estate and the rare breed had almost died out. By diligent search Santiago had finally located a pair on the Mora and brought them in triumph to Rio Brioso. It was almost like a miracle. Legend had it that if the breed was allowed to die out at El Cerrillo, so too would the fortunes of the family of de Vasquez. It might have come true, but for Quint Kershaw.

The mountains were alive with mule deer, white-tailed and black-tailed deer, huge antlered elk, turkeys, and black bear. Topmost on the heights were mountain sheep with huge curling horns. Eastward on the plains of the Canadian River and beyond, pronghorn antelope abounded. Numberless buffalo ranged for hundreds of square miles. The vast "Texas Herd" was beyond the Llano Estacado, the "Staked Plains." Its domain extended from near the Clear Fork of the Brazos west to the Upper Pecos and from south of the Arkansas four hundred miles to Canyon Diablo. Twice yearly the *ciboleros*, the buffalo hunters of Rio Brioso and the Mora, hunted the buffalo—in September when their meat was fat and the hair thick and fresh for robes, and in April when the meat was good only for jerking and the skin for hides. Buffalo hunting was a dangerous business but a necessary part of the local economy.

The village of Rio Brioso was situated on the north bank of the river using parts of the foundations of the original and second settlements but extending about twice as far to the north. The adobe and stone buildings formed a hollow rectangle. They were joined one to another by contiguous walls whose outer sides were windowless but pierced with loopholes. The roofs were parapeted to protect riflemen in case of attack. Two huge, ponderous gates, one on the east side and the other on the west, afforded entry into the plaza. They were closed and barred at dusk, not to be opened until dawn. The only means of entry into the plaza when the gates were closed was by small wicket doors cut into the thick timber of the gates. A small chapel stood within the plaza for the use of visiting priests. Defensive towers guarded the northeast and southwest corners, extending beyond the walls to afford enfilading fire along the two adjacent walls.

The community corral lay just west of the village. Its high walls were planted with spiked cactus to repel thieves. It had one gate. A sentry stood guard each night in a small tower over the gateway. Beyond the corral was a water-powered sawmill. It was the only one in New Mexico. Kentucky-bred Luke Connors had once helped his father and grandfather construct a similar mill on Connors Fork of the Licking River. The parts had come from Saint Louis. The river had been diverted into a ditch, then a millpond, and finally flumed to a twenty-foot waterwheel to power the saw. There was plenty of fine timber to feed the saw; its locust whirring had become a familiar sound along the Rio Brioso. People came from miles around to see the *yanqui* wonder and buy or trade for the precious sawn lumber.

The Rio Brioso was a good place, but it had somehow failed Quint. The thought haunted his mind. Guadalupe, or "Lupita," as he preferred to call her, had spent little time there, particularly after the birth of the twins Francisco and Rafaela six years ago. She preferred El Cerrillo, where she had been born and raised like so many generations of de Vasquezes. It was settled, luxurious—at least for New Mexico—and above all civilized. With the arrival of the twins her visits to Rio Brioso had become less frequent and much shorter. She absolutely refused to spend a winter there. Her last visit had been for a few weeks in April before Quint left on the spring buffalo hunt. (Perhaps, if he had not gone, she might have stayed on.) Furthermore, she saw no reason why he should spend so much of his time there instead of being with her and the children. In her opinion, that of a *rico*, a *gente fina*, the work he felt compelled to do could easily be taken over by others. That included the twice yearly buffalo hunts. They had become the particular bane of her existence. The trips were dangerous; this she well knew from her own single experience seven years ago. And they took Quint away for weeks. But worst of all, she considered the buffalo hunt degrading work for a man of his position.

It was Luke Connors who clarified the principal reason Guadalupe stayed away from Rio Brioso. Well oiled by a half pint of Taos Lightnin', he had pointed out, "She's jealous of the drawin' power of the wilderness to yuh, Big Red. It's somethin' she and the kids can't compete with. When yuh were first married it didn't matter much. She wanted to please yuh so she accepted the rivalry of the wilderness. But in time it became worse than the threat of another woman. *That,* she could handle. New Mexican wimmen are expert in such things. But she knows she's fightin' a losin' battle unless she can get yuh back at El Cerrillo. Right now she's doin' something wimmen in her position do—rumor has it she's turnin' more and more to her religion for comfort. So yuh better get her and the kids here at Rio Brioso or yuh might lose her and the twins. Yuh won't lose Davie but then she ain't his real mother. He ain't got a drop of greaser blood in him." He rolled his eyes upwards. "Half Scots and half Shoshoni. My God! What a combination!"

"So, what's your sage advice, Wandering Wolf?"

Luke was silent for a moment. He knew what he was about to say would in time work against his great friendship and deep love for Quint. He could keep his mouth shut and perhaps things would go on as they were now, but in honesty, he could not do such a thing. "Build her that fancy *plazuela* here at Rio Brioso. The one yuh talk about now and again. That *might* hold her with yuh, Quint."

Quint studied Luke. He knew what it might mean in time to him. He nodded. "You're right," he agreed quietly. They finished the bottle together.

★ THREE ★

Santiago Zaldivar, *segundo* and *viejo,* or "Old One," of Rio Brioso, was usually consulted first on matters of importance. Quint had been accepted by the people, but still he was not of the same blood. In such an isolated settlement custom ruled with blinding force and innovation was suspect. The old ways had the deepest of Spanish roots. Therefore, when Quint decided to build the new *plazuela* for Lupita and the children before he left for Taos, he turned to Santiago for advice. Perhaps such a new home as Quint had envisioned for Lupita might lure her back to Rio Brioso and hold her there.

"There is only one place such a *plazuela* as you described to me should be built, Don Quintin, as you well know," the old man said thoughtfully.

The site was a low, flat-topped hill standing like a miniature mesa on the gently sloping ground half a mile south of the river and roughly in a line north-south with the settlement on the other side of the river. It was a perfect viewing site. To the west rose the majestic Sangre de Cristos. To the north the upslopes of the river valley, and beyond them more of the Sangre de Cristos. To the south were low, rolling foothills, backdropped by the hazy Turkey Mountains. Quint planned to have the house facing east, his favorite view, a magnificent panorama of vast limitless plains stretching toward the hazy infinity of the Canadian River Valley. The faint trace of the Santa Fe Trail could be seen coming from the north and Raton Pass, while to the east-northeast was the Cimarron Cut-Off.

Quint planned to leave for Taos within a matter of weeks. He was willing to try Lupita's way of life there for a time at least. He knew he could never remain there long despite the powerful hold she and the children had on him. El Cerrillo was truly representative of the old, static New Mexican way of life. That life was dying. It would soon be extinct what with the overpowering influx and influence of American merchants and traders in the province. There would be more to come; a flood of vital new blood pumped into the old Spanish veins. He knew if he returned to El Cerrillo to live the way of life to which Lupita was desperately clinging, he would become an anachronism among the Americans now living, doing business, and working in Taos and Santa Fe. He had married a de Vasquez, but he was still his own man. His place was truly on the Rio Brioso, and when that place too became static, as it surely would, he'd need a new frontier to conquer. Before that time came, he wanted to bring his family to Rio Brioso. Having a great house was not a matter of much concern to him. He had never been one for ostentation or the servitude of others, something to which Lupita had been born and bred. She considered it her right and due beyond question and never could understand why Quint didn't feel the same way. He had never been exposed to that sort of life, therefore he had not missed it. The *plazuela* he now planned would be an experimental compromise to win Lupita away from El Cerrillo and perhaps her newfound religious devotions. God willing, it might work.

Santiago walked about the proposed *plazuela* site. He pointed out low, badly eroded adobe ridges. "There, Don Quintin," he said almost reverently, "the remains of the original walls raised here thirty-five years ago by the orders of Don Sebastian himself, God rest his tough old soul. The footings are of rocks set three feet deep in loose stones and mortared together. The walls were twelve feet high and three feet thick. The *hacienda* had been but partly roofed. . . ." His hoarse voice died away. He shook his head. "Ah, but you know the story, Don Quintin and Senor Luke. It is legend."

Don Sebastian, Lupita's grandfather, had established the first settlement on the Rio Brioso. It was succeeding until one chill, gray dawn the Kotsoteka Comanches struck. Don Sebastian had been severely wounded. Santiago had saved his *patron*'s life at the risk of his own, sustaining severe wounds himself. Rio Brioso had been destroyed. All adult males except Don Sebastian and Santiago had been slain. Older women and grown boys had been slaughtered. Young women and children had been taken captive. Don Sebastian died, for he had no further wish to live. Only the land eternal remained of Rio Brioso.

Santiago's thoughts were far away. "Don Sebastian's son Don Francisco rebuilt the village and the *hacienda* twenty years ago. Most of the able-bodied men left for the early summer buffalo hunt. I was with them. When we returned we found the *hacienda* and village burned to the ground. Comanches had raided here and on the Mora. Don Francisco and a few people survived. He returned to El Cerrillo with a bullet in his leg and a permanent limp: He was never the same. Don Quintin, it is bad luck to build here again."

Quint shrugged. "You said yourself it is the only place."

"It may be more than just bad luck. Perhaps it is the will of God." Santiago quickly crossed himself.

Quint ignored the old man. "Build it the old, traditional way but with a few changes I'll tell you about. I want only the best. I want a fine place to shelter my family and me as well as future generations of Kershaws."

Santiago slanted his eyes sideways to look at Quint. "Like El Cerrillo, *patron?*" There was no guile apparent on his wrinkled features. He knew of the silent struggle going on between Lupita and Quint; two strong-willed, determined people who knew *their* way, and only *their* way was right.

"Not exactly, *viejo*," Quint replied. "Who can match that jewel of the mountains?" The truth was he did not want a duplicate or even an imitation of that place of legend and fixed tradition. That was the place of the de Vasquezes and always would be. His place was to be the place of Kershaw and that alone.

Quint had drawn up a plan of the proposed *plazuela* during the snowbound winter. It was to be a smaller version of Bent's famed fort on the Arkansas, eighty yards square with a large inner quadrangle or courtyard seventy-five yards square. Three sides would have twelve-foot walls. The rooms would be single-storied. The west side would have two stories. The northeast and southwest corners were to have two-storied towers jutting out from the walls in order that cannon and small arms could deliver enfilade fire along them in case of attack. Each tower was to have a brass 3-pounder cannon. The walls facing the outside were to be loopholed. The main entrance was to be on the east side and large enough to admit carriages and wagons. It would be closed by a large double gate composed of two thick layers of hardwood planks. One of the doors would have a wicket gate for entry when the gate was closed and barred. The corral was to abut the south wall and would measure about half the size of the main structure. It would contain a barn and stock buildings. The old well in the center of the original *hacienda* was to be dug out and faced with stone. Living quarters for the family would be the rooms on both stories of the west wall. The *sala,* or "formal living room," would be the largest room at the north end of the ground floor. The master bedroom would be the room adjacent to it. Both rooms were to have board floors, a rarity in New Mexico. Each room was to have large beehive fireplaces in diagonally opposite corners. The remaining rooms throughout the fort were to have but one fireplace and their floors were to be of adobe surfaced with smooth clay mixed with animal blood. All walls would be mud-plastered and finished with a thin coat of whitish clay. The stables would compose the south wall with a passageway to the corral. The north wall rooms were to be the kitchen, the *dispensas,* or "storerooms," and quarters for the cook and domestic servants. The east wall rooms were to be a combination library and sitting room for Quint and a room planned for Luke Connors, when and if he wanted to use it. With Guadalupe living in the house, it was likely Luke would prefer his old quarters in the village. The remainder of the east wall rooms were for guests.

Santiago drafted every available able-bodied man from Rio Brioso and many from the Mora to build Kershaw's Fort, as Luke had dubbed it. Rumor had it that Doña Guadalupe wanted Don Quintin to remain permanently at El Cerrillo, taking his rightful place there as *patron.* Those who thought they knew him better than most were willing to bet she would not be able to keep him there. Was he not a *Montero Americano* and not a *rico* and a de Vasquez? Still, there was Doña Guadalupe, the "Lupita" many of them remembered from years past. She of the shapely body, dark flashing eyes, and silken, lustrous hair with which to net *any* man, even Don Quintin. The results should be interesting. Odds were even, with a slight edge allowed Doña Guadalupe.

Quint left Rio Brioso just before dawn accompanied by Luke and the eighteen-year-old orphan Jesus Martinez, his *mozo* or "manservant." Jesus was a Genizaro, or "one begotten by parents of different nations," in short—a half-breed. Martinez was not the name of his father but that of his mother, first cousin to Padre Jose Martinez the vicar of Taos. She had been captured twenty years ago by Moache Utes and taken as squaw by one of the subchiefs. Jesus had been the product of that union. When he was five years old, Santiago Zaldivar had led a retaliatory raid against the Moaches. He had found Jesus in their burned-out *rancheria* and had taken him from there to raise him as his own son. He had been eleven years old when Santiago had brought him from Taos to live at Rio Brioso. The people of Rio Brioso had never fully accepted him, but, after all, he was blood/kin to Padre Martinez and the good vicar had allowed the boy to use his name. The church records at Taos had the word "coyote" next to the boy's name, meaning one of mixed blood, but no one at Rio Brioso referred to it, at least within his or Santiago's hearing. In time there was good reason to treat Jesus with respect. It was his attachment to, and acceptance by, Don Quintin himself. The *patron* treated the young lad as an equal, as he did all men and women, irrespective of their birth and social status. Therefore Jesus, who had no trade or calling, attached himself as *mozo* to the *patron*. In his own mind he considered himself not only a manservant but a bodyguard as well, and he let that fact be thoroughly known throughout the Valley of the Rio Brioso. One might smile faintly at such a self-imposed designation. Bodyguard for Don Quintin? *Valgame Dios!* Did ever such a one *need* a bodyguard?

Jesus led two pack mules heavily laden with bulky hide *aparejos* tightly packed with furs and other gifts for Doña Guadalupe, the twins, and David. They were the finest of furs from wolf and bear and a beautiful, reddish buffalo cow robe, a real "silk." The animals had been shot or trapped by the *patron* himself. He also led two of the Jerusalem burros, a male and a female with the mysterious markings of the Holy Cross on their backs. They were to be for Francisco and Rafaela. Best of all was a sprightly chestnut sorrel pony of the coloring *"alazan tostado,"* so called by the Spaniards, with a creamy blaze on its forehead. The pony was for David, Don Quintin's elder son, the one many suspected of being part Indian.

The sun was up an hour when they drew rein at a place on the trail overlooking the Valley of the Rio Brioso. It was a pleasant-looking, productive land stretching as far as the eye could see. Thin smoke rose from

the chimney pots of the settlement. The sun flashed
from the blade of an earth-polished spade at the new
hacienda, and glinted from fast-moving river ripples.
The *hacienda* and adjacent corral looked like a huge
squared figure eight sharply defined on the tawny ground.

"It is a good place," Quint said at last, almost as
though to himself.

"It is a good place, *patron,*" Jesus echoed.

Luke said nothing. His sharp bottle-green eyes flicked
at Quint. Quint sounded like he was trying to convince
himself. There had been a restlessness in him ever since
they had returned from the spring buffalo hunt. Nothing
too apparent, but it was there all the same. Quint had
been happiest when they had trailed the Cochetopa Utes
north to Cimarron Canyon. That's when he was at his
best.

They camped that night under a towering facade of
cliff reflecting their flickering, flaring firelight. Jesus went
to the robes early. Quint and Luke lay on their robes
beside the fire smoking their short Dublin pipes and
passing a leather flask of Pass brandy back and forth. It
was good. It brought back many memories of which there
was no need to speak. Each of them sensed what was in
the other's mind.

Luke refilled and lighted his pipe, then offered it to
the sky for the first puff. He drank deeply of the potent
brandy, wiped his mouth on the back of a hand, and
waited complacently for the deep, silent explosion within
his lean gut. *"Wagh!"* he grunted at last.

Quint studied him. "Talk, Wandering Wolf," he suggested. "Ye have more than *aguardiente* in that lean gut
of yours."

"She wants yuh to succeed at Rio Brioso, Big Red."

Quint looked surprised. "Lupita? Ye canna mean that!
Seems as though she wants me to have little or nothing
to do with it."

Luke studied him. "I was thinkin' of La Tules."

La Tules! The famous, or notorious, owner of the finest
and most profitable monte *sala* in Santa Fe and all New
Mexico, with the favor of her *querido,* none other than
His Excellency Don Manuel Armijo, governor of the
Province of New Mexico. La Tules was the orphaned
baby daughter of Joaquin Barcelo, a soldier of Andalu-

sian stock from the Right People, and Luz, a Sonoran peon. He had been slain in battle by Apaches.

La Tules! A real *rubia,* a coppery gold redhead with flashing wide green eyes, both attractive features inherited from her father. Christened Maria Gertrudis Barcelo, called "Tu-les" for short, until she had achieved the status of successful courtesan and monte dealer, when it had become a respectful "La Tules." She was a survivor, a barefoot *pelada* born into a life of poverty, harshness, tumult, cold, hunger, and the constant menace of Navajo raiders. Married young and widowed young, she had risen from a vendor of cheap *jaboncillos,* small perfumed cakes of cheap garishly colored soap, in the *mercado* at Santa Fe to the exalted position of mistress to the governor, and queen of the monte dealers.

"Why La Tules, Luke?" Quint asked.

"Last time I was in Santy Fee I had a lot of words with Doc Tom Byrne. We talked about the possibility of war between Mexico and the United States, and the fact that the U.S. might eventually take over New Mexico."

"Manifest Destiny again. Does he ever talk about anything else?"

Luke grinned. "Only around Mexicans. He thinks Armijo's days are numbered. If the U.S. conquers New Mexico, Armijo will have to leave in a hurry. La Tules, on the other hand, will certainly throw in her hand with the U.S. She's cleanin' up in that monte *sala* of hers. Don't care nothin' for property. Believes only in good hard cash. Figgerin' both she and Armijo have a quarter interest in the Rio Brioso grant, she'll likely buy him out at bottom peso if he has to leave New Mexico. She'll have him by the short hairs. So, in that case, she'll own half the Rio Brioso. Then, when New Mexico becomes American, she can sell her half to you and Doc Byrne and come out smellin' like a rose."

"Which leaves me out," Quint said dryly. "Ye know as well as I there's never much cash in ranching business. Certainly not enough for me to pay my share in such a transaction."

"Wal, you've always got Doc Byrne behind yuh with cash, ain't yuh? He had the mortgage on the major part of El Cerrillo, didn't he? He made it easy for yuh to pay him off. He's a good friend to yuh, Quint. Yuh shouldn't have any trouble."

"Maybe not, but ye know my quarter share of the Rio Brioso was based on my acting as *hacendado*. I put no cash into the deal. Further, it's Lupita who really owns El Cerrillo."

Luke stared at him. "What the hell do yuh mean?"

"It's legally hers. All I've got in it are my quarter share profits from the Rio Brioso, which we used to restore El Cerrillo after we regained the land mortgaged to Tom Byrne by Lupita's father."

"Mostly ,to pay off her dear brother Bartolome's gambling debts."

Quint nodded. "Exactly."

"Still, I'm sure the doc will make some kind of deal with yuh, Quint. He's a wealthy man who doesn't seem to care much about money."

"There's a damned good reason for that."

"Such as?"

"Where do ye think he got his money originally?"

"Why, he came to New Mexico, started a practice, put his money into trade goods, opened a store, and invested in merchandise brought in on the Santy Fee Trail. Mebbe did some Chihuahua tradin' too."

Quint shook his head. "Not exactly. He never had that much of a practice in Santa Fe, at least not enough to finance his trading business and that fine house of his in Santa Fe."

Luke shrugged. "He could have brought it with him."

Quint nodded. "That he did, aye, but it wasn't *his* money."

Luke stared at him. "Yuh mean that it was U.S. money."

"You're right quick, Lukie. More specifically funds supplied by his old commanding officer in the Dragoons, Colonel, now Senator, Alexander Jamieson Allan, so that Tom could act as an undercover agent for the United States in New Mexico. Which simply means if Armijo leaves New Mexico after selling his quarter share of the Rio Brioso to La Tules, and she sells her half share to Tom Byrne, for God knows I can't pay my share of the deal, that means the real owner of the Rio Brioso will be Senator Allan. Further, the Rio Brioso, as ye well know, is in an ideal strategic position for the establishment of a military post to guard the junction of the Santa Fe Trail and the Cimarron Cut-Off. The Mexicans have always known that, but they were never able to establish a post there."

"Until you came along."

"It's not a military post . . . *yet*, Lukie."

"It's the next thing to it, especially now that you've built Kershaw's Fort. Chances are, yuh might lose it in time, to Senator Allan, who'll likely sell it to the U.S. government at a damned handsome profit."

"Aye," Quint murmured.

"Then why did yuh go ahead and build the fort?" Luke demanded.

"First, to get Lupita and the kids away from El Cerrillo. Second, there's no real sign of war between the U.S. and Mexico. A great deal can happen between now and a possible war. La Tules always gambles for the biggest stakes. If the U.S. takes over New Mexico, she wins. If the U.S. doesn't go to war with Mexico, or does and loses, that would be the end of La Tules, her monte *sala*, money chest, and the diamonds she is rumored to have cached somewhere. If the U.S. wins, she'll need every American friend she can get in order to survive under the new government. I will be one of them, so, to retain that friendship, she'll have to consider my interests as well as her own. Too, the United States will have to depend on Americans with some power and authority in New Mexico. I will be one of them. Whichever way the ball bounces, I'll need bargaining material. *That*, my friend, will be Kershaw's Fort on the Rio Brioso."

"Sometimes I think you're a bigger gambler than La Tules."

"You and I are survivors, Wandering Wolf. We'll make it."

Luke shook his head. "I have nothing but my rifle, hoss, and clothing."

Quint shook his head. "Ye know damned well everything I have is yours if ye need it."

Luke shrugged. "Mebbe. I believe yuh, of course, but there's one major problem always in the way."

"Guadalupe?"

Luke nodded. "Then, there's that eternal itch workin' under yore hide like a botfly."

"What makes ye think I've got such an itch?"

Luke studied him. "Sometimes, lately, I think yuh fergit who you're dealin' with. We've been together how many seasons now?"

"Ten?"

Luke shook his head. "Twelve. Trapped beaver together from the Yellowstone south to the Gila. Fought Blackfeet, Crows, 'Patches, Comanches, and Comancheros: Shared our likker, food, money, and wimmen. I fergit how many times we saved each other's lives. We been here together on the Rio Brioso buildin' it into what it is today. Now, here we are, sittin' about a fire in the good mountains sharin' our likker and tobaccy, talkin' about our problems, hopes, and old times, and *you got the eternal guts to ask me how I figger yuh got an itch!*"

Quint grinned. He drank deeply, wiped his mouth on the back of a hand, and passed the flask to Luke. "Forgive me, partner," he pleaded. "I get mixed up too much in my own thoughts these days."

"So, what's the itch? Lance the boil, son! Out with it! It's Ol' Wanderin' Wolf talkin' here!"

"Aided and abetted by at least a pint of Pass brandy."

"That too! Out with it, Big Red!"

"El Cerrillo," Quint said quietly.

"Yuh really mean Lupita, don't yuh?"

"Aye. Sometimes El Cerrillo and Lupita seem to be one and the same. My little Lupita is no longer the girl we saved from the Comanches in '38. Now she can't forget she is a direct descendant of one of the Conquerors. Now, so help me God, she's Doña Guadalupe de Vasquez Kershaw, *patrona* of El Cerrillo de Vasquez, very much the grand lady, as her mother was, and her grandmother before that, and so on, *ad infinitum*."

"So? Let her play the grand lady. You can still run the show, that is, if I know you, and *sometimes* I think I do. Lately, I ain't so sure."

Quint shook his head. "She isn't content to let me spend part of the year at Rio Brioso. She's upset because I still lead the twice yearly buffalo hunts. She thinks that should be left to the menials. She wants me to play the role of Don Quintin, *patron* of El Cerrillo de Vasquez. A man of property, substance, and position, a pillar of Taos society and a loyal citizen of Mexico, with a great deal of emphasis on that last. Maybe I made a helluva mistake by marrying into the *rico* class in their little isolated world of dry rot. Their old-fashioned way of life is dying out and they haven't got the sense, and maybe the native intelligence, to realize it. Once Lupita and I were married and the honeymoon was over at El Cerrillo, she started trying to mold me into the image of her father and grandfather, and every direct male ancestor of hers since Rodrigo de Vasquez established the line of de Vasquez and the grand *hacienda* of El Cerrillo. In short, instead of her becoming a Kershaw, she wants me to become a de Vasquez, not in name, but in every other sense. *That*, I cannot and will *not* abide by!"

"Seems to me there's something basic yuh should think more about, Quint," Luke said thoughtfully.

"Such as?"

"Do yuh still love her as a woman and not as a de Vasquez?"

"I'd like to think so."

"But, yuh don't know for sure?"

Quint nodded. "Aye."

"Yuh want my advice?"

"I'd value it."

"Rio Brioso can run for a time without yuh. Yuh been away from your family too long as it is. Try *her* way for a time. If you're needed at Rio Brioso, yuh can be there in two days. Yuh don't have to tell Guadalupe yuh aim to bring her and the kids back to Rio Brioso in time."

"My God! Don Quintin de Vasquez Kershaw, *hacendado* of El Cerrillo!" Quint rolled his eyes upwards as he reached for the brandy flask.

"Well, what do yuh say?"

"I reckon I owe her that much at least," Quint admitted grudgingly.

When the flask was empty, they crawled unsteadily under their robes. They lay quietly. "Big Red?" Luke said after a time.

"Aye?"

"Does Lupita know La Tules owns a quarter share of Rio Brioso?"

There was a short trenchant pause. "No, Luke. At least, not yet. . . . Somehow I never got around to telling her."

"My God," Luke murmured.

They fell asleep listening to the night wind soughing through the tall pine tree tops.

★ FOUR ★

Quint reined in his *barrosa* where the road descending from Palo Flechado Pass afforded a panoramic view over the tree tops to where Hacienda El Cerrillo de Vasquez sprawled covering much of a low, flat-topped hill overlooking the Valley of Taos. It was early afternoon. The air was fresh and pure in the rarified atmosphere, and a limitless clarity of light intensified color and seemed to shorten distance so that the mountain peaks many miles away appeared to be much closer. The air was spiced with piñon and juniper. Sunlight reflected from the whitewashed *casa* walls of Don Fernandez de Taos and turned the crumbling church towers a warm golden hue. Faint bluish-gray smoke rose from many chimneys and hung in a cloud over the town. The clanking of flat-toned church bells mingled with the barking of many dogs.

"I'll be gettin' on my way to Touse," Luke said.

Quint turned. "You're welcome at El Cerrillo."

Luke shrugged. "With you anyway and the kids."

Quint did not press the matter. The early friendship between Guadalupe and Luke seven years ago had slowly deteriorated despite the fact that Luke had been one of those instrumental in rescuing her from the Comanches. The gap had widened the more she matured into Doña Guadalupe instead of the girl-woman Lupita. Two reasons for the estrangement might be her jealousy of Quint's close relationship with Luke, and her growing coldness toward David, who had always been Luke's prime favorite. Not that Luke had ever slighted the twins—quite the contrary—but there was a noticeable closeness between him and the half-breed boy.

★ 29 ★

Luke dismounted and stripped off his trail clothing. He dressed himself in his "brave" clothing—a brass-buttoned hunting coat of golden-brown smoked elkskin, fringed and beaded, with patterns of quill work on the sleeves and diapers of black velvet let into the full skirts. The collar was of rich brown marten fur. His buckskin leggings were Cheyenne made, the best obtainable trimmed with scalp hair. The moccasins were Ute. His black hat was flat crowned, wide brimmed and banded with plaited leather studded with silver conches. The feather of a gray eagle had been stuck behind the band for luck. Luke's long braided hair was wrapped in otter fur for good fortune.

"Wagh," Quint murmured.

"*Que hombron!* What a man!" Jesus cried.

Luke preened himself. "Lookout Touse! Here comes Luke Connors! Ol' Wanderin' Wolf hisself! King of the hill! Brave as a buffler bull in the spring! Mean as a bee stung grizzly! Fat and sassy as a wolf pup and ready to howl, I am! Fact is, I think I will!" He threw back his head, cupped his hands about his mouth and war-whooped deep throated, "*Howgh-owgh-owgh-owgh-h! Howgh-owgh-owgh-h! Howgh-owgh-owgh-h!*"

Luke mounted his sorrel. "I'll be partin' from yuh here, Big Red," he said.

Quint nodded. "Ye won't change your mind?" He knew better.

Luke shook his head. "I'll stay with Francois Charbonne. How long might yuh be stayin' here?"

Quint shrugged. "*Quien sabe?* If Lupita has her way it would be semipermanently."

Luke rolled his eyes upwards. "God forbid!"

"I'm still hoping to get her to Rio Brioso, at least to see the new *hacienda*. Maybe she'll like it and stay or at least spend more time there."

They both knew the odds of her staying there would be mighty slim. If she did decide to spend a long time there, that would be the end of Quint and Luke's close relationship. There would be no place for Luke in that narrow, constricted world of domesticity, a static existence built exclusively along the lines laid out by Lupita. At least, if she split her time between El Cerrillo and Rio Brioso, Luke's presence at Rio Brioso would be assured as long as Quint was there. He'd just have to get along with her when she was at Rio Brioso. As long as Quint stayed there, Luke and he would have the freedom they loved—the open plains, buffalo hunting, hunting for predators in the mountains and staying there weeks on end looking to the horizons of untamed land of which there was virtually no limit.

"How long will ye stay in Touse?" Quint asked.

"For a while, then I might take the Old Spanish Trail to Californy. Always had a hankerin' to see them king-sized *ranchos* and the *señoritas* ridin' them fine hosses sidesaddle wearin' them long ruffled skirts."

"But, you'll come back?"

"Maybe in the spring for the big buffalo hunt."

Quint held up his right hand palm outward. "*Vaya* then, Wandering Wolf!"

A bend in the road took him out of sight. A moment later his hoarse war whoop echoed down the slopes. Birds fluttered up from the trees in panicky flight, and dogs began to bark and then howl in imitation.

"He's like a wolf, *patron*," Jesus said admiringly.

Quint nodded. "He *is* a wolf."

They rode toward El Cerrillo.

The *hacienda* seemed like a detached fragment of Andalusia in Old Spain. It had been built over two hundred years ago for Don Rodrigo de Vasquez. The lands had consisted of a generous grant in the Valley of Taos and the much vaster territory of the Rio Brioso grant. El Cerrillo had some of the finest arable land in the valley. Peon labor and Indian slaves had built the *hacienda*, dug the irrigation ditches and tilled the fields. The house had originally been built like a squared figure eight around a family patio and a walled corral. Over many decades it had been added to in a sort of checkerboard fashion to accommodate a growing family, the families of sons and daughters and other relatives. El Cerrillo had actually been a small community rather than a single-family dwelling until the de Vasquez fortunes waned. The relatives had gradually left. There were none of them there now.

The elements working with their ally time had softened the original outline of the *hacienda* into a moundlike structure of golden brown adobe glinting on bright days from the tiny bits of mica embedded in the walls. In time El Cerrillo had blended into the surrounding terrain like the natural camouflage of a huge panther lying on the hills which was its territory. The estate had been immensely wealthy in its day. Fifty thousand *churro* sheep grazed in the hills. The finest irrigated land surrounded it. Fifty Indian slaves worked looms making rugs, blankets, serapes, and yard goods. De Vasquez woolens were valued throughout the province. Another half-hundred servants and slaves serviced the house and the family. Hundreds more tilled the fields, shepherded the flocks, and herded the cattle. Each spring the vaunted *ciboleros* of El Cerrillo crossed the mountains to hunt buffalo along the Canadian and beyond the Llano Estacado for hides and meat in the spring, meat and robes in the fall. It was lucrative business.

If there had been an acknowledged aristocracy in the province, the de Vasquez family would have ranked among the highest due to their early origin, vast lands, accumulated wealth, and intermarriage with other high ranking families.

From where he and his grandson Jose irrigated the vegetable garden, old Jose Vaca saw the dust on the road. He narrowed his eyes. "Joselito!" he called to the boy. "Can you make out who that is?"

The boy shaded his eyes. "Two horsemen. One is a very big man. The other man is smaller. He leads two pack mules, two burros, and a pony. I think the big man is Don Quintin."

The old man took off his sombrero and mopped his seamed forehead. "Let us pray to the Virgin that he has come to stay," he said quietly, as though to himself.

The boy looked up at Jose. "Will he make it easier for us here, grandfather?"

Tomas Valdez, a field hand, came to stand by them. He leaned on his spade. "Why don't you answer the boy, *viejo*? Are you afraid to tell him the truth? Tell him we peons have no choice between one taskmaster and another. They are all the same—cruel, grasping, and intolerant."

Jose shook his head. "Watch your big mouth, Tomas," he warned. "Your voice carries like the bellowing of a bull."

"Maybe someone will hear me."

"You didn't answer my question, grandfather," Jose said.

The old man looked toward the *hacienda* almost as though he might be overheard. "Anything will be better than working under the hand of Doña Guadalupe. It was never like this in the time of her father, Don Francisco. He was a hard man in his way but just. *Ojala!* Would to God he was still alive." He quickly crossed himself. "The way things are now was not so in his time nor in the time of his father. It was not so before that she-panther in the *hacienda* changed from the sweet and lovely Lupita we all worshipped into the Doña Guadalupe. But, enough! Run and tell Federico, the majordomo, Don Quintin comes. He will notify Doña Guadalupe the *patron* is here."

"She's not here today," Tomas said. "She's in Taos for some church affair. Maybe Don Quintin will be surprised at the change in her since she's taken to religion in a big way. I wonder if she'll act different in bed with that stud husband of hers."

Jose was horrified. "In front of the boy! Shame, Tomas!"

Tomas shrugged. "He'll learn soon enough." He walked slowly back to his work.

Jose leaned on his spade idly watching the horsemen. "Come to think," he murmured, "we here would be happy to see a *Montero Americano* come here to lighten our load. A redheaded *gringo*. . . ." He shook his white head and started back to work.

The great house of de Vasquez was shielded from the cold winter wind by a green domed *bosque* of giant venerable silver-barked cottonwoods whose restless leaves formed patterns of light and shadow on the earth. A cold, racing stream flowed noisily past the *bosque* into an *acequia madre*, or "mother ditch" from which many branch *acequias* spread out to water the wide spreading cultivated land. Cottonwoods, willows, wild plum trees, and Roses of Castille with their profusion of yellow and pink blooms lined the banks of the *acequias*. Mockingbirds flashed through the air. Blackbirds strutted on the furrowed ground hunting for insects. Meadowlarks ceaselessly trilled liquid arias close by the water while mourning doves crooned soft incessant undertones.

The *hacienda* itself was a home and a citadel. It had sustained many Indian attacks. It was now a large and intricate complex of many rooms, corridors, and patios of varying sizes. The corral and service quarters behind the house had ten-foot walls surmounted by spiked cactus to thwart thieves. As designed there had been no windows in the outer walls, only narrow loopholes, but in time they had been converted into small windows paned with sheet mica. Beyond the house and its walled corral there spread a complex of buildings—barns, stables, toolhouses, storerooms, workshops, a blacksmith shop and a carpenter shop, weaving rooms, and quarters for the field help. There were many corrals, sheep and goat pens, chicken houses, cattle yards, pigsties, and a shed for milch cows.

"El Cerrillo did not look this prosperous when I lived here as a boy, *patron*," Jesus said. "Padre Martinez had me indentured here as a stableboy. The place was rundown in the days before you came to New Mexico and marrried Doña Guadalupe. Don Francisco's health had failed and his son Don Bartolome spent most of his time in Santa Fe after he left the Military Academy in Mexico City. He gambled day and night borrowing money from his father against his inheritance. The old man could not keep up the place and Doña Guadalupe either, although God knows she tried like a man. It is rumored Don Bartolome is still in Chihuahua although some say he has been seen in Santa Fe and once even here in Taos."

"Where did you hear that?" Quint demanded.

Jesus shrugged. "It is perhaps just a rumor."

"Are you sure?" Quint demanded harshly. "Or are you just repeating idle gossip? I want to know the truth!"

The *mozo* was startled at the look on Quint's face. "Who knows about such idle talk?"

"If it *is* idle talk."

"*Patron*, as I said, it is just rumor. Would he dare to return to New Mexico after having tried to kill our governor?"

"I doubt it," Quint replied. "I don't want him here at El Cerrillo in any case."

Jesus looked sideways at Quint. "If he does come again what would you do, *patron?*" he asked boldly.

The look in Quint's eyes was like a blow across the face. Hoofbeats thudded on the road. "Here comes the majordomo, Don Quintin," Jesus said harshly, glad of the interruption. He hadn't realized how much the possible presence of Don Bartolome in Taos and above all at El Cerrillo would anger the *patron.*

Federico Casias was the majordomo of El Cerrillo, and a distant and much older cousin to Guadalupe. He had known Quint in the old days when the *Montero Americano* beaver trappers had come to Taos. He had met Quint again when Federico had been in the Canadian River country hunting buffalo for Don Francisco. He had fought Comanches beside Quint and his partners in order to save Guadalupe's life. When Quint had become *hacendado* of the Rio Brioso, Federico had wanted to work there, but Quint had prevailed on him to stay at El Cerrillo as majordomo. He was one of the best. Federico adored Guadalupe and the children.

Federico waved his sombrero. "*Hola,* Don Quintin!" he shouted.

Quint reined in. "*Que tal,* Federico? How goes it?"

Federico drew up his horse, leaned over and threw his arms about Quint, pounding his back in the customary *abrazo.* He would not have dared to do such a thing with Don Francisco or Bartolome in the old days, but Don Quintin was more a companion than a *patron.*

"How are Lupita and the children?" Quint asked.

"Doña Guadalupe is in Taos for a religious procession. The children are here. God help you when they see you. They'll swarm all over you." There was a suspicious break in Federico's voice. He was a very emotional person.

"Lupita not here? Did she not get my message?"

Federico nodded. He did not look Quint in the eye. "Perhaps she forgot you were coming today," he suggested quickly.

Quint knew better. "Perhaps. No matter," he murmured.

They rode together to the corral. Quint dismounted. Little booted feet pounded on the hard ground. "Father! Father! Father!" Francisco and Rafaela shrieked. Two fast moving, solid little bodies struck Quint's long legs like a pair of miniature battering rams. "Francisco! Rafaela!" Quint cried. He lifted the sturdy six-year-old twins and seated them one on each forearm, grinning back into their delighted little faces.

They were not identical twins, being born in separate sacs, but there was a remarkable resemblance in certain respects. While Francisco had the dark blue-black hair and immense dark smoldering eyes of the de Vasquezes, particularly like his uncle the handsome, haughty, and arrogant Don Bartolome, Rafaela's dark hair had a coppery tint to it inherited from Quint, and she had immense clear gray eyes, certain legacy of her Scots blood. They were a beautiful little pair of human beings.

Francisco had been named after his maternal grandfather. Rafaela had been christened after the formidable Doña Rafaela, her maternal grandmother, whom the peons and slaves believed was a witch. The twins were much alike in character except that Francisco was a spoiled charmer, strong-minded and adamantly persistent in getting *his* way whatever the cost to others or himself. Rafaela was independent, self-confident, but without her brother's self-centered stubbornness. She was vivacious, lively with a touch of the tomboy, but at times completely feminine withal and adept at switching instantly from one role to the other. She too had a will of her own but one that was more pliant and resilient than that of Francisco. Still, it would not crack under adversity. The two children were absolutely devoted to each other.

Francisco's eyes widened as he saw the chestnut sorrel pony. "Is he for me, father?" he cried as he wriggled to get down to the ground.

Quint placed Rafaela on her feet. "He's for David. The burros are for you and your sister."

Rafaela placed a small hand over her open mouth in awe, Indian style, as she looked at the pair of burros. "Which one do you want, Francisco?" she asked excitedly.

Francisco looked up at his father. "I don't want a burro," he said quickly. "I want the pony."

Jesus unpacked two small silver-mounted saddles. "The burros are for you and your sister," he explained. "The pony is for your brother David."

Francisco kicked Jesus on the shin. "You bastard half-breed! Genizaro! Coyote! Who do you think you are to tell *me,* the son of the *patron,* what is mine and what is not?" he shouted.

Jesus slowly closed and then reopened his fists. His face was set and hard as he looked over the raging boy's head at Quint. Quint shook his head as though to say, "Leave the boy to me."

"Damn it! I want the pony! I don't want a God-damned burro!" Francisco shrieked.

Quint ignored him. "Pick out the burro you want, Rafaela," he suggested.

She shook her head. "Let Francisco have first choice, please."

"No. Do as you're told," Quint ordered.

Rafaela knew that tone of voice. She looked from one to the other of the burros.

Francisco wavered. "I'm to have first choice!" he cried.

Quint shook his head. "No longer, son."

"Rafaela *always* lets me have first choice!" he yelled.

"Rafaela, take your pick," Quint said firmly.

She didn't want to do it. She tried to figure out which of the two Francisco might want. "The littlest one? The female?" she asked tentatively.

He nodded. "If you are sure. Don't take her because you think Francisco might want the other one."

"I do!" Francisco snapped.

Quint gently pushed the girl toward the smaller of the two burros. There was hardly that much difference in their size, in fact it was hardly noticeable. She put her arms about the burro's neck and rested her smooth cheek against her furry one. Her eyes were moist. "Thank you, thank you so *very* much, father. How do you call her?"

Jesus placed a saddle on the burro's back. "We called her Bonita," he suggested.

Rafaela's face lit up. "Bonita! That's it!"

Francisco stomped determinedly toward the male burro.

"Wait," Quint said.

The boy turned. "You won't let me have the pony. So this one is mine, isn't he?" he demanded hotly.

Jesus held the other saddle. He looked at Quint. Quint shook his head.

"Give me that saddle, you!" Francisco shouted at Jesus.

"He has a name, Francisco," Quint said.

"He's a *mozo,* isn't he? Mother says peons don't have names."

"This one does," Quint said quietly.

"All right then, dammit!" Francisco whirled. "Jesus!" he snapped. "Saddle my burro!"

Quint shook his head. "Not like that, son. I don't like your attitude and the tone of your voice. Jesus, put the burro in a corral, *por favor.*"

Francisco stared unbelievingly at Quint. No one, *but no one,* not even his mother dared treat him like that. He turned and stomped toward the house.

"Oh, David!" Rafaela cried. "See what father brought for us! Burros for Francisco and me and a sorrel pony for you!"

David had the same reddish-auburn hair and gray eyes of his father. He was developing the rather prominent nose and solid, determined jaw like his father, but he had the brown skin, high cheekbones, and rather broad underjaw of his Shoshoni mother. He was a quiet boy, bidding fair to be self-confident and capable; the sort who might learn slowly but would retain what he learned. He kept much to himself, although he could be equally at home with other children. There was one major exception to that; his younger half brother Francisco. It was through no fault of David; it lay entirely with the demanding, self-centered Francisco. The situation often caused the warm, sensitive Rafaela to suffer for she loved them both equally well.

Rafaela scrambled up into her saddle. "Come on, David!" she cried. "I'll race you to the big cottonwood by the *acequia madre* and back here!"

Quint watched them race. "You were always the master horseman, Federico. You've taught them well."

"They learn well."

"Francisco too?"

Federico nodded. "He learns faster than both of them but is always too impatient. He'll wear out his mounts more quickly. In that case, Rafaela is the better rider of the two."

"And David?"

"His blood tells. He rides like a *Montero Americano*, or . . ." His voice died away.

"An Indian?" Quint asked.

Federico shrugged.

The children rounded the big cottonwood in a flurry of flying clods and dust. Rafaela held the lead.

"He's not trying," Quint said. "The pony could easily outrun the burro."

"He'll let her win. He always does."

"Francisco too?"

Federico shook his head. "Never. There is already bad blood between the two of them. Even at their ages it is obvious. In time to come . . . Who knows?"

Rafaela's burro hammered past them. "I won! I won!" she shouted.

David reined the pony to a sliding halt. "Thank you, father. He's a beauty. I'll call him Blaze."

Quint waved a hand. "*Por nada*, Davie."

Rafaela leaned toward David and kissed him on the forehead. "It's no fun racing you, Davie. You always let me win."

They rode off to the fields, chattering happily.

"How long has this feud been going on between the boys?" Quint asked.

"Quite awhile."

"I didn't notice anything the last time I was here."

"It was there. Lupita kept it quiet."

"She did well then. I had no idea."

"David never looks for trouble. Francisco does. There are times when he reminds me of his uncle Don Bartolome."

"So soon? God forbid!"

Federico nodded. "It's already noticeable. Can't you feel it?"

"At such a tender age," Quint commented. "Jesus said there was a rumor Bartolome had come back to New Mexico and had been seen here in Taos and El Cerrillo. Is that true?"

"Yes, he was. I didn't actually see him. I was away at the time. Rafaela told me. Francisco said he had not been here. David said nothing either way."

"I'll look into it," Quint said quietly. "Now, tell me more of the trouble between the boys."

"Francisco always starts it. David avoids him. He walks away even when Francisco strikes or kicks him as he did Jesus."

"Is it cowardice on David's part?" Quint demanded.

Federico shook his head. "David is much like his father." He smiled faintly. "Not one to start a fight but more than capable of finishing it. There will come a day when he will turn on Francisco and then his revenge will be powerful."

"Does Lupita treat him as well as she does the twins?"

Federico shrugged. "I'm not one to carry tales."

"Tell me," Quint insisted.

"Very well. When you brought him here seven years ago she treated him well, as you know. I believe she really loves him. After all, he is the son of the man she loves. It is only been since the twins grew up that she began to pay more attention to them than to David, particularly in the case of Francisco. As David reminds me of you, so Francisco remind me of Bartolome. The same headstrong, self-centered arrogance is slowly revealing itself in the boy."

Quint took his saddlebags and Hawken from his horse. "Have Jesus bring the *aparejos* to the house, Federico."

As Quint walked toward the house, he thought about El Cerrillo. It was a good place for those who favored the old times—static, set in its ways, slave to custom and tradition, and infested with dry rot. He knew for his own sake and future as well as that of Lupita and the children he'd have to break them away from it and take them back with him to the clean, progressive atmosphere of the frontier.

Quint struck the butt of his rifle against the thick, bolt-studded door set in its tunnellike entrance through the thick wall.

"Quien es?" a throaty feminine voice called from within.

The key turned in its lock and the door bar was removed. The heavy door creaked open. An awed servant girl looked up into Quint's scarred face with its eerie alien eyes said by the locals to be like the devil's own. She was hardly more than sixteen but already full figured. She was pretty in a pronounced Indian way with a skin like dark moist earth, high cheekbones, and a somewhat broad face with a strong jawline. Her hair was glossy jet black. It was her eyes that attracted attention. They were huge and like dark bottomless pools a man could seemingly fall into if he wasn't careful, and never quite recover from the experience. For a fraction of a second Quint felt he was looking at someone he had known and made love to years ago. Then, as swiftly as the memory occurred, it vanished.

Quint smiled. "Did I frighten you, little one?"

She shook her head while managing a cheerful little smile. "No, *patron*," she replied as she curtsied.

"You're new here. How are you called?"

"Cristina, Don Quintin."

Quint entered the *sala*, kicking the door shut behind him. He hung his saddlebags over the back of a chair. Cristina struggled to lift the heavy bar back into its brackets. Quint helped her, feeling the weight of one of her unhampered breasts against him as he did so. Her loose, white blouse had fallen away from her breasts so that he could look down and see the big, brown nipples, then almost down to her crotch past the silver cross pendant about her neck. She did not move away from him. She looked up. There was no fear or shyness in her eyes, rather what seemed to be a flicker of interest.

She watched him as he leaned his rifle in a corner. This *gringo* giant was already a legend in New Mexico. She had heard many stories about him. In such a place as El Cerrillo the head of a house was next to God; his will was law in everything. He could make free with the serving girls and female Indian slaves if he so desired and his wife would think little of it if anything at all. She wondered, with a faint feeling of delicious fear, what it would be like to be taken to bed by a man like him.

"When will Doña Guadalupe be back, Cristina?" Quint asked.

"I am not sure, *patron*."

"What do you mean?"

"Sometimes she stays overnight with her cousin Josefina Jaramillo, she who is married to Senor Kit Carson. Doña Guadalupe has been spending much time at the church receiving religious instruction from Padre Martinez. Is there anything the *patron* requires?"

"Plenty of hot water. I want to bathe and change my

clothing before I ride into Taos this afternoon to search for my wife," he said dryly.

"Will you bathe in the kitchen?" she asked, almost hopefully. He was said to be a veritable stallion. The serving men who had been severely warned by Doña Guadalupe not to make passes at her had contented themselves by whispering to Cristina what would happen to her when he called her to his bed some night when the *patrona* was not inclined and he had too much to drink. He was like a bull, they said, and her a *virgin* too. *Madre de Dios!*

Quint looked curiously at her. "In the bedroom, girl. What are you thinking about?"

"Nothing, *patron*." It was almost as though he had read her mind. That was said to be another skill of his. Perhaps he was a *brujo*, a male witch.

"Have my *mozo* help you with the water buckets, Cristina," Quint said. He smiled. "And watch where he puts his hands. If I were you I'd make sure he keeps them filled with bucket handles." He watched her interesting and unconsciously sensual hip action as she left the room. It had been many long months since he had bedded a woman. One of them had been a buxom whore in Pueblo when he had been there on business. Before that he had slept with La Tules when he had gone down to Santa Fe to see Tom Byrne. Both times he had been quite drunk. In fact he didn't have the faintest recollection what the Pueblo whore had looked like. However, who could ever forget La Tules?

Quint poured himself a brandy and looked about the *sala*. The room was like a small, private museum displaying an encapsulated history of the de Vasquez dynasty. No male who had ever married a female of the family had ever been able to assume a dominant role. That privilege was the inherited right of the direct line of descent. An outsider became more or less of a figurehead. His de Vasquez wife was always behind him, dominating him with a will of steel. In time he became a de Vasquez in all but birth and surname, succumbing to the background, tradition, power, and wealth of the family. Eventually he would accept his position as a great honor. Now the only direct male descendant was Don Bartolome, elder surviving brother of Guadalupe. He had lost the Rio Brioso grant to La Tules in a monte game and later fled New Mexico after an attempt on the life of Governor Armijo. In time the *patron* of El Cerrillo and *hacendado* of Rio Brioso was a redheaded *gringo*. Quint had always stood on his own two feet, refusing to accept the great honor tendered to him by marrying a de Vasquez woman. In a broader sense he had contributed to the dynasty with the birth of Francisco who, because of his Uncle Bartolome's self-imposed exile, would in time inherit the leadership of the de Vasquezes, but with the alien name of Kershaw.

The *sala* was typical in the homes of wealthy New Mexicans. Carved *vigas* upheld varicolored, peeled aspen poles set in herringbone pattern. The polished earthen floor was hard as stone. The walls were whitewashed. Huge beehive fireplaces stood in diagonally opposing corners. The furniture was heavy, dark and formal. Two huge intricately carved wooden chests fitted with large iron hinges and complicated locks were said to have been brought from Mexico City by Don Rodrigo.

Deep-cut niches in the walls held carved wooden *bultos*, stolid-faced saints whose Indian-like features betrayed the partial natal origin of the *santeros*, or "saint makers," who had carved them. A larger niche contained a severe-faced Saint Francis of Assisi made by the Franciscan Third Order. He was kept clothed in the fashion of the day by the expert needlework of the household women including the *patrona*. Another niche held a garish painting of the Virgin of Guadalupe. A candle in a red glass cylinder burned continually before it. A solid gold crucifix from Spain hung over a fireplace mantel with a spray of pink feather flowers beneath it.

But it was the weapons that fascinated Quint. One was the buffalo lance of Lupita's grandfather Don Sebastian. The blade was two feet long of Toledo steel fitted to a six-foot shaft of hard black wood inlaid with silver figures of two coiled rattlesnakes, two vinegaroons or scorpions, and a pair of herons. Beside it hung a silver-mounted bridle and bit. A long-haired scalp hung from the bridle. It had been taken from a famous Comanche war chief by doughty Don Sebastian in his youth. The Comanches had never forgotten. It had taken them almost forty years to gain their vengeance.

Don Rodrigo's famed Toledo sword and *main gauche* dagger, or short left hand sword used in conjuction with the sword itself, hung above the buffalo lance. Tom Byrne had once told Quint how these fabulous weapons were fashioned. The sword was an extension of a Spaniard's right arm. One of the great Toledo masters Hortuna de Aguirre had made Don Rodrigo's weapons. The core was of old iron forming of *alma,* or "soul" of the blade. New steel cheeks were welded one on each side of the core. The blade was born only on the darkest nights, the better to let the true or false temper show when the metal was red-hot and only on nights when the south wind blew so that in passing the glowing steel from fire to quenching water it might not cool too rapidly as in a north wind. It was quenched six times with exact timing in water from the Tagus River, then finally heated again and smeared with fat cut from the sac about the kidneys of a male goat or sheep which would burst into flame darkening the blade as it cooled. The next day the blade was sharpened and polished into a masterly creation of deadly beauty.

Quint drew the sword from its scabbard. One side of the blade was inscribed *"Por my Rey"* and the other *"Por my Ley,"* swearing protection to king and law. The hilt was of well-turned iron wrapped with silver gilt wire. Evidently Don Rodrigo had not been able to afford studding the hilt with smooth jewels or inlays of gold and silver. His only fortune had been his aristocratic blood, indomitable will, stubborn courage, and the sword. With the sword in his strong right hand, the promise of becoming a hidalgo if he succeeded, eyes on the horizon, he had won El Cerrillo and created a small empire of his own in the Valley of Taos. It had never occurred to Quint that Don Rodrigo and he had much in common.

Quint made a few tentative thrusts and passes with the weapon. The balance was perfect. Something spiritual, perhaps from his Celtic and Viking warrior ancestors, seemed to travel from the fine steel through his hand, up his arm and then into his very soul. Before God! With such a weapon a fighting man might well-nigh be invincible!

Quint wandered about the room, sword in one hand, brandy glass in the other. It was in this *sala* seven years ago that he had first seen Lupita dressed other than as a young girl; later she had worn rough trail clothing and lastly had been clothed in deep mourning for her father. It had been when he had come to El Cerrillo as he had promised to ask her hand in marriage. She had worn a short-sleeved white linen bodice baring smooth shoulders and arms and revealing much daring cleavage. The short skirt was of bright red wool hanging just below her knees. Her legs had been bare with fragile silver-buckled black slippers on her tiny feet. A silver-mounted comb of finest tortoiseshell was thrust into her luxuriant black hair. The shawl was of bright yellow silk worked with an intricate design of red flowers. Her earrings were of soft pure gold, a betrothal gift Quint had sent her. He had never told her where he had gotten the gold for them. The perfume she wore, as always, was intriguing and alluring. He half closed his eyes as he thought of her. It was the way he saw her most often in his dreams.

Jesus came into the *sala* carrying a pair of *aparejos*. He eyed the sword. "Where shall I put these, *patron?*" he asked.

"Empty them here. When you're done help the serving girl Cristina bring in the water for my bath."

Jesus nodded. He looked about the room. "This is like a museum, *patron*."

"Two hundred years of history, Jesus."

"And now they are all gone, the men of de Vasquez."

"There is still Don Bartolome."

"Who is outlawed."

"Leaving a redheaded *gringo* in charge."

They grinned at each other.

"I hope the *patron* doesn't intend to stay here long," Jesus said rather boldly as he paused at the door.

Quint shook his head. "Only for a time. My home is Rio Brioso."

Jesus and Cristina brought in the huge, wooden bathing tub and placed it in the bedroom. When they left, Quint heard Cristina squeal a little as they passed through the patio. Jesus was a bit of a hand with the women.

The master bedroom was dominated by a massive canopied four-poster bed. Guadalupe's grandfather Sebastian had been born in it. Her grandmother had given birth to

Guadalupe's father, Francisco, in it. Guadalupe and her brothers and sisters had first seen the light of day in that bed. Only her elder brother Bartolome and herself had survived. One sister had been stillborn, another had died at birth, and a younger brother and sister had died when still quite young. A younger brother Sebastian had died at fifteen while valiantly resisting a Navajo raid on Taos.

Black and white patterned rugs of thick, woolen *jerga* covered the floor. The de Vasquez coat of arms was inlaid in colored stones over the fireplace. The whitewashed walls had the lower halves hung with dull red cotton cloth to protect clothing from it. A wooden wardrobe of black walnut towered to the ceiling. A pair of Castilian *vargueños*, wooden chests supported on high legs and honeycombed with little drawers and compartments, stood on each side of an alcove. The wood was cunningly inlaid with ivory and nacre and studded with worked metals. The alcove was illuminated by two windows paned with mica through which the afternoon sun shone bringing out faint opalescent tints on the snow-white coating of the walls. A round table was covered with spools of thread, needles, scissors, tape, skeins of yarn, and fragments of cloth. A low bench upholstered with polychromed leather trimmed with faded velvet and gold bullion lace lined the alcove. Several *santos de retablos*, images of saints painted on small panels of wood, hung on the walls. Two tall, straight chairs with leather seats and backs of crimson velvet stood on each side of the sewing table. The only contribution Quint had made to the room was a large liquor cabinet.

Quint stripped to the skin before he opened the liquor cabinet to get a drink. At that moment Cristina, reliable if not well trained, kicked open the door to the patio and staggered in with two bucketfuls of steaming hot water. Quint whirled, brandy glass in hand, and instinctively picked up one of his Colts. He leveled and cocked it without spilling a drop from the glass.

Cristina stared openmouthed, too awed to be frightened. The contrast between his mahogany-hued complexion, dark reddish hair, and white body skin was startling. That, and his hard gray eyes, the curly bush of red hair at his crotch, and the whitish scar on his left cheek made him the extreme opposite of any man of her people she had ever seen. And the body scars! *Madre de Dios*! There were parallel claw marks on his left shoulder where some powerful beast had dragged its talons down from his face to his shoulder. There was a faint furrowed scar on the right side of his head. A puckered bullet hole was just below his right ribs, a two-inch scar was on his right bicep, and there was the deep dimple of another scar on his left forearm. But, most fascinating of all, his great penis and full testicles: *Por Dios!* The man was a stallion!

Quint could not help but grin as he saw the wide-eyed astonishment of the girl. He lowered the pistol in front of his privates. "Leave the water, Cristina. Come! Come! I won't harm you."

She poured the water into the tub, not daring to look at him. The mistress was in Taos for the day. The children were playing in the fields. There were no other servants in that part of the house. Jesus the *mozo* didn't matter. It was Don Quintin's right to take her to bed. How would it be to lie naked under that lean, sinewy body marked with scars of bullet, knife, and claw? The very thought was enough to send a shiver up her spine, erect her nipples, and cause a loose moistness up between her sweating thighs. She was still a virgin. Doña Guadalupe had insisted on that when she had hired her. Cristina had expected to be deflowered by the *patron*, with the permission of the *patrona*, of course. Cristina's opinion had no weight. It was the custom. So she had been told by her contemporaries, although Doña Guadalupe had never mentioned it to her.

"You can leave now," Quint said.

She carried the empty buckets to the door, then turned slowly with lowered head. "I can scrub your back if you like, *patron*," she suggested boldly.

Quint shook his head. "Perhaps some other time."

When she left he drained his glass. There was something about that girl. Perhaps he had seen her before? No, he was sure he had not. Still, there was someone like her.

Jesus brought two bucketfuls of water and emptied them into the tub. "She's a Genizara, *patron*. A coyote, like me."

Quint handed him a glass of brandy. "So? How do you know?"

"One could be half-blind and not mistake her."

"It takes one to know one, eh? Did you know her before?"

Jesus shook his head.

"Then how?"

"Simple, *patron*. I asked her."

"Navajo? Apache? Comanche? Ute?"

"Moache Ute, like me."

"Mountain Comanche."

Jesus shrugged. "I don't like to think of it that way."

"Still, it's true. They're basically the same people."

Jesus sipped his brandy. "She's afraid of you."

"No reason to be. Have you got your lustful eye on her?"

The *mozo* shook his head. "Josefina the cook warned me to leave her alone. She said the *patrona* allows only virgin serving girls to wait on the family."

"Like the good Josefina? Maybe Josefina told you that to turn your interest from Cristina to her."

Jesus shook his head. "But a man could do worse. She's already invited me to sleep with her while we're here at El Cerrillo."

Together they watched Cristina as she brought in more water and poured it into the tub. She did not look at them. Jesus eyed her shapely rump as she left and slowly shook his head. "Just my luck," he murmured.

When Jesus left, Quint relaxed in the tub sticking his long legs over the side. He reached for the soap and the memory came to him. "Dotawipe," he said softly in Shoshoni. "Mountain Woman." *That's* who she looked like. He was ashamed of himself for not remembering sooner. The Cheyennes considered the Utes as Mountain Comanches, and the Shoshonis were the same basic family as the Utes, so that would put them in the same category. The indistinct, shadowy face of Mountain Woman seemed to float before him out of a hazy mist. "You make my heart big, En-Hone," she seemed to whisper. The vision faded away. That was what she had always said to him in moments of great tenderness. En-Hone, "Big Red Badger," a name given Quint in honor by the Yellow Noses, the famed fighting military society of the Shoshonis.

Quint shaved and trimmed his beard and mustache. He studied himself in the mirror. Hard gray eyes, bold nose, reddish hair and beard, and the scar welting his left cheek. "By God," he said quietly. "No wonder these New Mexican women seem to fear me, and at the same time have a fascinated curiosity about me."

He dressed in fine linen drawers, cambric shirt ruffled at throat and wrists, black leather trousers split from the knee down and loosely laced to reveal the drawers. His dove-gray jacket was of the charro type embellished with swirls and arabesques of black braid. The saddle-yellow boots were of finest Chihuahua workmanship. The blunted spurs were silver inlaid. He slid one of his Colts into the left side of his waistband concealed by the front of his jacket. He dropped a double-barreled derringer into his left jacket pocket. His gray ranchero hat was wide brimmed, flat topped, and banded with leather studded silver conches.

Quint eyed himself again in the mirror. No wonder many of the people of New Mexico sometimes thought of him as one of Satan's henchmen striding ruthlessly over the sacred soil of the province. He shrugged. "Don Quintin Douglas Ker-Shaw, *patron* of El Cerrillo de Taos and *hacendado* of Rio Brioso, Province of New Mexico. *A sus ordenes.* At your service," he said in his clipped Scots tongue. He bowed his head slightly and grinned askew.

★ FIVE ★

Quint and Jesus rode down the sloping road from the higher ground at El Cerrillo. The Valley of Taos spread out before them illuminated by the bright sun of late afternoon. The valley was at seven thousand feet altitude, extending north-south for nearly forty miles in a nearly semicircular shape hemmed in to the north, east, and south by the Sangre de Cristo Mountains. The terrifying black gorge of the Rio Grande del Norte bounded the valley to the west beyond which was the great plateau La Otra Banda, "The Other Side," a sagebrushed, windy domain for countless herds of wild mustangs. The valley was seventy-five miles north of Santa Fe, accessible through the Canyon of the Rio Grande with its huge cliffs of igneous rock, through which passed a broad well-traveled trail used by white men for three hundred years.

The valley held three principal communities—the earthen villages of Don Fernando de Taos rather centrally located, the Indian Pueblo de Taos to the northeast, and the old Pueblo Indian farming community of Ranchos de Taos. Don Fernando de Taos had long been a trading center, a meeting place of Pueblo and Plains Indians and traders from Mexico. For thirty years the mountain men, mighty trappers of beaver and powerful drinkers of whiskey, had come to "Touse," famed for "brown wimmen and white likker," the latter being the notorious Taos Lightnin', a mind-blowing whiskey distilled from wheat.

Foreigners as well as Americans came to Taos to avoid corrupt Santa Fe officials and replenish their supplies. It was ideal for their purpose. It was the northernmost town in the Province of New Mexico and closest to teeming beaver streams. Thus it had become the center for foreign-born residents, principally Americans, who eventually gained great influence and became proficient at intimidating local officials. Inevitably there was an American "veneering." It was smaller and more remote than Santa Fe but much more cosmopolitan. Many Americans became Mexican citizens and married local women. They became established in business. But some of them lived on credit, always broke and talking incessantly of the "old days" when beaver was king. There was no work for them in Taos, and they would not stoop to do the mean labor of the local *paisanos.* So they did little or nothing at all, waiting for God alone knew what. Despite their Mexican citizenship and wives, their business or lack of it, they all remained American at heart waiting and hoping for New Mexico to become part of the United States as part of the powerful burgeoning sentiment sweeping the country—Manifest Destiny.

Don Fernando de Taos was the center of the valley

surrounded in every direction by cultivated fields
crisscrossed with numerous *acequias* flowing brightly
with clear cold water from the melting snow of the mountains. The roads from out of town eventually turned into
the narrow, unpaved, winding alleys the Taoseños called
streets, which inevitably led to the plaza in the center of
town. During daylight hours the byways and particularly
the plaza were alive with people and activity. Diminutive
burros roamed foraging for refuse. Packs of gaunt wolflike dogs prowled. Herds of goats pattered by. Bleating
sheep were driven in from the hills. Woodcutters drove
strings of tiny mouse-gray dinkeys concealed under enormous halos of copper-red cedar firewood or yellow
pitch-pine faggots. Slow-moving *carretas*, huge crude
two-wheeled carts drawn by oxen, creaked, groaned, and
squeaked under their heavy loads. *Muladas,* packtrains
of mules laden with huge leather cargo packs called
aparejos, trotted to the plaza and warehouses.

The plaza was treeless, dusty in dry weather, muddy
in wet with no other condition between the two extremes.
Everywhere pedestrians had to dodge wandering domestic animals, their excrement, and puddles of voidings.
The stench was ever-present. The fiercely mustachioed
men showed their habitation between mountain and
desert by their costumes of heavy glazed sombreros, gay
serapes, brightly colored shirts and leather pantaloons
unlaced or unbuttoned halfway up the leg to reveal white
drawers. Their boots were of yellow leather armed with
immense roweled spurs. These men, seemingly indolent
afoot, were some of the finest of horsemen. The young
women of Taos attracted the eye, particularly the
women-hungry mountain men and traders far from the
sedate females of their own kind. They were exotic, sloe-
eyed creatures who thronged the plaza in good weather.
The younger women usually wore short, red skirts fastened about their slim waists with silver-ornamented
belts. The skimpy blouses were white with nothing worn
beneath them and revealing plenty of cleavage. Their
bare, brown shoulders were half-hidden beneath gayly
colored shawls. They wore their black hair plastered behind the ears then plaited into a long queue hanging far
down their backs. All of them wore crosses of gold or silver hung about their necks and nestling in the warm

cleavage. Their fans and shawls were used with alluring and coquettish skill. A shawl was symbolic of a woman's taste and wealth. It was a great deal more than just part of a costume; it was always kept in motion to express her mood. If drawn close in a certain way it might denote aversion, assent, or coquetry. It could be flung wide as a challenge or perhaps invitation. A young woman of Taos need not speak to convey her feelings toward a young man. Her fan, shawl, and great dark eyes more than satisfactorily portrayed them.

Quint and Jesus rode toward the plaza. They reined in their mounts to let a holy procession pass slowly by. The copper bells in eroded church towers clanked dolefully out of rhythm with the procession musicians playing irregular music on *bandolins, heacas* (a species of guitar), and tom-toms.

"*Penitentes*," Jesus murmured. He rolled his eyes upward in mock humility.

Thin dust rose from under the plodding feet. Most of the penitents were women or very old men. Their dusty bare feet were stained with manure and flecked with blood. Some of them shuffled painfully on their knees with agonized eyes fixed in adoration on the holy images in tinsel painted brightly to the point of grotesquerie and carried tossing above the heads of the people.

Quint and Jesus dismounted, baring their heads in respect. The women were heavily veiled. One slender woman's features were concealed behind a veil of silk. The sun shone on a large cross of exquisite workmanship that hung from a gold chain about her neck. Quint recognized the cross at once. It was an ancient heirloom of the de Vasquez family said to have been brought from Spain by Don Rodrigo. Lupita stumbled and seemed to shudder in pain. Her feet were thick with dust, stained with manure and blood. If she saw Quint, she gave no sign of recognition. The procession moved on toward the road leading to Taos Pueblo and its massive church three miles to the north.

"Was that the *patrona*, Don Quintin?" Jesus asked.

Quint nodded. "Doing penance."

Jesus shook his head. "It must be hard on her. She's not used to such pain and suffering. It must a terrible sin for which she is atoning."

Quint shrugged. "I have no idea," he lied.

"Perhaps I could hazard a guess about that, Don Quintin," a cultured voice spoke in Spanish from behind Quint and Jesus.

They turned quickly. Jesus dropped to his knees and bowed his head. "Padre Martinez," he murmured.

Padre Antonio Jose Martinez the Curate of Taos sat in his carriage. He was a tall, broad-shouldered, burly man with an immensely large dome-shaped head and features to match. Charles Bent, who hated and distrusted him, had dubbed him "The Calf" because of his large head and broad features. He was the head of the Church in New Mexico and one of the two most politically important men in the province next in importance to Governor Manuel Armijo. Padre Martinez had great intellectual gifts and social consciousness, was brilliant, controversial, and liked the ladies. He had always championed the cause of his people and was outspoken in his dislike of Americans. One exception to this last was Quint.

"I am happy to see you in the good company of Don Quintin, Jesus," the padre said, indicating that Jesus should rise. "Your mother, my cousin, God rest her soul, would be proud of you for serving such a man as he."

Quint smiled. He genuinely liked the padre. "It is good to see you again, Padre Martinez."

Martinez leaned from the carriage and embraced Quint. "It is good to see you again." He released Quint and studied him appraisingly. "The life at Rio Brioso suits you well. But, one must spend time with his wife and family, eh?"

Quint nodded. "That is why I am here, padre."

"I have just come from El Cerrillo. They told me you had just returned from Rio Brioso and had come into town to find Guadalupe. Did you find her?"

Quint gestured toward the receding procession. "There, padre. I didn't quite expect this."

"In penance resides virtue, my son."

"I'll have to try it some day," Quint responded dryly. "Was this penance your suggestion?"

The priest raised his eyebrows. "Me? Why no. Why do you suggest that?"

"I heard you were giving her religious instruction."

★ 53 ★

"At her request only. I knew nothing of her marching this day. She is a troubled young woman, Quintin."

"How can that be? She has everything. El Cerrillo was saved for her and her children. It prospers now. Rio Brioso does well and will do much better. We have three fine children. All of us are blessed with excellent health."

The padre narrowed his eyes. "So?" he murmured.

Quint studied him. "Is there something wrong with Guadalupe or the children? Is there something I don't know?"

The priest shook his head, too quickly it seemed. "All is well, to the best of my knowledge. But come, tell me of conditions east of the mountains. As you know I have some interests over there and have suffered great losses in sheep, horses, and mules to the Utes and Jicarillas. The story of your pursuit and recovery of many horses and mules has spread throughout northern New Mexico."

"They were stolen by Cochetopa Utes and some Comancheros."

"Those vermin! But I have always thought your presence east of the mountains was a deterrent to them."

Quint shrugged. "At least to the Moache Utes, the Jicarillas, and particularly the Comanches. We taught the Kotsoteka Comanches a bitter lesson seven years ago when they raided Rio Brioso. They haven't forgotten."

The padre smiled. "I've heard it said that the hostile Indians and even many New Mexicans believe you are the devil in human form."

Quint grinned. "All to the good. Let them think so. It's good insurance."

"Unfortunately many Taoseños have that same belief."

"Does that include yourself, padre?"

Martinez smiled. "Some of your American friends think the same of me. However, I do not believe in devils although at times, I must confess, I am somewhat doubtful."

"And, in *my* case, padre?"

They studied each other. The tall, rangy Scot who had become somewhat of a legend in the province and the brilliant, domineering priest who had become a legend in his own time.

Padre Martinez waved a hand. "I haven't given it

★ 54 ★

much thought, Quintin. But there are times when I do wonder just *who* and *what* you are. I speculate on the reason for your presence in New Mexico. An *escocés* turned American who has become a Mexican citizen. Now owner with his wife of El Cerrillo. *Hacendado* of Rio Brioso with such prestigious partners as Governor Armijo, Doctor Tomas Byrne, and, rumor has it, perhaps the notorious La Tules. Also, you are a friend and confidant to the American Party, who would like nothing better than to see New Mexico become part of the United States, and yet are trusted and respected by many prominent and *loyal* New Mexicans."

"Does that last include yourself, padre?" Quint asked with a winning smile.

The padre shrugged, but smiled. "As I said, I *wonder*. . . . But, enough of speculation. In time we will know all. I am happy to see you here in Taos with your wife and family, but I wonder if it might not be wise to return to Rio Brioso as soon as possible? We property owners of land and stock east of the mountains look upon you as our primary defense against Indian raids as well as any attempts by foreigners such as the Texans in 1841 to invade the province."

"I've just arrived here, padre. I haven't seen my family in months. There are good men back at Rio Brioso in case any such problems arise."

"Agreed, but always remember you are considered to be the mainstay of the northeastern frontier defenses."

Quint became nettled. "I'm a little tired of the task. I'll decide when and if I return there."

Martinez studied Quint. "It is a fact that one of the conditions of your part ownership of the Rio Brioso is that you are also a member of the active militia of the province with the rank of *subteniente*. Thus, in time of emergency or war you can be charged with the duty of recruiting a militia company from the able-bodied men of Rio Brioso, the Mora, and other frontier communities for active duty."

"Isn't that considered a formality?"

The padre raised his eyebrows a little. "It can easily be enforced. A mere word in the governor's ear will substantiate it, Quintin."

"From you or any of the other large property owners

with grants east of the Sangre de Cristos," Quint said dryly.

Martinez smiled. "So, would it not be more convenient to return there under your present status rather than under orders as an officer of the active militia subject to the beck and call of those same large property owners?"

"You've a valid point there, padre," Quint admitted. "But there is also the problem of Guadalupe. She doesn't want to live there. And, as you well know, once a de Vasquez makes up his or her mind about what they will do or don't do, Jesus Christ himself couldn't convince them otherwise."

The padre quickly crossed himself. "I don't profess to have such spiritual authority, but in my own way I can be quite convincing. Leave it to me, my son. When you wish to leave I'll speak privately with her. Now I must be on my way to the Church of Taos Pueblo. By the way, not long ago I baptized one of your former Delaware friends by the interesting name of Black Beaver who married one of the Pueblo women."

"A good man. One of the best. His brother Black Moccasin and son Joshua still work with me from time to time. At present they are with Lieutenant Fremont of the United States Army on his third expedition to the West. Kit Carson and Dick Owens are with him too."

The padre nodded. "I know," he said quietly. "An interesting man this Lieutenant Fremont. Is it not foolhardy for him to stray so close to or into Mexican territory?"

Quint shrugged. "Who truly knows where the boundaries are?"

"He certainly knows California is part of Mexico."

They looked at each other eye to eye. At last Martinez raised a hand in blessing. "Go with God," he murmured, then drove off.

"A powerful man," Jesus said quietly.

Padre Martinez had been born a *rico*, married and became widowed in his teens, then studied for the priesthood. He had opened his mission at Taos in 1826. He established a seminary to educate young men for the priesthood and a school for boys and girls, the first coeducational institution in the Southwest. His life had been devoted to fighting the vice and superstition so prevalent among his flock. He had brought the first printing press in New Mexico to Taos and published *El Crepusculo de la Libertad,* the "Dawn of Liberty," the first newspaper in the province as a voice for his strong political opinions. The press also turned out textbooks on grammar, rhetoric, Spanish and Mexican law and other subjects to instruct his students as well as political pamphlets written by him. He had served for six years as a member of the Departmental Assembly of New Mexico. The padre had a close association with the *Penitentes,* members of an order dating back to the Thirteenth Century, and had gone so far as to publish a pamphlet in their defense. He was not unaware of the power of primitive religion among his backward people. On the more earthy side he was known to keep concubines and had fathered a number of children whom he acknowledged openly and supported.

"It is good to have such a man as a friend," Jesus said. He studied Quint out of the corners of his eyes.

Quint nodded. Still, he wondered where Padre Martinez would stand when and if the United States attempted the annexation of his beloved New Mexico and his devoted flock.

★ SIX ★

Guadalupe returned to El Cerrillo at dusk, half expecting to find Quint there. She had known he was due to come home from the Rio Brioso that day, but had perversely decided not to be found patiently waiting for him like a dutiful wife, as passionately as she wanted to see him. She had seen him watching the penitent procession that afternoon. She hadn't really wanted to walk in it that day. She wasn't quite *that* repentant of her sins; in fact she wasn't repentant at all, but some quirk in her proud character had made her march. Now that he had returned at last, the hunger for him that had been eating into her very vitals was worse than ever. She had seen him out of the corner of her eye standing beside his horse watching the procession. *Por Dios!* He was as tall as a young pine, with those saturnine good looks about him and complete air of masculine independence that seemed irresistible to women, particularly to herself. In their years of marriage that feeling had strengthened, despite his long absences from her side. Paradoxically, she sometimes regretted her passion for him and at the same time was secretly and deeply frightened almost to the verge of panic that it might burn itself out over the years. She could not, must not lose him!

The old chapel at El Cerrillo had fallen into disuse in the time of Guadalupe's grandfather and had remained so during the time of her father. The men of de Vasquez had never been known to be particularly religious. When the children had grown old enough for religious instruction, Guadalupe felt the need for a private chapel. The original chapel had been small and dingy, plagued over the years by unstopped leaks until it was useless for anything. It had been abandoned to the mice and occasional owls who hunted them. Guadalupe had consulted with Padre Martinez on the matter. The good priest, longtime friend and confessor of her family, had suggested the use of her old bedroom because of its size, proximity to the master bedroom, and the fact that one wall abutted the old chapel. It had been a simple matter to gut both rooms completely, knock out the wall between them, and restore the chapel roof. Padre Martinez had agreed to consecrate it, but only in the presence of Don Quintin which was altogether fitting. That momentous occasion had not occurred as yet, pending the expected arrival of Don Quintin.

The new chapel was a small masterpiece of which any church might well be proud. A huge cross of carved mountain mahogany dominated the rear wall. The crucified Christ hanging on it had been carved by Jose Rafael Arago, a *santero* of Taos, past master of his craft. In the dim light and soft shadow the agonized facial expression of Jesus seemed to be formed by warm flesh and blood rather than cold wood and paint.

Guadalupe came to the chapel often, day and night. In her confused search for someone, or something, to substitute for Quint, she had turned to Him who has compassion for the poor, weak, all repentant sinners, and in Guadalupe's case one who needed faith, for something in which to believe.

She was no longer the passionate and loving girl-woman whom Quint had married. Now she was the dignified Doña Guadalupe de Vasquez Kershaw *patrona* of El Cerrillo, a keeper and guardian of the symbol, tradition, and legend of the family of de Vasquez in the Valley of Taos and all of northern New Mexico. It should have been the responsibility of her elder brother Bartolome, but he had alienated Governor Armijo, attempted his assassination, and when that had failed through the interference of Quint, he had exiled himself from New Mexico. But, even before that, he had failed their father Don Francisco by refusing to take the load of responsibility from him, a sick and aging man. Don Francisco had placed his hopes on Bartolome. Bartolome would have none of it. He had left El Cerrillo to live in Santa Fe, an inveterate gambler, insatiable womanizer, and complete wastrel.

The estate had fallen on hard times despite Guadalupe's attempt to fill the place her brother should rightly have taken over. It had always been the responsibility of the eldest son of the family to conduct the important spring and fall buffalo hunts far out beyond the Llano Estacado, haunt of the Comanches. In the continued absence of Bartolome, Guadalupe, although hardly more than a girl, had accepted that responsibility. It had been during the spring hunt of 1838 that she had come into contact with Quint. She had first seen him in Taos when she was but a child. The tall *rubio* with the hard gray eyes that belied the sensitivity and humanity of the man. She had never forgotten him. Her namesake, Our Lady of Guadalupe, to whom she had often prayed, had seen to it that they would meet again and in time become man and wife.

She had hoped then that Quint would be the man to revitalize El Cerrillo and restore it to its former glory. This he had done. But something had gone wrong. He was proud as a Spanish grandee of his strange-sounding name and alien heritage of the heretic *escocéses,* the Scots, a wild and fierce warrior breed of semi-barbarians, or so she had been told. He loved her and the children, but there was no great pride within him that he had married into the family of de Vasquez. *He did not, or could not understand the great honor conferred on him by being accepted into the family of de Vasquez!* Not for him had been the life of a grandee at El Cerrillo with her at his side. For him life was to be lived in constant struggle, fulfillment, and accomplishment. There must always be a far horizon, an untamed frontier; he thrived on that challenge. He could not stand the stifling confinement of the quiet *hacienda* on the hill overlooking the Valley of Taos. "Walls are for winter," he would say, and ride off, much more at home in the open than behind thick adobe walls.

It was the Rio Brioso that was Guadalupe's great rival. She had slowly realized it during the first years of their marriage. Now that the Rio Brioso was well established, would the lure of the untamed frontier take him farther away from her and the children? She hated the Rio Brioso. It was primitive, isolated, hot in summer and cold in winter. There was always the danger of Indian raids. There Quint was not Don Quintin of El Cerrillo, but rather Don Grande Rubio, the Big Redhead, admired, loved, and respected by the people. There he was eminently successful, a leader, and more than that, already established as a legend. Guadalupe? She was merely Doña Guadalupe, wife to Don Grande Rubio, respected but not loved. Perhaps Quint preferred it that way although he would never admit it. She must have him here at El Cerrillo. He had come home at last. She must use every means of persuasion at her disposal to hold him there. With that, and the lure of the children whom he loved, she might net him forever.

Someone tapped at the outer door of the chapel.

"What is it?" Guadalupe called.

"It's Cristina, *patrona*. Don Quintin is on his way to the house from the corral."

Lupita walked into the master bedroom. She studied herself in a mirror, rearranged her hair, dried her eyes, and renewed the subtle, alluring French perfume she wore, of which Quint always said, "It excites me, Lupita. I can't be responsible for my actions when you use it." She smiled a little. It had always worked on him; pray God it would work again.

The patio had been the place Guadalupe loved most in

all the sprawling *hacienda*. Here she had solved her childhood problems with the help of her beloved mother; and after her early death, Guadalupe's aunt Doña Filomena, hunchbacked, wizened, ugly spinster sister of her father, had taken her place. She had been a woman whose soul was as beautiful as her body and features were ugly. Here Guadalupe had spent many idyllically happy days when she had first been married. It became Quint's favorite place as well. Here he read his beloved books, while she sewed; they did not speak much to each other, but were intensely content, and (sinfully!) a few steps away was the master bedroom. Mother of God! What had happened to change their lives so greatly? In the past few years during which they had slowly drifted apart, she had made the patio, master bedroom, and chapel her citadel of defense against the changes that were gradually overcoming New Mexico and her marriage. Here she could be safe and secure, alone or with the children, and pray God, always with her husband.

There was no finer patio in all New Mexico. It was paved with large flat stones around a fountain that overflowed into a pool in which tiny fish darted about the mossy stems of huge water lilies. There was a covered well of pure cold water. Small trees and shrubs in wooden tubs lined the sides of the patio. Vines and clay pots filled with colorful flowers hung from the *portale* eaves. A large cottonwood overhung the roof and part of the patio. A seventeenth century bell hung beside the chapel doors. A mockingbird whistled in a bent amole cage hung from a projecting *portale* beam. Here and there tin lanterns pierced with many holes emitted a soft and smoky light from scented candles.

Quint walked noiselessly across the dimly lighted *sala* to the doorway leading into the patio. He paused in deep shadow to look at her. She was not yet aware of him. She was twenty-six now, seven years younger than he. Her once slim, almost boyish figure with its lovely uptilted breasts had filled out after the birth of the twins and the sedentary life at El Cerrillo. She wore a high-necked, black silk dress with jet buttons down the back and blond lace ruffling at throat and wrists. A fine, black tortoiseshell comb decorated with silver filigree was thrust into her blue-black hair. The soft light seemed to warm the earrings of pure gold Quint had given to her as a betrothal gift.

She had her shapely back toward Quint, while listening enthralled to the mockingbird. She turned her head a little, presenting her profile, and for the briefest dreamlike flash of time she was again as he remembered her best.

He walked toward her, his soft footfalls muffled by the fountain and the silver-toned song of the mockingbird. The mockingbird stopped singing. Guadalupe turned suddenly to face Quint.

Quint raised his eyebrows and whistled softly. "Doña Guadalupe de Vasquez Kershaw *patrona* of El Cerrillo, I, Don Quintin Douglas Ker-Shaw am at your service," he murmured as he continued walking toward her. Suddenly she was so close her firmly upheld breasts pressed against the lower part of his broad chest. She looked up into his eyes. The intriguing scent of her perfume seemed to envelop him. He noted the faint dark circles under her great eyes and the hairlike stress lines across her forehead, at each side of her nostrils, and the corners of her soft, full mouth. They were new, come since he had last seen her.

"You walk like a hunting cat and smell like Turley's Distillery at Arroyo Hondo!" she cried.

He swept her into his arms, lifting her so that she stood on the tips of her black satin slippers, crushing her against his hard, muscular body. She stiffened in resistance for a fraction of a second, then relaxed as he sought her lips with his. Her arms crept up to and around his neck. Her breathing was quick, spasmodic, and it seemed that between them all was as it had been before.

Suddenly she tried to draw away. "The children. The servants," she murmured. She touched her hair quickly, nervously. "I . . ." He smothered her mouth with his. At last he released her, but kept his arms about her. She could feel his hard manhood pressing firmly against her soft belly. "The children. The servants," she repeated breathlessly, uncertain what to do or say next.

Quint shook his head. "No fear. The children are in bed, are they not? The servants are in their quarters. They know better than to break in on us this night. We have this part of the house to ourselves, as it should be, Lupita."

She turned her head a little away from him. "Francisco is terribly upset with you," she said, for want of anything better to say.

He held her by her slender shoulders. "Forget him for now. We've too much to talk about between ourselves."

She broke away from him and went to stand by the pool with her back toward him.

"Not the warmest of welcomes, *querida,* I'd say," Quint ventured.

"What did you expect?" she asked over her shoulder. "You've been away for months."

"Building up the Rio Brioso," he said, his voice hardening almost imperceptibly. It hadn't taken long to get to the crux of their difficulty with each other.

She turned. "Must you stay there so much? This is your home, Quint. Here, at El Cerrillo, with your wife and family. You're a man of standing here in New Mexico, a gentleman, not a foul-smelling trapper wearing animal skins and living like one of them. Another thing—I've worked just as hard here at El Cerrillo as you have at Rio Brioso."

He could not resist it. "With the profits from the Rio Brioso paying the way here," he reminded her. "El Cerrillo hadn't supported itself in years. It was in a state of advanced decay. A large part of the land was mortgaged to Tom Byrne. If I had my way, that money could have been used to further develop Rio Brioso."

She narrowed her eyes. "I was the one who brought El Cerrillo to you as a dowry! Does that mean nothing to you?"

Quint shrugged. "I've been damned tired of listening to the past glories of El Cerrillo and the noble family of de Vasquez. I've no intention of staying here and changing into a de Vasquez in all but name over the years. Or do you want *that* too? By God, woman! I'm a *Kershaw!* Not a member of an almost extinct New Mexican family of *gente fina,* so enamored with what they *were,* they can't see what they *are!*"

"So, that's it! So, now it's out in the open!" she snapped.

He shook his head. "It's always been out in the open, as far as I'm concerned."

"Kershaw," she sneered. "There are times when you speak that name as though it was of the nobility. *My* family came from the nobility of Andalusia! You have no such background!"

He grinned irritatingly. "No need. I'm my own man. I make my own way, always have, and always will. I'm building the Rio Brioso into something for the two of us. I've never thought of El Cerrillo as being *ours*. Damn it, woman! It's *yours!* I want no part of it if I have to go through the rest of my life thinking I've been triply blessed because I was allowed to marry into the the de Vasquez family and reside here at El Cerrillo."

"The Rio Brioso is not truly yours!" She was thoroughly angry now. "You got into it because of that damned cheat La Tules and that crooked lover of hers, Manuel Armijo! La Tules! That gilded redheaded whore with her diamonds and cheap *gringa* fashions!"

Quint couldn't help but grin, although he knew it would irritate her still further. "My God, I should say you're beautiful when you're angry, Lupita, but truthfully I can't. Lupita, *querida,* it makes you look ten years older than you truly are!" He leaped backward with a grimace of mock fear on his face as she sprang forward and swung a fist at him.

"Can't you ever admit La Tules cheated?" she demanded hotly. "She drew the winning cards from the top of the deck."

He shook his head. "You weren't there; I was. I was standing right there when she paired the gold five from the bottom of the deck against Bartolome's ace of swords. She did not cheat!"

"That's a damned lie! You liar! You cursed liar!" Her voice died away as quickly as it had risen. She instantly regretted her burning desire to hurt this man whom she truly adored and loved, even more than her two natural children.

Quint turned on a heel and walked toward the *sala* door.

"Are you leaving?" she faltered, tiny hand at her smooth white throat.

He turned. "Do you want me to stay?"

She was uncertain. What was he up to now? She knew him of old. A man of swift decision and sudden action, *always* action.

Quint smiled. "In there, *por favor?*" he asked, pointing suggestively toward the bedroom door.

She shook her head. "Not until we straighten out this matter that stands between us."

He shook his head in turn. "There is nothing standing between us that is of my choosing, but rather yours. *I* am supposed to be the master in this family. Now, please get into our bedroom." He raised his right hand slightly, as though warning of a possible blow.

Still she hesitated. She was almost positive he'd not raise a hand to strike her. He had never done so before. She didn't think he would now. She was *almost* certain.

Lupita walked quickly, with a slightly sensuous swagger, glancing archly over her shoulder with a deceptively devastating smile, then stepped suddenly into the bedroom, whirling quickly to slam the door shut and drop the bar into place. She sped to the door that opened into the *sala* and turned the massive key in its lock, then across the darkened bedroom to the chapel and through it to lock the door leading into the patio. She returned to the bedroom, turned her back on the door into the patio, and placed her hands palms flat against the door as though to signify she was now secure againt Quint.

It was very quiet. She pressed her ear against the door and listened. She heard nothing, but that meant nothing: Quint moved as noiselessly as a cat. She hurried to the door into the *sala* and listened. Nothing. . . . Perhaps he had left in one of those rare fits of temper of his. Mother of God! She hadn't thought of *that!*

Minutes drifted past. She was bewildered. Now that she had him back after long, lonely months, had she driven him away again? It wasn't like him to be that impetuous, but then he was a proud and stubborn man, with a hidden sensitivity few people other than herself—perhaps the blond *gringa* woman of seven years past, or even his Shoshoni squaw—had ever experienced. Always he treated women of any class gently, courteously, and with consideration, and yet he would not run after any of them at their beck and call for any small favors he might receive. He was a *man!*

Quint heard Lupita bar the doors opening on to the patio. She'd likely do the same with the door into the *sala*. He got a bottle of Pass brandy from a saddlebag. The liquor he had drunk in Taos had begun to wear off, not that he had been anywhere near drunk. He had just managed a pleasing glow that had stayed with him until he reached El Cerrillo. He sat down at the table with the brandy flask before him.

Long minutes ticked past. The brandy level was considerably lowered. The key turned slowly in the bedroom door lock. The door creaked gently as it was opened a trifle. "Quint?" Lupita whispered.

Quint stood up, a towering figure in the dimness.

She quickly closed the door and turned the key in the lock.

"I'll be God-damned," Quint murmured. He drank again.

He crossed the room to the door and tried the handle. "Lupita! Open this damned door!" he cried.

The bedroom was quiet.

Quint took his Hawken and loaded it. He struck a hard fist on the door. "Can you hear me?" he called.

There was a short hesitation. "Yes," she replied.

"Open the door!"

"No!"

"Then get away from it. I'm going to shoot through the lock!"

"You wouldn't dare!" she cried.

"In my own house? Don't delude yourself. Are you away from the door?"

"I don't believe you?"

"I'll count to three! One! Two! *Three!*"

Just before he pressed the trigger he heard another door slam inside the bedroom. The Hawken flashed and bellowed. The bullet drove into the keyhole and knocked the key clattering to the bedroom floor. Acrid powder-smoke swirled about Quint as he kicked open the door. He ran across the room to the door opening into Lupita's old bedroom. The door handle turned easily. He threw open the door and stopped short. The soft flickering light of a single large candle shone on the massive wooden cross with its agonized Christ. Quint's eyes quickly roved the walls scanning the *bultos, retablos* saints, Christs, and religious subjects. Lupita knelt before a small carved altar with her back toward Quint.

"Mother of God," Quint breathed. "What's this?"

She did not answer, only murmured her prayers.

"I want you in the bedroom," he said quietly.

"I'm not ready yet," she replied without turning.

"How many times have you prayed there that I might return and make love to you as we did in the old days, Lupita?"

She turned slowly, ever so slowly. Sometimes he was like a *brujo,* a male witch, in such matters.

Quint crossed to her in three quick strides, picked her up under one arm, and carried her from the chapel, leaving the door partly open. He dumped her unceremoniously on the big bed. She quickly swung her legs over the side and stood up, so close to him her breasts rubbed fully against him from navel to chest. The top of her head just, but not quite, reached his chin.

He tilted her head back and sought her lips, pressing full against them, but with no response from her. He turned away from her, walked to the bedside table, and lighted the candles on a triple candelabra. He walked through the dissipating powdersmoke into the *sala* and got the brandy flask. He opened the bedroom liquor cabinet (one of his first innovations of El Cerrillo) and took out a bottle of wine and two glasses. He turned quickly just before she reached the *sala* door, stepping in front of her, and looking down into her flushed face.

Lupita retreated a little. "Get out of the way," she demanded.

He shook his head. "Get undressed." He held up the flask and bottle. "Brandy or wine?"

"Neither!" she flung at him as she turned her back.

Quint filled a glass with brandy, downed it in one gulp, wiped his mouth on the back of a hand, and flung the glass into the fireplace. She turned a little at the sound. He gripped the high neck of her dress at the back and ripped the fine material down to her waist, scattering the tiny jet buttons over the floor. He whirled her about, tore the dress from neck to crotch, scooped her up, face downward under his left arm, and stripped the dress from her, throwing it into a corner. She was allowed to wriggle free. She tried to run but a big hand ripped the fine lace and cambric of her undergarment and tore it down about her waist, followed by her flimsy and almost transparent brassiere. Her full, brown-tipped breasts swung invitingly as she struggled to free herself from those powerful, denuding hands of his. Then she modestly tried to cover her breasts with crossed arms, giving Quint the opportunity to peel the ruined petticoat down about her slim ankles. She stepped out of it, naked except for her thigh-length black silk hose, lacy garters, and satin slippers.

She battered at his chest with her fists. "Bastard! *Cabron!* Sonofabitch! Whoremonger!" she screamed.

"Tsk, tsk," Quint murmured, grinning at her with his sardonic, scarred face. "That's no talk for a lady, and the mother of my children, Doña Guadalupe." He reached over her flailing arms to pluck out her fine silver-mounted tortoiseshell comb. Her lustrous hair cascaded down about her smooth white shoulders, falling below her waist. Quint whirled her about and shoved her toward the bed, smacking her lightly on her finely rounded bottom. She shrieked as though he had hit her with a shingle. She turned. He shoved her, and she fell back onto the bed. She quickly rolled over onto her belly and buried her face between her crossed arms while kicking her toes into the soft bedding like an angry child.

Quint eyed her creamy white nakedness, accentuated by the wild disorder of her hair and the black silk stockings. The soft glow of the candlelight highlighted the faint rosiness of her flesh. "Jesus Cristo," he murmured. "Where the hell have *I* been all these past months?"

He stripped quickly, throwing his clothing in wild disorder over the floor. Suddenly she rolled over on her back with a forearm over her eyes, seemingly quiescent. Quint eyed her breasts, the roundness of her belly, the fine curly hair at her crotch, the shapely legs, and the ankles he had sometimes encircled between thumb and forefinger.

"Look, Lupita," he invited.

She shook her head and rolled over onto her belly again. He smacked her bottom. She looked sideways and up. Her eyes widened. "*Dios mio!* Good Lord!" she exclaimed in awe as she saw his proud erection.

Quint smiled. "*A sus ordenes, senora.* At your service."

He blew out two of the candles, leaving but one flickering flame casting faint light beside the bed. He lay down beside her, but not touching her, with full brandy glass in hand. "Drink, *querida*," he said softly.

She shook her head. "I'm not thirsty."

"It's not to quench your thirst, soul of my soul."

He rolled her over, raised her head, and touched the glass to her red lips. He sang softly to her,

> "*Por todo mal, mescal;*
> *Por todo bien, tambien.*
>
> Brandy helps everything bad,
> And the same for everything glad."

"You want to get me drunk so you can have your way with me," she whispered against the glass.

"You're right," he whispered back. "Drink."

She held his big hands with her small ones and drained the glass, looking sideways at him in triumph as she accomplished the feat.

Quint raised his eyebrows. Lupita had never really learned how to drink. He placed the glass on the table, re-filled it, and then rolled over close beside her. He passed his hand up and down her sweat-dewed body. The warmth and scent of her, coupled with the brandy he had drunk, began to inflame his senses. He gently molded and caressed her breasts and kissed the nipples into stiffness. She relaxed a little with the sensuous attention and the effect of the potent brandy. He leaned over her and looked down into her shadowed face. She lifted her head and met his lips with hers. They clung together, kissing so repeatedly, it seemed like one long kiss. Quint began to feel impatient. It had been many long months since he had bedded a woman.

He rolled half over on Lupita and forced his knee in between her soft thighs, prying them apart, so he could get his hands in between them to press them outward. Suddenly he rolled quickly over on top of her and in be-tween her legs as she opened up to him.

"For the love of God!" she cried. "You stallion! Can't you wait just a little?"

"Why?" he asked. "I've waited too long already." Just

the same he paused. She was willing enough, but he sensed something might be wrong.

Lupita closed her eyes. What was it Doctor Tomas Byrne had said some months past when she had gone down to Santa Fe to see him? "No more pregnancies, Guadalupe," he had warned her. "You have had all the births you must ever have. It might be dangerous to have more."

"But I've only borne the twins!" she had cried.

"Be satisfied that you did have twins. If you are impregnated again, you might conceivably give birth to a normal child, but it might be too much for you, even dangerous, perhaps even fatal. Do you want me to tell Quint?"

She had shaken her head. "I'll tell him," she promised. But how could she do that? She must keep him at El Cerrillo, and hold him with her and the children. Having another child with him might give added, perhaps permanent assurance of that.

Quint cupped his big hands about her small oval face. "Well?" he asked softly.

She tasted the good brandy on his lips. "Give me the flask, *querido*," she requested sotto voce. She drank, and drank again, so that some of the brandy leaked from the corners of her mouth onto her chest and breasts, mingling with her perspiration then trickling down her belly to her crotch.

Quint drank and then pressed his mouth against hers. She spread her legs outward as high as she could, then guided the hard head of his erection into the soft, inviting moistness between her thighs.

They had always worked well together in bed, except for the first time and for some months later, when he had returned from the north to marry her. She had been virginal then, and *small*. Sometimes she remembered that first night and many nights after that first experience, striving to submerge the pain beneath the intensity of pleasure.

They achieved full rhythm. He became more aroused. She tried to meet his thrusts strongly and please him, forcing Doctor Byrne's warning from her thoughts. They achieved full orgasm together, trembling spasmodically, then fell weakly apart, bathed in sweat, their legs still intertwined. Quint lay back on his pillow with his left arm still cradling Lupita's neck. He reached for the bottle, drank deeply, then fell back on the pillow, breathing heavily.

She stirred. *"Madre de Dios,"* she murmured.

He brushed the sweat-damp hair back from her pale face. She seemed taut and strained instead of relaxed. "Well?" he asked.

She slanted her great eyes at him. "I needed that, my heart. And you?"

He nodded. "You're better than ever, Lupita, if that's possible."

They lay silent for a long time. The house was tomb-quiet. Quint closed his eyes and drifted off to sleep. She lay still, staring up at the ceiling. Something was wrong. She had never felt this bad physically after intercourse, and even the emotional part of the act somehow seemed different. She eased her right hand down to her belly and pressed hard, wincing a little at the reaction. She felt about between her thighs. She raised her hand and held it before her face. It seemed to be gloved. Her eyes widened. It was dark blood! *Mother of God!* What now? She had had her period two weeks past.

Quint moved in his sleep. If she knew her man, he'd not sleep long. He slept like a cat. She eased out of the bed and tiptoed to the bathing tub. She swiftly laved herself, washed the blood from her hands, dried quickly, and crept back to bed. She could not sleep.

The candle guttered out. The only light in the room came from the partly opened door of the chapel. Quint moved a little. He opened his eyes and fumbled about for the bottle.

"Give me some," she said in a strange little voice.

They drank together. He kissed her full wet mouth and then began to explore her breasts and belly. His fingers crept spiderlike down to the thick mat of curly black hair at her crotch.

"So soon, *querido?*" she whispered.

He shook his head. "No hurry, *querida.*"

She snuggled closer to him. "We've months and years ahead of us here at El Cerrillo, my heart." She instantly sensed a sudden change in him.

Quint sat up and swung his long legs over the side of the bed.

"What is it?" she asked quickly. "Did I say something wrong?"

He shook his head. He shaped cigarettes and placed one of them between his lips. He lit both cigarettes, looking full into her eyes as he did so. It had always seemed to him a man could tilt right over the brink of those eyes and plunge down into an abyss of love and emotion from which he might never have the desire or will to escape.

She sat up. "You have come to stay, haven't you?"

Quint shrugged. "For a time," he replied cautiously.

There was a not-too-subtle change in her demeanor. "How long, Quint?" she asked quietly.

"Who knows. There's still much to be done at Rio Brioso."

"There's much to be done here. The children are here. *I'm* here."

"Dammit! I can't be in two places at the same time!"

"Dammit!" she snapped back. "You've never tried, have you?"

Quint grinned. "Pretty good trick," he said dryly.

"You know what I mean! This is your place! I'm here! If that's not enough, you should think of the children! They need you. I'm their mother. I can do much for them, but they need a father." She hesitated. "Especially David," she added slowly.

He studied her. "What is the problem with Davie?"

She looked quickly away.

He cupped a hand under her chin and gently turned her head so that he might look into her eyes. "Tell me," he said.

"You saw him when you arrived here."

"I did. I saw nothing wrong."

"What about the matter of the pony?"

"It was Frank who started the trouble."

"His name is *Francisco*," she reminded him tartly. "After my father. Everyone calls him that, I insist upon it, all except you. Frank is an outlandish *Yanqui* name."

"Perhaps you mean *gringo*? He's half *Yanqui*, or have you forgotten?"

"This is New Mexico!"

He nodded. "So you've always insisted, but the New

Mexico of your father's time and his father's time, and those who came before them, which seems to be the way you want things to be, at least here at El Cerrillo."

"And why not?" she demanded.

"There is a wind blowing across this land," he said quietly. "A wind of change. It's only a matter of time before New Mexico, and indeed, the Far Southwest will probably become part of the United States."

Her face grew taut, etching the fine lines across her forehead and the sides of her nose and mouth. "That is treasonable talk," she accused.

He shrugged. "Perhaps. But it's inevitable."

They looked at each other, two proud, stubborn people, neither of whom would give an inch on such a matter. They had been over this ground many times over the past few years.

"We were talking about David," he reminded her. Talk about Manifest Destiny was always a touchy, perhaps almost dangerous matter with native New Mexicans, including Guadalupe, her relatives, and most of the *rico* class. He couldn't blame them, but he could not accept the fact that New Mexico would not, in time, become part of the United States.

"I want to talk about New Mexico," she insisted.

He stood up. "Later, if you must do so. Let's get back to David. I brought the pony for him, the burros for the twins. Francisco insisted on having the pony. I refused to give it to him. I'm not blaming the boy, in a sense, for the way he acted. He's been badly spoiled. He's basically headstrong, self-centered, and domineering. He should be gently disciplined and taught otherwise."

She leaned back against her pillow and blew a smoke ring. "By whom?" she asked sweetly, with the slightest hint of acid. "His father, whom he *occasionally* sees?"

"*Touché*," he murmured.

"Sit down here beside me," she ordered.

She placed a hand against his left cheek and traced the course of the cicatrix from the corner of his eye to the hard line of his mouth. Nothing in a full lifetime of weathering could even darken that scar. "*Que hombron*," she murmured. "What a man." She touched his lips with hers.

He smiled. She could always work her way around him. "What is it you really want?"

"Nothing for myself. It is for the children."

"Meaning Francisco and David?"

She nodded. "Particularly David."

"I've not noticed this problem before. You've always treated David as if he were your own. I've never thought of you treating him otherwise. I'm sure Rafaela loves him."

She shrugged. "She adores him, but then too, she adores Francisco." She smiled a little. "Rafaela simply loves everyone."

Perhaps she had entrapped herself, although Quint had not intended it to be that way. "Then, if Rafaela gets along with David, and he gets along with her, and she gets along with Francisco and David doesn't, what's the root of the problem?"

She tilted her dark head to one side. "Would you mind repeating that?" she asked quietly, with a half smile.

He shook his head and grinned. "I doubt if I can, and moreover, I'm not sure at all what I intended to say."

She drank a little. "There's Indian blood in David. Perhaps it's bad blood. It wasn't apparent when he was younger, but in past months while you were not here it showed more and more. Quint, it *shows*. . . ."

"What do you mean?"

"Perhaps Francisco gives him trouble now and then, but nothing more than other children might do. Even when it goes beyond a childish prank David does not fight back with words or actions. He walks away, keeps to himself, says nothing, but I am quite sure he broods about it."

Quint narrowed his eyes. "I see nothing wrong in David's walking away from Francisco. Francisco is smaller and younger than he is. Perhaps that's the reason David does not fight back."

She shook her head. "Some day, perhaps soon, when least expected he *will* strike back, and it will be a terrible thing to see. That is what I'm worried about. It's the Indian in him. Of that I'm quite sure, Quint."

"Are you not speaking of vengeance now? You Mexicans of hot Spanish blood were never ones to forget a slight or injury."

"Perhaps you're right, but we are not like Indians!"

Quint shook his head. "They're not different than we are. There is no such thing as bad blood, and if the boy is like his mother, that is all to the good."

"The boy might forgive, at least for a time, *but he will not forget*," she insisted.

Quint reached for the brandy. There was something his father had told him when Quint was a boy in Scotland. "Trust not the Scot. For he will touch pot and flagon with ye, until ye are lulled into believing all is well between the two of ye. Then some dark night when ye least expect it, the Scot will even the score between ye with the point of his dirk."

"Quint? What is it?" she queried.

He drank slowly, then placed the flask back on the table. "It might not be the Indian in him after all," he said quietly, almost as thought to himself.

She studied him as though she understood, but perhaps she had not wanted to believe. "Whatever it is, it is buried deep within him, waiting to emerge when the time comes."

Quint shrugged. "Well, if there is trouble between them, one must look for causes in both of them, not just David."

She smiled sweetly. "Exactly! And that, my love, is one of the many reasons you are needed here at El Cerrillo!"

By God, she *had* him!

"How is your brother Bartolome?" he asked suddenly.

"He seems well," she answered absent-mindedly.

He studied her. "When did you last see him?"

"You tricked me," she accused.

"He has been here, hasn't he?"

She nodded.

"Why did he come?"

She shrugged. "He wanted to see the twins. You know he had never seen them."

"Not unless you held that back from me too."

She shook her head. "I didn't lie about his being here, Quint. I just didn't mention it."

"The man is an outlaw."

"He's still my brother," she said simply.

Quint kissed her. She passed her smooth hands down

the sides of his face, over his chest, and down his lean belly to his crotch. She opened her mouth against his and thrust her tongue into his mouth. She manipulated his privates, gently squeezing, pulling, and pressing until he came to full life again. They joined together with an almost savage abandon, reminiscent of their early days of marriage, the full product of which had been the premature birth of the twins seven months later. She thrust Doctor Byrne's dire warning from her mind, as she had done earlier that evening, and gave herself as fully and passionately as she could. It seemed to her Quint had come home at last to stay. *Maria Santissima!* How could it be otherwise?

★ SEVEN ★

Doctor Tomas Byrne came up to Taos from Santa Fe with his young Genizara woman Luz, at the invitation of Guadalupe to attend a dinner party and *baile* she was giving at El Cerrillo in honor of her husband's return from "the frontier," as she termed it. Everyone was to be there, that is everyone of importance then living in Taos who was considered to be of the American Party, or at least sympathetic to the aims and hopes of that rather nebulous group, in short, the annexation of New Mexico Province by the United States. It was an open secret, at least in Taos, which was far more "Americanized" than Santa Fe. Guadalupe herself was not sympathetic with the views of the American Party—in fact she felt quite the opposite—but she knew better than to mingle that faction with those prominent New Mexicans, such as Padre Martinez, who were devoutly loyal to Mexico, especially when wine and brandy were freely flowing.

Tom Byrne was highly skilled in medicine and surgery. In fact, at that time, he was the only surgeon in all northern New Mexico. He had been thoroughly educated in medicine at Trinity College Dublin. He was Catholic by birth and had been a Mexican citizen for fifteen years. Before coming to New Mexico, he had served for a time as a contract surgeon with the United States Dragoons until he had been disabled for military service by wounds sustained in action while saving the life of his commanding officer. That officer had been Colonel Alexander Jamieson Allan, an immensely wealthy Kentuckian, now senator from that state and chairman of a special military advisory committee to the president and his cabinet. Senator Allan was a man who believed fervently, almost fanatically, in the United States and Manifest Destiny, living only for the day when the Stars and Stripes would fly over the entire Southwest and California. In Tom Byrne he had found a willing convert to this point of view. It had been the senator who proposed to Tom that he emigrate to New Mexico, become a Mexican citizen and merchant trader, and firmly establish himself in the province as a loyal citizen of Mexico. This he had accomplished. He had acquired wealth, position, and prestige. His private library was undoubtedly the best north of Chihuahua City, Mexico and west of Saint Louis, Missouri. It was quite likely no man in Mexico or the United States had the three-dimensional knowledge of New Mexico acquired by Tom Byrne. At one time he had held the mortgage on El Cerrillo. With Governor Armijo, Quint Kershaw, and Gertrudis "La Tules" Barcelo (that most silent of silent partners) he owned the vast Rio Brioso. He was a powerful undercover agent for the United States on the personal payroll of Senator Allan. Last, but not least, Quint owed Tom a great deal for the help the good doctor had offered him when he had first come to New Mexico, a penniless mountain man.

Tom Byrne had received a private note from Guadalupe along with the invitation to stay at El Cerrillo as a house guest and to attend the dinner party. Upon his arrival she had arranged for Quint and the children to be away for the day so that Tom might examine her. She wanted another child from Quint, a holdfast, so to speak, to keep him at El Cerrillo, at least as much as possible during the coming winter. Day and night since Quint's arrival she had prayed to Our Lady of Guadalupe that Tom's diagnosis might be revised from the one he had given her after the birth of the twins, that under no circumstances must she incur another pregnancy. Her prayers had been to no avail. This time he had not merely warned her; he had adamantly insisted she must *not* have another child. The child might be stillborn, or even worse, deformed in body or mind, or both. Further, Guadalupe herself would suffer, possibly ruin her health, or *die*.

They walked together in the lovely patio, already being prepared for the forthcoming *baile* and dinner. "You must be satisfied with what you have, Lupita," Tom advised her. "I don't believe there's need for another child to hold Quint. He loves you. It might not be too apparent. He's never one for a great show of emotion. But, as sure as I am standing here, he loves you."

"If that is so, Tomas," she argued, "why does he insist on spending so much time at the Rio Brioso rather than staying here with his family?"

Tom shrugged. He studied Guadalupe with keen blue eyes. "Because there he is his own man. You can't take a mountain man away from his love of the wilderness and challenge of the untamed frontier and reshape him into your image of a New Mexican *don*, taking his place in *gente fina* society as the husband of Guadalupe de Vasquez, heiress of the de Vasquezes, first family of Taos. You must learn to compromise, to share Quint with his way of life rather than to attempt taking him away from it altogether. If you persist in this, Lupita, you'll lose him. Compromise is the word, little one."

She nodded. It was what she expected from him. She had told her fears to the two wisest men she knew— Padre Martinez and Doctor Byrne. It was amazing, almost eerie how closely they had agreed without ever speaking about the subject with each other, bound by their professions to keep such matters private between themselves and the confessor or patient. They were not friends. No matter how well Tom Byrne had established himself in New Mexico, gaining the respect and friendship of many powerful native New Mexicans, Padre Martinez still looked upon him as one of the so-called American Party, whose unofficial leader was Charles Bent. The padre respected Doctor Byrne, in common with those others of the American Party he also respected, but he still distrusted them as thinking more of their personal interests and ambitions in New Mexico than of the province itself, and beyond that their hope in the ultimate annexation of his beloved province to the United States.

Tom watched Guadalupe covertly as she gave instructions to the many servants who were preparing the patio for the dinner party. She was a beautiful woman, maturing early, very much the *patrona* of El Cerrillo. Here she was absolutely in her element, a daughter of the de Vasquezes doing her duty to carry on the traditions of that once great family of New Mexico, perhaps without fully realizing that without Tom Byrne's finances—through Senator Allan, of course, and by way of Quint—the estate would have been lost long ago, as the great de Vasquez Grant east of the mountains had been lost.

El Cerrillo meant nothing to Tom; the Rio Brioso meant everything. It wasn't because of his quarter partnership. Land had no personal value to him. None of his three partners in the Rio Brioso knew this, of course. Manuel Armijo was interested only in how he could profit from such a venture. La Tules cared for nothing but gold and silver. Her well-known motto was, "With silver nothing fails." Quint seemed to love the Rio Brioso only as long as it was a challenge to him. Now that it was well established, though far from static, there were times when his interest in the grant seemed to wane. But he had to stay there! He had to hold that land! There were most important reasons for that. Whatever Tom could do to make Quint return to the Rio Brioso as soon as possible he would have to do. The most pressing problem at present was Guadalupe, her love of El Cerrillo and her deep-seated aversion to the Rio Brioso. Tom had to take advantage of his position both as family friend and doctor to convince her, subtly but very firmly, to return to Rio Brioso with Quint and their children.

Guadalupe had invited Francois Charbonne to the dinner party. She didn't care too much for him, this quarter Cree Canadian, just as she disliked all Quint's old partners and associates from his beaver-trapping years; but Francois was an incomparable cook who knew how to tease the palates of those who had been invited to the dinner. Francois had been one of the quartet of trappers, partner with Quint, Luke, and the Delaware Black Moccasin. They had been the elite of trappers, the independents who trapped for themselves rather than work for one of the fur companies. They had formed an invincible, now legendary quartet in their time. Francois had done most of the cooking. He had earned his nickname "Boudins" because of his skill in preparing that most succulent of delicacies from buffalo meat and intestines. When the beaver trapping had waned in 1837, the four had broken up their long partnership. Francois had come to Taos to partner his cousin Henri Charbonne, a minor trader married to a Taoseño woman who had inherited large properties in the Mora River area, where Henri ran much cattle and many *churro* sheep. Henri had not long to live and was well aware of it. With his blessing Francois had inherited Maria Charbonne, her two small children, and the trading business. In recent years he had opened a small restaurant and lodging house in Taos, combining French-Canadian, mountain man, Indian, and Mexican dishes in a cuisine whose fame had spread throughout northern New Mexico, particularly among the Americans and other foreigners.

Everyone of importance in the American Party came to El Cerrillo for the dinner party and *baile*. Charles "Carlos" Bent was generally considered the political leader of the Americans in Taos. He also held the respect and friendship of many prominent native New Mexicans. Now forty-five years old, he was of Puritan stock. His grandfather had been one of the leaders of the Boston Tea Party. Charles had started out as a trader in Saint Louis, later joining his three younger brothers and Ceran St. Vrain to form the fur trading company of Bent, St. Vrain and Company. They had built Bent's Fort on the Arkansas in the early 1830s, 530 miles from Independence, Missouri and 280 miles from Santa Fe. The company had become a virtual monopoly. William Bent had eventually taken charge of the fort. Charles had moved to Taos to open a company trading store, but he had not taken Mexican citizenship. Charles had married the nineteen-year-old strikingly beautiful widow Maria Ignacia Jaramillo, a woman of prominent New Mexican parentage. Her mother had been a Vigil. Ignacia had borne Charles five children, two of whom had died in infancy. Her younger sister Josefa had married Kit Carson.

Charles Hipolyte, or Charles Beaubien as he was known in New Mexico, was another honored guest. He was Canadian-born, descended from French nobility. He had studied for the priesthood but had left the seminary to become a Hudson Bay trapper. He had opened a Taos trading store in 1827, become a Mexican citizen, and married Maria Paula Lobato of an influential New Mexican family. His marriage allied him to many prominent New Mexican families—the Maxwells, Trujillos, Abreus, Couthiers, and Mullers, names reflecting the presence of American, French, Mexican, and German born citizens of Taos. He had become a transition figure in the history of the Santa Fe Trail by bringing in bulk trade goods to Taos. He was a remarkable man, a man of the times, merry, natural, genial, shrewd, and immensely popular. His ability, charm, and marriage ties helped him prosper. Politically he had assumed an unofficial role as leader of the non-Mexican members of the Taos foreign colony.

Ceran St. Vrain, like Charles Bent, was an old friend of Quint. Now forty-eight, he was Missouri-born of aristocratic French stock. He had been a mountain man and trapper before becoming a partner with the Bent brothers. He had come to Taos in 1825 and took a Mexican wife the following year. In 1831 he became a Mexican citizen to facilitate the firm's business and had opened a branch trading store in Taos, also serving as United States Consul there in 1834. He was a powerful, impressive giant of a man, with a broad open face, thick black hair and beard, and wide-set eyes. Gifted with great energy, he was a natural and experienced leader of men, and he had the open frankness of the mountain man coupled with natural charm and courtly characteristics. His old friend Kit Carson had given him the accolade of his peers: "All mountaineers look to him as their best friend and treat him with the greatest of respect."

There were many other prominent native New Mexicans and foreigners present—Steven Lee, Cornelio Vigil, James Leal, the Jaramillos, Trujillos, Mullers, Leitensdorfers, Abreus, and other representatives of well-known and established Taos families.

The dinner was a huge success. The *baile* was in full

swing. The guests danced to the continuous music of the Indian drum, or *tombe,* the *heaca,* and *bandolin.* The moon had just risen to illuminate the patio when Federico the majordomo brought Santiago Zaldivar and Blas Galeras of the Mora to the *hacienda.* Both men were exhausted. They had ridden the fifty-five miles from the other side of the mountains without rest. The two men entered the patio smelling of stale perspiration, oiled leather, unclean wool, the odors of horses and manure. They were ill at ease upon encountering such prestigious, well-dressed company. Although Santiago had worked many years for the de Vasquez family, he had never been within the *hacienda.* He was uncomfortable under the cool gaze of Doña Guadalupe, knowing he might spoil her fine party.

Santiago turned his dusty sombrero round and round in his gnarled hands. "Don Quintin, there is bad news from Rio Brioso and the Mora, as well as the entire northeastern frontier from Las Vegas east to the Canadian and north as far as Raton Pass," he reported hoarsely. "Many sheep, cattle, horses, and mules have been stolen by Utes, Jicarillas, and Comancheros. A small wagon train was taken by Comanches and all the people killed."

"Senor Bovian," Blas said to Charles Beaubien, "three trappers outfitted by you were killed by Apaches. Many of your stock have been driven off. Senor Charbonne, your newly built *estancia* has been looted and burned."

So it went on. Those present who were owners or partners of ranches east of the Sangre de Cristos had all suffered losses never before seen.

Santiago continued, "We have been so busy repelling and pursuing the raiders, the animal predators seemed to have sensed it. Wolves have gotten in among the flocks of sheep. A huge grizzly hunts and kills our calves, twenty or so just this year. The giant mountain lion we call Long Tail has reappeared. Colts are his favorite food, but he has been known to drag down and kill big strong California mules."

Cold fear crept through Guadalupe. She was quite sure the only answer to the vital problems reported by Santiago and Blas would be the return of Quint to the Rio Brioso much sooner than she had anticipated. She had been trying to convince herself she was willing to go there in time despite her aversion to the settlement. She had almost succeeded, but certainly she had not intended it to be so soon.

Quint himself was not quite ready to return to Rio Brioso. He had begun to enjoy the long leisurely days at El Cerrillo, seeing old friends, getting to know his children, and above all regaining his love for Lupita.

"What can be done, Don Quintin?" Santiago asked.

"Couldn't you have kept things under control for the short time I've been gone?" Quint demanded testily. He instantly regretted it as he saw the embarrassed look on the old man's face. To be shamed thus in front of all these fine people, many of them whom he had known for many years. "I'm sorry, *viejo*," Quint added quickly.

Guadalupe tapped a foot on the flagstone. "Perhaps he's far too old to be *segundo* at Rio Brioso," she suggested coldly.

Hurt was soul-deep in the old man's eyes.

Quint shook his head. "Not so, wife. He has done a fine job these past seven years."

Now Guadalupe was hurt. Besides, she did not like to be corrected in front of her guests. She sniffed. "Certainly he does a fine job as long as you are there to oversee him, husband."

Santiago had always loved Guadalupe, but now she was no longer the adorable, laughing child he so well remembered. "Doña Guadalupe," he said with simple dignity, "it was not so in the time of your father and his father before that. No one has ever served the family of de Vasquez with greater devotion and loyalty than I. The *patrons* have changed over the years, but I have remained the same."

"Listen to him!" Guadalupe cried. "And you say *you* have not changed! Come, look into my mirror and tell me you are not an old man who is no longer of use to anyone, including himself! In the time of my father and grandfather you would have been whipped naked and bleeding off the land of the de Vasquezes for speaking so to one of your betters!"

Quint took Santiago by the arm. "This is not the time of your father and grandfather, wife. The Rio Brioso is no longer the land of the de Vasquezes." He almost added, "Nor is he speaking to a better, but rather an equal as all of us here are."

"I don't like to be spoken to thus by a servant or even by my husband in front of our guests and the servants!" she snapped.

Quint shrugged. "Then leave, *señora*," he suggested coolly.

Guadalupe stared at Quint in utter disbelief then spun on a heel and stalked into the master bedroom slamming the door shut behind herself.

"I meant no affront, *patron*," Santiago said.

Quint shrugged. "No matter. Blas and you come into the *sala* with me." He looked about at the sober-faced guests. "Do continue to enjoy yourselves, ladies and gentlemen. Doctor Tom and Luke, I'd appreciate it if you would come with us to the *sala*."

Quint closed the *sala* door behind himself. He filled cups with brandy and placed them on the table. "Let's talk this matter over," he suggested. "Sit down all of you, please."

Blas and Santiago were nervous. This was a great honor for such simple men as themselves. To sit at the same table with the great Doctor Tomas, Senor Luke, and greatest of all, Don Quintin himself! No one but him would allow such a liberty. In the old days of the Mexican *patrons* such an honor would have been unthinkable. But to Don Quintin all human beings were equal. It gave him great popularity and respect among the common people. It did not increase them with the Mexican *rico* class and even more of the better-class Americans.

The good brandy warmed Santiago and loosened his tongue. "You understand that without the Delaware hunters and Senor Luke the animal predators are difficult to keep in check. We might have been able to do so if we had not been chasing Indian and Comanchero raiders. Up until recently they had been kept away because they feared you, Don Quintin."

Quint shrugged. "Perhaps. But did not the Cochetopas and some Comancheros steal many horses and mules from the Mora and Rayado not more than two months ago?"

Santiago nodded. "Agreed, Don Quintin, *but not one of those horses or mules were from the Rio Brioso!*"

Quint stood up and walked to the table near the master bedroom door to get another bottle of brandy. As he did so, he noticed the door was slightly ajar, and he caught the faint scent of Guadalupe's perfume.

Santiago was in fine form. "Did you not pursue them with Senors Kit Carson and Luke, with your Delawares and get back *all* the stolen herd? How many of those thieves got back to their den in the mountains? Did you not fight the Comanchero Jake Stow in fair combat and hurl him to his death from the towering palisades of Cimarron Canyon? *Madre de Dios!* What a story! It will be legend! Ah, if I had only been there to see it!"

Quint had not told Guadalupe of that adventure, and he had warned Luke and Jesus not to mention it.

Tom looked up at Quint. "Jake Stow. The name rings a bell. Wasn't he one of the four Comancheros who looted your beaver plews and raped that Shoshoni woman in '38?"

Quint nodded. "It took me seven years to get him. He was the third to die at my hands. I got the loco Indian Jose and the half-breed Antonio back in '38. Now, with Stow gone, that leaves Kiowa, part white, part black, part Kiowa, and all bad. He hasn't got a single redeeming feature of any of the three races. He was at Cimarron Canyon but escaped me. But I'll get him. He'll not escape me. I'll bide my time."

Kiowa was notorious in the Province of New Mexico; an amoral monster in human form. The people could not believe that such a thing was human. To them he was a devil incarnate haunting the earth in human form, delighting in utter cruelty and bloody murder, impossible to kill. Men suffered much at his bloodstained hands; what women endured before he finally killed them was unspeakable. Nothing that could be said against him was exaggeration. If any man had reason to avenge himself on the beast called Kiowa, it was Quint Kershaw.

Quint sent Santiago and Blas for food and rest, then invited Charles Bent, Charles Beaubien, Ceran St. Vrain, and Francois Charbonne into the *sala* for brandy and cigars.

"What do you intend to do, Quint?" Tom asked. "Return to the Rio Brioso or stay here?"

"I hadn't figured on returning there before Christmas,"

Quint replied. "Perhaps not until early spring for the buffalo hunt."

Tom shook his head. "That won't do. You'll have to get back there as soon as possible. I have a premonition the whole northeastern frontier might be going to hell."

Ceran nodded. "It's never been the quietest place I've ever been, but at least when you're there, Quint, you keep a lid on it."

"Can't Governor Armijo send troops?" Charles Beaubien asked.

Charles Bent laughed. "That damned corrupt mountain of fat? He needs his Vera Cruz Dragoons, Presidial Companies, and the Santa Fe Company of the Active Militia Cavalry to stand guard over him in case the people rise up and overthrow him."

"Well, he's got *some* other militia, Charley," Beaubien said rather lamely.

"Peons riding burros armed with rusty flintlock *escopetas?*" Charles asked scornfully.

Tom nodded. "Besides, he figures he's already got some of the best rural mounted militia led by one of his best men on the northeastern frontier."

They all looked at Quint.

"The Rio Brioso is one-quarter his," Quint said. "If he doesn't want to send troops, he's only hurting his own pocketbook."

"And you, by avoiding a return there, are hurting yours," Tom said. "You've done a vast amount of work there these past seven years, Quint. It would be a shame to risk losing it now."

Ceran nodded. "Amen to that."

Quint eyed his guests. "There seems to be a helluva lot more concern about this situation than meets the eye," he suggested dryly.

Charles Bent waved his cigar. "The northeastern frontier must be kept under control *whoever* does the job."

"With you and Kit there, Quint, we had hopes it might remain quiet," Ceran said. "We lost some good men to Fremont. Kit, Dick Owens, and Lucien Maxwell. That leaves you."

Tom studied his cigar as though he had never seen one quite like it before. "Duty is a stern mistress, Quint."

"You feel it's my duty?" Quint demanded.

Ceran leaned toward him. "Do you remember the after-dinner conversation we had with William Bent at Bent's Fort in June of '38?"

Quint nodded. He wondered if Guadalupe was still listening. "I think you're referrring to two words of it anyway, Ceran," he said. What did it matter if she did overhear? "Manifest Destiny," he added.

Each of them was secretly looking forward to the day when the United States would take over New Mexico and perhaps California as well by peaceful means or armed force. There might be some justification for the annexation of New Mexico based on the original claim of the Texas Republic before it became part of the United States that the Rio Grande was indeed the western boundary of Texas rather than the Nueces 250 miles further east. The difference would be perhaps 175,000 to 200,000 square miles of territory. Furthermore, if the Rio Grande was accepted as the western boundary, that would include the three largest towns in New Mexico— Albuquerque, Santa Fe, and Taos.

Tom got up and checked the door into the patio to make sure it was closed tight. "Whichever way the United States eventually takes over New Mexico, there is only one way an armed force from the United States can invade the province. By way of the Santa Fe Trail through Raton Pass or over the Cimarron Cut-Off. Both routes form a junction not far from Rio Brioso and the Mora. The Rio Brioso is the first place beyond Bent's Fort on the Santa Fe Trail where an invading force may obtain forage, food supplies, horses, and draft animals. It is also the only place they can fall back upon in case they are driven back by the Mexicans."

Luke grinned. "Fat chance!"

Tom shrugged. "We must consider every possibility. Further, Quint, we Americans here in New Mexico must be able to hold the northeastern frontier of the province until an invading force has need of our services."

"When and if," Quint added.

Charles Bent nodded. "Exactly. Until that time you might stand to lose a great deal or all of that which you have built these past seven years if the Indians are allowed to run loose. You'll get no help from our esteemed governor in any case, and it might be a long time before the United States does invade. But I don't think there's any question about that, Quint."

Quint looked from one to the other of them. They were right. Each of them, as well as himself, stood to lose a great deal if the frontier was lost to the Indian raiders. If it was not under his control, the theoretical invasion by the United States might fail. The whole weight and responsibility of controlling the frontier had come to rest on his shoulders. He began to realize in a small way the absolute and terrible loneliness of commanders faced with crucial decisions. His whole future might depend on the decision he must make now.

Quint stood up. "Are ye still of a mind to go to California, Wandering Wolf?" he asked.

Luke grinned. "Only if yuh aim to stay here, Big Red."

"I'll be ready to leave when ye get back here with your possibles," Quint said.

The outer door clicked shut behind Luke.

Charles Beaubien stood up. "Is there anything we can do to help you, Quint?"

"Each of you write out an authority for me to take anything I might need from your *estancias*—men, horses, weapons, and supplies." Quint drained his cup. "Goodbye then, gentlemen." He strode from the room.

In a little while the *hacienda* was emptied of everyone except Quint and his family, the servants, and Tom Byrne and his Luz.

Guadalupe watched Quint as he dressed for the trail.

"You heard everything?" he asked.

She nodded. "Everything."

"Then there is no need to explain, Lupita."

"It is not necessary," she agreed quietly.

He looked at her in surprise. "You *agree*?"

"It is your patriotic duty to hold the frontier, my husband."

"You heard the conversation about Manifest Destiny."

She shrugged. "The Americans are not here yet. They may never come. We'll face that decision when and if the time comes. Meanwhile we can't afford to lose Rio Brioso." She studied him. This would be the way she would remember him, always with his deadly Hawken rifle in hand. "You look now as you did when I was a young girl here in Taos, and again later at Cañon Chacuaco, my heart." She smiled quickly and for a moment she herself looked as he had seen her then. He warmed to her. She looked so small and alone.

He drew her close and sealed her mouth with lingering kisses. He held her at arm's length and studied her. "You'll join me at Rio Brioso with the children when it is quiet again?" he asked curiously. There were times when she was a complete mystery to him, as now. He had expected a tearful protestation or a fiery verbal blasting, certainly not a quiet, loving, and dutiful wife. Lupita had an uncanny knack of always retaining a touch of feminine mystique; something held deep within her soul which he knew he'd never be able to reach no matter how hard he tried.

"I'll come as soon as it's safe for the children," she promised.

"Winter will come soon, Lupita. I may have to stay at Rio Brioso until spring."

She smiled. "Then we can have an American Thanksgiving and Christmas together, my love."

Tom Byrne and Luz accompanied Guadalupe and the children to see Quint and Luke leave. "Can I ride with you, father?" David asked quietly.

Quint shook his head. "Not this time. Be patient, Davie lad. Your time will surely come. It won't be long before you'll be at Rio Brioso."

Quint held each one of them close, kissed them, gripped Tom's hand, then mounted his *barrosa* dun. He rode beside Luke followed by Santiago, Blas, and Jesus toward the road leading to Palo Flechado Pass and the Sangre de Cristos. He looked back. A young woman stood under the front portal. She came out of the shadow into the moonlight. It was Cristina. She came partway down the gentle slope in front of the *hacienda,* then paused while looking directly at Quint.

Quint turned and waved. *"Vaya!"* he called.

In a little while the five horsemen were out of sight among the shadowed trees.

Guadalupe herself put the children to bed that night. She retired to her room. It wasn't until she was on her knees before the little altar in the chapel that she broke down completely.

★ EIGHT ★

Subteniente Quintin Kershaw, Rural Mounted Militia of Rio Brioso and Mora, formed a unit of twenty-five picked men armed with Leman Nor'West trade rifles and a brace of single-shot pistols. In fact his company was better armed than the government troops stationed at Santa Fe. Their first duty was to guard the cattle and sheep being driven down earlier from the summer pastures so that they could be more closely watched.

The company ambushed a small horse-thieving party of Kotsoteka Comanches near the junction of Vermejo Creek and the Canadian. The sole survivor was a young untried warrior on his first raid. A .60 caliber ball had "barked" his skull just enough to stun him. When he regained consciousness, Quint prevented his men from killing him as they would a rattlesnake. "We'll give them some of their own medicine, *compañeros*," Quint explained. "Ninety years ago they defeated a big war party of Pecos Pueblos near here. They allowed one survivor to return with news of the disaster as a permanent warning to the Pueblos. So we'll do the same. Let him carry the news back to his people that we men of the Mora and Rio Brioso are ready to meet them whenever they have the courage to cross the Canadian. Tell him so, Wandering Wolf."

Luke had once spent some years with the Kotsotekas, supposedly because he liked their nomadic life, but in reality searching for a legendary gold deposit. They had named him Isa-nanica or Wandering Wolf. It fitted him well, both from appearance and inclination. He had left the band and his young squaw in a hurry after killing the chief's brother in a dispute. Luke spoke quickly in the slurring, gutteral tongue of the Comanches aided by much sign talk. When he was done, the youth looked at Quint with fearful respect, covering his open mouth in awe. He left in a hurry, looking back fearfully over his shoulder.

Quint shaped a cigarette. "What did ye tell him, Luke?"

Luke grinned, just like a hungry wolf seeing easy prey. "I told him who yuh were. The redheaded warrior with the scar on his face who fought the Kotsotekas to a standstill from behind a fort of dead mules near Cañon Chacuaco. I told him you had also defeated a large raiding party at Rio Brioso seven years ago. I said bullets can't hit you, nor arrows strike and that you shoot your small guns many times without reloading. Maybe that will keep his people on the far side of the Canadian."

Quint passed the makings to Luke. "That, maybe, and the coming winter."

Blas shook his head. "Perhaps it is not so good, Don Quintin. Perhaps now every Kotsoteka warrior who wants to a great hero among his people might come looking for you to test his good medicine against yours."

A combined raiding party of Jicarillas and Moaches struck along Ocate Creek, gathering up cattle, sheep, horses, and mules, then headed north. Near Cimarroncito Creek they attacked a *mulada* of thirty-six pack mules. Twelve Mexican packers were killed and two women captured. The raiders headed north again for the Vermejo Valley.

Kershaw's Company were watering their mounts at El Vado de las Piedras, the Ford of Stones where the Cimarron Cut-Off crosses the Rio Colorado. Scouts brought in Ike Parrott, a drifter bound for Bent's Fort with his Arapaho squaw and three half-breed children. He had encountered the raiding party.

"I was once friendly with some of the Moaches, Big Red," Ike related. "Otherwise I wouldn't be here with my woman, kids, animals and best of all, my ha'r. They wanted to kill my woman. They hate Arapahoes. They were raidin' along Ocate Creek and caught a Mex *mulada*. Killed the muleteers, took the pack mules and two wimmen. Headed north toward Vermejo Valley, I'd say." He grinned. "They were sure proud of themselves. Figgered they had outsmarted yuh, Big Red."

Quint shrugged. "Can't win them all, Ike. Were there any Comancheros with them? Maybe ye saw a rough-face? Dark-skinned, thick-lipped man with one eye? A mix breed known as Kiowa?"

Ike shook his head. "No. There were Jicarillas and Moaches. I know Kiowa. He wasn't with them."

"How fast were they moving?"

"Easy-like. Figgered they'd save their hosses and stock."

"How many of them?"

"Mebbe a score or so. I didn't bother to take a census, Big Red." He flashed a snaggle-toothed grin. "I just wanted to get the hell out'a their way."

"Vermejo River, yuh say?" Luke asked.

Ike nodded. "The Valley leads them home."

Quint looked to the northwest. It would be dark in less than an hour. The horses were fresh. Darkness would cover their movements and revealing dust. The valley was at least twenty-five miles from the ford. If they left right away they just might reach the valley ahead of the raiders.

"They wasn't in no hurry, like I said," Ike offered. "They mentioned you, Big Red. They thought you was away over to the northeast around Carrizo Creek hunting Comanches."

"Even if we don't get ahead of them, Don Quintin," Blas Galeras put in, "we might be able to catch up behind them."

Quint shook his head. "I don't want that. They could abandon their loot and scatter. We'd have a helluva time catching any of them. No, I want them *all*, if possible."

They rode northwest until darkness, then dismounted and led their horses, trotting alongside them for an hour, then remounted and rode for an hour, stopping every three hours for a breather. They were in position two hours before dawn. Quint quickly made his dispositions. Ten men, the best marksmen, were situated five each on opposing sides of the shallow river. Luke and Jesús waited for the raiders at the valley mouth. Blas and four men moved up the valley to halt a possible stampede of the stolen stock and eliminate any of the thieves who might escape the ambush. Quint and the remaining eight men waited within the valley mouth for Luke's report.

It was cold in the darkness. The only sound was that of the wind and the occasional thudding of a hoof or chinking of a bit.

The false dawn was just pewtering the eastern sky

when Luke and Jesus returned. "Listen," Luke said. The faint thudding sound of many hoofs came on the wind. "They likely won't be stopping," Luke added. "Not with daylight comin' on, even if they think we're still at Carrizo Creek."

Quint sent Jesus up the valley to warn the rest of the command and remind them to watch out for the two women.

The gray sky was diffused with faint pearly iridescence. A mule brayed. A steer bawled. The bleating of many sheep mingled with the thud of hoofs. Three horsemen appeared. The mingled herd followed them filling the valley from side to side splashing through the shallow water, trying to drink but pushed on by the herders anxious to get much farther up the valley before stopping for water and rest. Thin dust rose and drifted on the wind. The herd drag appeared, followed by the herders. Quint and his men mounted and rode after them. None of the herders looked back.

The light grew. The herd neared the ambush. "Now!" Quint said. He placed his reins between his teeth, cross-drew his Colts, then drove his heels into the flanks of his big chestnut.

The sound of the charge was muffled by the noise of the herd. Quint opened fire, pressing both triggers alternately, and as the pistols recoiled up and back, hooked his thumbs over the spur hammers letting the falling weight of the 9-inch barrels cock the hammers. He fired until each 5-round cylinder ran dry. He removed the empty cylinders and replaced them with loaded ones from his jacket pockets all at full gallop.

The staccato gun reports of the command sounded like the ripping of heavy canvas echoing from the valley sides. By the time the fire slackened, only a few of the raiders were untouched. The women had been rescued. The motley herd was in full stampede up the valley. Three of the thieves tried to outdistance the herd. Gun-flashes sparkled from the valley sides. Three riderless horses ran ahead of the herd. The herd pounded the three fallen raiders into the ground. Blas and his men opened fire to turn the herd, then rode hard against the flank aided by some of Quint's men. The herd slowed down and began to mill. Pistols popped as the wounded raiders were finished off.

Quint dismounted to reload his pistols. "Any of them escape, Luke?" he asked.

"I doubt it, Quint."

The herd was started back down the valley through the settling dust and dissipating powdersmoke. The militiamen watched their leader as he inspected each of the dead, hooking a foot under those who lay face down and flopping them over on their backs, cursing softly, then moving on to the next one. He returned and mounted his horse.

"How can you tell about those three trampled by the herd, Don Quintin?" Blas asked. "Perhaps one of them is Kiowa?"

Quint looked up the valley. "I can tell," he replied quietly.

They ate their cold rations while the animals watered. By the time the sun was fully up, they were on the way back to Rio Brioso and the Mora.

The last week of duty for the militia company Quint sent newly promoted Acting Corporal Jesus Martinez and his squad to Taos to escort Guadalupe, the children, and her personal servants to Rio Brioso. Jesus and his men had been instructed not to tell Doña Guadalupe about the newly built *hacienda*. It was not yet complete, but the living quarters were ready. All that remained was to complete the two corner towers and build a barn in the corral. That would be done by the time the first snow fell.

★ NINE ★

OCTOBER 1845. LONG TAIL.

David led Blaze into the small corral built especially for him at the rear of the *hacienda*. He unsaddled the pony, rubbed him down, made sure there was fresh water in the trough and feed in the lean-to shed built against the rear of the house. He left the corral with his saddle slung over his shoulder, secured the gate, and then trudged to the house, a small, sturdy, and perhaps lonely-looking figure.

Francisco peered furtively around the other side of the house. David was out of sight. The sun was tipping the mountains to the west. Just enough time for him to sneak a ride on Blaze. He opened the gate. Blaze looked toward him. Francisco approached slowly. Blaze was a one-man pony, dedicated to David. Even Rafaela was only accepted by him when David was close by.

The pony moved away as the boy approached. He pricked his ears forward and raised his upper lip from his teeth. He widened his eyes, showing more of the whites. Francisco took the halter from its peg and walked slowly toward Blaze, talking to him in a low, persuasive voice as he had seen the *vaqueros* do. Blaze paused. Francisco tried to put the bit into his mouth. The pony swung his head sideways, striking the boy solidly alongside his head, then quickly nipped his left shoulder.

Tears flooded Francisco's eyes. "God damn you!" he shouted. He lashed out viciously with the halter across the pony's eyes. Blaze bolted to the unlatched gate and through it, galloping in panic down the slope. Francisco felt the rising lump on the side of his head and the teeth marks on his shoulder. He hung up the halter, ran to the gate and fastened it quickly, then vanished around the side of the house. In a few minutes Blaze was out of sight among the trees.

"Long Tail" came noiselessly down the forested mountainside. The mountain lion was a monarch among his kind, a magnificent, amber-eyed brute nine and a half feet long from nose to tail tip. He had a big, rounded gray head with rounded ears. His back was brownish-red, the sides tawny. The belly was white, the stout legs were grayish-hued, and his long tail was tasseled in black. He moved into the wind, without a sound on well-padded feet, concealed by the growing shadows—a big horse-killing cat, a lord of stealthy murder intent on his prey, a chestnut sorrel pony marked with a creamy blaze on its forehead. The man-place was further down the valley. There was no sight, sound, or scent of man creatures.

Blaze grazed alone close to the edge of uncut timber

clothing the lower slopes of the mountainside. Now and then he raised his handsome head to sniff the cool wind of dusk. When the wind shifted, as it always did with the coming of darkness, he caught the faintest hint of wild, alien scent which should have alerted him, but he was young and inexperienced and had lived too sheltered a life. Even had he not, he was being stalked by a master predator. Blaze moved closer to the timber. Long Tail reached blurring speed almost the second he sprang from cover. His powerful jaws snapped the pony's neck with a single bite. Blaze died without an outcry.

The trio of white wolves threaded their way through the forest tangle just before the rising of the moon, an old bitch and two of her offspring, nearly grown males. They paused downwind from the sheep pen and waited. There were no man creatures near the sheep herd. The wolves easily cleared the crude, sagging fence and were in among the sheep with rending fangs. Their hunger was quickly sated by partially eating three sheep who were still alive as they were being devoured. Then the fun began. There was no escape for the terrified, pitifully bleating animals. Round and round they ran, the wolves easily overtaking and dragging down their prey. It became a shambles, with the maimed and wounded sheep in dumb agony, flanks ripped open to the bone, greasy, shining entrails dragging on the blood-soaked ground as they still sought to escape. By the time the moon was fully risen, over half the herd of 150 sheep were dead or mortally wounded. The wolves leaped back over the fence and padded noiselessly into the timber, blood still dripping from their mouths.

"Old Clubfoot," *ursus horriblis,* a monstrous grizzly, moved silently as a hunting cat despite his half a ton of weight, and deformed left rear foot. He was armed with powerful jaws, teeth and razor-sharp six-inch talons. Hunting was good near the settlement of the man creatures. The small herd of cattle stood heads down, tails to the evening breeze, oblivious to any danger. Then some of them caught the fearsome scent of the wind. They stampeded too late. The deceptive, lumbering speed of the grizzly outran a clumsy calf. One powerful paw swipe almost tore off its head. The rest of the herd thundered down the slope to safety. Old Clubfoot dragged the calf carcass into the timber where he had a clear moonlit view of the slopes descending to the river and settlement. There he dined in leisurely comfort.

Buzzards swung in wide, ever-lowering circles over the sheep corral, their black silhouettes sharp and clear against the bright azure of the morning sky. Coyotes hovered in the timber shadows eyeing the remains of the calf left by the grizzly. The gnawed carcass of Blaze had been covered wtih dead leaves in the fastidious fashion of the mountain lion.

Santiago Zaldivar despondently shook his head. *"Pero como, como?* But how, how?"

Quint sat his dun horse, eyeing David sideways. The boy's eyes were fixed on his dead pony. He would not cry. He rarely cried, if ever. It had been a terrible blow to him, for he had loved that pony, not only for itself, but also because his father had given it to him. Yet he showed no emotion, bottling it up inside. It wasn't a good thing, but it was his way, Indian fashion. There would have to be an outlet for the grief and growing anger within him. Perhaps a blood purge. He was far too young for a drunk and a woman.

Luke dismounted and took out the makings. "What's the butcher's tally, *viejo?"* he asked Santiago as he shaped a cigarette.

Santiago squatted, studying the dim tracks about the dead pony. "Eighty sheep these past two days. The week before, twenty of them in one night. Tracks of a full-grown wolf, likely a bitch, accompanied by two younger wolves, males possible. This is their territory. Twenty-two head of cattle these past two weeks, including the calf killed by the grizzly last night. The tracks are the same as those made by a grizzly who kills one calf each night. His left rear foot is deformed, maybe from tearing it loose from a trap. He drags it as he walks."

Luke nodded. "What about the pony? Painter kill, ain't it?"

Santiago looked up the shadowed forest slopes into the thick tangle of timber and brush choking the canyon. *"Leon fantasma,* phantom lion, a ghost of the mountains," he replied quietly. "It could be the same one who dragged down two big, strong California mules last week."

Luke whistled softly. "Must be a big, strong sonofabitch to drag down one of them. Yuh figger it might be the same one we was talkin' about a coupla weeks back?"

Santiago nodded. "Long Tail."

Luke looked at Quint. "Can't let this go on, Big Red. Couple more weeks of this and yuh might be out'a business."

Santiago nodded. "I'll take Jesus and the half-breed Jose. Jose is almost as good a tracker as your two Delawares."

Quint looked at his taut-faced son and then up at the mountain bright in October sunlight. "You're needed here, *viejo*." He did not want to tell the old man the mountains would be too much for him.

David spoke up, "You mean no one will go after those killing bastards, father?"

"I didn't say that, Davie."

"Then who will go?"

Quint glanced sideways at Luke. "Ye game for some varmit hunting, Wandering Wolf?"

Luke grinned. "I've been waitin' for yuh to ask. I'll swear I need to get out of this valley for a while, smell a campfire, kill a few varmits, eat some good venison, and mebbe if we're lucky some prime painter meat if we get Long Tail."

Quint kneed his dun away from Santiago. "We'll be gone a couple of weeks, more or less, *viejo*. Odds are you won't be bothered by stock thieves this late in the year."

Santiago nodded. "There are lookouts posted from the Mora and on up to the Cimarron. The cattle and sheep are down from the high pastures. We'll be all right." He looked down at David, then up at Quint. Something unspoken passed between them. His meaning was plain. It was getting to the time when David should begin his transition from boyhood to manhood. Boys all too soon became men on that frontier.

"Well, Davie, are ye no coming with us?" Quint asked. "From the looks of things Luke and I will need all the help we can get."

Guadalupe was waiting for Quint and David in the

sala. "Where are you going this time?" she asked rather abruptly.

Quint smiled. "Up into the mountains for some pest hunting, Lupita. Wolves got in among the sheep. The slaughter was terrible. A grizzly has been killing calves. We found what was left of Blaze. A mountain lion got him."

Quint did not wait for her reaction. He went into the bedroom and changed into his well-worn trail clothing. Last, but not least, he hung his good medicine about his neck, the grizzly claw necklace. Lupita hated the sight of that necklace. She knew its history and of the Shoshoni woman who had been an integral and vital part of that history.

Quint came back into the *sala*. "Change into your trail clothing, Davie. We'll have to move fast to get up the canyon before dusk."

David looked at Lupita. "Is it all right for me to go, mother?"

Francisco strode into the *sala* from the patio after riding his burro, slapping his quirt against the side of his thigh, aping the hard riding *vaqueros* of the Rio Brioso.

"Get moving, Davie," Quint said.

"I don't think mother wants us to go," David said.

"Get dressed," Quint ordered.

"Shall I wear the mountain man clothing Uncle Luke got for me at Bent's Fort?" the boy asked eagerly.

"Aye, with the Ute moccasins and all. We've hard trailing and hunting ahead of us."

"I'll need a bigger-bored rifle then, father."

Quint nodded. "That will be taken care of before we leave, laddie."

David darted from the room, passing Rafaela as she was entering the *sala*. "Where are you going, Davie?" she called after him.

"Hunting up the mountain with father and Uncle Luke!" the boy shouted.

"How long will you be gone, husband?" Guadalupe asked, rather formally.

Quint shrugged. "A week. Ten days. Maybe more. As long as it takes us to finish the hunt."

"Just like that? A week? Ten days? Maybe more? Is it always necessary for *you* to go on these expeditions?

★ 99 ★

Sometimes you forget you are the *patron* here. You've got peons to do that hard and dirty work. Send some of them and make them earn their keep for a change. Or that man Luke and some of those damned half-breeds around here you like so well."

Francisco snickered. "David is a half-breed, isn't he? Send him along with the others, father."

"Can I go with you and David?" Rafaela pleaded.

Quint shook his head. "Not for this kind of hunting, lassie. It can be dangerous."

Guadalupe nodded. "All the more reason the boy should not go with you. Besides, you are needed here more than up the mountain. Why can't those greasy Delaware friends of yours go? Isn't that their job here?"

Quint opened the liquor cabinet and poured himself a drink. "They have *names*, wife. Perhaps you've forgotten they went to California with Kit Carson and Lieutenant Fremont."

"And I suppose you wish you'd gone with them?"

Quint turned slowly to face her. "The thought *had* crossed my mind," he admitted thoughtfully. "Would you like a drink?"

"At this time of day?" she asked archly.

Quint shrugged. "Good as any time. I'm not needed here now, Lupita. The sheep and cattle are down from the high country for the coming winter. There has been no sign of stock thieves. The *vaqueros* are keeping an eye out for them. Besides, I need to get away from here for a while."

Her face tightened. "From what, or *whom?* Is it *me*, Quint?"

He almost said, *"Perhaps. . . ."*

"You've never learned your true position in life."

Quint shook his head. "Not *my* position, wife, but rather the position *you* want me to accept."

David stalked noiselessly into the *sala*. His Cheyenne leggings were of buckskin, the jacket of elkskin, his moccasins were Ute of smoke-tanned leather, the finest kind of mountain footgear. His hat was like Quint's, rather shapeless, broad-brimmed and banded with the skin of a big diamondback rattlesnake he had killed, skinned, and cured himself. A jaunty grey eagle feather was stuck underneath it for luck.

Quint's eyes widened. He placed his hand in front of his mouth in awe, Indian style, murmuring, *"Wagh.* It is Old Gabe Pritchett come back from an unknown grave to haunt me?"

Luke came to the door, rather reluctantly removing his hat when he saw Guadalupe. "Ready to go, Big Red," he said.

Guadalupe's face grew taut. *"Don Quintin,"* she corrected.

Luke shrugged. "Whatever," he said casually. He stared with feigned amazement at David. *"Wagh!"* he cried. "A sure-enough mountin' man, but without the stink! Waal, we'll take care of that up the mountin'."

David smile proudly. "I told father I don't have a big-bore rifle, Uncle Luke. Only a little small-bore popgun."

"He's not your uncle!" Francisco shouted angrily.

Luke looked questioningly at Quint. Quint nodded. "Go get it, Luke." Luke left the *sala.*

"He's not your uncle," Francisco repeated.

"He is too," David insisted quietly.

"Who says so?" Francisco demanded.

David raised his head a little. *"I* do, and Luke does."

Francisco laughed. "He hasn't got Indian blood in him like you do. How can he be your uncle?"

Quint looked over Francisco's head at Guadalupe. She, Luke, and the Delawares were the only people at Rio Brioso who knew David's mother was Shoshoni. Luke and the Delawares would not have told Francisco. Guadalupe turned away under Quint's steady gaze.

Luke returned loaded with a double armful of accessories and a small rifle. David's eyes widened at the sight of the rifle.

Quint took the rifle and held it out to David. "This was to be yours for Christmas, but ye have greater need of it now. It's a .31 caliber percussion lock custom made by Sam Hawken himself! It's an exact copy of my 'Auld Clootie,' except for size and caliber. I had a rough time talking Sam into making it for ye, but he finally gave in. Likely, it's bound to be the only one in existence; there may never be another one quite like it. Luke, give him the rest of the gear that goes along with the Hawken."

Luke dumped his load on a chest and sorted it out. "Everything yuh need is here, Davie. Possibles bag, chest strap with attached powder horn, Green River knife and sheath, whetstone, bullet bag, wire worm, single ball bullet mold, and Galena bar lead to run balls when yuh need 'em. Percussion caps, awl, nipple pick, firesteel and flint, and all the odds and ends yuh need to keep alive in the mountins and on the plains, mebbe someday in hostile Injun country."

David hung the gear about his person, almost as reverently as a newly knighted squire arraying himself for a quest. He looked up at Quint with moist eyes, but he could not speak.

Quint shook his head. "There is nothing to say, lad."

Rafaela threw her arms about David. "Oh, Davie!" she cried excitedly. "Now you look just like Daddy and Uncle Luke!"

"He needs a scar on his flat Injun face to look like Daddy!" Francisco shouted as he rushed at David with upraised quirt.

David shoved Rafaela to one side out of danger, parried the slash of the quirt with his rifle, then quickly handed it to her for safekeeping. He hit Francisco in the mouth with his left fist, then rammed his right into the belly. Francisco involuntarily doubled over; as he did so David raised his right knee to meet his downcoming face. Guadalupe screamed as Francisco fell sideways, half-stunned with blood gushing from his nose and leaking from his mouth. Luke snatched David back, fended off a solid punch thrown at him, then dragged the white-faced boy out of the *sala*.

"That damned half-breed might have killed him!" Guadalupe cried hysterically. She knelt beside Francisco and cradled his head in her arms.

Quint held Francisco's head between his two hands and examined his face. "Hold him closer," he said to Guadalupe. He quickly set the boy's dislocated nose and pulled two broken teeth from his mouth.

Rafaela closed the door. Her eyes were wide; she was frightened but she did not cry. As Quint stood up, she wormed her hand into his. She looked up into his set face. "Will he be all right?" she whispered.

Quint nodded. "The nose might eventually be a little askew, but I doubt it. He would have lost the teeth anyway. He got off easy."

Guadalupe looked up. "What do you mean by that?" she asked coldly.

"It could have been worse. David might have bent his rifle barrel over Frank's head. Instead, he fought fair."

"Fair? Where did he learn to fight like that? It is not the way of *my* people."

Quint smiled thinly. "No. He didn't use his knife. He fought mountain man style. Luke gave him some lessons."

"So, it was Luke! Get rid of that man! You hear me? He's got to go! He should have been sent away long ago! He's got to go, I say!"

Quint poured himself another drink. "He stays," he said flatly.

"After something like this? He's a savage! A white Indian! A damned renegade! He's like a Comanchero, only worse, and what is more, he stinks as bad as they do!"

Quint couldn't help but grin, just a little. "Not *quite*, maybe, Lupita."

Guadalupe stood up. "He goes, *I* say!"

Quint shook his head. "*I* say he stays. Besides, it wasn't just Luke who taught David how to fight and defend himself. I taught him a few tricks myself. I want him to grow up into a man who can take care of himself in this country. Boys must grow up fast here. The passage from boy to man is hardly apparent. If he doesn't learn fast and well, he won't live very long."

She stared at him, this ofttimes gentle giant of a man she had married who could be as relentless and savage as any Apache or Comanchero if the need arose; an implacable and efficient killing machine. One of her hands crept slowly up to her smooth white throat, a habit she had when thoroughly distraught.

"I'll be leaving with David now," Quint said. He started toward her as though to embrace her and kiss her good-bye, but she turned quickly away from him.

Quint turned at the door. "Frank will be all right," he said. "Maybe he learned something to his advantage this day."

"What do you mean?" she demanded.

"To leave quiet men alone. Do not start trouble with them. They rarely start fights; they usually finish them."

"Get out!" she shouted. "Be sure you have plenty of

aguardiente for yourself and that drunken friend of yours! You hear me?"

Quint wisely closed the door on that.

Guadalupe looked at Rafaela, as though for support.

"Father is sometimes right on such things," Rafaela said, very grown up.

"Get to your room! You're all against me!"

The little girl shook her head. "No one is against you, mother. We all love you, and none of us more so than father."

"Get to your room, I tell you!" Guadalupe cried. Her voice broke, followed by a deluge of hot tears.

Quint, Luke, and Dave rode from the *hacienda*, leading three packhorses. When they started the long, steep climb up through the river canyon, Quint looked back. He took his telescope from its buckskin case and focused it on a small figure seated on a little burro. Rafaela. . . .

Luke let David pass him leading the packhorses up the trail. He rested his crossed forearms on his saddle horn. "She will be the one to suffer most," he said quietly, almost as though to himself. "She dearly loves both those boys, and Guadalupe and you, of course. By God, Quint, I think she even loves *me*."

Quint nodded. "The wee lassie is all heart," he agreed. "You're right, Luke. She will be the one to suffer most."

"I hardly recognized Davie as he fought," Luke said thoughtfully. "The grip of hate on his face was so powerful. Like he couldn't feel any pain himself, only a rage to destroy his enemy." He looked sideways. "Reminds me of someone I've known for a long time."

Quint cased the telescope and took out the makings. He shaped two cigarettes and handed one to Luke. They lighted up. "Go on," he urged.

"There's much of you in him, Big Red, and mebbe much of his mother too. She was a gentle one, as I recall, but I remember her fighting alongside the warriors against the Crows at the Medicine Lodge Fork fight back in '37." He looked up the trail to where David was riding ahead of his charge of pack mules. "He's not one to start trouble. He'll be a sonofabitch to straighten things out."

They rode up the trail together.

The wolf bitch lay complacently in the bright, early morning sunlight of a high mountain meadow idly watching the two nearly grown males playfully tussling with each other over an old dry bone.

"One hundred and seventy-five yards," Quint whispered. He closed his telescope.

Luke nodded. "Give or take ten."

"I'll take the bitch. You take one of the others."

"Who gets the other one?" David asked quickly.

Luke looked sideways at the boy. "Yuh game to try?"

David nodded.

Quint shook his head. The boy must be taught the discipline of the hunt. "All three of the wolves must die. *Now.*"

"Why can't I try, father?" David asked.

"We can't miss, laddie. It's taken two days to track them down. We might never get another chance like this. They're killers, not satisfied with simply killing to eat. If one of them escapes he'll run with others who'll likely follow his example. Ye still want to try?"

Dave shook his head. "You're right. I'm not ready yet."

Luke grinned. "Ain't quite like huntin' rabbits, Davie."

Quint nodded. "After all, Davie lad, it was the mountain lion who killed Blaze, not the wolves."

David looked quickly at Quint. "Will you let me kill him?"

"Sure, laddie, if we can track him down."

Luke yawned. "While you're discussing the details, partners, them killers out there in the sunlight might take it in their minds to skedaddle."

Quint popped a rifle ball into his mouth and poured an extra charge of powder into his left palm. "Bet a flask of Taos Lightnin' I get the third wolf."

Luke nodded. "You're on. I'll take the bold bitch to start."

"Time," Quint said.

They stood up, raising their Hawkens in easy fluid motion. The two rifles cracked as one. The bitch wolf simply dropped her head in instant death. One of the males leaped high, then fell thrashing to the ground, soon to die. The surviving wolf loped at speed for the timber. Powder charges poured down muzzles; bullets were spat down the bores and rammed home; rifle butts thudded on a log to seat the charges; hammers were cocked and percussion caps were pressed on nipples. Both rifles were raised as one while triggers were set. Hawkens flashed and cracked simultaneously. The wolf died instantly at the edge of the timber.

Luke spat to one side as he reloaded. "Thrown cold," he said laconically.

The shot echoes died thundering down the canyon. It was quiet again except for the soughing of the wind through the towering pines.

David's eyes were wide, his mouth gaped open. "Jesus Christ, I never seen anything like that before," he murmured.

"*I've* never seen anything like that before," Quint corrected.

David nodded. "Where'd you learn to shoot so fast, then reload before you do anything else?"

Luke grinned. "Ol' Bug's Boys taught us that the hard way, Davie lad. You know—the Blackfeet."

"I didn't know they were friendly yellowskins."

Luke shook his head. "Weren't. It was a case of them or us. Neither side took prisoners. Do or die. Yuh learned fast in the beaver-trappin' business, or yuh didn't live long enough to cash in on your plews at the rondyvoo."

They walked to the wolves. Luke rolled over the last one killed.

"Who won?" David asked.

Luke poked a finger into a pair of bullet holes, either one of which would have been sufficient to kill the beast.

David covered his open mouth in awe.

Quint and Luke each skinned a wolf, leaving the third for the boy. It was a hell of a job for him, but he persisted, making in the process a bloody, greasy mess out of his clothing by wiping his Green River knife on it.

Luke grinned. "Waal, nubbin', now yuh look more respectable. Coupla more months in these mountins living off the land and the game you'll sureenough look, and what's more important, *smell* like a real child of the mountins. *Waagh!*"

Grizzlies are territorially inclined. Woe betide the ignorant stranger who inadvertently or willfully wanders into their private domain. Quint explained this vital fact to David after they found the tracks left by the grizzly who had slain the calf five days past. The tracks were unmistakable, the deformed left rear foot plain to be seen.

"He's old and crippled," Quint said. "That's why he risks raiding so close to the settlement."

"One helluva brute," Luke added. "From the track depths on the softer ground, I'd estimate Old Ephraim weighs at least half a ton."

"Why is he called Old Ephraim?" David asked.

Quint semiconsciously traced the course of the brutal scar on his left cheek. "Ephraim is wedded to his idols, leave him alone. It's in the Bible, son."

They found Old Ephraim complacently digging for wild onions at the far end of a wide mountain meadow. They watched him from downwind, a good one hundred yards away, just within the edge of the timber.

"His primary tools of war are not his teeth, Davie," Quint whispered, "but rather his terribly armed forepaws. In order to strike he rises on his hind feet. When ye see that, shoot fast and straight, or get to hell away from him, standing not upon the order of your going. His loving embrace is certain death."

Just as though he had heard Quint whisper, the bear turned and looked directly toward the three hunters.

"Better try for him now, Big 'Red," Luke whispered. "Cripple or not, he could still be fast enough to jump over his own shadow if need be."

Just as the two Hawkens cracked, the grizzly threw himself to one side. He roared, *"Wa-a-a-agh!"* It was at one and the same time a horrific grunt, boast, and warning of sudden death. He charged directly toward the revealing cloud of powdersmoke. He covered fifty yards before the Hawkens flashed again, slamming a pair of half-ounce Galena pills into him, seemingly with little effect. Twenty yards away he rose on his legs, roaring like an avalanche in full descent.

Quint spat a bullet into the smoking muzzle of his rifle. *"Vamonos!"* he yelled at David.

David paused just long enough to fire his rifle point-blank at the towering mass of roaring mayhem and death, then vamoosed as fast as he could go, bounding over fallen logs with his smoking rifle at the trail.

Two more slugs thudded into the beast. Quint and Luke parted, darting right and left to get big pines between them and the charging bear. Old Ephraim roared insanely. Big drops of blood mingled with reddish foam flew from his gaping mouth. His razor-sharp claws ripped bark from the tree behind which Luke had taken cover, only inches from his face. Quint whipped out his pair of Paterson Colts and emptied them, ten .36 caliber balls at fifteen-foot range, directly at the spine of the beast. The bear shuddered spasmodically. He fell slowly sideways like a toppled pine and crashed to the ground. The air was thick with acrid powdersmoke. The last of the shot echoes died away.

Luke poked a white face around the side of his pine and stared at the furrowed bark stripped from the tree by the murderous claws.

Quint leaned weakly against his tree, peering through the swirling powdersmoke at Luke. He smiled wanly. "Old Ephraim is wedded to his idols. Leave him alone. Maybe we should have taken our own advice, eh, Wandering Wolf?"

Luke pulled the cork from his brandy flask with his teeth and drank deeply. He handed the flask to Quint. *"Madre de Dios,"* he murmured. "He mebbe got between fifteen and seventeen Galena pills in him afore he went down for good."

David came slowly and cautiously through the shadowed timber. He paused a respectful twenty feet from the huge carcass, his eyes wide in his pale face.

Quint reloaded his rifle. "We'll camp here tonight. We can move on up the canyon after we skin him."

After two days they moved camp to a narrow canyon with a clear trout-filled stream lined with willows and alders. A colossal granite-faced, double-humped mountain rose sheer above the canyon. It had at least a nine-thousand-foot summit and towering reddish-brown cliffs a sheer two-thousand feet high. The area was trailless, wild, and primitive, uninhabited and almost impenetrable to the inexperienced. It was terrain to be avoided, but it was probably the solitary territorial domain of Long Tail.

Luke finished bundling the fleshed grizzly hide. "We been in the mountains two weeks, Big Red. Got the wolves and Old Clubfoot. Two out'a three ain't bad, leastways in this tangled up country. Mebbe time to call a halt? They's a smell of snow in the air these past few days or I miss my guess." He slanted his green eyes toward David as he spoke.

David was honing his Green River knife. He tested the edge on the pad of his thumb and looked slowly at Luke.

The sun was setting, the wind getting colder. Quint threw wood on the fire. "It's good to be in the mountains again," he said. He lighted his pipe with a smoldering twig.

Luke nodded. "Still, in a couple of days we'll have to head out. Big snow due any day now. Don't want to get snowed in. Might have to *invernar* for the winter in this canyon."

David looked steadily at his father.

"Ye forget we haven't got Long Tail yet, Luke?" Quint asked.

"No. Yuh still aim to try for him?"

"I do."

"Who'll back yuh? I will, of course, like I been doin' the past ten or twelve years. Seems like every time I let yuh get off on your own hook yuh get a bullet in yuh, or get stuck with a knife, or clawed by a ba'r, or somethin' bites yuh. Still, I think we ought to pull foot soon."

"Well, if ye won't back me, Wandering Wolf, I'd better not try for Long Tail alone," Quint said resignedly.

Luke squatted by the fire and filled his pipe. It was coming up father-and-son time.

David sheathed his knife. "I ain't leaving this country until I get Long Tail," he said quietly. He looked at Quint. "If Uncle Luke is too old and tired to back you, father, I'll do it."

Quint nodded. "That's generous of ye, lad. I was

★ 109 ★

hoping you'd say just that. After all, it was your Blaze the panther killed."

Luke solemnly shook his head. "Rough country up thar," he warned dolefully. "No place for greenhorns."

"We'll make it all right, won't we, father?" David asked.

Quint grinned. "No question about it, son."

David's grin matched his father's.

Later, as the boy slept bundled up in a cocoon of Navajo blankets covered by a buffalo robe, Quint and Luke split the potent contents of a flask of Pass brandy.

"Thanks, Luke," Quint said. "Ye worked that beautifully. We'll take two of the packhorses. The sorrel and the old buckskin."

"That buckskin won't hardly make it up the mountain."

Quint shrugged. "He'll make it. I'll need bait for the panther. The buckskin should do."

"I'll trail after yuh with the rest of the horses and the gear. When I hear the shootin', I'll stop and make camp."

"Good thinking."

Later, as the pipes went out and the fire was but a thick bed of ashes, Quint rose to go to bed. He looked down at his partner. "Thanks again, Lukie," he said.

Luke looked up. "For what this time?"

Quint studied him. "Just for being yourself all these years, and particularly tonight." He knocked out his pipe, yawned and stretched, then went to his blankets and robe.

Luke emptied the flask. He hiccuped. "Waal, I'll be Gawd-damned," he murmured. He grinned, well pleased with himself and life in general.

The high country was all up-and-down like a temporary relief map made by tightly wadding a ball of newspaper and then partially spreading it out, but that could not give the true overwhelming impact of its chaotic ruggedness. The mesa surrounded by immense granite outcroppings could only be ascended by a hard climb of three thousand feet in a mile and three-quarters. The lower slopes were thickly clothed with aspen and oak brush, mingled with groves of huge pines and some blue spruce while the higher-up forests of pine and fir were mingled with aspen and scrub oak spread in tangled profusion. To the west, towering above the closer elevations, were the majestic Sangre de Cristos. Despite the seeming vast isolation the mesa was not much more than fifteen miles from the Rio Brioso as the crow flies.

Quint padded noiselessly through the thick stand of timber upslope from a wide mountain meadow. He glanced back over his shoulder at the small figure aping his walk. He smiled as he turned back to the faint trail they had been following since early morning. He halted suddenly, half turned and placed the fingertips of his left hand over his lips, then inclined his head slightly, Indian sign language for silence. He knelt and beckoned David to him. He pointed to the ground. There were two parallel markings on the loose soil terminating in two small piles of earth and pine needles about four inches high. Quint pointed to his nose and then at David's, then to the piles. The boy knelt and sniffed, wrinkling his nose as he did so.

Quint led the way to cover in a jackstraw pile of fallen timber drifted thickly with fallen leaves. He and the boy crouched low. "Those are mountain lion territory marks, Davie. The home ground of a lion, male or female, is marked by their making short, heavy backward strokes, first with one hind foot and then the other, forming piles of debris, then urinating on them.

David wrinkled his nose. "I *know*, dad."

"These 'scrapes' are markers for their personal territory. So, we must be between two territories. Problem now is which of them belongs to Long Tail."

"Can't we cover both territories?"

Quint took two pieces of jerky from his possibles bag and gave one to David. "Problem is, son, a winter range can be as much as fifteen to thirty square miles, which leaves maybe thirty to sixty square miles for us to cover, and we haven't got hounds to track them down for us. The snow will start falling any day now."

They sat there gnawing at the tough dried meat. David took the cork from his gourd canteen and passed the canteen to his father. "Which maybe leaves us nothing for this lion hunt but a beautiful view," he said quietly.

Quint finished his jerky, drank deeply, wiped his mouth on the back of his sleeve, and stood up. "Why?" he asked. "Ye ain't quitting, are ye, laddie?"

David was up on his feet immediately. "What do we do now?" he asked.

"Look for sign, Davie. Look for sign."

There was a brushy section at the lower north end of the mountain meadow where the ground was soft from rainwater. Quint pointed to the faint tracks. "Lion was stalking here, maybe. See how he placed his hind feet in the imprints of his forefeet, thus lessening the chance of snapping a twig or dislodging a stone?"

Quint looked out over the long, wide sunlit meadow. "He hunts around here when he's not dining on our veal."

"Are you sure?" David asked.

The wind shifted. The warbling, whistlelike sound came faintly from somewhere on a ridge beyond the south end of the long meadow.

Quint gripped David by the shoulder and forced him to the ground. "Listen!" he hissed. The warbling sound changed to shorter, more intense tones, repeated several times, then stopped abruptly.

"Birds?" David asked. "Sounds more like a big loud house cat."

Quint shook his head. "Painter talk," he whispered.

They lay silent and motionless.

The sounds came again, farther away this time.

"We're right on top of some of them, Davie," Quint whispered. "Go back and get the buckskin. Turn him loose in the meadow."

David looked back at the shadowed, darkened woods.

"You're not afraid?" Quint asked. "They rarely attack man. Will try to escape first."

David smiled wanly. "That's a comfort," he said dryly.

Quint grinned as he watched the small figure vanish noiselessly into the thick brush. He hoped to God they were in the territory of Long Tail. Time was running out. A few more days and they might get caught in the first snowfall.

They camped that night in the pile of fallen timber overlooking the meadow and the grazing horse. As the moon rose, Quint's memory took him back eight years to just such a place many miles to the north in the Rockies, a great valley where he was to winter. He quickly shook his head to dispel the memory. It was not good to dwell upon. He looked down on the sleeping boy. David's mother had been there.

The aged buckskin was partially blind. He drifted slowly grazing. The moonlight was almost as clear as day.

The buckskin whinnied, then neighed sharply.

Quint gripped David by the shoulder, clamping a hand over his mouth to prevent any sudden outcry. The boy was awake at once. He followed Quint over the fallen logs. They ran lightly and noiselessly downslope toward the edge of the meadow.

The buckskin was quiet now. He stood close to the timber on the west side of the meadow looking into the shadows. He was nervous, unsure but seemingly more curious than frightened.

Quint uncased his telescope. He focused it on the horse. He handed the telescope to David. "Watch his ears, Davie," he whispered. "A horse talks with his ears. There's something suspicious in among those trees."

The panther made his move so quickly he caught Quint off guard. The lean, tawny shape launched himself with blurred speed from the shelter of the timber. He landed with the forepart of his heavy body on the rump of the buckskin. The horse jumped forward and reared, shaking loose the powerful grip of the mountain lion. Long Tail slid backward while digging in with his talons raking them deeply from withers to hips. The buckskin screamed like a demented woman. Inch-long fangs sank into the ham of the horse and tore loose a blood-dripping chunk of hide and flesh. The lion struck the ground. The frenzied horse bolted toward the south end of the meadow. The moonlight shone on the bright, dripping blood.

Quint stood up. The mountain lion bounded after the horse. He leaped again, trying for the horse's back. Quint's Hawken roared throatily. The .53 caliber ball struck Long Tail and seemed to hurl him sideways. He hit the ground, rolled over twice, regained his feet, and streaked toward the north end of the meadow. Another Hawken spat flame and smoke with a thinner, whiplike

★ 113 ★

crack. The lion jerked and fell sideways kicking spasmodically. David's shot was echoed by Quint's second. The lion stiffened and lay still.

Quint looked down at David. The boy was pouring a charge of powder from his left palm into the smoking muzzle of his rifle. He spat a bullet into the muzzle, started it down the bore, then rammed it home with his wiping stick. He capped the nipple, then looked up at his father.

"I'll be damned," Quint said. "Fast time there, son."

"You and Luke told me always to reload at once when in Indian country."

Quint nodded seriously. "So we did!" he said emphatically.

David shook his head. "Then why haven't you reloaded yet?"

Quint laughed as he quickly reloaded. "You're right, laddie."

"Of course," David added conversationally, "maybe it ain't 'zactly Indian country. The Jicarillas and Moache Utes are pretty quiet now, 'ceptin for some sheep stealin' now and again, but not at the Rio Brioso, after the lesson we taught them. But you never know. Still, there may be some Utes around, but we won't know unless they show themselves. Luke always says the only way to find a Ute in the mountains is to let him find you, but, make damned sure you know when he's getting close."

Quint studied the serious, little Indian-like face with the incongruous gray eyes so like his own. "Aye, lad," he agreed. "Come on! Let's take a look at that painter!"

The buckskin was a pitiful sight. Blood glistened on his trembling sides. He stood with head down and splayed out legs, shivering spasmodically.

"Did you *have* to use him as bait?" David asked, almost accusingly.

Quint suddenly felt guilty and ashamed. He hadn't figured on the panther moving so lightning-quick on the attack. "We hadn't much time left to hunt for Long Tail," he explained rather lamely. "The buckskin was the best way to lure him into the open." He didn't sound very convincing, but it was the truth all the same.

Quint rested his Hawken on the body of the panther. He walked slowly toward the buckskin, talking in a low, persuasive voice. "Hoh, hoh, hoh, hoh. . . . Hoh, hoh, hoh, hoh. . . ." It brought back a night years past along the Arkansas when he had accomplished an unheard-of feat for a white man by stealing two Southern Cheyenne horses right from under their noses; one of them had been a prized bay mare marked with the split ears of a buffalo-runner.

The buckskin turned to look at Quint. He moved slowly toward Quint for comfort and solace. Quint knew the old-timer couldn't be saved. The Colt was drawn, cocked, and fired so fast David hardly saw the action. The buckskin was dead before it hit the ground.

Quint raised the heavy head of the mountain lion. There were two bullet holes in it. Either one of them could have killed the beast, but Quint's bullet had probably struck while he was either dying, or already dead and kicking only from reflex action.

"Did I do well, father?" David asked.

Quint nodded. "Ye paid him off for Blaze, laddie." He shook his head in amazement. "Seventy-five-yard head shot on a moving target, and by moonlight at that."

David casually inspected his fingernails, aping his rifle coach Luke Connors. "Closer to a hundred," he said.

Quint grinned. He drew the boy close and squeezed him hard. "Ye'll do, laddie, ye'll do," he murmured. He turned his head away from the lad so that he might not see the tears glistening in his eyes.

The moon was on the wane by the time they finished skinning the panther together. Quint cut out some choice parts of the meat, to some mountain men the best part of their varied cuisine.

"Will we camp here?" David asked.

Quint stood up. He handed the meat to the boy, then picked up his Hawken and the raw pelt. "Listen," he said softly.

A wolf howl had broken the brooding stillness.

They located Luke by the odor of woodsmoke where he had established camp two miles from the meadow. A cooling deer carcass hung from a tree branch. He nodded in appreciation, covering his open mouth in awe as Quint spread out the panther's magnificent pelt, already winterizing with luxuriant fur.

"I figure about one hundred and eighty pounds, Luke,"

Quint said. "Three balls in him. "My first shot just wounded him slightly. He was streaking for cover while I was reloading. Davie fired. Maybe a hundred yard head shot on a moving target by moonlight. He went down and I put another ball in his head to keep him there, but he might have been dead already."

Luke nodded. "It's Long Tail all right, or I miss my guess." He looked proudly at David. "Yuh did right well, pup. We could have used yuh on the Seeds-kee-dee Agie or the Yellowstone when we trapped beaver and fit Blackfeet and Crows."

"Maybe we could go back again?" the boy suggested eagerly.

Luke shook his head. "Them days are gone forever. No call for beaver pelts anymore since they started making hats out'a Japanese silk. Hell ought'a fill up with hats made out'a silk." Luke looked at Quint over David's head, a look exchanged between them fraught with great memories.

Quint nodded. " 'Where are the snows of yesteryear?' " he murmured.

Later, when an exhausted David went to his robes and fell instantly to sleep, Quint stood over him looking down at the brown-skinned little face with its high cheekbones. When David was asleep with his clear gray eyes closed, the resemblance to his Shoshoni mother was striking.

Quint and Luke lay on robes beside the fire long after David had gone to bed. Luke looked at the boy. "When he's a man, likely there will be few enough of us left who'll know what a tipi smells like, or how to set a beaver trap proper and case, stretch, and flesh a plew. En-Hone, seems-like it ain't in human nature not to trap beaver and have an Injun squaw to cook for yuh and keep yuh warm under the robes on cold nights."

They looked thoughtfully at each other across the dying fire. The first snowflakes drifted down silently from the darkness to hiss in the embers and powder the cold ground.

ELEVEN

MARCH 1846 - CRISTINA

Cristina was alone in the big kitchen. She shivered as the late winter storm howled about the *hacienda*, sucking the smoke, flame, and sparks up the kitchen chimney and driving them at right angles from the top off into the snow-swept darkness to the south. Now and again hard sleet battered at the loophole shutters. It was long after dusk. Don Quintin was a week overdue from Pueblo. Cristina had waited up for him until midnight each night that week, shivering some from cold but mostly from fright. She was alone in the *hacienda* except for young David, who had been left in her charge by Doña Guadalupe when she had left hurriedly for Santa Fe with Francisco and Rafaela. Josefina the cook had gone with the *patrona*. The live-in servants were all in their quarters outside the *hacienda* quadrangle. They had been in bed for hours. Even old Tomas, the porter, had left for his bed after dusk, saying none but a damned fool would be abroad that witches night. Cristina had tucked David in much earlier, although he had protested that he wanted to wait up for his father. But Cristina had a way with him. He was like a younger brother to her. He adored her, and the feeling was reciprocal. There seemed to be only four people who were close to David—his father and sister, Luke Connors and Cristina.

Don Quintin had been gone only for a week when Doña Guadalupe had decided to travel to Santa Fe, as she said for a little gayety and comfort. Cristina knew better. During the long winter months the *patrona* had changed, losing weight and color and aging perceptibly before one's very eyes. It had been Josefina who tipped Cristina off that it was some sort of female trouble, that her intercourse with Don Quintin had become increasingly painful until she had reached a point where the very thought of such an act was almost horrifying. Each day Don Quintin was supposedly due back at Rio Brioso added to the dark circles under Doña Guadalupe's beautiful eyes, and the tiny hairlike tension lines had become etched deeper into her smooth, creamy skin. A trader bound from Pueblo to Santa Fe had brought word Don Quintin would be delayed a few more days on business. It was then the *patrona* had made up her mind to go to Santa Fe, ostensibly for some pleasure and creature comfort, but actually to consult with Doctor Tomas Byrne. She would stay with Doctor Byrne, if Don Quintin wished to follow her there, but it wouldn't be necessary, for she would return to Rio Brioso as soon as the weather cleared into spring.

Cristina had spent increasingly more time with Doña Guadalupe since the first of the year, and although the *patrona* was very haughty and aloof with the other help in the *hacienda* (she completely ignored the field workers and ranch hands), she had slowly begun to treat Cristina almost like a younger sister, telling her little confidences, listening to her troubles, and virtually taking her into the intimate family circle even to the extent of allowing her a room in the *hacienda* itself. It was small, it had been planned as a storeroom, but it was actually in the same building where Don Quintin lived with his wife and children. Carefully and patiently Doña Guadalupe had taught Cristina English, better manners and deportment, how to read and write (a miracle among her class), to sew and take care of the children. Cristina learned quickly. Of late, she had noticed Don Quintin watching her when he thought she was not aware of it. Her original awe, and even fear of the *patron*, had gradually diminished until now there was little of it left, replaced by something of which she herself was not fully cognizant. Perhaps she loved him? If so, it would be a hopeless thing. He was happily married and loved the children. How could she contend with Doña Guadalupe? Not that she had ever dreamt of such a thing in her wildest thoughts. Or, had she . . . ?

The wind seemed to slam itself against the north wall of the *hacienda*, driving icy needlelike blasts through cracks in the loophole shutters. Cristina stacked more firewood vertically in the huge, bell-shaped corner fireplace. The wood supply was rapidly diminishing. It took four men with two *carretas* and four yoke of oxen to provide daily firewood for the *hacienda* alone during the winter. That day they had not been able to get the *carretas* through the drifts and had to pack as much as they could on burros to bring it, but there had only been enough for the kitchen and the master bedroom. The remaining rooms would be like tombs. David would be snug enough under his Navajo blankets and the thick pelt of the huge grizzly his father and Luke had hunted down in his company last fall.

Cristina stood with her back to the fireplace, lifting her full, red skirt and many gayly colored *enaguas*, petticoats of homemade flannel, to warm the backs of her sturdy legs in their thick, white woolen stockings.

She had wanted to go with the *patrona* to Santa Fe. She was deeply concerned about her. Doña Guadalupe had shaken her head. "You must stay here and take care of David, and Don Quintin when he returns. You must devote yourself to the *patron*, and grant his every wish. You must foresee things that he might want, without his having to ask for them. In everything, you understand, *everything*. . . ." Cristina had looked into those great, lovely eyes of the *patrona*, searching for the exact meaning in what she had just said, then slowly, ever so slowly it had crept into her mind.

Doña Guadalupe had paused, seemingly to look into the distance. Then it had come, as Cristina half expected. "I am sure you are still a virgin, eh, my child?" Cristina had nodded, then replied, "Yes, *patrona*. No man has known me." After Doña Guadalupe had left, Cristina had several times thought back to the first time she had seen Don Quintin, when he had come to El Cerrillo the summer before. She had only been in service a short time, handpicked by the *patrona,* who had made sure she was still a virgin. The men servants of El Cerrillo had been severely warned to keep their hands off her. Doña Guadalupe wanted her for the *patron*. It was merely custom, although the *patrona* had never spoken about it to Cristina. Cristina had figured it out herself, with the help of the admirable Josefina. Over the long months of her servitude she had often wondered when she would be summoned to the bed of Don Quintin. One her age should have been married by now, or at least taken as a mistress by some *rico*. There were times when

Don Quintin studied her with a strange expression on his scarred face, almost as thought he had known her before.

The wind slackened. A muffled thudding noise came to Cristina. She ran to the door and placed her ear against it. She heard the noise again. For a moment she wasn't sure what it was, and then she realized something was hitting the big carriage gate. She threw a thick woolen shawl over her head and shoulders, snatched up the loaded double-barreled shotgun that àlways stood behind the door, and opened the door.

"Madre de Dios!" she cried as the icy wind drove needlelike particles of hard snow against her face. She ran across the wide quadrangle, staggering now and then as the wind caught at her, lifting her skirt and petticoats and feeling about her bare thighs and privates with icy fingers.

The thudding noise was repeated against the carriage door. A horse whinnied faintly.

"Quien es?" Cristina cried.

"Don Quintin! Gawddammit! Get this damned gate open!" Quint shouted above the moaning wind.

It was all she could do to open the wicket gate. She saw him then, standing muffled in a buffalo coat, a thick scarf tied over the top of his hat, over his ears, and under his chin. Frost was in his nostrils, mustache, and beard. His horse stood head down, legs splayed, with vapor about its frosted nostrils.

Quint pushed Cristina back inside, then followed her. He lifted the heavy gate bar and pulled back one of the double doors. He led the exhausted horse into the quadrangle, then rebarred the gate. "Get out of this damned storm, girl," he said over his shoulder.

"There is food in the kitchen, Don Quintin," she offered, speaking her newly learned English as she had been taught by Guadalupe.

He nodded. "Aye. Get in there, lassie. *Andale!*"

She looked back as she reached the kitchen door. He was leading the horse to the stable. She entered the kitchen, threw off the shawl, and placed an earthen pot of *carne de olla*, boiled meat, and another of *albondigas con asafran*, meat balls seasoned with herbs, on the stove to heat, along with some large pots of water, in case Don Quintin wished to bathe. He'd have to do so in the kitchen. A shivery feeling coursed through her at the thought.

Quint came into the kitchen, peeling off his buffalo coat. "The poor beast is about done," he said. He took off his hat and stood near the fire, warming his big hands, sniffing at the appetizing aroma of the food. She came to stand beside him, bending over to stir one of the pots. He looked down at her glossy jet-black, braided hair, and inadvertently down inside her white blouse as he had done when he had first seen her at El Cerrillo. He could see her full, firm-looking breasts and their big brown nipples, and almost, but not quite, down to her crotch past the silver cross pendant in her cleavage. She turned her head sideways and looked up knowingly at him with her immense black eyes.

Quint sat down and began to tug at one of his boots. She came to help him, hiking up her skirts and petticoats to place the boot between her thighs, wincing at the icy harshness of the rough leather. She gripped the boot while Quint placed his other foot against her well-rounded bottom and pushed while she pulled. She staggered a little as the boot came free, then sprawled on the floor in a wild tangle of skirt and petticoats, with sturdy wool-clad legs thrusting out. She smiled at Quint. He grinned back. She exploded into merry laughter.

Quint's expression changed quickly from a smile into a faraway look. There was another whose laughter had been like that, a sound as of a swift running mountain stream during the spring breakup, tinkling like tiny silver bells over the fragments of ice and rocks in its bed.

She stood up slowly with the boot in her hands, looking at him a bit fearfully. "Did I displease you, *patron?*" she asked quietly.

He slowly shook his head. "No, lass. No. It's just that, for a moment there I . . . Never mind. It is nothing. Help me with the other boot, please."

He warmed his socked feet at the fire. "Has Doña Guadalupe gone to bed, Cristina?" he asked over his shoulder.

"She's not here, *patron*," Cristina replied.

Quint turned slowly. "What do you mean, not here?" That displeased look was in his gray eyes.

"She has gone to Santa Fe for a little while."

"The children?"

"She took the twins. David is still here."

He nodded. "That figures. And she left you in charge of the household, is that it?"

"That's right, *patron*."

He was too proud and stubborn a man to ask the girl why Guadalupe had left. He had expected to find her here, but then again, perhaps it wasn't so strange that she had gone. She had never learned to like Rio Brioso, even with the new *hacienda* he had built for her.

He slammed a big fist into the palm of his other hand. "She left a child in charge here in this big empty house?" he said, as though to himself.

Cristina drew herself up. "I am not a child, *patron!*"

He turned slowly and studied her. "No, by God, you're not, Cristina. But, supposing there had been a raid on this place? What would you have done then?"

She shrugged. "The Indians would not raid in this weather. Besides, are they not afraid of you, Don Quintin? Even in better weather since you killed the Comanches on the Canadian and the Utes and Jicarillas in the Vermejo Valley, they have not dared raid Rio Brioso."

"I was thinking perhaps, of the Comancheros, Cristina. Both you and David would be a prize for them, to trade or sell to the Comanches."

She paled a little.

"I'm sorry if I frightened you, Cristina," Quint apologized. "But, in this frontier country, one should be prepared for anything." He smiled. "Is the boy all right?"

She nodded. "Sound asleep in his room, under three Navajo blankets and the grizzly robe."

He studied her. "He did not want to go to Santa Fe?"

She shook her head. "He wanted to stay here until you and his Uncle Luke returned from Pueblo."

"The two of you got on well, eh, Cristina?"

"Yes, *patron*. He is like a younger brother to me."

She drew a small table closer to the roaring fire and placed a chair beside it, then set out the food.

"Have you eaten?" Quint asked.

"Hours ago, *patron*."

Quint placed another chair at the table. "Then dine with me, if you will, Cristina."

Cristina shook her head. "It is not for me to sit at table with my betters, Don Quintin."

He eyed her. "Do you really accept that, lass?"

For a moment she was a little frightened. She knew her station in life; there was no chance she could ever elevate herself. Even if she was accepted as a mistress to one of her betters, at least while she was young and attractive, she would lose that position to another, younger woman when she grew older and fat. It was the way of life in New Mexico. She knew she was considered little other than a piece of property, or one of the animals on the *hacienda*, to be used and disposed of when unwanted, as part of the social system.

Quint shook his head. "You don't believe that at all. Come, sit with me. Or is it perhaps that you think you would be the one lowering yourself?" He grinned askew.

She clasped a hand over her open mouth, then saw the brief glint of warmth in those cold gray eyes of his she had learned to look for and anticipate. She burst into that spontaneous laughter of hers, so beloved by young David and the twins.

They chatted and laughed together, sometimes at the simplest thing, almost as though it was the greatest of jokes. To Cristina it was like Christmas of the past year when she had been accepted as part of the family, something she had never before experienced, being without family herself. It was warm and comforting in the kitchen despite the storm battering against the north wall, howling across the roof and moaning down the chimney.

When the meal was finished, Quint filled a cup with brandy and lighted his pipe, sitting beside the fireplace while the bathwater was heating. Cristina cleared the table and washed the dishes and pots, softly singing to herself all the while, watched pleasurably by Quint. Memories of a crude lodge high in the Rockies came back to him. He had spent many such nights there, eight long years past, just Mountain Woman and himself. He slowly touched the great cicatrix on his left cheek; track of the grizzly claw. Mountain Woman had saved his life that dusk in the snow-filled woods beside a beaver stream.

She had nursed him back to health and run his string of beaver traps at the same time. "Dotawipe," he said aloud.

"Yes, *patron?*" Cristina asked.

Quint turned and looked at her. Her skin was like dark moist earth, with high cheekbones on a broad face with a strong jawline characteristic of northern tribes. The resemblance there was strong to Mountain Woman; it was the eyes that clinched it. *They were exactly the same,* as he well recalled.

"Did you want something?" Cristina asked curiously.

Quint shook his head.

"The water is ready, *patron,*" she said.

"You can go to your bed now, lassie," he suggested.

She hesitated. "The *patron* might want something?"

"I'll need some fresh clothing, but I wouldn't want you to go out into the storm for it."

"I'll go!" she cried. "It's not that far."

He took his heavy buffalo coat from the hook and draped it about her shoulders, snuggling it tight up under her chin. "Stay under the *portales,*" he said. He looked down into her eyes. She made no effort to go. Suddenly he looked away. "Aye! Get moving then, lassie! *Andale!*"

Cristina hurried from the kitchen keeping close to the front wall of the row building, then scurried across to the *hacienda* proper. She slammed the *sala* door shut behind herself and felt her way through the darkness to the master bedroom. She lighted some large candles, then started the fires in the two corner fireplaces. The chimney drafts immediately sucked up the flames. She took his clothing from the wardrobe and hurried back to the kitchen with them.

He was standing naked in one of the larger wooden tubs sponging himself off when Cristina returned. She averted her eyes as she laid the clothing on a chair. She slanted a glance toward him. His back was to her. She had no need to see what he looked like naked from a frontal view. She had seen him so last summer when he had returned to El Cerrillo. Cristina remembered him well from that time, the hard muscular body, the curly reddish hair on his chest and at his crotch, the scars marking his firm flesh, and above all, his privates.

She rolled her eyes upwards. *"Maria Santissima!"* she murmured.

He looked back at her. "Did you say something?"

She shook her head.

"You can go to your bed now, lassie. Look in on Davie first, if you will. Goodnight."

Quint dried himself after Cristina left. He drank several cups of the potent brandy and felt a warming glow course through his body. Make drunk come, he thought. He dressed slowly, keeping close beside the fire. He had been thinking of Lupita all that day as Luke and he rode over Raton Pass and down to Rio Brioso. A good meal, plenty of brandy, a fine cigar, and then into bed with her. . . . "Damn!" he said. He drank from the bottle this time.

Quint sat down beside the fire as it began to die out. He looked into the thick bed of embers, now thickly powdered with ash through which secretive red eyes winked quickly and then closed. The sight of Cristina's full, firm breasts with their brown nipples came forward in his memory. He thought of her as she had pulled off one of his boots, gripping it firmly between her rounded thighs, and the feeling of her shapely bottom against his foot. He forced the thoughts out of his mind and drank again. A chill was advancing into the room as the heat of the dying fire retreated.

She had fallen as the boot came free, sprawling on the floor in a colorful melange of full red skirt and vari-colored petticoats like a huge blossom through which her sturdy, white-clad legs had thrust themselves out like pistils.

They were alone in the *hacienda* with the exception of David, who'd be lost to the world until daylight. There was nothing or no one to stop Quint from bedding her. It was his right. Despite her acceptance more or less into the family circle, she was still a servant, a peon, in the New Mexico of that day a female chattel to be used when and if the *patron* was so inclined.

Quint stood up and drank again. He wiped his mouth on the back of a hand and stared moodily into the bed of embers. "By God," he murmured, "maybe I *am* so inclined. It's been months since Lupita was so inclined, and then I had the feeling that it was more duty on her part than anything else. Further, I'm damned sure she did not enjoy it as she usually does."

He blew out the candles. The fires were almost dead. He took his rifle and pistols, opened the door, and plunged out into the storm, along the front of the building under the icicle hung *portale* and then across the short open distance to the *sala*. He slammed the door shut behind himself and dropped the bar into place. The *sala* was lighted by one candle flickering uneasily in the draft from one of the unlit fireplaces. The door to the master bedroom was open and he could see the firelight flickering against a wall. Good girl! She had thought of everything.

Quint blew out the candle and walked into the bedroom. He leaned his Hawken in a corner, hung his belt with twin holsters from a hook near the bed, then withdrew one of the Colts from its holster and put it into the drawer of the bedside table. He quickly stripped, snatched a full brandy bottle from the liquor cabinet, pulled the cork out with his teeth, spat the cork into one of the fireplaces, drank deeply, placed the bottle on the bedside table, stripped back the bedcovers and the buffalo robe on top of them, and got into the bed, pulling the covers up about him. The bed felt warm. He rolled on his side and came up against a warm, soft body, facing away from him. Maybe he was drunker than he had thought, but the subtle, tantalizing perfume was familiar.

"Lupita?" he asked slightly bewildered through a glowing brandy haze.

The woman turned slowly to face him closely. "No, *patron*," she murmured. "It's *Cristina*." Her breath was redolent of good brandy.

"Jesus Christ!" Quint cried.

She laughed happily. "No, *patron! Not* Jesus Christ! In bed with you? It's *Cristina!*" She could not stop laughing.

He could feel the firm nipples against his chest, firm belly to belly, and her rounded thighs pressing against his. His full and sudden erection poked hard against the mound above her crotch.

So this was it at last, Cristina thought. The great moment she had thought too often about in the long months since last August when she had first seen him. What came next? She closed her eyes, slid her rounded arms about his neck, and held up her full, soft wet mouth to be kissed.

Quint drew back from her sensuous searching mouth. He pushed her back a little, feeling his proud erection rising like a Cheyenne twenty-skin tipi pole.

"Do I displease you?" she asked with a slight catch in her voice.

"God no, lassie!" he cried in English. "What the hell are ye doing here! Why are ye not in your ain bed?" The broad Scots had a tendency to reveal itself in his voice when he was up against an imponderable situation. This time he was truly up against *something*—a full-blossomed sixteen-year-old female body waiting to be taken, and likely a virgin at that!

"What would Doña Guadalupe say," he said in mock horror. Somehow it didn't sound convincing.

She placed a cool little hand against the scar on his left cheek. "Shall I tell you what she instructed me to do? You must stay here and take care of David, and Don Quintin when he returns. You must devote yourself to the *patron,* and grant his every wish. You must foresee things that he might want, without his having to ask for them. In everything, you understand, *everything.* . . ."

"You've not been with a man before?" he asked.

She nodded quickly. The dancing firelight shone on her long glossy black hair, undone now and falling about her smooth, bare shoulders.

"This is what you want?" he asked softly.

"It is what the *patron* wants," she said humbly.

He rose up on one elbow and studied her. "Would you believe I would have *you* want it as well as I?"

She turned her face away from him and reached down with an exploring hand, feeling its way down his hard belly into the tangle of reddish curly hair, to firmly grasp his penis.

Before God, Quint thought. There is no going back now. "Would you like some brandy?" he asked rather lamely. "It will help perhaps, when the pain comes."

She nodded, but she didn't let go her grasp. She turned back toward him and rose up on one elbow. The covers fell away revealing her pair of full, firm, brown-tipped beauties. He reached for the bottle and held it to her mouth. She greedily sucked in the brandy. *"Wagh!"* she grunted, as she had often heard Quint and Luke do.

He drank again. He suddenly stripped back the covers. The flickering firelight played on her soft brown skin, the thick mat of curly dark hair at her crotch, and her lovely rounded thighs, slightly dewed with sweat.

She studied him with huge dark eyes. "Do I please you?" she asked in a strange little voice.

He lay down beside her, rolling her onto her back, with his torso atop hers, feeling those fine breasts against his chest. He pressed his mouth on hers. She crept her arms up about his neck and then crossed them, pulling him closer to her, arching up her belly and thighs against him. They kissed and kissed again, their brandy wet tongues thrusting in and out. She learned quickly, as in everything she did. He worked a hand down her sweat-damp belly to her crotch. She spread her thighs. He gently worked and manipulated her as she spread her legs farther and farther apart. She began to moan a little. He rolled fully on top of her, manipulating with one hand, while the other molded and shaped her breasts, kissing the nipples until they were stiff and erect. Her moaning became faster and more erratic. He probed his knees in between her thighs, forcing them farther apart, to an almost painful limit.

"Guide it in," he whispered. "It will be easier on you. Take only as much as you can at a time."

She held the tip of his shaft across the slit of her vagina, just enough to push apart the soft, slippery wet lips. He shoved his hips forward, then pressed her knees outward as she tried to work him into her. Then his restraint broke. He pushed and pushed. She grunted, gasped, turned her head from one side to the other, moaning. He pushed, deeper and deeper. It seemed in her ecstatic agony that this stud of a man would surely tear her apart and penetrate right up into her belly. She stifled a scream. There was no stopping him now. She relaxed as much as she could rather than resist him.

Quint stroked in and out, roughly at first—his experience of the virgin tightness of a young woman had last been with Lupita seven years ago.

The sweat dripped from his face and splashed on Cristina's breasts, mingling with hers and trickling down her belly to her crotch to join the slippery moisture there.

"Mother of God!" Cristina gasped. "Oh, stop, *stop, patron!* You're tearing me to pieces inside!"

"Too late, woman," he grunted, and drove in ever harder.

Something gave within her. She felt a searing flash of pain and a great wetness, as he shuddered and trembled, gasping incontrollably, then he rolled sideways from her withdrawing his organ, spewing wetness over her sweating belly.

She closed her eyes. A tension that had been slowly building up within her for several years was gone. So, that was what it was! The need for a man, and what a *man!*

Quint lay still beside Cristina, panting and breathing deeply. He reached for the brandy bottle and drank deeply, spilling some of the brandy down his chin and chest.

She passed trembling hands down to her crotch and felt gingerly about the moist aftermath. She raised her hands to look at them. The dark blood shone in the firelight.

Cristina looked at him. "Are you in pain?" she asked sympathetically. "I thought it was only women who suffered from this."

He grinned crookedly. "The Indians call it The Little Death," he said quietly. "Did you like it, lassie?"

She thought for a moment. "I know I'll get used to it, Don Quintin." She slanted her great eyes at him. "You'll have to see to that."

He studied her, then nodded. "One thing, lassie."

"Yes?"

He leaned over and kissed her. "I think we now know each other so that you can call me Quint, at least when Doña Guadalupe is not around. Make damned sure you don't forget."

She laughed. "Brandy," she said. She drank deeply. "I'll build up the fires now."

"Why?"

She thrust her legs out from under the covers and stood up. "I'd like to try it next time without all those heavy covers in the way."

He stared at her. "Tonight?"

She nodded as she walked to the fireplace, then turned, warming her bare, rounded bottom. "And in the morning, if you want it, Don Quintin."

"Quint!" he said.

She stacked wood vertically in both fireplaces, ran to the bed, snatched up the brandy bottle and drank, then crawled in beside him. "I'd like a *cigarillo* now," she requested.

Spring came late that year. Guadalupe remained in Santa Fe with the twins, pleading against a return to Rio Brioso until the weather tempered itself. Quint was fully aware by now that she had long planned for Cristina to fill the role of bedmate, at least until she returned from Santa Fe. It was the custom in New Mexico. To Guadalupe it meant nothing that could possibly come between them, so sure was she that she still held Quint's love and devotion. She was right in that respect, but wrong in another. Perhaps subconsciously she was still endeavoring to remold Quint into her image of a *rico patron*, in short, a carbon copy of a de Vasquez male. In that case, a young mistress was fully acceptable. She had badly miscalculated in another major sense—she had not reckoned with Quint's damnable Scots conscience and inborn sense of fair play, coupled with his sensitivity to the underdog. He could not accept Cristina as a mere plaything, an amusement, someone whom he could use when the need arose and set aside or discard when so inclined. He was a lusty man, but not an animal, insensitive to the fact that Cristina was a female and a human being. He realized after some weeks that he should never have accepted her in his bed, but, God help him, what man could have resisted such a temptation? The deed was done. It was not a time for regrets. In May he would leave for the spring and early summer buffalo hunt. Guadalupe showed little sign of returning to Rio Brioso before then. He missed her and the twins, but David and Cristina filled the lonely gap. The days he filled repairing and restoring the damage of winter and preparing for the buffalo hunt. The evenings he filled happily with Cristina, David, and Luke. The nights were devoted to Cristina.

TWELVE

MAY 1846. CIBOLO!

The immense "Texas Herd" of countless buffalo would be moving slowly from their wintering area around the Upper Pecos and Conchos Rivers on their annual spring migration, a seasonal march of between 250 and 450 miles to the Canadian and Arkansas Rivers for summer grazing. It had been an unusually dry spring after the final blast of winter in March. The seasonal watering places were expanses of cracked and drying mud. Now, on the burning, savage stretches east of the pitiless Llano Estacado, the "Staked Plains," determined buffalo plodded on day after monotonous day into the wind as they always did. There was enough water to keep them alive, but just barely.

The *ciboleros*, buffalo hunters of the Rio Brioso and the Mora, 100 men and almost 350 animals, horses, riding mules, pack mules, and oxen were under the overall command of Don Quintin Kershaw. There were forty *carretas*, great wooden carts with huge cottonwood wheels as tall as a man, made in the style of two hundred years before with little or no iron used, held together with strips of rawhide and wooden pegs. The oxen that slowly drew them were yoked together by a straight piece of wood laid across their heads behind the horns and lashed fast with rawhide. The carts creaked and groaned across the *llano*, their discordant noise a respectable tenor for a double bass horse-fiddle. They could carry many hides. The big California pack mules could be loaded with three hundred pounds of dry hides or jerked meat. The hunters were to remain on the plains for six weeks to two months depending on their hunting luck. They had traveled over one hundred fifty miles sighting distant scattered groups of buffalo hardly to be dignified with the title "herd." Quint was after much bigger game— the Texas Herd itself. As a rule summers on these plains, at least during times of good rainfall, could be a hunter's paradise. This year two perennial factors were missing east of the Llano Estacado. One was an asset, the other a liability—rain, and the Kotsoteka Comanches, the Buffalo Eaters, whose usual domain was the Canadian River Valley.

Quint, Luke, Moccasin, and Joshua left the caravan camped at an unnamed creek by a welling seepage spring whose bright band of water trickled half a foot deep between banks of glistening salt-filled sands. Usually at this time of year the creek would be running bankful from heavy rains, a reddish, turbid flood more sand than water. The *ciboleros* threw up banks of earth to dam the creek, forming *charcos*, or "pools" for water storage. There would be just enough water for a week or so of waiting until the herd was located and to fill the water kegs and canteens for the return home. It was up to Quint and his companions to find water and buffalo, in that order.

They rode eastward finding occasional buffalo wallows filled with filthy, muddy water covered with green scum which had to be strained before being at all potable. Their mouths became sore and slimy, lips and tongues swollen, talking difficult through mouths parched constantly by hot sun and dry wind. Here the plains were so level and smooth that if one looked at buffalo in the distance, sky could be seen beneath their shaggy bellies. There were no distant hazy smoky-looking mountains to be seen. The horizon was clear and flat, the light was stunning, distances deceptive, and everything enlarged in the clear air. Occasional thunderstorms moved swiftly across the parched land depositing a few inches of water in hollows and buffalo wallows. The water evaporated quickly leaving a thick solution of "buffalo tea," loose mud stinking of buffalo piss and manure, alive with repulsive wrigglers.

The four mule-mounted buffalo scouts fanned out individually to cover as much territory as possible, sometimes meeting at midday, and always rendezvousing before dusk at some predesignated area. By this time they had passed through the vaguely undefined territory of the Kotsotekas into that of the Kwahadis, or Antelope Eaters. The difference in their names didn't make any change in their hostility. They were Comanche kin, all related like girls in Georgia.

Quint rode Demonio, his seemingly tireless mule. Trim as a deer, with little round hoofs as hard as flint, he had been sired by a big burro and damned by a half-broken mustang. Quint never dared turn his back on him while afoot. He could kick like a medieval catapult. The midday rendezvous was in sight, a lone wide *bosque* of dusty gray cottonwoods, willow, stately white oak, black walnut, and mulberry trees bordering both banks of a wide, deep dry creek. Turkeys in huge flocks feeding on grasshoppers and seeds blackened the prairie in every direction as far as the eye could see. The ground under the trees was thick with their guano. By dusk the branches would be covered with roosting birds with not an inch to spare, sometimes bending too far under their weight and snapping off, tumbling their squawking load to the guano-covered ground.

It was top grazing country. The ground was covered with the graceful sickle-shaped heads of nutritious grama grass, so parched it crunched like snow underfoot. The bright spring and early summer flowers had wilted and died under the unseasonable killing heat. Here and there in the hazy distance were quail, whirring grouse, dainty little prairie plover, prairie chickens, and curlews, whose pink underwings were lovely as a flash of sunset cloud as they flitted and swooped about.

Quint unsaddled Demonio and rubbed the caked sweat from his back with handfuls of dried grass. He looked into the distance as he worked. Not one buffalo, even a crippled stray, was to be seen. The Texas Herd ranged from near the Clear Fork of the Brazos west across the Staked Plains to the Upper Pecos and from south of the Arkansas four hundred miles to Cañon Diablo. *Damn!* Everything was about right—the season, the route they always traveled, and the good grama grass already curing on the stem. *Where were they?*

The slightly sloping ground between the *bosque* and a low saddle-backed ridge due south was marked by buffalo trails established over countless years. The trails were about a foot or so wide, just enough to let the small hoofs pass with ease. Buffalo always followed the level of valleys and plains, crossing and recrossing stream beds in order to avoid grades. As a rule, when the trails in use became deeper than six inches, whether by wear or washout, they were no longer comfortable; whereupon they were abandoned and new trails started. There were exceptions. Quint had seen some north of the Arkansas so deep as to rub the sides of the buffalo. Within sight from the *bosque* in all directions were so many trails side by side, the ground seemed to be a gigantic piece of dun-colored corduroy covering hundreds of acres.

To the east of the *bosque* and athwart the course of the dry creek lay a huge oval depression of hardpan which would fill several inches to several feet deep during heavy rains, draining into the creek bed for some miles before the waters sank into the sandy bed. Now it was inches deep in thin dust. Maybe that was one of the reasons the herd had not as yet reached this far north. That, and the fact that the wind had been uncertain for days, boxing the compass now from the north then shifting to the east, dallying to the south, then sweeping back to blow intermittently from the north and northeast. Now, but almost imperceptibly at times, it seemed to steady northeast. A buffalo herd *always* marched and fed into the wind. This instinct would sometimes lead them into casual annual circles many hundreds of miles across. Thus, with a northeast wind the main herd might very well head away from the *ciboleros*.

Quint had coffee boiling by the time Luke, Moccasin, and Joshua reached the *bosque*. None of them had cut recent buffalo sign. They squatted on the guano-covered ground, soaking flint-hard *bizcocho* into the bitter, alkaline-tasting black java, after trying to sweeten it with melted brown sugar cake.

"Ye didn't work south, eh, Luke?" Quint asked around a mouthful of biscuit.

Luke shook his head. "Just easterly. Wind shifted. If they're anywheres south of us, which they must be, as they ain't passed this way yet, they'll head into the northeast wind. I thought I saw a dust cloud miles to the southwest, but warn't dust *or* cloud. Miles off, anyways."

Moccasin scratched inside his shirt. "No sign anywhere."

Joshua nodded. "Nuthin' but last season's bullshit."

"No water hereabouts for them anyways," Luke added, "and damned little for us."

They looked at each other out of the corners of their eyes. Born hunters to a man, they hated to leave a game trail no matter how faint it was. This day fresh buffalo sign was nonexistent.

The dry wind died away. With its passing the midday sun beat down upon the hapless earth like sledge blows on an anvil. The air seemed breathless.

Moccasin walked slowly away into the depths of the *bosque*.

Luke nodded at him. "Gone to take a leak?" he asked facetiously. He knew better.

Josh shook his head. "Prayin' for rain."

"We need buffalo, not rain, Josh."

"We pray for buffalo with no rain, we get no rain and no buffalo. We pray for rain, we get buffalo."

"Irrefutable logic," Quint murmured.

A vast hush came over the burning land.

Quint dozed with his back to an oak.

The wind began to blow from the south.

Josh stood up quickly. "Look!" he cried, pointing south.

A thickening grayness was sharply defined against the clear sky. A great rolling darkness moved swiftly to the north directly toward the *bosque* and the creek valley. Zigzags of chain lightning forked into a distant mesa. A whirling funnel of black cloud continually scarred by eerie-looking sheet lightning moved with frightening speed as though aiming for the *bosque*.

Black Moccasin dashed back. "Get away from the trees! I think mebbe I pray *too* much! This storm gonna be a real sonofabitch!"

They led the nervous mules out into the open plain. Great fat drops of rain plopped on the dry ground raising tiny spurts of dust. Then the cloudburst was on them with full fury dropping a massive, blinding deluge of icy rain mingled with hailstones that stung like whiplashes. The four men stood holding out their arms when the hail stopped, faces upturned, soaked to the skin, reveling in every minute of it, ankle-deep in the runoff water covering the plain.

"Gawd dammit, Moc!" Luke yelled. "Did yuh have to ask for it all at once?"

"Gawd dammit, yuh wanted buffalo, didn't yuh?" Moccasin bellowed back.

It took only a matter of thirty minutes. The empty, dark clouds drove on to the north as swiftly as they had appeared. The sun came out revealing the rare phenomenon of a double rainbow. Where the huge, bone-dry, dusty hardpan depression had been was now a shallow lake, many acres in extent, reflecting the cerulean blue of the rain-washed sky.

They led the steaming mules to the full running creek and watered them. The sun beat down again, raising a rank stench from the mules and men's clothing alike.

Moccasin looked south. "Buffalo come mebbe tomorrow. Thousands. Send Joshua for caravan, Big Red. By the time they get here, we mebbe got enough hides and meat to load up all them *carretas* and pack mules." He grinned.

At dusk the turkeys returned to their roosts. The humid, windless air was thick with gnats and mosquitoes who mercilessly plagued the mules causing them to hit their picket ropes first on one side and then the other. Gouts of blood spotted their hides from myriads of biting flies. Smudge fires had to be lighted, risking the smoke being seen by prying Comanche eyes.

A huge, silvery moon inched slowly up into the sky to light the terrain like a gigantic Japanese lantern. The moonlight sharply defined light and shadow like silhouettes cut from black paper. The *bosque* was like a long narrow island rising from a motionless sea of grass. The night was alive with sound. The insistent, humming sound of mosquitoes mingled with the booming sound of arrow hawks diving on them. Now and again ground owls called. Faintly at a distance there came the thin, tremulous howl of a young gray wolf or the bark of a coyote pup. Noiseless owls swooped down on velvety wings seeking the shy, little white jumping mice who were all but invisible in the clear moonlight. The ubiquitous coyotes were out in full force that lovely night. Their commingled bark, whine, and yelp was broken now and then by a spasmodic laugh, now tenor, now basso; then one would attempt a treble solo. After an ear-piercing prelude every coyote within hearing would join in the chorus, an indescribable discord that would die away as suddenly as it came. A period of silence would follow, only to be broken again by the whole gamut of barks, whines, yelps, solos, and choruses.

About midnight a lonely, light little breeze wandered into existence from the northeast. It carried the faint scent of fresh rainwater to the southwest.

Miles to the southwest of the new lake, on the hot, dry moonlit plain a four year old buffalo cow lifted her ugly head and swung it slowly this way and that, moist nostrils testing the northeast wind. *Water.* . . . She moved slowly and deliberately into the wind. The plain was covered with buffalo, one black, uneasy mass extending to the horizon in all directions. One after another, those of the trotting buffalo cow's immediate division of the vast herd began to move after her, singly at first then in twos and threes in long steadily moving files, planting their small hoofs into the narrow trails. There were huge bulls, spikehorns—the young bulls, aging cows, pregnant cows, and "light" cows, those that had just calved. Calves closely followed their mothers. The newborn calves were reddish-yellow in color; the older calves were browning into maturity. The calves were fat, romping and adventuresome, running this way and that, sometimes lagging until their impatient and thirsty mothers turned back to hurry them up, or the huge sentry bulls who traveled on the outside of their particular herd unit might drive them back into its protection.

Hundreds of wolves came running through the moonlight, necks outstretched, with sharply outlined uplifted heads, gaining at every stride in swift, noiseless pursuit of the herd.

When the first pearl-gray nuances of dawn light tinted the eastern sky, the rolling, undulating plain was covered in every direction for miles with moving buffalo. They moved with great humped shoulders thrusting forward, shaggy heads down, black tongues out, tails upheld like a scorpion, dewclaws rattling, and thousands of hoofs beating up a deep rumbling from the hard-packed earth. They were not afraid of anything that was not straight upwind from their wet, flaring nostrils. Nothing on those vast plains could stop them once they were in full pounding motion, bobbing up and down with the rolling motion of the humps like corky vessels in short seas.

Quint was standing guard as dawn came up in a vast silent explosion against the eastern sky. He watched the mules. Mules and horses talk with their ears. Something was bothering them. They slanted their long ears to the south, always to the south. Quint walked to the edge of the *bosque* and studied the low saddle-backed ridge dominating the southern skyline. The turkeys were abandoning their roosts for the day's feeding in the open. They moved out until the plain between the *bosque* and the ridge was carpeted black with them.

He sensed something rather than heard it. The sound began to grow out of the earth itself, swelling, traveling for miles through the ground like an earthquake tremor.

Luke raised his head. "What is it, Big Red?"

Quint turned. He grinned. *"Cibolo! Cibolo! Buffalo on the wind!"*

A herd of antelope suddenly appeared on the ridge top. They leaped down the slope, bewildered, running in swift wide circles only to break off and dash away in all directions, then plunged onward toward the creek and lake. They stampeded the vast flocks of turkeys, who took wing, the roar of their flighting sounding like a tornado moving over the plains.

One fraction of a second the ridge crest was sharply defined against the clear dawn light, then a dark flood overlapped the crest and poured down the slope. *Cibolo!* Thousands upon thousands of them blanketed the ground, a vast thundering herd, a solid mass of the grandest ruminants in all nature. The dusty, shaggy heads and rumps rose and fell like the rise and fall of a dark, menacing sea.

Luke yelled, "Drift, yuh son-of-bitches! Drift or they'll go right over and through us!"

Quint shook his head as he ran for his Hawken. "Grab your irons! Here we stand or get trampled into bloody pulp!"

They had seen buffalo stampeding before, but nothing that could approach in awe this oncoming, stinking avalanche of thousands upon thousands of tons of meat on the hoof. The front ranks had swung out to both sides and began to outdistance the main mass of the herd, like crescent horns which were already even with the edge of the *bosque*. There could be no escape for the three hunters now. They double-tethered the panic-stricken mules behind stout cottonwoods. They took their stand where several stunted oaks had grown so close together their tops were interlaced. Three Hawkens came up as one. The earth swayed under the pounding of the hoofs.

"Make meat, Gawd dammit, or we die here!" Moccasin yelled.

"Don't miss, partners!" Luke shouted.

"Tell me about it," Quint bellowed.

It was the last they were to speak to each other for hours. The din was overwhelming from the pounding of hoofs, the incessant bellowing of the bulls, and the throaty roaring of the Hawkens. Two bulls crashed into the twin oaks. Hawken muzzles almost touched them and flamed, piling them against the trees. A big cow turned sideways as she was struck, snorting blood in a thick spray all over the three shooting, cursing men, then went down to one side. The rifles crashed as one. A bull died on top of the cow. A dusty, shaggy, stinking barricade of dead, wounded, and dying buffalo formed about the twin oaks, causing the herd to part and flow around it. No need to aim true. It was shoot, pour part of a palmful of gunpowder down the smoking muzzle, spit a ball after it from a supply held in the mouth, slam the butt hard on the ground to seat the charge, raise, cock and cap, then pull the trigger.

Moccasin's mule disappeared under the sharp pounding hoofs. Demonio broke his tethers and vanished into the herd. Luke's mule Sonofabitch stood with splayed-out legs, head down, shivering incessantly from head to rump and back down legs to hoofs. The world became a microcosmic hell of yellow dust, acrid powdersmoke, hot stinking blood, and the overpowering stench of the herd itself.

The barricade held. To each side were crushed and macerated humps of bloody flesh and bone where the young, the wounded, and the weak had gone under the insensate stampede to water. The heaps of fallen buffalo wreathed thickly in dust and powdersmoke cut off the terrifying sight of the oncoming herd, but the noise and stench were there to stay.

Hour after hour passed. The sun was well up, its hot light veiled and hazed by the immense dust cloud, but its enervating heat penetrated to the earth just the same. Bedeviling insect hordes came with the herd—greenhead flies that stung like red-hot needles and buffalo gnats like whirling clouds of fine, clinging dust about the nose and eyes of man and buffalo alike. They were tiny black insects who attacked faces and hands, insinuated themselves under clothing and stung breasts, arms, and any other place they could creep. They were much more annoying than mosquitoes and more frequently met with along prairie streams. Their bite was poisonous, leaving a mark like a pustulated varioloid that itched incessantly. There was no way to avoid them, kill them, or drive them off. Flight was the only recourse, but there was no place to run that day of hell.

The solid mass of the herd began to thin out. It degenerated into lines and small groups between which would be the old, weak, injured, and the very young, the usual trail drag of any herd. The wolves and coyotes closed in behind them. After them the cleanup crews would show up—scavenger buzzards, ravens, and long-tailed magpies. Few buffalo ever died of disease other than the bloody murrain. Old age, predators, and man were the greatest enemies of the buffalo.

The herd encircled the five-acre lake, heaving and shouldering in their struggle to get to the water. From a distance they resembled a mass of blackish-brown maggots in decaying meat. The banks were destroyed, trodden, and kneaded into a thick paste of water, mud, urine, and manure. Beyond the lake on the low hills east of the creek a herd of mustangs moved nervously about waiting for their leader, a dazzling sorrel beauty of a mare to lead the way to water. The antelope had returned after their precipitate flight. The lure of water was too much for them. They were still nervous. They ran here and there, then back again, then suddenly coming to a rigid halt gazing toward the lake.

At last some of the buffalo leisurely moved across the creek to a vast, limitless expanse of rolling prairie thick with grama grass. Once watered the herd would settle down to rest, lethargic and careless from the watering. They might rest for a few days, certainly no more than a week, before continuing on their determined northern migration to the Canadian and the Arkansas.

Quint studied the herd through his telescope. "This will be the place to stand hunt," he said. "I wonder how much time we'll have before the Comanches find out we're here?"

Luke shrugged. "One way to find out. Start huntin'."

Luke picked his way gingerly through the mush of blood, flesh, and bone marking the remains of fallen buffalo and one of the mules. He placed his hat over the eyes of shivering Sonofabitch and talked soothingly into one of his long ears. When the mule seemed calmer, Luke dug a leather flask of *aguardiente* from his possibles sack and turned to plod toward his partners. He grinned. "See? Ol' Sonofabitch ain't as ornery as yuh think he is." At that instant both hind hoofs of the mule hit Luke square on his lean rump, driving him forward to fall flat on his face inches deep in the gory muck. Sonofabitch's triumphant bray echoed through the *bosque.*

Moccasin broke up. He bent his knees and slapped his thighs, shaking his head speechlessly. Quint grinned widely. The grin faded as Luke came up on his feet like an uncoiling spring and plunged toward his Hawken. Quint snatched away the rifle and stopped Luke with a hand against his chest. Luke's gory face was almost unrecognizable in his fury. He swung his fists at Quint until Moccasin hammerlocked him from behind and threw him to the ground. Quint and Moccasin sat on top of Luke, waiting for him to cool down.

At last Luke lay still. "Damn yuh both!" he shouted. "Yuh should'a let me kill that sneaky sonofabitch!"

Quint got off Luke and squatted beside him, teetering on his heels. "Look, ye stupid idiot! I'd feel the same way, but he's the only mule we have left and one of us has to scout for Comanche sign!"

They squatted on the ground drinking, silently passing the flask from one to the other. After a time Luke looked back over his shoulder at Sonofabitch. He grinned. "He's some punkins, ain't he? By God, he euchred me neatly into that one. I should'a known better to *ever* turn my back on him."

They all drank to that. They filled their short Dublin pipes to get the stench of the *bosque* out of their nostrils. They lit up, carefully offering the mouth of the pipe to the sky for the first whiff of tobacco.

Quint stood up. Six mature bulls, a pair of spikehorns, two young cows, and a number of calves had piled up against the oaks and each other in front of the stand position. Quint drew his knife and began to hone it. "We can get started on these until the skinners get here."

"Oh, my God," Luke murmured. "I'm a hunter, not a skinner."

"Stay and skin, Wandering Wolf, or look for the Comanches alone."

"Great choice. Either way I lose."

Quint shook his head. "I'm the real loser. This stupid *gringo patron* has to stay and skin. The choice is between Moc and ye."

Moccasin and Luke eyed each other. "I'll go, Big Red."

"Why you?" Luke asked.

Moc grinned. "I'm smarter than you are."

Luke shrugged. "Smart enough to ride Sonofabitch?"

Moccasin studied Luke for a few seconds. "Not *that* smart."

Quint and Moccasin worked as a team for speed. The big cow had fallen on her belly, legs spread out sideways. A transverse slit was made across the nape of the neck and the boss, a hairy lump about the size of a man's head which projected from the back of the neck just above the shoulders. When boiled it tasted much like marrow and was tender, nutritious, and appetizing. Another cut was made along the spine from boss to tail. The skin was separated from the body on each side and pulled down to the brisket to which it was still attached. The skin was then freed from the carcass and placed to receive the meat and the attendant swarms of greenhead flies.

The shoulder was severed. The fleece, a thin layer of flesh covering the ribs, was removed from along the backbone. The belly fleece was stripped away. The so-called hump ribs, which weren't really ribs at all but flat vertical bones about a foot or more in length projecting above the spine, were chopped off next. The *depuis*, or back fat, a broad layer of fat extending from hump to tail, was removed, followed by the tenderloin and fine pale tallow. The belly was opened to allow the intestines, or *boudins* containing the chyme, to fall out. *Boudins* when emptied could be turned inside out, sketchily cleaned and cut into eighteen-inch lengths, then packed with a mixture of minced tenderloin, kidneys, brains, a pound or so of quarter cut close to the bone, marrow, suet, grease, wild onion juice, and salt. Knotted into a sausage ten inches long and broiled in the coals or simmered in an iron spider, with the rich fat cooking inside, *boudin* was a most delicious dish and one that its admirers never tired of.

"Remember Francois' *boudins?*" Moccasin asked, reminiscing. "Best damned cook on the High Plains."

Quint wiped the sweat from his face with the back of a grease-soaked sleeve. His wool shirt was saturated with perspiration, blood, and tallow. Stinging sweat ran down his face and body, dripping on the carcass. The stench of buffalo and gory death hung throughout the *bosque*. The flies and gnats made life there a living hell.

Moccasin looked curiously at Quint. "Well?" he asked.

Quint shook his head. "Now you ask me? *Now?*"

Moccasin shrugged. "You ain't got an Indian's guts." He cut off a slice of liver, sprinkled it with gall, and offered it to Quint.

"Hell no! Thank God I *haven't* got an Indian's guts!"

Moccasin chewed away, rolling his eyes up in ecstasy. "Oh, I don't know. Sure as hellsfire it don't limit your menu, as you white folks say."

Quint excised the big tongue while Moccasin cut out the huge marrow bones which resembled thick, pink-touched wood. "Best way to cook these, Big Red," the Delaware said conversationally, "is to light a fire at both ends. Heat travels through the bone to heat the marrow. Top splits open like a box lid when ready. Delicious."

They cut out the shoulders, hams, and side ribs. The meat was pretty close to 'mean meat," or spring cow meat, and much of it would be flyblown or spoil if not jerked as soon as possible.

Moccasin teetered back on his heels and reached for the *aguardiente* flask. He drank deeply and then wiped his greasy, sweat-streaming face with the back of a sleeve. "I've had enough of this, even for an Injun, Big

Red. We're gonna lose all this meat anyways if the skinners don't get here soon."

Quint raised his head. "Listen," he said.

The wind had shifted to the northeast. Faintly, ever so faintly, came the horrendous shrieking, groaning, grinding noise of the huge ungreased *carreta* wheels.

Quint reached for the brandy flask.

★ THIRTEEN ★

The hardpan lake temporarily delayed the thousands of buffalo from their annual spring migration northward. Perhaps some instinct warned them the country toward the Canadian and Arkansas was still held in drought. The new lake attracted birds and wildfowl of many species—curlews, ducks, cranes, shitepokes, and loons were numbered among them. Dragonflies poised above the new grass already sprouting beyond the muddy lake margin. White and yellow butterflies drifted over the backs of the grazing buffalo. Rabbits appeared, seemingly out of nowhere. Antelope and deer drank side by side with buffalo and mustang. Wolves and coyotes came in their hundreds doubly attracted by the water and the huge masses of meat on the hoof.

The buffalo grazed on the wide plains beyond the creek and lake. It was still the rutting season. The bulls usually mated at three years and were fully grown at five. They spent half their waking time chasing cows and the remainder fighting other bulls. Thousands of calves frisked and romped about their more sedate elders. They ran, jumped, butted, and rolled in the dust. The bulls, more so than the cows, liked to roll in the dust as well, stretching out at full length while rubbing their heads hard on the ground, then rolling over on their other side as easily as a horse to repeat the process, raising a cloud of dust.

Quint, despite the protests of his veteran *ciboleros,* had made a firm decision to change from the traditional centuries-old style of hunting to his own method. He would not let them ride their swift, half-broken mustangs, plunging into a stampeding herd at full gallop killing with lance or arrow. The usual result was a madly stampeding herd scattered to hell and gone over many square miles of open plain, and the buffalo carcasses dropped helter-skelter for the skinners. The old system was too hit-or-miss and too much of a hardship on the hardworking skinners, besides exposing them to Indian attack without the nearby support of other hunters and skinners. Quint's method was simplicity itself. He and Luke using three rifles apiece, would make a stand, so called because the buffalo would gather, or stand around the dead and wounded not knowing what to do, thus setting themselves up for the kill. By Quint's canny calculations he and Luke could kill perhaps five times as many buffalo in about the same amount of time required by the mounted hunters. In addition the stand method would keep the carcasses bunched together for the convenience of the skinners, and themselves close enough to each other and the hunters for mutal protection in case of Indian attack. The system lacked the wild dash, color, and raw, atavistic excitement of the chase so beloved by the mounted New Mexicans, superb horsemen to a man. Essentially, the stand method was more practical and a great deal more profitable. Quint had to make some concessions to the mounted *ciboleros*. He had converted most of them to skinners, but he agreed that if the herd, or any part of it, stampeded or began their northern trek again, the mounted men would have their day. Quint hoped that day would not come. The stand method was faster and more efficient than the chase method, and the sooner they filled their quota of hides and meat the quicker they'd be able to head back home and away from this dangerous country.

The first day of the stand hunt Quint and Luke approached the herd from downwind in the predawn darkness and cached half a dozen large gourd canteens at their individual stands. Their contents would be used for cleaning and cooling their rifles after excessive shooting. Quint had originally planned to have Moccasin and Joshua, superb marksmen both, stand hunt too, but the possibility of a surprise Comanche attack required that scouts be kept out at all times making wide patrolling sweeps from north to south and back again. He had delegated the Delawares to that duty. Now it was up to Luke and Quint to get as many kills as they could as quickly as possible, get the hides cured, the meat dried, and haul tail out of there pronto.

It was almost dawn. A cool northerly wind was blowing. Quint had already cached two of the three rifles he intended using. He had a new Mills recommended to him by Kit Carson and an old but excellent J. Henry rifle converted from flintlock to percussion. Quint bellied toward his first stand, a slight hollow on a sweeping slope commanding a panoramic view of the herd. From his experiences of the year before he had worked out three rules for a good stand: not to shoot fast enough to heat a gun barrel to overexpansion; always try to hit the outside buffalos; shoot any that tried to walk off.

He carried his prized "Auld Clootie" within the crook of his left arm as he crawled in a direct line, not deviating to one side of the other. Buffalo were notoriously weak-eyed, but where they might not be able to detect details, they certainly could notice suspicious movement. Alert sentinel bulls constantly patrolled the herd perimeter. If he was detected by sight or scent, there might be no hides that day, at least from his first stand.

Quint swore softly under his breath as he tracked his chest, belly, legs, and the buttstock of his Hawken through a massive pile of fresh buffalo droppings still warm and steaming slightly in the cool air. There was no way to sidetrack it with a suspicious sentinel bull looking in his direction. He froze into position, feeling the warm moisture of the droppings and urine soaking through his jacket, shirt, and leggings to his skin. The bull moved on at last, nose to the ground, grunting softly then belching up a cud into his mouth to chew on again. His small weak eyes were practically lost in a thick matting of hair, but his keen sense of smell served him just as well.

Quint slithered into his hollow. While he plucked out the burrs sticking in his fingers and knees, he checked his gear—telescope, a pair of *bois-d'arc* sticks swiveled together to form a rest for keeping the muzzle of his rifle up off the ground, three large powder-horns each of which held a pound and a half of gunpowder, precut greased wads, several bags of bullets, some tins of expensive English percussion caps, the very best, and a supply of hard biscuit and jerky.

He focused his telescope on the herd. The closest buffalo were a pair of sentinel bulls he estimated to be about three-quarters of a ton each on the hoof. Both of them were standing with upraised heads looking to the north, in the general direction where Luke was getting ready to make his stand about double gunshot range from Quint's position.

Quint loaded his pair of extra rifles. The sky was lightening. The plain was covered with buffalo like a vast, dark-colored, loosely woven blanket. Some of them were feeding, others were lying down chewing their cuds. A steady procession of them trotted to the lake or returned from the lake to the grazing area. It was the season when the winter hair changed to a sort of down like that of lion skin. From late November to late December the robes were at their finest. Then the buffalo were sleek and fat, their winter pelage of thick and glossy dark fur ranging from a dark umber color to a liver-shining brown. The mature bulls had much longer and more luxuriant hair on head, neck, and forequarters. The massive, magnificent head never lost its frontlet and beard at any season. The calves were a smooth brown color. In the spring and early summer, however, bleaching hair gave the buffalo a rusty, seedy look. The dead hair still clung to them in ragged, dirty tufts. It took months to rid themselves of the vermin-infested hair. To do this they rubbed themselves against rocks, trees, or cutbanks like snakes changing their skin. The new hair pushed the old off the hump and shoulders as it came in, dark and well matured as early as June, but the rest of the body was still often nude as a badly scalded hog until mid-June. The skin was raw, scabby, and tender, an irresistible lure to flies and the hordes of gnats that clung like dust clouds about the moist nostrils, eyes, and in the sores of the exposed sunburnt skin. The only remedy to this maddening plague was flight, or retreat to the nearest mudhole where they would roll in it like a great pig coating themselves all over. Mud gathered in thick lumps on the long hair of the forequarters, head, and beard creating an appallingly hideous creature.

Quint shook his head. "Ugly, by God, monstrous ugly, but truly magnificent all the same," he murmured.

The light was right. Quint crumbled some dried grass, then sifted it through his fingers to test the windage. He selected his first kill. She was a big cow one hundred fifty yards away trotting slowly to the north into the dawn wind. She was a leader. Here and there a few buffalo were rising awkwardly with cracking joints to follow her.

Quint rested his Hawken on the swivel sticks, holding them with his left hand to keep them from separating. He centered the silver blade front sight in the upward curving horns of the rear sight, cocked the rifle, and set the trigger. He aimed just behind the shoulder blade and two-thirds of the way down the hump, just a few inches above the brisket, the only truly vulnerable point. Unless shot through the heart, lungs, or spine buffalo took a great deal of killing. One might flatten bullets against the broad forehead all day, or shoot at the huge carcass in general with no more result than the loss of a lot of lead and burnt-up gunpowder.

Quint squeezed off. The throaty roar of the heavy rifle echoed along the creek flats and died away. A puff of white smoke drifted downwind. The cow gave a violent start forward and then stopped short. Blood streamed from her wide nostrils. She swayed unsteadily, staggered and tried to keep her feet, then lurched sideways and fell heavily. Her body rocked a little as she kicked, then she stiffened and lay still. The buffalo nearest the stricken cow ran off a hundred feet or so, then stopped as suddenly as they had started. A young spike bull hooked at the cow with his horns, more interested in her sexually than for any other reason. Buffalo are stupid. "Buffalo savvy" is utterly unpredictable, except for one important fact—their intense curiosity. A group of them gathered slowly about the cow, staring and sniffing in wide-eyed wonder. They chewed, coughed up new cuds, and started chewing again while grunting, grunting all the time.

Luke's rifle flatted off, hollow-sounding like the slamming of a distant door. An old cow jerked. She stood with legs braced, eyes glazing while she slowly bled to death. Other buffalo smelled the blood and milled about her, bunching up accommodatingly for the deadly green-eyed marksman who dropped them one by one until the entire group was down in a patch of ground no more than fifty feet square. Not one had made an effort to escape. The cow was the only one to suffer and not very long at that. She went down on her foreknees, striking her head on the ground. A bright crimson flood poured from her mouth and nose. She stiffened and lay still.

Quint dropped five cows and two spikehorns. He poured water down the bore of the Mills. A huge bull, a monarch among his kind weighing over a ton, had become infuriated at the sound of shooting and the smell of hot blood on the wind. He began to walk at a swinging pace, then broke into a trot and finally a rocking gallop.

"Bastard," Quint murmured. "Ye'll stampede them all."

The old J. Henry roared next. The bull crashed to the ground, kicked his legs sporadically, then began to crawl off by using his forelegs, dragging his paralyzed hindquarters. A slug from the Hawken stopped him forever.

Some of the nearby buffalo bunched together, ponderous shoulders side by side, little eyes rolling, anger deep in their throats. Two old bulls pawed the earth, angry at the stink of gunpowder and the smell of sudden death. They hooked their horns this way and that, threatening the unseen enemy, long mud-caked beards wagging angrily. Some cows started a sustained, mournful bellowing. One of them began to lead out. She picked up speed, rocking along leading a few confused followers. Quint's bullet smashed through her lungs and the bottom of her heart. She stopped, switched her tail, and walked off alone. She lowered his head, coughed up blood, went down on one foreknee then the other, dropped suddenly on her hindknees, rolled over and died.

Quint stopped firing to let the accumulated powder-smoke drift off. A few sentinel bulls had been curious about the concentration of smoke. They raised their heads and stared uncomprehendingly, not associating this phenomenon with the leaden death striking among them. Living buffalo clustered stupidly about the many dead sniffing at the warm blood and bawling in bewilderment. Quint lay belly flat and watched them. They were doing everything but what they should have done—*run away*. He shook his head at their great stupidity. Yet, in a way, he was sorry for them, dying in bunches because they did not know how to deal with the unseen danger.

The sun was fully up. Every time a new leader started north into the wind, a ball brought him or her down and the herd came to rest again. So it went on all day, hour after hour, shot after shot, buffalo after buffalo going down. The smell of stinking powdersmoke, fresh blood, and violent death hung over the plain like a plague miasma. Three times Quint and Luke moved their stands that day, each of them leaving thirty to forty dead at each stand.

The skinners had come up from the camp further along the creek where they had thrown a crude dam across it to hold back the runoff water from the lake, creating their own private little reservoir. They worked in pairs, finishing the still warm carcasses within twenty minutes to half an hour. The *carretas* creaked up to collect the green hides and meat for transport back to the camp. There teams pegged out the hides for drying and sliced the meat with the grain into thin sheets for the drying racks.

The bold wolves and the more timid, but no less predatory, coyotes moved in on the stripped carcasses, or hovered about the old, disabled, the weak, and the young. Calves who stayed close by their downed mothers were torn down and sometimes half devoured before they died in terrible agony.

By midday the scavenger birds were in full force. Long-tailed magpies with red and white on their wings, and western ravens bigger than the smaller, rustier, and noiser crows came in cawing flocks. *Zopilotes* hovered high in the eye of the sun. They hung almost invisible, riding the wings of the wind with motionless black, white-tipped pinions, like scraps of charred paper rising from a bonfire.

The gunfire was so steady and regular that in time the buffalo seemed to become accustomed to it, not knowing it was steadily diminishing the herd. What did it really matter? For every bull or cow that fell there were thousands to take their place.

It was late afternoon the last day of hunting. The buffalo started moving north about midday. The tail of the herd was passing beyond the creek valley under a huge cloud of yellowish dust. The ground throbbed from the pounding of thousands of hoofs. Hundreds of wolves splashed through what remained of the lake, now a churned-up, stinking mass more solid than liquid. Their long hair dripped with water and mud. They loped on after the herd. The hunt was over.

Quint laid aside his smoking, overheated Henry rifle. The last of the gunsmoke drifted off. His eyes ached from the intense heat and the glimmering of the sun from the whitish saline patches on the valley floor. He laid his throbbing, pounding head on his crossed forearms and closed his burning eyes. His right shoulder ached intolerably from the incessant heavy recoil of the three big-bored rifles. His moutch tasted like corroded brass. His thirst seemed unquenchable. Quint's clothing was stiff with stale perspiration, dried blood, and tallow, crawling with itching vermin and infested with buffalo mange. He was deathly sick in a spiritual sense from the ceaseless slaughter. As Luke had said dryly at the end of the second day of shooting, "Stand huntin' is a lot more practical and profitable than buffalo runnin' on hossback but it shore takes the shine out'a life."

A snorting and grunting came on the wind. Quint raised his head. One huge old bull was on his feet among the motionless humps of the slain, an ancient, isolated patriarch perhaps a quarter of a century old. He was gaunt and stiff from age, spotted and torn with long-standing scars. He stood defiant, angry little eyes rolling within a circle of sinking coyotes. Perhaps he thought the dead about him were still his to protect. He was fearsomely angry, pawing the earth and tossing up bunches of sod that silted down on his mane and back. As long as he kept his feet he lived and the nearby dead were safe from desecration.

The coyotes surely weren't after him for his meat. They had been sated all week. This was sport. They were safe as long as they didn't get too close to him. They worried at him, gave him no rest, closed in behind him to nip playfully at his hamstrings, then scattered yelping gleefully when he turned to face them. Then the rest of the team dashed in behind him, nipping with sharp fangs or slashing at his massive sides, whirling away before he could turn and charge. Bright blood dripped from his aged hulk. He had no chance of survival. He could not get past them to join the rest of the herd even if he had wanted to do so. His tormentors would win in the end. As he tottered from wounds and exhaustion, all alone among the dead, his many enemies would at last close in, bite and hold fast to drag him down. He'd be torn to pieces while he still lived.

Quint rested his chin on his forearms and watched the unequal, preordained struggle. The bull's hide was useless, his meat too tough and stringy for jerking. How much was he really worth? At least a half-ounce lead ball, ninety grains of powder, and a percussion cap.

Quint stood up. He took Auld Clootie and swiftly loaded it. He cocked it, capped it, set trigger, aimed it, and fired all in one fluid motion. Powdersmoke plumed from the muzzle. The throaty shot echo ran along the creek flats and died out against the distant ridge. The bull was dead before he hit the ground. In an instant he was buried under a mass of snarling, snapping, slashing coyotes heaving like a squirming mass of dirty yellowish-brown maggots.

Quint reloaded. He gathered his gear, slung the three rifles over his shoulders, and turned his back on the scene of slaughter. Skinners moved across the open plain to finish the last of the buffalo. One of them was leading Quint's riding mule. Quint mounted, kicked the mule in the ribs with his heels, and rode toward the distant camp. He did not look back.

★ FOURTEEN ★

The long straggling line of heavily laden *carretas* and pack mules crawled across the heat-hazed plain. A plume of thin dust rose from under hoofs and wheels to be driven off by the dry north wind. Beyond the course of the caravan a scattering of antelope were in the distance, their white rumps barely showing through the haze. Dimly seen to the north were the twin notched volcanic peaks of Rabbit Ears Mountain. The temperature was 110 degrees.

The dust could be seen for many miles. It was Kotso-teka country. The caravan was fifteen miles short of Carrizo Creek, the next watering place, and eight to ten miles south of the Cimarron Cut-Off of the Santa Fe Trail. During July and August the Carrizo and the main branch of the Canadian were slow-running streams discharging a volume of water about the thickness of a man's waist. The Mexicans said, "He who leaves the edge of the Canadian or its tributaries must make a good day's march to find food, water, or grass." But it had been a very dry spring. Would there be water in the Carrizo? Once the caravan reached there the Rio Brioso was only eighty miles west.

It was nearing late afternoon. Luke rode up beside Quint and drew down the dusty bandanna covering his nose and mouth. He shifted his tobacco chew and spat dryly. "Still no Comanch, Big Red."

Quint shrugged. "Maybe something more valuable than we are drew them off."

Luke snorted. "All of the weeks we been in their country, killin' hundreds of buffalo, cured their hides and dried their meat, then turned around and rode this far west and they didn't *know* we was here? What drew them away? It ain't right. It just ain't right!"

Quint grinned, wincing as his lower lips cracked. "Maybe our medicine is just good."

"Shit!"

Antonio Zaldivar stood up in his stirrups. "*Mira! Mira!* Look! Look!" he shouted.

Dust was rising on the flat plane between the caravan and a long ridge this side of the Rabbit Ears.

"Indians! Indians!" Blas Galeras cried. "Should we corral the *carretas,* Don Quintin?"

Quint reined in his mule and drew his telescope from its case. He focused it on the dust. "Two horsemen. Probably the Delawares." He thrust up an arm. "*Parada! Parada!* Halt! Halt!"

The caravan came to a dust-shrouded halt. The dust drifted south on the brisk wind.

The Delawares trotted their mules up to Quint and Luke. Moccasin pointed northwest. "Comanches at last.

This side of Carrizo Creek and about five miles from it along a ridge overlookin' the Cut-Off."

Quint nodded. "Looking *this* way?" he asked casually.

Moccasin shook his head. "They can't see the caravan because of the ridge behind them."

"What about our dust?" Luke asked.

"The wind is blowin' south, ain't it? Besides, they don't seem much interested in what's goin' on behind them. It's somethin on the Cut-Off they're interested in."

"Such as?" Quint asked. "Caravan maybe?"

Moccasin looked back over his shoulder. "No. They're waitin' for some soldiers comin' from the east."

Quint looked quickly at Moccasin. "Soldiers? What kind of soldiers? Mexican?"

"American. About thirty of 'em."

"Guardin' a caravan?" Luke asked.

"Ain't no caravan. They got five mule-drawn wagons and a *caballada* of forty mules and horses."

Quint and Luke looked at each other in puzzlement.

"Exploring party?" Quint asked.

Luke shook his head. "On Mexican territory?"

"How many Comanches?" Quint asked.

Joshua held out a short stick cut with notches. "Each notch, ten, Big Red."

Quint counted eighteen notches. He whistled softly.

Luke shifted his chew and spat. "Now we know where at least *some* of 'em are. Watchin' for loot along the Trail."

"Them soldiers keep marchin' the way they are, the first Comanches they see will be the ones killin' 'em," Joshua said quietly.

Moccasin nodded. "No scouts out except a few soldiers ridin' within sight of the rest of 'em."

"What do ye think, Moc?" Quint asked. He could foretell the answer.

"They ain't got a chance, Big Red."

The dust had drifted off. The drivers and *ciboleros* squatted in the hot shade of the *carretas*. Mules bawled and thirsty oxen lowed.

Quint looked west. He could just make out the haze-faint line of basalt-capped mesas called the Don Carlos Hills. They were the line of demarcation for the caravan. Once past them the caravan was comparatively safe, with reasonable caution. One never let his guard down in that country. Quint and the people of Rio Brioso and the Mora needed those hides and dried meat. They could not afford the loss of horses, mules, and oxen. His men were watching him intently. He was the *patron;* the leader. The decision was his and his alone.

Quint looked at Moccasin. "How much time for the soldiers to reach the creek?"

"Late afternoon, Josh?" Moccasin asked.

Joshua nodded. "Mebbe about dusk."

Quint shaped a simple map in his mind. The Cut-Off and the route of the caravan formed the north and south sides of a truncated isosceles triangle. The base to the east formed the line north-south. The truncated western end was formed by the line of Carrizo Creek and the Don Carlos Hills. It would take the soldiers perhaps five hours to reach the creek for water and bivouac. The Comanches would never let them reach it.

"How far are the Comanches from the creek, Moc?" Quint asked.

"Mebbe three miles. They can't hide closer to the creek because there ain't enough cover for them. Ground too open. Even a Delaware would have a hard time findin' cover there."

"How soon before our caravan might be seen by the Comanches?"

"Couple of hours mebbe. By that time they might be so busy killin' soldiers and runnin' off their stock they won't even notice our dust."

The lowing of the oxen, braying of the mules, and whinnying of the horses had increased in volume. The men were quiet, in the way of those expecting imminent danger.

"Blas Galeras! Antonio Zaldivar!" Quint shouted. They came running. "I'm going to take a look at those loco American soldiers riding on Mexican territory in Comanche country with no scouts out," Quint explained. "Blas, you'll take charge of the caravan. Antonio will be *segundo.* Close up in two parallel lines. Keep outriders between the caravan and that ridge to the north. If you see dust rising and moving toward you, corral your *carretas* until you can verify who it is. If that doesn't happen, keep on to the creek as fast as you can go, cross it, water on the far side, then continue on to Rio Brioso. Do not, under any circumstances, camp for the night. Force march all night. By that time, the danger will probably be over and you can rest for half a day, then continue on. Understood?"

"How many men will you need, Don Quintin?" Blas asked.

"Only my partners."

Blas stared. "Only four of you? For the love of God, Don Quintin! There are almost two hundred Comanches on the other side of that ridge."

Quint nodded. "And thirty American soldiers. I don't want to risk the caravan by taking any men from it." He smiled thinly. "Don't worry, *companero*. We'll do what we can, but we must do *something*. . . ."

They changed their riding mules for fresh mustangs from the *caballada*. Quint mounted a *barrosa*, a smudgy dun-colored horse. Such a breed had a reputation for stamina. They rode north.

"There is a madness in such people," Blas said gloomily.

Antonio shrugged. "God or the devil watches over Don Grande Rubio. He will return."

The dust rose again as the caravan moved out, but the north wind held good, drifting the dust plume to the south away from the distant ridge. Quint idly speculated on what would be the choice of the Comanches if they saw the dust and the caravan. Would they choose the soldiers with their fine weapons, mounts, *caballada*, and the loot from the wagons or the caravan? The hides and jerky would have little value to them. They would want the horses and mules first and then the weapons of the *ciboleros*. It would be safer to attack the caravan. The soldiers were usually good shots and would fight to the death. On the other hand the Comanches had nothing but sheer contempt for New Mexicans. "The Mexicans raise our horses and mules for us," was their arrogant boast. They had made it good over the centuries.

Joshua looked up, *"Zopilote,"* he said quietly.

The sky was cloudless that day, an inverted bowl of hazy brazen blue. High above the Cimarron Cut-Off a black speck like a scrap of charred paper seemed to hang motionless. The great land buzzard rode the wind on outstretched motionless wings, moving only the white-tipped fingerlike feathers at the end to hold its position. Was it a harbinger? How could it know to be there at that particular time? The Delawares had not reported anything dead or dying along the Cut-Off, sure to draw such a scavenger. *How did it know?*

★   FIFTEEN   ★

COMANCHE!

The Cimarron Cut-Off was arrow-straight across a dry, grassy plain. Carrizo Creek was three miles west marked by a low line of dusty trees. South of the trail a low ridge of naked volcanic rock extended to within several miles to the creek. Below the ridge the wind rippled the endless grass like choppy waves beating against a shore of black sand and rock. The column of soldiers with their five mule-drawn wagons and *caballada* of horses and mules moved slowly toward the creek, trailing a fine skein of powdery dust raveled out by the wind. The brave red and white guidon snapped at the head of the column. Occasionally polished brass and steel glinted through the dust. Regulars for sure. They seemed to be the only human beings for hundreds of square miles so vast and lonely was the empty plain.

Luke held his hat to shade Quint's telescope, to keep the sunlight from reflecting off the brass and lens, a dead giveaway to their position. Quint studied the column. Luke and he lay bellyflat on the ridge to the south of the trail. In a hollow below and behind them Moccasin held the horses. Half a mile to the west hidden in a deep, wide cleft on the north slope of the ridge were almost two hundred Comanches painted for war. Not far from them, watching them, was Joshua.

The column had two troopers riding point half a mile ahead. Two flankers rode on each side of the column, about three hundred yards from it. The *caballada* was herded along behind the wagons. A dust-eating rear guard of three troopers followed the *caballada*. At a discreet distance, about extreme carbine range behind the rear guard, where wolves, loping easily along waiting for the dead, dying, or dropout horses and mules. The remainder of the troopers led their horses, plodding wearily along, their hopeful eyes on the line of dusty trees along the creek.

The fine German telescope lens picked out details. The soldiers had the lean and rangy style of veteran horse soldiers. They wore snug-fitting jackets of dark blue with a single row of brass buttons. The jacket trimmings were yellow tape. Trousers were sky-blue with a single yellow stripe along the outer seam. Forage caps were dark blue with short leather bills and banded with orange cloth. Belts and carbine slings were white leather. The pair of soldiers who marched afoot just ahead of the troopers had two yellow stripes along the seams of their trousers. They were officers.

"Well?" Luke asked.

"United States Dragoons, Lukie."

"In Mex territory."

"I'd figure them for an escort to a trader's caravan if there was a caravan."

"There ain't any caravan."

"Exactly."

"Ridin' right into a Comanche ambush."

Moccasin crawled up beside Quint and Luke. "What a target," he murmured. "What do we do about it? Warn 'em?"

Quint shook his head. "No time. The instant we do the Comanches will be down on them and us."

"Even if we did warn them," Luke added, "they'd have no time to corral those wagons and make a stand. It'd only be a matter of short time afore the Comanches would go right over them and *us* if we was down there."

"Twice we whup them Kotsotekas and never lose a man," Moccasin reminded Luke. "Our hearts were big and our medicine was good."

Luke looked sideways. "That true now, Moc?"

There was no reply from the Delaware.

"Are ye both with me?" Quint asked.

They nodded.

"Moc, go get Josh," Quint ordered. "Luke, give me a hand."

★ 158 ★

Quint and Luke pulled many double handfuls of dry grasses and tied them together with thrums, the long fringes they cut from their jackets. They led the horses into a hollow closer to the trail and waited for the Delawares. The north wind was rising, booming over the hollow. The grass rippled and undulated from the blast.

Moccasin and Joshua came to the hollow.

"Who's got the fastest horse?" Quint asked.

"Me," Joshua replied.

"When I give ye the word, ride like the wind to warn the soldiers. Tell them to ride for the creek and fort up within the trees."

"Right in front of the Comanches? They'll never make it, Big Red!" Joshua cried incredulously.

Quint smiled wryly. "It'll be up to the three of us to keep the Comanches busy while ye warn the soldiers and they get on their way to the creek."

Luke studied Quint. "Are yuh goin' to let me and Moc into how yuh plan to do this?"

Quint took three big blocks of lucifer matches from his possibles bag. "When I give Josh the word, each of ye will light two bundles of dried grass and follow me. I'll lead the way between the trail and the position of the Comanches. The grass is tinder dry. The wind from the north should fan one helluva blaze right up that slope and into the faces of the Comanches and their horses. The warriors will try to ride through the flames, but they'll never force their horses to do it. It won't take long for the grass to burn away, so we won't have too much time. If those horse soldiers down there have any sense, they'll hightail it for the creek, and I hope to God they make it before the Comanches get reorganized."

The three of them studied Quint. "Yuh figger these angles out yourself, or do yuh get help?" Luke asked.

Quint began to stuff bundles of the dry grass inside his jacket. "Oh, I do it myself, Wandering Wolf," he replied casually.

Luke shook his head. "Dry grass and a block of lucifers. What a helluva way to fight nigh on to two hundred wasp-mean Comanches."

"Ye got any better ideas, Lukie?"

There was no answer from Luke.

The column was now several hundred yards from

reaching a point on the trail abreast of the ambush. The tips of feather bonnets showed now and then along the lip of the arroyo as the Comanches mounted and lay low on their ponies' backs.

Quint mounted. He placed the reins between his teeth and nodded to Joshua. Josh was out of the hollow like a stone flung from a sling. Quint lighted two bundles and held one in each hand. He rammed his spurs into the flanks of the mustang and raked them back and forth. The half-wild brute hammered up out of the draw into the open. The wind caught at them.

The *barrosa* ran like a lightning streak, its drumming hoofs hardly seeming to touch the ground. Quint tossed a burning bundle far to his left and went on, hurling the second bundle fifty feet beyond the first. The grass seemed to flash as it caught fire. The wind caught at the tiny flames and fanned them as it drove them up the slope. Luke and Moccasin at full gallop followed Quint, casting their burning bundles in rotation beyond the point where he had dropped the second of his bundles, igniting a continuous line of burning grass clear across the front of the imminent Comanche charge. The fire licked up the grass like so much gossamer, a long line of flame crackling like the reports of a thousand pistols, moving upslope in terrible rapidity, while sometimes flames shot several feet into the air like the forked tongue of a serpent.

Quint set fire to another pair of grass bundles and hurled them as far as he could up the slope. As he did so his eyes widened. "Jesus Christ!" he cried.

The rim of the arroyo was lined with feathered horsemen urging their half-wild painted mounts up and out of the deep hollow. Their faces and lean muscular torsos were painted red, vermilion, ochre, white, and black. Horned and feathered warbonnets rippled in the wind. Shields were a glaring white, made of the thick, toughened rawhide of a buffalo bull's neck slowly smoke-dried and hardened with layers of glue boiled from buffalo hoofs. They were light of weight, could easily turn an arrow or lance and even a bullet from a smoothbore musket if turned obliquely. Their powerful bows were laminated pieces of bone and horn from buffalo, elk, or mountain sheep, spliced and glued together, wrapped in wet buffalo sinew which bound the bow iron-banded tight as it dried. Lance blades and polished ornaments of brass and silver glittered with reflected sunlight. The nervous mustangs were striped, flared, patterned, and blotched with fresh bright paint. Feathers fluttered from their manes; scalps dangled from their bridles. The Lords of the Plains—*Comanches!*

Isa-tai—End of a Wolf—was a great medicine man of the Kotsotekas. He had once ascended to the abode of a Great Spirit high above the Heaven of the White Man's Father. He could control the elements and produce rain, cause drought and bring forth as many bullets from his stomach as the Kotsotekas might need this day. His black magic could so influence the guns of the white men that they could not shoot Comanches. He had touched each of the warriors with some of his magic paint so that they could not be seen and killed by white men's bullets. This day he stood naked, painted all in white from head to toe with cabalistic signs marked on his gaunt body. He wore only a cap of sage stems as he stood to the right of the Comanche line chanting his incantations.

An angry, swiftly moving scar of bright flame ate its irregular way up the slope directly toward the warriors. Flame, sparks, and thick smoke blew against them and their excited mounts. Quint reined in his mustang in a hoof-pawing rear as he threw his last two incendiary bundles. Luke and Moccasin hammered toward him bending low in their saddles as they hurled the last of their flaming grass bundles.

The entire area between the trail and the arroyo was a billowing, smoking, and flaming mass of burning grass leaving black smoking ruin behind it. Horses, no matter how well trained and disciplined, would not face those flames. The front rank of warriors broke and turned back against the main mass of those still urging their panicky mounts to get up out of the arroyo. The advancing and retreating lines crashed into each other in wild confusion.

"Now!" Quint shouted as he yanked his Hawken from its saddle scabbard and wheeled back the way he had come followed by his two whooping companions.

Joshua had warned the dragoons; he had not convinced their commanding officer to make for the creek with all possible speed. The commanding officer snapped out orders with machinelike precision. The taut discipline of Regulars took over. The wagons were driven into an irregular oval with gaps between them. The dragoons led their mounts within the oval. One man in each four held the horses. The rest of the dragoons cocked and capped their Hall carbines and took up defensive positions. The rear guard closed up to help herd the *caballada*. Some of the excited horses and mules broke loose and stampeded to get away from the fire.

Joshua joined Quint and his companions. The four of them opened fire through the drifting smoke. The fire reached the arroyo lip and jumped it to ignite the grass on the far side. The arroyo and the ground in front of it was a tangle of fallen horses and warriors. Bullets hummed wasplike through the smoke, striking flesh or ricochetting off rock or hard-baked ground.

Quint stood up in his stirrups, waving his smoking Hawken. "Keep up the shooting, *compañeros!*" he shouted. He set spurs to the dun and plunged downslope toward the corralled wagons. He drew back on the reins, rearing the sweat-lathered mustang. "Get this Goddamned column moving!" he roared. "Once those Comanches get organized, they'll ride right over ye! Head for the creek, dammit! *Head for the creek!*"

"I'm in command here, mister!" the dragoon captain shouted.

Quint fought to control his excited mount as the dun turned in circles while rearing and plunging. "Then *command*, God dammit! Move out! *Carajo! Carajo!*"

The officer stared at Quint for a few seconds as though recognizing him, then spat out orders. A single file of mounted dragoons formed along the length of the wagons, between them and the Comanches. A squad spread out fanwise in front of the wagons. Other dragoons tried to drive the panicky *caballada* behind the wagons.

Quint galloped toward the *caballada*. "Each of ye take as many lead-ropes as ye can and get to hell out of here! Let the rest of them fend for themselves! Maybe they'll follow their mates to the creek."

"They're government property!" a sergeant yelled.

Quint shook his head in disgust. "The lot of ye will be *dead* government property if ye don't get your asses out of here! We can't hold off those Comanches for long! Now *git!*"

The Comanches struggled out of the arroyo and formed up, then plunged downslope toward the trail. Gunfire smoked and sparkled along the line of dragoons. Hawken rifles and Hall carbines began to take effect on the warriors.

The Comanches were now in their element. They flung themselves over the offsides of their mounts, clinging to hair ropes woven into the manes, hooking heels over rumps while firing muskets or loosing arrows from under their horses' necks.

"Shoot the horses!" Quint shouted. At that instant a Comanche bullet struck his mount square in the forehead. Quint hit the ground running as the dun went down. A knot of Comanches veered toward him. Some of them might have recognized him, because of his size, auburn beard, and the scar on his face. They knew him of old. Twice seven years ago he had been their nemesis. They forgot about the prize of wagons, horses, mules, weapons, and scalps. To count coup on this man was a far greater prize.

More Comanches boiled up out of the arroyo, perhaps sensing victory. Quint's *compañeros* dashed about in the smoke and dust, half-obscured while firing repeatedly. They did not know he had been downed.

A slug shattered Quint's powder horn. The powder flowed to the ground and was instantly ignited by smoldering sparks. A quick flash of fire singed Quint's left moccasin and legging. He slung his Hawken and drew his twin Colts under cover of the thick powdersmoke. He stood his ground behind the fallen horse. Comanches hammered toward him, lances down, razor-sharp two-foot blades flashing in the slanting sunlight.

Quint raised his Colts and opened fire.

Crisp, staccato commands cracked out behind Quint. "Dragoons! Sling carbines! Draw pistols and sabers! Follow me! *Charge!*"

The dragoon captain pounded so close past Quint his left stirrup brushed Quint's elbow. His reins were held in his teeth. The glistening saber was in his right hand, a pistol in his left. He was closely followed by half a dozen dragoons, reins in teeth, heavy brass-hilted "wrist breaker" sabers gripped in right hands, single-shot Aston pistols in the left. They shouted into action against three times their number of warriors.

The big dragoon mounts crashed into the smaller Comanche ponies. Dragoon sabers fended off, parried, or slashed lance shafts. Pistols cracked. Sabers thrust and slashed. It was too much for the Comanches. This was not their kind of war. The survivors broke and fled. Another Comanche charge formed.

The officer had taken a lance thrust through the breast of his shell jacket, exposing the lining of a pocket which hung out and flapped as he rode toward Quint, holding out his crooked right arm. Quint rammed his smoking pistols under his belt. Just as the officer neared him a small, dark object flipped out of the torn pocket and sailed directly toward Quint who neatly fielded it, then hooked his right arm within the officer's, gripped his saber belt, and vaulted up behind him, seating himself on the blanket roll strapped to the saddle cantle. They rode after the wagons followed by the dragoons, Luke, and the Delawares.

The officer spoke over his shoulder. "Are you all right, sir? No wounds?" There was a soft Virginian quality to his voice. It sounded vaguely familiar.

"Aye, I'm fine, captain," Quint replied. "Do I know ye?"

"You do, Quintin Kershaw. I'm Captain Shelby Calhoun, First United States Dragoons, at your service."

Quint nodded. "We meet again. I owe ye my life, sir."

Shelby shook his head. "All in the line of duty. You owe me nothing. You saved my command from possible defeat and massacre this day. In addition, you will recall saving my wife's life and mine eight years ago from the Pawnees at McNee's Creek. Remember?"

"Aye, I remember."

The Comanches pursued for a time but were held back by rifle and carbine fire until at last they slowed down and came to a halt. Shelby reined in his bay within the shelter of the trees and shouted for his orderly. He turned to Quint as he dismounted. "They'll not attack well-armed dragoons shooting from cover. I'll send my second-in-command back for the stampeded horses and mules. Can I use your men to help?"

Quint smiled slowly. "There are only four of us, captain."

"You mean to tell me you came to help us with just four men against hundreds of Comanches?"

Quint shrugged. "That's all there were."

Shelby studied him. "It's said you are somewhat of a living legend in New Mexico now."

Quint grinned. "Where did ye hear that interesting fable?" he asked dryly.

"We've kept close track of you, Quint."

"Through the good Doctor Byrne, no doubt."

Shelby nodded. "There's not much going on in New Mexico of which we are unaware."

Quint looked out across the smoky plain. The sun was gone. "If ye send your men out there you'll never see them again—alive."

"The Comanches should be gone by then." There was a hint of steel in Shelby's voice. He was used to command.

Quint shook his head. "They'll be back after dark to round up your stampeded stock. They've got to show some profit out of this disastrous day, or lose face."

"Dammit! Those animals are government property! I'm responsible for them!"

"Jeeesus Christ!" Quint exploded. "Would ye trade off some of your beloved dragoons and their mounts just to prove ye might be right? I tell ye, Calhoun, if ye do send them out, ye'll not see a man jack of them, *or* their mounts this side of hell!"

Shelby rubbed his jaw. He plucked at the front of his torn jacket. "Perhaps you're right," he admitted slowly after a pause. "After all, you are the more experienced Indian-fighter." He stripped off his gauntlets and pulled them under his belt. "Jean speaks about you now and again," he added.

It was she who had prophesied Quint's destiny, all those years ago. *"The future is here for you in New Mexico, Quintin Ker-Shaw,"* she had said.

"We heard, of course, that you had married that lovely Mexican *rico* child, Quint. Can't recall her name."

"Ye knew her only as Lupita. She was Guadalupe de Vasquez."

"You've children?" Shelby queried.

It seemed to Quint that he must know about the children. Over the past seven years there had been much secret coded correspondence between Doctor Tom Byrne and Senator Alexander Allan, Jean Calhoun's father, former colonel of the First Dragoons, and now senator from Kentucky and a power in the government of the United States. The correspondence was to feed information to the United States on the political, economic, and military situation in New Mexico. Quint knew that he and his activities had been included in much of that correspondence.

"I've three children, Shelby," Quint said. "My oldest boy David, now nine years of age. The twins, a boy and a girl, Francisco and Rafaela, now seven years."

Shelby narrowed his eyes. "The oldest boy is nine?" There was unspoken curiosity in his voice.

"Guadalupe is not his mother. You've a son, I've heard."

"Alexander. He's eight. He knows a great deal about you from his mother and grandfather. They've made quite a hero out of you. The boy thinks more of you than he does of your great contemporary and friend Kit Carson."

"A great honor, I'm sure," Quint murmured.

Shelby nodded. "He talks of nothing but becoming a dragoon and coming West to fight Indians and Mexicans."

"Mexicans? Why Mexicans? Possibly he listens to you and his grandfather a great deal on that touchy subject."

"He does. He's the apple of his grandfather's eye."

"Ye didn't answer my question."

"About Alexander wanting to fight Mexicans? It's obvious now, isn't it?"

Quint was puzzled. "Not to me, Shelby."

"But, the *war*. Haven't you heard about the war?"

Quint stared. "War? We've been buffalo hunting east of the Llano Estacado since May."

"My God! No wonder! Congress declared war on Mexico the thirteenth of May. My command here is an advance reconnaissance party for the Army of the West, under the command of Colonel, Acting Brigadier General Stephen Watts Kearny, First United States Dragoons, with whom I have the honor of serving as aide-de-camp.

My unit is the first United States force to enter the Province of New Mexico."

It seemed to Quint that it had suddenly become much quieter within the *bosque*, but he knew it was merely an illusion brought on by the impact of Shelby's announcement. War had finally come to New Mexico. The swift prairie dusk had begun to gather over the bivouac, with its wavering firelight and shifting shadows. The astringent odor of burning firewood mingled with that of boiling coffee, cooking pork, fresh manure, and the ammonia smell of the mounts. A moment past the scene had seemed normal, routine, an army unit preparing its mess and camp for the night. Now it was different somehow, not more purposeful, but certainly more intent, as though a great event was in the offing, even in this little temporary bivouac of a score and a half of dragoons, lost in the vast immensity of the plains. War had been half expected for years. Now it had come at last—*War!*

"I must see to my command, Quint," Shelby said. "You'll dine with me tonight. I have some important papers that were to be delivered to you at Rio Brioso. I think you'll find them interesting, to say the least." He stalked off into the shadows, a tall spare figure, every inch the ideal dragoon soldier.

It wasn't until Shelby was gone that Quint remembered the small object that had fallen from the officer's torn jacket. He took it out from within his shirtfront. It was a small, green, plush velvet case held shut by a tiny gold hasp. He opened it. It was a daguerreotype of a woman, a young girl, and boy. There was no question in Quint's mind about the identity of the woman. Her immense blue eyes held quick intelligence and an innate sense of humor. Her soft-looking, lustrous hair was the shade of corn silk. The face was lovely, oval-shaped with a clear complexion. He recalled it freckled and tinted by the burning suns of the Santa Fe Trail. Her nose was slightly bold, the mouth wide, with perfect teeth and soft, full lips. Jean Calhoun, nee Jean Louise Allan, like a bright sunlit day in comparison to the soft, lustrous, moonlight beauty of Lupita. Quint remembered how Luke had once compared the two young women: "*Too damned bad Big Red Badger couldn't take* both *of 'em. Good lookin' wimmen. One bright like sunlight; one dark*

★ 167 ★

like moonlight. Sunlight got lots of money; moonlight got lots of land. Both mebbe got lots of lovin'. Make tipi nice and warm on cold winter nights. Wagh!"

Quint thumb-snapped a lucifer into flame and cupped his hand about it so as to study the features of the boy and girl. The girl seemed to be slightly older than the boy, perhaps a year or so at least. She bid fair to be a beauty of the fragile type, pale and transparent of skin, dark of hair and eye, and vaguely familiar to Quint. Slowly it came back to him. Eight years ago Jean Allan had accompanied her older, pregnant sister, Catherine, to Santa Fe so that the child would be born there in the presence of Charles, Catherine's merchant and trader husband. Frail Catherine had died in childbirth. Charles wanted no part of raising an infant daughter. Jean had just married Shelby Calhoun and was about to return with him to Washington. She had agreed to take the infant Catherine back with her to raise in the proper environment. Charles had died of drink a few years later. There was little question in Quint's mind but that the girl in the photo was young Catherine Williston.

The boy was a handsome lad, bidding fair to be a bold one in his time. He had fine, light hair like that of his mother, a strong nose and firm chin. But it was his eyes that caught and held one's attention. And there was no mistaking *their* origin.

Quint blew out the match. "Mother of God," he murmured.

★ SIXTEEN ★

"Could ye use a cup of issue java, Quintin Kershaw?" an unmistakably Irish voice asked from behind Quint.

Quint turned. "Mike Quinn! It's been a long time!"

The sergeant grinned as he held out a ham of a hand. "Bent's Fort. May of '42. I was there with Captain Cooke on escort duty when ye passed through on your way to Saint Looey."

Luke nodded. "That was the time we all 'made drunk come' together and lost a day in the process."

Mike held out two cups of coffee. He looked back over his shoulder, then withdrew a black pint bottle from inside his jacket. "A bit of the crayture to kill the night chill," he said in a low voice. He laced the coffee. "The captain himself is not much of a drinkin' man, especially in the field, lads."

A pistol cracked as a dragoon put his wounded horse out of its misery. Shelby's voice rang as he reamed out another for not properly cleaning his weapons before he messed.

"Bit of a stinger ain't he, Mike?" Luke asked.

Mike nodded. "Horses, mules, weapons, wagons, and dragoons are only important to him in that order. But, he's one helluva soldier. Ranked third in his class at the Academy. Served with honor and distinction on the Plains for three years. I shud know. I was a corporal in his platoon in those years. The rigimint presented him with a cased pair of fine silver-mounted pistols for his service in them days." He slanted his blue eyes at Quint. "I often wondered what happened to them." He grinned.

"They belong to a Pawnee chief now," Luke said. "Courtesy of the Big Red Badger here."

Quint shrugged. "His life and that of his future wife were at stake," he said quietly.

Mike nodded. "I know the tale. That was in '38. He was on his way to Santa Fe and Chihuahua, supposedly on sick leave from the army."

"But actually eyein' the Santa Fe Trail, New Mexico, and Chihuahua with the thought of some day the U.S. might want to move troops, artillery and supply trains there," Luke added dryly.

"Is that why he's in command of this reconnaissance?" Quint asked.

"No better man for the job, Quint."

"Is that how come he happened to ride right into a Comanche ambush with no scouts out?" Luke asked.

Mike shrugged. "He refused some Shawnee and Delaware scouts back at Fort Leavenworth. Said he could handle his own scoutin'. He was told the Comanches had declared war on all white men because disease had come among them supposedly brought on by soldiers. Said the soldiers blew evil breaths on their children. Bull shit! They just figured on easy pickings like the Kiowas and

Pawnees was already doin'. Anyway, ye can't tell the captain much if he's already made up his mind."

"He told me Colonel Kearny commands your Army of the West. Wasn't he in command of a reconnaissance to South Pass last year, Mike?" Quint asked.

"Aye! The finest officer in the whole damned army! Stephen Watts Kearny! Officer and gentleman. Commanding officer of Fort Leavenworth and the crack First Dragoons, elite rigiment of the army. New Jersey man fifty-two years old. Distinguished for bravery at Queenston Heights on the Niagara River when he was lootenant in the 13th Infantry, War of 1812. Thirty-four years in service. A 'soldier's soldier' he is. A real professional and master of his job. Some say he's as good as Winfield Scott and Zachary Taylor. I say he's better than the two of them together."

"What's Calhoun's assignment?"

"One of Kearny's staff. Some say he got his captaincy and assigned to the staff of the Army of the West through his father-in-law, Senator Allan. Before this assignment he was stationed in Washington on the General Staff as advisor to the Military Affairs Committee."

"Helps to have relatives and friends in high places," Luke observed. "What's the word, Big Red?"

"Nepotism. Both Washington and Santa Fe are infested with it."

Mike shrugged. "Kearny would not have accepted the captain for his staff had he not been a first class soldier, all the same."

Shelby Calhoun had disciplined himself to fare no better than the enlisted men, at least while in the field. Officers' mess was served on battered tin plates, the powerful coffee in chipped granite cups. His second-in-command was young Lieutenant Claiborne Griffin, Topographical Engineers, a Pennsylvanian one year out of the Military Academy, a blond, gray-eyed, smiling young man. The officers and their two guests sat on fallen logs balancing their plates on their knees.

"How many men do ye have in your Army of the West?" Quint asked conversationally.

Shell put down his empty plate. "No offense, Quint, but you might be considered as a loyal Mexican citizen."

"So what if I am?"

Clay Griffin looked quickly at Quint. "There's a possibility you might inadvertently reveal such information to the Mexican authorities."

Shell nodded.

Quint smiled faintly. "If your war has been in effect since early last May, don't ye think the Mexican authorities by now will know your Army of the West is on its way, its exact numbers, how much artillery it has, and how big a wagon train?"

"In the weeks you were organizin' at Fort Leavenworth travelers and traders bound for Santa Fe would know about it. News travels fast on the plains. Indians call them 'moccasin messages,'" Luke added.

"Ye said I *might* be 'considered' as a loyal Mexican citizen. Ye seemed doubtful? Why?" Quint asked.

"My answer to that question depends on whether or not you accept the claim of the former Republic of Texas that the Rio Grande del Norte is its western boundary, as opposed to the Mexican claim that it is the Nueces instead. A difference of roughly two hundred fifty miles east to west. You know of course the Republic of Texas is now part of the United States by their willing annexation. At the time of annexation all Mexican citizens in the republic were allowed one year to become citizens of the United States. If they did not, they were required to leave Texas. Therefore, Quint, if you accept the premise that the western boundary of the Republic of Texas was the Rio Grande del Norte, that means you are no longer a citizen of Mexico but rather of the United States."

Luke whistled softly. "By God. If the Rio Grande *was* the western boundary of the Republic of Texas, and Texas is part of the United States, that will include your El Cerrillo property in the Taos Valley as well as the Rio Brioso grant."

Quint nodded. "Don't forget Santa Fe, Albuquerque, El Paso Del Norte, and about fifty thousand New Mexicans."

Shell smiled. "Exactly. So, you see, it's not really an invasion at all, merely the United States occupying territory rightfully ours since the annexation of Texas."

"Manifest Destiny," Quint murmured.

"We're thinking along the same lines, Quint."

Quint shook his head. "Not quite. Mexico has never

accepted the Rio Grande as the western boundary of Texas. To me, it seems to be a matter of arbitration between the two governments rather than war, invasion, and occupation."

Clay shook his head. "Too late. The Army of the West is on its way already to take possession of New Mexico and California."

Quint raised his eyebrows. *"California?* That's a helluva long way *west* of the Rio Grande."

Clay poked up the fire around the big coffeepot. "Manifest Destiny, Quint. Your own words."

"I didn't say I agreed with it."

Clay looked up. "There's really not much you can do about it, is there?" he asked coolly.

Shell nodded. "The Mexicans probably won't resist. They haven't got the troops, weapons, and will to fight. If they are foolish enough to resist, we'll brush them aside like so many straw men."

"Manuel Armijo is no coward. Neither are the New Mexicans as a whole. They will fight if well led."

Shell shook his head. "Suicide. We know almost to a man how many troops he has, including a certain *Subteniente* Quintin Kershaw, commander of the Rural Mounted Militia of Rio Brioso and the Mora. Kershaw's Company, in short." He smiled. "Any resistance will be suicide. As long as you are quite sure the Mexicans know our numbers, the quality of our troops, and the number of guns we have, I see no reason why we can't inform you as well. We've a splendid little army marching on New Mexico to fight a splendid little war. Three squadrons of the First Dragoons. The First Missouri Mounted Volunteer Regiment. The Laclede Rangers, a spare troop of cavalry from Saint Louis, attached to the First Dragoons. Two companies of Regular infantry. A battalion of Missouri Volunteer Infantry. Two artillery companies formed into a Light Artillery Battalion with 6-pounder guns and 12-pounder howitzers—sixteen guns in all, capable of firing solid shot, spherical case, and canister. Captain Fischer's artillery company was recruited from German emigrants living in Saint Louis. There are the usual staff troops, a detachment of Topographical Engineers, and fifteen Delaware and Shawnee Indian scouts. About seventeen hundred men in all.

"There are two more units forming, one cavalry and one infantry. The cavalry are the Second Missouri Mounted Volunteers, now forming at Fort Leavenworth. The infantry will be unusual, to say the least."

"Five hundred Mormons," Clay Griffin murmured wryly. "My God. . . ."

"Saints?" Luke asked incredulously.

Shell nodded. "Brigham Young ordered them to serve the United States. Colonel Kearny wasn't anxious to have them but we were top-heavy with cavalry and short on infantry. The 'Pukes', the Missourians, refuse to walk when they can ride. So, we were forced to take the Saints."

"Mebbe have a problem handlin' them?" Luke suggested.

Shell smiled. "The colonel took care of that. He sent one of his best officers to command them. Captain James Allen of the First Dragoons. If anyone can whip the Mormons into something resembling soldiers, he's the man to do it."

Luke shook his head. "How will they get along with the Pukes? There never was any love lost between them."

"They hate each other worse than they hate Mexicans," Clay said. "The Army of the Lord marching with us Gentile sinners. Oh, my God!"

Shell leaned toward Quint. "Do you remember the interesting discussions we had in Doctor Byrne's library in Santa Fe when we were there in '38?"

"I've never forgotten them," Quint said. The lovely face of Jean Calhoun suddenly appeared in his mind's eye. She had been present at those highly informative sessions.

"At that time," Shell continued, "there didn't seem to be much doubt in your mind, or the minds of such Americans as Doctor Byrne, Ceran St. Vrain, the Bent brothers, and many others that the United States should and must annex New Mexico."

Quint refilled his coffee cup. At that time Quint had been penniless. Born a Scot, raised a Canadian, matured as a mountain man in the American West, he considered himself an American without benefit of official naturalization. Both William Bent and Ceran St. Vrain had recommended New Mexico for his future. Their estimate of the time required for the United States to take over New Mexico, one way or another, had been between five and seven years, certainly no more than ten. That had been in June, 1838. It was now July, 1846. Eight years since Manifest Destiny had been explained to him.

"There are some important facts concerning your position in New Mexico I am quite sure you already know," Shell said.

"*My* position?" Quint smiled faintly. "Is this in reference to the United States annexing New Mexico?"

Shell nodded. "Your Rio Brioso grant is in a vitally strategic position for invasion, with access west through the passes of the Sangre de Cristos to the Taos Valley, and adjacent to the Santa Fe Trail, with its route to Santa Fe. Your *hacienda* and settlement could serve as a temporary fort and base until such time as the United States can establish permanent facilities. You've immense flocks of sheep, herds of cattle, horses, mules, and oxen, as well as access to those of the Mora Valley. The able-bodied men would make excellent irregular mounted rifles if enlisted in the service of the United States. There are other considerations, *if* you're interested."

"Do continue," Quint said dryly.

Shell opened his dispatch case and withdrew two papers. "These are official documents for your consideration. One is a requisition for food supplies, forage, and draft animals from your Rio Brioso property. The other is a temporary commission for a lieutenancy of volunteer mounted rifles in the Army of the United States. It is signed by the Secretary of War. There is no name filled in as yet on this commission. I have the authority of Colonel Kearny to fill in your name and swear you into the service of the United States of America. What say you, Quintin Kershaw?"

Quint studied the papers for a few seconds, then looked up at Shell. "Ye know that Rio Brioso is a vital part of the defenses of the northeast frontier of the province. In fact, sir, they are the *only* defenses of that frontier. By Mexican law, at least in the opinion of Governor Armijo, I am a *subteniente* of rural mounted militia, sworn to the defense of the province in time of emergency or war. I have acted in that capacity, which is

★ 174 ★

tantamount to accepting that commission and responsibility for the defense of the northeast frontier. In that case, I can't accept a commission in the service of a foreign government."

Clay stared at Quint. "You consider the United States a *foreign* government, sir?" he demanded coldly.

Shell stayed Clay with an outthrust hand. "This is the same issue as before, Clay: Whether or not Mister Kershaw recognizes the sovereignty of the United States in New Mexico as far as the Rio Grande."

Quint smiled. "You haven't given me time to consider that fact, Shell."

Shell nodded. "Granted. I assume this will also apply to the requisitions?"

"Ye certainly know from your reliable sources of information that the Rio Brioso is not wholly mine. I am one of four partners, although the only active one, acting as *hacendado* these past seven years."

Clay looked puzzled. "I didn't know that."

Shell looked at him. "The other partners are Doctor Byrne, Governor Armijo, and Gertrudis Barcelo, more familiarly known as La Tules, the notorious monte dealer of Santa Fe."

"And all three of them are Mexican citizens," Quint added. "Even if Tom and I agreed, La Tules might not, and Armijo certainly wouldn't. Further, the governor certainly must know by now his province is due to be invaded. He probably already has sent his requisitions to the Rio Brioso along with my orders for active duty."

Shell shrugged. "So, it seems we are right back where we started. The question of the western boundary of the new State of Texas."

Quint nodded. "Full circle, Shell."

"There isn't much time, I must remind you. New Mexico will be invaded by August. The Rio Brioso will be occupied by the Army of the West. That, sir, is *absolute certainty!*"

The decision was solely up to Quint. There was no one to whom he could turn.

"Any resistance is useless," Shell added. "More troops will come. They will be irresistible. New Mexico will be ours and then California. American settlers hungry for land will come in their hundreds of thousands. Tough frontiersmen who will spread across the Southwest like an avalanche. In twenty years the United States will completely occupy the West from the Mississippi to the Pacific Ocean and from Canada to the Mexican border."

Clay stood up. "Manifest Destiny!" he cried dramatically. He was very young. He looked at the two cynical mountain men and flushed deeply.

Shell stood up. "Will you not reconsider your decision and accept this commission, Quint?"

Luke was out of Quint's line of sight. He caught Shell's attention, shook his head, and silently formed words with his lips. "Give him time."

Shell nodded. "I think I understand your position, Quint. It is a major decision, perhaps the greatest decision you'll have to make in your lifetime. If you accept the commission, and by the remotest of chances the Army of the West is defeated by the Mexicans, you'll be considered a traitor and stand to lose everything, perhaps even your life."

Quint stood up. "Ye don't really believe you'll be defeated, do ye?"

"I'd like to think it won't happen."

"My decision won't rest on such a remote possibility. It's not my property or my life that is in question here. It is a question of principle, perhaps even honor, sir." He suddenly realized how hypocritical that statement was. Never, at any time, during his eight years in New Mexico had he ever felt other than that in time the United States would eventually possess New Mexico. It was Guadalupe and the children he must consider. He had come to New Mexico with nothing but his Scots determination, courage, ambition, and his Hawken rifle. Now he was Don Quintin Kershaw, owner of El Cerrillo and *hacendado* of the Rio Brioso. He could do without the property. Wealth, as such, meant little to him. There was more land to be had. But he could not do without his wife and children. In truth, his concern was not so much over the children as it was over Guadalupe. The children were too young to care much in the long run whether or not they were Mexican or American. It was not so with her. Heart and soul she was New Mexican, direct descendant of Rodrigo de Vasquez, one of Onate's 130 "Orphans."

"I'll leave ye one of my Delawares as scout, Shell," Quint offered. "Young Joshua is not acceptable as a Mexican citizen, nor even as an American, but ye won't find a better man or a more loyal one." He half smiled.

Shell nodded. "Many thanks. I take it this means you won't resist us on the Rio Brioso?"

"It means nothing other than that I am concerned for your safety and that of your command." Quint smiled. "As yet I haven't received any orders from my governor."

"They might be there when you reach Rio Brioso," Shell suggested.

"Perhaps. We'll cross that bridge when we come to it."

They gripped hands and looked into each other's eyes. They respected each other even though they were not friends, nor was it probable that they ever would be.

Quint, Luke, and Moccasin rode through the darkness following the line of trees along the creek.

Luke looked sideways at Quint. "He's right yuh know."

Quint rested a hand on his saddle cantle and looked back at the bivouac.

"It was bound to come, Big Red."

Quint turned and looked forward into the windy darkness of the plain. "I know, Luke," he said quietly. "I *know....*"

★ SEVENTEEN ★

The late afternoon sun flashed from something polished brightly. A faint dust skein was wind raveled. A trumpet sounded faintly.

Quint thrust up his right arm. *"Parada! Parada!"* he shouted.

The caravan came to a dust-shrouded halt. It was less than five miles from Rio Brioso on the last day's march from Carrizo Creek.

Luke stood up in his stirrups, shading his eyes against the sun. "Soldiers, Big Red. Can't be Americans, *yet,* anyways."

★ 177 ★

Quint uncased his telescope and focused it on the distant moving column. They were moving faster. The faint drumming of hoofs sounded. The trumpet was blown again. A line of troopers galloped out in front of the column and spread out into a skirmish line.

"What the hell is goin' on?" Luke demanded.

The advancing horsemen moved down a long gentle slope toward a wide, dry streambed. The powerful telescope lens began to pick out details. The soldiers wore sky-blue coatees with scarlet collars and cuffs, dark blue trousers with deep red stripes, and leather half boots. Their shakos were of dull black leather topped by crimson pompoms. A red-white-green guidon snapped in the wind.

Quint closed the telescope. "Santa Fe Company of Active Militia Cavalry. Commanded by Captain Diego de las Casas, aide to Governor Armijo, first cousin to my wife from her mother's side of the family, and an arrogant, self-important sonofabitch. I can't stand the sight of him."

"What's he doin' out here?"

"Guess."

Quint looked back over the dusty caravan. His *ciboleros* had survived two months of hell's own time tracking down the Texas Herd, skinning and curing the hides, and jerking the poor meat, only to be met by a company of Mexican cavalry before they even reached home. There was no doubt in Quint's mind as to *why* the cavalry had come out to meet the caravan. Diego de las Casas was there to mobilize the resources of the northeast frontier and especially the Rio Brioso settlement to resist the forthcoming American invasion. Further, he was there to check up on the loyalty of one Don Quintin Kershaw.

"Calhoun and his dragoons might be here in a few days," Luke reminded Quint. "Nice reception."

"Ye'd best back-trail then, Luke. Make them stay out of sight until the Mexicans are gone, or at least until Calhoun is strongly reinforced. I don't want any fighting at Rio Brioso if I can prevent it. Not yet, in any case."

Luke nodded. "Have yuh made up yore mind about whose side yuh plan to fight on?"

"Why?"

★ 178 ★

"If de las Casas finds out yuh sent me back to warn Calhoun, that's something like treason against Mexico, ain't it, Big Red?"

"Well, Wandering Wolf, it still hinges on the important fact as to whether or not the western boundary of Texas is the Nueces or the Rio Grande."

"So?"

Quint looked sideways at Luke. "That's a good question. I'm glad ye asked me. Now, get the hell out of here!"

Luke turned his mustang on the forehand, kicked him hard with his heels, and seemed to shoot off down the long length of the caravan, hoofs drumming and thin dust rising.

The trumpet blew. The column and skirmishers halted. An officer riding a splendid black stallion single-footed forward, followed by a trumpeter and the guidon bearer. The sun glinted from his silver-mounted saddle and sword hilt.

Captain de las Casas was resplendent in sky-blue cape flung back over his shoulders, sky-blue coat with scarlet cuffs, turnbacks, and epaulets. His trousers were dark blue with double dark red stripes down the seams, and foxed with antelope skin on the seat and inside of the thighs. He wore the scarlet silk sash of a staff officer, aide to Governor Armijo. His long, elaborately brass-hilted, straight-bladed sword with its red sword knot hung at the left side of the saddle. A pair of pistols hung in pommel holsters.

Diego casually raised his right hand to touch the stiff brim of his shiny black leather shako, with its brass shield stamped with the national arms of Mexico above which was a tricolor cockade in the national colors of red, green, and white topped by a crimson pompom.

Quint raised his right hand in salute. "A pleasant surprise, Diego de las Casas," he greeted.

Diego was arrogantly handsome, noble-nosed, dark of eye, with a thin line of mouth, and dark skin lightly pitted with the scars of smallpox.

Diego looked toward the thin skein of dust rising behind Luke's galloping horse. "Greetings, Quintin Kershaw," he responded. "Who was that horseman?"

There was no use in lying. "Luke Connors, Diego," Quint replied.

Diego looked quickly at Quint. "The *Montero Americano?* The one with the look of a hungry wolf about him?" He smiled, but only with a mechanical movement of the facial muscles and not the eyes.

"He left something at last night's camp," Quint explained. "He went back to get it."

"At the Carrizo?"

"We couldn't have gotten this far from there since dawn."

The dark eyes studied Quint. How much did Diego really know? Diego looked at the caravan. "The hunting was good?" he asked.

"You can see for yourself."

"Any trouble with the Comanches?"

Quint almost walked into that one. "A little," he admitted. "They were too busy hunting to bother us."

"So? Is that not unusual?"

Quint shrugged. "Who knows? Our medicine was good, Diego. Here we are home again, safe and sound."

"You know of the war?"

"Yes."

"Who told you?" Diego shot out.

"Some Comancheros on their way to Bent's Fort. Is the war the reason for the pleasure of your company out here, cousin?" Quint replied easily.

Diego studied Quint. The scarred face seemed guileless enough. Yet, one could never understand these damned *gringos;* these abominable *Montero Americanos.* They could lie straight-faced and have one believe they were telling the truth. No matter, later he'd have the Mora *ciboleros* questioned surreptitiously. It was useless to interrogate the Rio Brioso *ciboleros,* and, for that matter, any of the people at the settlement. Their loyalty to their *patron* was unquestionable.

Diego smiled thinly. "I have been at the Rio Brioso under the express orders of His Excellency Governor Armijo to mobilize the resources of the Rio Brioso and the Mora to resist an anticipated invasion of New Mexico by forces of the United States, the so-called Army of the West."

Quint nodded. "It was to be expected."

"I have also brought an order signed by the governor promoting you, Don Quintin Kershaw, temporary captain in the Active Rural Mounted Militia of the Province of New Mexico. You are also to be charged with the duty of swearing in a company of mounted rifles of the rural militia from the able-bodied men of Rio Brioso and Mora for the defense of the northeast frontier of the province."

"How soon am I expected to do this, Diego?"

"Immediately."

"But, I've been gone hunting over two months. I must see to the division of the hides and meat between Rio Brioso and Mora. I must see to the grant. It's been in good hands, but one knows that unless the *patron* himself is here things sometimes go unattended and the people become a little slack. . . ."

Diego stopped Quint's objections with a cut of his right hand. "Those matters can be attended to whether or not you accept your promotion and the mobilization of the militia company. In addition, I have the authority of the governor to requisition horses, mules, oxen, certain foodstuffs, forage, and any surplus firearms you may have."

Now Quint suddenly realized why Diego had come out from Rio Brioso to meet the caravan. His command outnumbered the *ciboleros,* making it easier to force his demands on Quint than if Quint was at Rio Brioso, surrounded by his own stoutly loyal people. The governor had probably warned Diego of that fact. Manuel Armijo was partner in the Rio Brioso, and a friend to Quint, but he was not naive enough to believe that in time of war that partnership and friendship would be sufficient to insure Quint's loyalty to the governor and to Mexico.

Quint played for time. "I'll look over your requisitions when I get home, Diego," he promised warmly. "The horses, mules, and oxen are no problem, as are the foodstuffs and forage. The firearms are another matter."

"So? It is well known that the people of Rio Brioso are the best armed in the province. In fact, they are better armed than the soldiery of New Mexico." He smiled thinly. "As a matter of fact, I have already requisitioned sufficient of your stock of firearms, caps, powder, and ball to equip my company."

"I hope you left enough for me to equip mine," Quint said coolly.

Diego was not to be outsmarted. He waved a hand toward the caravan. "Your *ciboleros* will probably compose the bulk of your company, will they not? In that case, they are already well armed. In addition, I exchanged my issue arms for your requisitioned firearms."

"You have an order to do that?" Quint queried.

The Mexican's face tightened. "Damn it! No! It is not necessary!"

Quint shook his head. "I am afraid I'll have to disagree with you, Diego. Until you have such a requisition, signed by the governor, I request that you return my firearms. We'll be most happy to return your issue weapons." He almost said "junk weapons."

Diego looked back over his shoulder at his now well-armed troopers. "Would you like to try and take those weapons back by force, cousin?" he asked quietly. He turned and looked directly at Quint. "For, I assure you, before God, that is exactly what you will have to do."

It was quiet except for the murmuring of the wind, the stamping of a horse, and the occasional chinking of a bit.

Quint touched his horse with his heels and kneed him away from Diego. He turned and looked along the long line of the caravan and waiting men. This was not the time and place to start a private war with Diego de las Casas. Quint had been thoroughly outmaneuvered by him. There might be other Mexican troops at Rio Brioso, many of them. This was not the time to make a hostile move.

"Well, cousin?" Diego asked dryly. There was a slightly triumphant note in his tone.

Quint raised his right arm and pumped it up and down and forward. "*Adelante! Adelante!*" he shouted.

The caravan began to move slowly forward down the long slope. Quint did not look at Diego as he rode to the head of the caravan. He was afraid of what he might say or do.

Diego smiled. He turned to his trumpeter. "Blow Assembly, Perez," he ordered.

The trumpet rang out. The company rode up the slope past the caravan, assembling behind their officer. Once the caravan had ground across the dry streambed and the dust had blown away, the company followed it toward the Rio Brioso.

"How did Don Grande Rubio take his orders, captain?" Lieutenant Hernan Calvillo asked. "Not well, I trust?"

Diego nodded. "I was almost hoping he'd resist," he said grimly.

"Would you have used force?"

"If I had to."

"He's a dangerous man, this *Montero Americano*."

"He can be handled."

"Not without cost."

"For that we are soldiers, Hernan."

"Which way do you think the *gringo* cat will jump once the American soldiers reach here?"

"Who knows? I am just going to make sure some of his teeth are drawn. If he resists, he can be killed like any other *gringo*."

As the caravan approached the settlement, two small figures raced their diminutive burros down the gentle slope. Quint smiled. Rafaela was holding a slight lead over Francisco. Francisco was always the more dashing and reckless rider, while Rafaela was more cool and calculating, and the better rider of the two.

A horsewoman riding sidesaddle on a beautiful black mare had appeared around the corner of the sprawling *hacienda*. She rode with leisurely dignity down the slope behind the twins. There was no mistaking her. Quint's heart seemed to leap a little and he drew in a short breath. *Lupita!* She had returned from Santa Fe to welcome him home.

Francisco reached Quint first and slid out of his saddle before his burro came to a halt. He sprinted to Quint, pulling and clawing his way up Quint's left leg. He wrapped his strong little arms about Quint's neck and pressed his downy cheek close to Quint's lean, scarred cheek. Rafaela drew rein close beside Quint's horse. He reached down with his right hand and drew her up close to him.

The caravan passed by on their way to the settlement,

the horsemen and drivers grinning at the sight of their tough, hard-pratted *patron* and his two beautiful children.

"Father, you smell like an old he-goat in the rain!" Rafaela shrieked, pinching her pert little nose between her thumb and forefinger.

"It smells good, like a *man* should!" Francisco shouted.

"Where is David?" Quint asked.

Francisco drew back a little. He lowered his eyebrows and thrust out his lower lip slightly. He shot a lowering glance toward the *hacienda*, then looked quickly away.

"There," Rafaela said, pointing to a small lone figure sitting a piebald pony about a hundred yards away. "David is shy, father. He likes to greet you when only the two of you are together."

Quint looked down at her. "Did he tell you that?"

She shook her head. "I just *know*," she said mysteriously.

Diego had ridden up beside Quint. "It's likely his Indian blood," he said carelessly. He did not look at Quint.

David had turned his pony, passing Guadalupe, and was now riding past the *hacienda* toward the low rolling hills to the south.

Guadalupe drew rein beside Quint, querying him with immense dark eyes. He leaned toward her to meet her kiss. Before God, she was beautiful! Her eyes were slightly shadowed underneath, faint smudging against the flower petal pink and white of her flawless skin. As their mouths met, she thrust the tip of her pink tongue between his dry, cracked lips as quick as a gecko lizard darting out its long, sticky tongue to snap up a fly. Infinitesimal as the action was, there was still a wealth of promise in it.

Guadalupe drew back, still holding Quint with her eyes. "Welcome home, my husband," she murmured.

He reached out his hard, calloused palm and touched her soft cheek. At that moment there was nothing he could say, so intense were his feelings toward her.

They rode together to the house. Diego's orderly came to take his horse. Diego removed his white gauntlets and used them to flick the dust from his beautiful uniform.

"I have offered Cousin Diego the hospitality of our

house while he is here on duty, my husband," Guadalupe said as Diego gave her a hand to dismount.

Quint nodded. He lowered the reluctant twins to the ground and then dismounted, taking each of them by the hand. "That is to be expected, my wife," he said. He looked at Diego. "My house is yours, cousin."

Guadalupe smiled. Perhaps after all Quint had forgotten his animosity toward Diego, or at least he had put it aside for the time being. "I'll see that your bath is prepared and there is fresh linen and clothing for you, husband."

Quint watched her as she walked, graceful as a fawn, toward the house. Before God, how many months had it been since they had made passionate love together?

Diego looked about at the magnificent panorama. "You've done wonders here, cousin. However, I can see Guadalupe's point of view."

Quint narrowed his eyes. "Meaning?"

Diego smiled, a smile only of the facial muscles, not of the eyes and certainly not of the soul. He was literally incapable of a true warm smile. "One must admit that Rio Brioso is not El Cerrillo."

Quint studied Diego. "And El Cerrillo is not Rio Brioso. I prefer it here, Diego."

Diego laughed. "The comparison can be quite dreadful, at least to a de Vasquez, one must admit. My sainted mother adored El Cerrillo. Ah, El Cerrillo de Vasquez! A gem of New Mexican *haciendas!* When I was a child oftentimes we stayed there many months at a time. I wonder why you do not prefer it over this frontier semi-fortress."

Guadalupe had been talking again. Always, one way or another, by devious means she worked to get Quint to return to El Cerrillo. "If it wasn't for Rio Brioso there might not be an El Cerrillo, at least in the hands of a de Vasquez and their multitude of relations," Quint reminded Diego.

Diego's face tightened. "Does that include the family of de las Casas?" he asked quickly.

Quint shrugged. He took his sheathed Hawken from the saddle and unstrapped his cantle roll. "I've seen quite a few of them there over the years, cousin. They seemed to think El Cerrillo was their right and privilege. I had something to do with them changing their minds."

Diego slapped his guantlets steadily into the palm of his other hand. "I do not care for your tone, sir. After all, *you* are *not* a de Vasquez. I am quite sure it was not the wish of my dear cousin Guadalupe that my family, at least, should be barred from El Cerrillo."

Quint looked over his shoulder. "Why don't you ask her?" he suggested.

"Your tone is insulting!"

Quint turned slowly. "Cousin, your tone has been insulting ever since we met today."

Diego was no coward. "I've thought more than once over the past few years I'd have to ask you for satisfaction one day. Were it not for this accursed war your *gringo* friends have brought upon this land, and my present official position and duties, I'd ask you out at once."

Quint smiled rather thinly. "Among us *gringos*, sir, we don't let a little thing like a war get in the way of settling personal difference. We have a custom of which you are probably unaware. If someone such as yourself has a difference with someone such as myself, they simply agree to meet beyond the corral and the difference is settled then and there."

Diego's eyes widened at the affront. "Why, damn you! You are armed! My weapons are on my horse!"

Quint shrugged. "Go get them, cousin. However, when I suggested meeting behind the corral I did not mean fighting with weapons. Bare hands, Diego, bare hands alone, unless you prefer to use teeth and boots as well."

"Only *gringos* fight in such a barbaric manner," Diego sneered.

"Do you prefer knives as being more cultured?" Quint asked dryly.

Diego knew much of this man. He fought only when goaded to the extreme, and when he fought, he always fought to kill.

"*Cobarde!* Coward!" Diego spat out in his cold fury.

A big, freckled hand shot out and gripped Diego by gathering together his uniform collar and the frilled cambric shirt collar beneath it. Quint twisted his hand hard to one side, tightening the material about Diego's throat so that he had difficulty breathing. Quint jerked him closer and thrust his face close to Diego's contorted visage. "You greaser sonofabitch," he grated. "I've had plenty of you for years, and enough of you right now! Now get on that fancy horse of yours and get to hell out of here and take those toy soldiers of yours along with you!" Diego stared back into those cold, gray eyes tinted like glacier ice, and a cold feeling crept through his whole being. For one agonizing moment he thought he was going to wet himself, both legs, and disgrace himself forever in front of this *gringo*.

Quint shoved Diego back, releasing his grip. "Now," he said in a low hard voice, "Go get your weapons if you like. I'll wait here for you. If you don't get back here within ten minutes, primed and ready for war, I'm going to come looking for *you*, and you'd better, by God, be ready for *me*."

Diego was badly shaken. He adjusted his collar. He walked away a few steps, out of reach of Quint, then turned. "I'll remember this," he warned. "You have attacked an officer of the Republic of Mexico on official duty. I'll report this to His Excellency."

Quint shrugged. "Be sure you tell him you goaded his good friend, and the man who once saved his life when my brother-in-law, your cousin and great friend, Bartolome de Vasquez tried to kill him. Who do you think he'll believe? He's never really trusted you, de las Casas."

Diego's face worked. He was speechless.

"By the way," Quint added, "I've heard rumors you still keep in touch with dear cousin Bartolome. Where is he now, cousin? Still plotting revenge on the governor, while hiding out in Chihuahua, or is it Texas?"

Diego turned on a heel and stalked off, the very picture of complete outraged dignity.

Quint could not help but grin as he stepped up on the verandah of the *hacienda*. He stopped short. Guadalupe stood just within the open door, staring at him wide-eyed, hand at her throat. "Mother of God! What have you done?" she cried.

"Did you hear what he called me?" Quint demanded.

She turned, slamming the door shut behind her.

"You did well, father," the brave little voice said from behind Quint.

Quint turned and looked down at his older son.

"I don't like that greaser sonofabitch either," David said.

"Why?"

"He always calls me the half-breed when you're not around. Is it bad to be a half-breed, father?"

Quint studied the serious little face, with its high cheekbones and dark skin, clear gray eyes and reddish hair. "Not to *me* it isn't, Davie lad. Why didn't ye come to meet me?"

"The others were there."

"Does that matter?"

David shrugged. "Not Rafaela."

"Is it still Francisco?"

David nodded.

"I saw you avoiding your mother. Why?"

"She's not my mother."

"But, she's my wife, Davie, and the mother of the twins. Hasn't she always treated ye well?"

David looked directly into his father's eyes, so exactly like his own. "She used to. But not after Francisco began to grow up, and I had that fight with him when he wanted to scar my face to look like yours."

"You're not jealous of him, are ye?"

David shook his head. Suddenly he pressed hard against Quint. "The next time you go buffalo hunting, take me along. I don't like this place."

"It's our home."

"Not with those others here. Except for Rafaela. She can go with us. Can't we go into the mountains and trap beaver like you and Luke done?" There was a catch in his voice.

"Did," Quint corrected automatically. He tilted David's head back and looked into the sober young face. He had thought the boy was crying, but it wasn't so. In fact, he could not remember the last time David had cried. "This is our home, lad. It's a good place, this Rio Brioso. There is everything ye want, or will need here. I've planned it that way for you and the others. Can't ye see that? Come now, let's go into the house, and while I bathe I'll tell ye about the buffalo hunt and how Moccasin prayed for rain and buffalo when there was none to be had."

"Then what happened?" David asked eagerly.

"There was a cloudburst, one of the most violent we'd ever seen. The next dawn thousands of buffalo came from the south. We had to make a stand in the timber, shooting them down as fast as they came to keep them from running right over us."

David's eyes widened. "God damn! I wish I'd been there with my Hawken!"

Quint grinned. "Well, it wasn't exactly a picnic. It was a damned close call. Too close for comfort." He turned and opened the door.

"Father," David said.

Quint looked at the boy. "Yes?"

"You said this was our home. That it's a good place. That we can have everything we could want or need here."

"So?"

"What will happen when the American soldiers get here?"

"Who said they were coming?"

The boy shrugged. "It's war isn't it? Don't the Americans want New Mexico? Cousin Diego talked a lot about the war before you came home. He said we New Mexicans could whip any *gringo* soldiers who had the guts to come here. Is that true?"

"We'll have to wait and see, eh?"

David hesitated before he spoke, "Will you fight in the war?"

"Yes, if there is to be fighting."

"On which side, father?"

Quint looked over the boy's head toward the plains, hazy in the late afternoon sunlight. Beyond sight, a score and a half of dragoons waited to advance to the Rio Brioso, while behind them somewhere along the Santa Fe Trail were another two thousand United States soldiers—the Army of the West.

"Father?" David queried.

"I can't answer that right now."

"Yes you can," the boy insisted boldly.

Quint smiled a little. "Supposing ye tell me, if ye know so much."

"It won't be on the side of the God-damned Mexicans."

The cavalry trumpet sounded as Diego de las Casas prepared to leave Rio Brioso. He was sure to return, this time with many more soldiers. The Rio Brioso was a key point in the defenses of northeastern New Mexico. If the Americans took it, there was little that could stop them short of Glorieta Pass, the gateway to Santa Fe.

Quint stepped into the doorway. "Are ye coming, lad?" he asked.

"I've got to corral my pony, father. You still didn't answer my question."

For a moment Quint studied David. "I don't have to, Davie. I think ye know the answer already." He closed the door behind himself.

The *hacienda* was much the same. Guadalupe had brought a few rugs, some bric-a-brac, and several pieces of furniture from Santa Fe. Tom Byrne had sent several boxes of books to Quint. There was, however, one major difference. Cristina was no longer there. Guadalupe did not mention why she was gone nor did the twins offer any help. It was David who told Quint that Guadalupe had ordered Cristina to return to El Cerrillo shortly after Guadalupe had returned from Santa Fe. Other than Guadalupe no one at the *hacienda* knew why. One day Cristina was there, happy at seeing the twins and Guadalupe again; the next day she was gone. The night before she left she had been closeted with Guadalupe for a long time. When she parted from Guadalupe, she did not tuck the children in bed as she usually did.

For a few days after his return Quint missed the smiling Cristina, but in time her memory faded somewhat with the pleasure of the warm and sensuous welcome home he received from Guadalupe. Even so, at times when he was making love with Guadalupe, thoughts of Cristina would fill his mind until he forced them out.

★ EIGHTEEN ★

Repeated blows thudded against the carriage gate, echoing dully through the house. A man's voice was shouting, but his words were indistinguishable through the gate and thick adobe walls. Quint threw back the quilt and rolled sideways and up from the bed onto his feet while reaching instinctively for one of the Colts on a bedside table. He thumb-snapped a lucifer and looked at his hunting-cased watch lying open on the table. It was just after ten o'clock. He lighted a candle and stalked naked to the door leading out to the patio.

"For the love of God, what is it, beloved?" Lupita cried from the bed.

Quint unbarred the door. The hammering on the carriage gate was louder. He opened the door. The voice was clearer now. "It's Luke Connors," he said over his shoulder. "Back from Bent's Fort." Luke had been nowhere near Bent's Fort, but Quint had previously told her that's where he had gone instead of returning to Rio Brioso from the buffalo hunt. The way she was feeling about United States troops on Mexican soil, he could hardly tell her Luke had gone to Carrizo Creek to warn the dragoons there about the presence of Mexican troops at Rio Brioso.

Quint stepped out into the dark patio. A cold night wind was sweeping down from the mountains. He shivered. "Tomas, you lazy sonofabitch!" he bellowed. "Where the hell are you!"

"Here, *patron!*" the night watchman cried as he ran toward the gate.

"Gawddammit!" Luke roared hoarsely. "Yuh want me to kick down this Gawddamned gate, Tomas?"

Quint grinned. He let down the hammer of the pistol to half cock.

"Your trousers, husband," Lupita reminded him.

Quint turned back into the room. He yanked on his drawers and trousers.

"Could he not have waited until daylight at least?" Lupita asked querulously.

"It might be important, *querida*."

"He has no manners, but that is to be expected from him. Pounding on his *patron's* door at this hour, with you asleep in bed with your wife. What are things coming to?"

Quint buttoned his shirt. "I've told you many times—I'm not his *patron*," he reminded her. "He's my friend and partner, Lupita."

She sat up as though impelled by springs. "He's a *servant*! No more! Further, he owns none of *our* grant! How can *he* be a partner? Another thing—why does he have to live in *our* house? I would not have him in the house at El Cerrillo! He'd have to come to the servants' entrance there with his hat in hand if he wanted to see you!"

Quint looked up as he pulled on the second of his boots. "Not as long as *I* am *patron*," he said firmly.

"We'll see about that, husband!"

He studied her for a moment, with her thick, lustrous blue-black hair tumbled about her smooth white shoulders. She looked like a luscious pearl on the half shell of the big bed. He was about to mention her shiftless or penniless cousins and other relatives who had often made a home for themselves at El Cerrillo, but thought better of it. Despite the physical warmth of her welcome upon his return from the buffalo hunt the past week, there was still a mental coolness he had not been able to warm at the fire of his sexual attention to her. He felt that there was more to her coolness than the resentment he had caused by his disagreement with Diego.

"Haven't you got the courage to tell him he's not wanted here?" she demanded hotly.

When he was dressed, he walked around the foot of the bed to her side and drew her close. She turned her face away from him. She was an alluring bundle of warm, soft fragrance. He cupped her chin in his hand and turned her face toward him, pressing his lips softly against hers. She resisted, but not too long, then responded as she always did, no matter how coolly she felt toward him. He lowered her, resting her shoulders against the big pillow. She drew him down to her, seeking his mouth with hers and arching her body up to meet his. She sought his mouth again and again, then slowly passed a hand down to his privates.

Quint disengaged himself from her. "Not now, Lupita," he said quietly.

"*Querido*," she pleaded. "*Mi vida. Mi corazón. Alma de mi alma.*" She writhed a little, almost as though she was in a pain that only he could alleviate with his body against hers.

Was it because she really wanted his lovemaking, or because she wanted to keep him with her and away from Luke? They had consummated their love for each other just the evening before, fully, as much as each of them could expect or hope for from each other. To him, at least, the act had been outstanding. But, still there was that mental reserve of hers.

Quint blew out the candle. "Sleep," he suggested. "There's no need for you to get up now." She did not speak. He closed the door softly behind himself.

Luke waited in the patio. "Didn't mean to bust up yore rest, Big Red, but it's important."

Quint nodded. "Figures. What is it?"

Luke pointed toward the gate. "Visitors, Quint."

"How does it go, Big Red?" boomed one of the four men standing just inside the gate.

Quint grinned. "*Hola*, Santiago! Jim Magoffin! Last time I saw ye, ye left here two years ago to farm at Independence, Missouri!"

The big Kentuckian's wind-narrowed eyes crinkled as he and Quint embraced each other in the customary *abrazo,* pounding each other on the back. James "Santiago" Wiley Magoffin had been a prominent Santa Fe and Chihuahua trader and United States Consul in Chihuahua. He had married Mary Gertrude Valdez, related by marriage to Governor Manuel Armijo, He had left New Mexico two years past to educate his six children in the United States. His wife had died of fever there.

"Meet Jose Gonzales, a trader of Chihuahua, Quint," Santiago said. "You already know Captain Shelby Calhoun. This other officer is Captain Philip St. George Cooke, First United States Dragoons. Captain Cooke, this is the famous, or notorious, as the case may be, Don Quintin Kershaw, otherwise known as Big Red to the rest of us *gringos.*"

Quint nodded to Shelby. He extended his hand to Captain Cooke. "I recall ye, sir, from Bent's Fort in '43. I was passing through on my way back here from Saint Louis. You and your command were on caravan escort duty at that time. Ye may not remember me from that time." Quint knew of him as a first-class soldier, a disciplinarian with a reputation as a martinet.

The officer nodded. "I recall you now, sir. I've heard a lot about you since then, certainly more than you've heard of me."

Quint gripped Shelby's hand. "We meet again. Have ye brought the Army of the West with ye, Shell?"

Shelby shook his head. "Just twelve of my dragoons as escort to Captain Cooke and Mister Magoffin. They are on their way to Santa Fe on official business."

Quint narrowed his eyes. "With twelve dragoons?"

"We're traveling under a flag of truce," Cooke explained. "I bear a letter from Colonel Kearny which declares that the United States government is seeking union and amelioration of the condition of the inhabitants of New Mexico."

"In short, sir, a warning of imminent invasion, conquest, and occupation," Quint said quietly.

"Are you in opposition to that, sir?" Cooke asked a little stiffly.

Quint smiled faintly. "I am not in opposition to you and your companions, Captain Cooke. In the matter of your mission, I find myself at present in the unfortunate position of a neutral."

Shelby shook his head. "Impossible. You are either with us, or loyal to Mexico. There can't possibly be any other recourse for you, Quint."

Quint studied him for a moment. "Perhaps not, but the decision is mine, isn't it? Meanwhile, you've had a long cold ride through the night. Ye must be tired and hungry. My house is your house, as we New Mexicans say. I offer ye my hospitality." He turned. "Tomas, awaken Josefina and have a meal prepared for these gentlemen. I want it served in the library. There will be twelve other guests, soldiers who will be served in the kitchen. See that our guest's horses are corralled and taken care of."

"My men will see to their own mounts," Shell put in

quickly. "Half of them will stay on guard with the horses while the other half are messing."

Captain Cooke slapped the dust from his clothing with his gauntlets. "It seems to me, Quint, by offering us your hospitality, officers and enlisted men of a nation at war with Mexico, you could be accused of offering aid and comfort to the enemy. In that case, I suggest that this means you are favoring the cause of the United States."

Quint opened the door of the library, while speaking over his shoulder. "Inasmuch as ye officers of a nation at war with Mexico are traveling under a flag of truce, I'm sure my act of hospitality cannot be considered as treason, and, I assure ye, knowing my good friend Governor Manuel Armijo as I do, he will offer ye the same aid and comfort when and if ye reach Santa Fe."

"Madre de Dios!" Santiago Magoffin cried in awe. "A guardhouse lawyer!"

Quint lighted the massive candles held in tall candelabra of wrought iron in diagonally opposite corners of the large room. Beehive fireplaces occupied the other two corners. The growing light seemed to touch the gold lettering on the spines of the many leather-bound volumes lining the bookshelves occupying the end wall. Other shelves held Pueblo pottery and various artifacts. A splendid Comanche lance and buffalo hide war shield hung over one of the fireplaces. A built-in adobe bench was covered with fine Navajo blankets. The furniture was heavy and solid, of polished dark wood. The table held a wrought iron candelabra and a small church bell green with the aging of many years.

Shelby Calhoun unclasped the throat catch of his long military cape and threw it on a chest. He studied the lean, scarred face of Quint in the growing candlelight. For some years he had known Quint was the true father of his son Alexander, now eight. The resemblance had grown more obvious the older the boy became and the more his features developed. Alexander had his mother's blond hair and fine skin, but his eyes were a clear gray. Both Jean's and Shelby's eyes were blue, while his hair was a dark brown. Jean had been honest enough to admit Quint's siring of her son.

Quint knelt before one of the fireplaces, struck flint and steel, and lighted the fire. The fat pine kindling caught fire readily. In the flare-up of bright flame Quint's strong features stood out plainly. Age Alexander, dye his hair a deep auburn, scar his left cheek, and he'd be a carbon copy of Quint Kershaw.

Quint looked up at Shelby. "The nights get cold here, even in the summer," he said. He smiled.

By God! The smile was the clincher.

"Make yourselves comfortable, gentlemen," Quint invited. "Luke, *compañero,* ye know where the liquor is."

Luke had been watching Shelby. He nodded. "Naturally, Big Red."

Shelby looked along the line of books. Milton, Chaucer, Shakespeare, many others, Burns of course, among the classics. There was a section of military works—Clausewitz, Jomini, and Napoleon, among others of less renown. Texts on tactics, gunnery, equestrianism, artillery, infantry, cavalry, and engineers. The library included books on astronomy, geology, zoology, and others of the sciences. History, philosophy, literature, and religion were represented.

Jim Magoffin spoke over Shelby's shoulder. "It's the best library in the province, after that of Tom Byrne and Padre Martinez, although neither of them have much on military works, particularly Martinez."

"It's quite impressive for a man with little or no formal education," Shelby admitted.

Luke handed them their drinks. "His father was a teacher in Scotland and Canada," he explained. "A domino, or somethin' like that."

"Dominie," Quint corrected. He smiled. "A learned man, who could not cope with the Canadian frontier. The love of books and learning was one of his legacies to me, gentlemen. Perhaps, if I had listened to him, I might have stayed in the Red River country of Canada and followed in his footsteps."

"And what prevented you from so doing, Quint?" Cooke asked.

Quint shrugged. "I was torn between a love of books and that of the wilderness. My mother and sister died young. My father did not last long. When he died I left Canada forever."

"At what age?"

"Sixteen, captain."

"And you never went back?"

Quint shook his head. "There were too many unhappy memories for me. I had no family left. There was always another pass to cross, another stream to trap, and a horizon that constantly intrigued me."

Quint turned to the second fireplace and prepared to light the fire. He did not realize the eyes of the two officers were still on him.

Guadalupe dressed hurriedly but carefully. When she was done, she studied herself in the mirror. There was little she could do to erase the fine stress lines on her forehead, at the side of her nose and the corners of her mouth. Cosmetics, no matter how heavily and skillfully applied, could not conceal those lines, or the faint dark circles beneath her eyes. Still, she was aging well. She was still quite beautiful.

The night was cool. She decided to wear a shawl. She opened the wardrobe and felt about for it. One of Quint's heavy wool shirts was in the way. She pulled it to the side and as she did so felt some small hard object in one of the breast pockets. Guadalupe, curious, unbuttoned the pocket and found a small, plush velvet case with a tiny gold clasp. She opened it. It was a daguerreotype of a woman, a young girl, and a small boy. She narrowed her eyes. The light was too dim to clearly discern their features. She took it to the nearest candle and held it close. The woman was more handsome than truly beautiful. Her light-colored hair seemed soft and lustrous. Her features were oval, clear complexioned, with a slightly bold nose and a wide, soft-looking mouth. *Madre de Dios*, Guadalupe thought, it's Jean Allan, she whom Quint had saved from the Pawnees at McNee's Creek eight years ago. There had resulted a strong attraction between the two of them, but Jean had left Santa Fe and New Mexico as the wife of Lieutenant Shelby Calhoun. Guadalupe had learned later from Doctor Byrne that she had given birth to a son. She held the daguerreotype close to the light and studied the boy. He was a handsome lad, perhaps seven years old, with fine light hair like that of his mother, and a strong nose and firm chin. It was the eyes that drew her close attention, them and something about the boy's features, something elusive she could not quite

★ 197 ★

place. Then slowly, ever so slowly, it came to her. "Mother of God," she said aloud. The eyes seemed almost identical to those of David, and perhaps, in a lesser sense, to those of Rafaela, but in combination with the features of the boy, it was clear the eyes were those of Quintin.

Guadalupe blew out the candle and placed the closed case within the bosom of her gown. For a little while she stood there, clutching the edge of the table, with her eyes closed, feeling a great fear and weakness working coldly through her system.

Josefina opened the library door for Guadalupe. Guadalupe paused in the doorway, seemingly for dramatic effect. She wore a black silk gown with a lacy shawl over her shoulders. Her attire seemed rather formal for such an informal occasion, but somehow, on her it didn't seem out of place.

"Don Quintin," she said, "please leave fire-making for the servants." She smiled and swished forward, extending her right hand, beautifully shaped, with tapered fingers to Jim Magoffin and Jose Gonzales. "Welcome to our home, gentlemen," she murmured. She glanced at the two officers. "Who are these gentlemen?"

Quint stood up. *Por Dios,* she was beautiful!

Shelby Calhoun bowed slightly from the waist. "Do you not recall me, Doña Guadalupe?" he asked in flawless Military Academy classroom Spanish. "May I refresh your memory? We first met on the Cimarron Cut-Off in 1838, and knew each other slightly in Santa Fe that same year."

Guadalupe stared at Shelby. She paled a trifle. "Yes, it was so. I recall my husband rescuing you and a lady from the Pawnees. I cannot recall her name at the moment," she lied.

"Jean Allan," Shelby said. "She is now my wife. You might not remember we were married in Santa Fe in 1838, just before we returned to the United States."

Guadalupe remembered quite well. She had never forgotten Jean Allan. She looked expectantly at Philip Cooke.

"Captain Philip St. George Cooke, at your service, madame," Cooke said. He had once heard vague gossip about something between Jean Allan and Quint Kershaw. The story was that they had a strong attraction for each other. Some said the attraction had been stronger on Jean's part. Cooke had wondered what damned fool would turn down Jean Allan. Now, face to face with Guadalupe de Vasquez, he could understand Quint's decision.

Guadalupe was the perfect hostess, a product of her breeding among the *gente fina*. There would be no business discussed during the late meal, despite the hour and the obvious urgency of Captain Cooke's mission. When the coffee, brandy, and cigars were brought to the table, Quint expected her to leave the room and the discussion of business to the men, as was customary, but Guadalupe was perfectly at home, charming the officers, Senor Gonzales and Jim while utterly ignoring Luke.

Philip Cooke looked at Quint as though to ask, "Is it correct to discuss business with the lady present?"

Quint nodded as he lighted his cigar. "How can I help you gentlemen?" he asked.

Guadalupe bent her dark head a trifle, as though to hide the slight look of triumph on her face. These officers had come to the Rio Brioso for more than just a stop on the way to Santa Fe. Whatever the reason, she intended fully to hear it for she was positive that the outcome would greatly affect her family.

"The government of the United States greatly appreciates the service rendered by you and your associates to Captain Calhoun and his command in the vicinity of Carrizo Creek, Quint," Cooke began, "and later the advice brought to him by Luke Connors about the presence of Mexican troops here at the Rio Brioso. There might have been some misunderstanding and a conflict between the two forces. I . . ." His voice died away as he saw the hard look Guadalupe shot at her husband. "Did I say something wrong?" he added.

Quint shook his head. "Go on," he urged, ignoring Guadalupe's intent stare.

Cooke could sense the sudden coolness between Guadalupe and Quint, but he had no choice. "I bear a letter from Colonel Kearny to Governor Armijo. I was on my way to Santa Fe when we arrived at Carrizo Creek. I had not expected to find Calhoun still there, on your advice to remain there instead of proceeding on the reconnaissance mission he had been ordered to perform by Colonel Kearny. In any case, his original orders had been to return along the Santa Fe Trail and meet us, to provide an escort for our mission to Santa Fe. I thereupon ordered Captain Calhoun, with twelve of his dragoons, to proceed with me to this point. Mister Magoffin had been highly recommended to Colonel Kearny in a letter from Secretary of War Marcy, at the request of President Polk. His experience while engaged in trade in New Mexico, Chihuahua, and other departments of Mexico, and his thorough acquaintance with the people and the country can be of eminent service to the United States in our military expedition against Chihuahua. In addition, he can be of great service in the matter of obtaining necessary supplies and livestock for the Army of the West upon its arrival in New Mexico. Mister Magoffin, in turn, recommended you highly, Quint, to accompany us to Santa Fe, due to your knowledge of the country, and the people, and your friendship with Governor Armijo."

"For what purpose?" Guadalupe asked quietly.

The two officers looked at Guadalupe in surprise. They had the impression that women of New Mexico did not interfere in the business of their men, at least openly.

"Captain Cooke?" Guadalupe queried again.

Cooke looked at Quint. Quint shrugged almost imperceptibly.

Guadalupe leaned forward. "My husband is a naturalized citizen of Mexico, a man of property, and a business associate and close friend of Governor Armijo and Doctor Tomas Byrne of Santa Fe."

Cooke smiled a little. "Of course we know that, madame. Please enlighten me as to your point of view."

"What you are requesting is that my husband take sides in a war that is not the choice of Mexico. If he goes with you to Santa Fe to help you in your mission, that will indicate that he has aligned himself with the United States, and would therefore be a traitor to his adopted country Mexico."

Cooke became uncomfortable. He had not expected this. He looked at Quint, seeking a way out of the dilemma.

"May I see the letter to Governor Armijo?" Quint requested. He did not look at Guadalupe.

The officer took the letter from his dispatch case and passed it across the table to Quint. "Read it aloud," he suggested, with a slight sideways glance at Guadalupe.

Quint moved a candle closer and began to read:

*"Headquarters of the Army of the West,
In Camp Upon the Arkansas, at Fort Bent, August 1, 1846.*

*To His Excellency, Governor and Commanding General,
Don Manuel Armijo, Santa Fe.*

Sir: By the annexation of Texas to the United States, the Rio Grande from its delta to the source forms now the boundary line between them (the United States and Mexico), and I am coming by order of my government to take possession of the country over a part of which you are presiding as governor. I come as a friend and with the disposition and intention to consider all the Mexicans and other inhabitants as friends if they should remain quietly and peaceably in their homes attending to their own affairs. All such persons shall not be molested by any of those who are coming under my orders in their person nor in their property nor in their religion. I pledge myself to the fulfillment of these promises.

I come to this part of the United States with a strong military force, and a still stronger one is following us as a reenforcement. I have more troops than I need to overcome any opposition which you may be able to make against us, and for that reason and for the sake of humanity I advise you to submit to fate, and to consider me with the same sentiments of peace and friendship which I have and protest for you and those under your government. Should your Excellency do this it should be eminently favorable to your interest and that of all your countrymen, and you will receive their blessings and prayers. If, on the contrary, you should

★ 201 ★

*decide otherwise, if you should make up your mind
to make resistance and oppose us, with such troops
as you may be able to raise against us, in that event,
I notify you that the blood which may be shed, the
sufferings and miseries that may follow, shall fall
upon your head, and, instead of the blessings of
your countrymen, you will receive their curses, as
I shall consider all of those your Excellency may
present against us armed, as enemies, and they
shall be treated accordingly.*

*I am sending you this communication with Captain Cooke of my regiment, and I recommend him
as well as the small party of twelve dragoons, to
your kindness and attention.*

> *With much respect I am
> Your Obedient Servant,
> S.W. Kearny, Colonel
> First Dragoons."*

Quint looked up. "To the point exactly," he agreed
quietly.

"Will you accompany us?" Cooke asked.

"These men have not come as visitors or envoys, husband," Guadalupe snapped angrily. "They are the
forerunners of a conquesting horde of *gringos!*"

Quint held up a restraining hand, although he knew
the gesture would further infuriate Guadalupe. "I apologize for my wife's outburst, Captain Cooke," he said.
"She is distraught. As ye undoubtedly know, she is a
direct descendant of the de Vasquez family, who have
lived in New Mexico for generations, settling here before
the Pilgrims first saw Plymouth Rock. Naturally, she
feels deeply about this proposed occupation of New Mexico. Her loyalty to Mexico is unquestionable."

"Would that yours were the same, husband!" Guadalupe spat out.

"No apology is necessary, Quint," Cooke said. He
looked at Guadalupe. "I also apologize for any misunderstanding I might have caused you, Doña Guadalupe."

Guadalupe did not respond. Her face had whitened
with tautness. Tiny lines etched themselves at the corners of her mouth and on her forehead. Her fists were

clenched under her breasts. In the quietness that followed Cooke's apology, a faggot snapped in one of the fireplaces, and the sound of one of Guadalupe's feet tapping the floor sounded exactly like the scrabbling of a mouse in one of the corn bins of the *dispensa*.

A mind voice seemed to speak within Quint. *"Manifest Destiny, Quintin Ker-Shaw. You are a part of that destiny now. Use it to your advantage. Do not let the opportunity presented you be lost forever. The time is now."* Those had been the prophetic words of William Bent to Quint in 1838. There had been another such prophesy in 1838, that of Jean Allan. *"The future for you is here in New Mexico, Quintin Ker-Shaw."*

Philip Cooke was a determined man, who, when he set his mind on some purpose, pursued it to the end despite whatever might stand in the way. "Will you accompany us, Quint?" he repeated.

Quint looked up. "In what capacity, captain?"

Cooke was slightly surprised. "Why, I hadn't considered that, Quint."

"*I* have," Quint said dryly. "If, by any chance, your invasion is resisted and your army defeated I'd be in one helluva fix. I'd have my property confiscated and might even be shot for treason."

Cooke studied Quint. "Is there any doubt in your mind that the United States will not be victorious?"

"Truthfully, very little, but there is always the possibility of defeat."

Luke downed his brandy. He wiped his mouth on the greasy cuff of his sleeve, ignoring Guadalupe's look of disgust. He grinned. "Reminds me of the time seven of us, Quint, me, three Delawares, a *cibolero,* and even the lady present here, held off over two hunnert Comanches from behind a fort of dead mules."

Shell smiled faintly. "You're not going to compare that legendary feat with the position of the New Mexicans against the force of the Army of the West, are you, Luke?"

Luke shrugged as he refilled his glass. "Just remindin' yuh such things are possible, providin' your medicine is good, and you're all center shots, and your hearts are big."

"Do you think the Mexicans can defeat us, Luke?" Cooke asked.

It was too much for Luke. He guffawed. "Them greasers with their playactin' uniforms and rusty, smoothbore *escopetas? Hawww!*"

Quint couldn't help it, despite Guadalupe's presence, but it was the good brandy working within him that brought it out. "They might do better with their buffalo hunting lances and bows and arrows," he said dryly.

Shell spoke quickly to prevent any more unpleasantness. "Quint, you must make a stand. We know you as a man of decision. If you turn down this offer to take a leading part in the annexation of New Mexico by the United States, you might regret it later. I assure you, nothing in heaven or hell can prevent us from doing just that."

Luke hiccuped. "He's right, Big Red. Come to think of it, Ol' Shell is *always* right."

Shell ignored Luke's jibe. At that, perhaps the uncouth mountain man was right. "If you are concerned about your position," he continued, "I have those two official papers entrusted to me by Colonel Kearny. A detailed requisition for supplies and draft animals from the Rio Brioso for the official use of the United States forces, and a temporary commission for a lieutenancy of volunteer mounted rifles in the Army of the United States. I have the authority to fill in your name on that commission and swear you into the service of the United States."

There was actually no question in Quint's mind but that the United States could take and hold New Mexico. His Rio Brioso would still be safe in his hands. He had not questioned that fact. He looked across the table at Guadalupe. It was she upon whom the matter hinged.

"Do you expect *me* to make your decision, husband?" Guadalupe asked icily.

"Don't try me before these guests, Guadalupe," Quint quietly warned.

Guadalupe looked at Shell. "Captain Calhoun, may I ask who instigated that commission for my husband?"

Shell was surprised. "Why, the secretary of war."

Guadalupe was not to be deterred. "And who, may I ask further, recommended my husband to the secretary of war?"

Shell could not reveal Doctor Tomas Byrne's clandestine role as an undercover agent of the United States for at least ten years.

"Well, captain?" Guadalupe asked impatiently.

"Senator Alexander Allan, chairman of the Military Committee to the president's cabinet."

Guadalupe arched her eyebrows. "So? I was not aware my husband knew, or had ever met the senator."

The usually cool Shelby was slightly nonplussed. "Well, actually," he said quickly, to cover his temporary confusion, "the senator is my father-in-law, and heard much about your husband from me."

Guadalupe sensed victory. A poor victory but it was hers. "You, captain? Or, perhaps it was your wife, the former Jean Allan?" she asked with mingled acid and sweetness in her tone.

Quint stared at her. *Damn her!* She had never forgotten! Not once in the seven years of their marriage had she ever mentioned her jealousy of Jean, but somehow Quint had always sensed that the acid of his former relationship with Jean was still eating away in her system. She still felt she had been second choice after Jean Allan, although Quint had never felt that way about the situation.

Quint drained his glass and refilled it with brandy. "I'll accompany ye to Santa Fe, Captain Cooke. I can initially supply your advance troops with about two hundred bushels of corn and oats. There is ample hay, as well. I can supply ye immediately with twenty draft horses, the same number of cavalry mounts, and about thirty good California pack mules. I have five double teams of oxen if ye have need of them for your artillery." He stood up. "Ye can swear me in now, Captain Calhoun."

Guadalupe rose to her feet. There was no expression on her face. She was sorely tempted to throw the daguerreotype on the table before Shelby and tell him where she had found it. She had no idea how Quint happened to have it, but that didn't matter. The fact was that he *did* have it. Still, she couldn't bring herself to do it.

The officers, Jim Magoffin, and Luke rose to their feet. She turned on a heel and left the library, slamming the door behind her. Quint had never seen her so deadly furious. At that moment he felt a vague and deep sense of loss; a part of his life that could never be the same again.

"Raise your right hand and repeat after me, Quintin Kershaw," Shell said.

Quint raised his right hand. *There could be no going back now*. The thought was in Quint's mind as he mechanically repeated the oath binding him at one and the same time into the citizenship and the military service of the United States.

The brandy was working well within Quint as he crossed the patio after seeing that the dragoons were quartered in the village, and escorting his houseguests to their rooms. A faint line of light showed under the door of his bedroom. He opened the door. Guadalupe sat up in bed, wearing her long-sleeved ruffled nightgown with lace at neck and wrists. She looked as prim as a nun, except for her set expression.

Quint kicked the door shut behind himself and dropped the bar in place. "It's cold as a tomb in here," he said conversationally. When Guadalupe did not reply he thought, Begod, it's as *quiet* as a tomb in here, too.

He walked to his side of the bed and was halfway through the process of taking off his jacket when he saw the opened velvet daguerreotype case on the table. *Madre de Dios!* He had forgotten all about it.

"Recognize her?" Guadalupe said sweetly.

He looked at her. "Of course."

"How long have you kept that in secret?" she asked.

He walked to the liquor cabinet and opened it.

"Haven't you had enough?" she asked.

He shook his head as he poured a stiff drink.

"You didn't answer my question, husband."

He looked at her. He knew her mood. No matter what he said, she'd not believe him, for in the perverse way of some women, she had already made up her mind to believe only that which she wanted to believe.

Quint dropped into a chair. "I doubt if you'd believe how it came about that I have that."

She smiled mechanically. "Try me."

He tried. She didn't believe him.

"It's the truth," he insisted.

She arched her eyebrows. "Did I say it wasn't?"

"You don't have to, Lupita."

She studied him. "You were sworn in?"

"I was."

"Was that what you really wanted, or was it the brandy speaking?"

He shook his head. "You know me far better than that."

"So, now you're a lieutenant in the Army of the United States, you've agreed to supply the enemy with our food, forage, and animals, and also to accompany them to Santa Fe."

Quint nodded.

"Without considering my wishes and the future of your family?"

"I am the head of this house," he said gravely. "As to your wishes, I had to make that decision on my own. The annexation of New Mexico is a foregone conclusion. Better that the children have a father who served and fought for the United States than one who served a defeated Mexico and perhaps lost everything, including his life."

She smiled fixedly. "Traitor," she said.

He downed the brandy, then studied her. "Is that what you really think?"

"It is."

He stood up. "We'll be leaving in the morning, Lupita. I'm not sure when I'll be back, perhaps ten days to two weeks, more or less."

"If you are not caught and executed as a traitor."

Quint shook his head. "We travel under a flag of truce."

"The officers and Santiago do. They are citizens of the United States. *You,* are *not*. Never mind Texas' claim that their western boundary is not the Nueces, but rather the Rio Grande, which automatically makes you a citizen of the United States."

"As it does you," he said dryly.

She shook her head. "Never."

"You've a year to make that decision."

"No!" she shouted.

Quint put on his jacket. He took his pair of Colts and

Hawken. He walked to the door and turned. "I'll be back, as I said, in about ten days to two weeks."

"What makes you think I'll still be here?" she demanded.

He studied her. "You had better be," he warned. "I'll not tell you again."

She lunged across the bed, grabbed the daguerreotype and hurled it at him. "Here! Take this with you!" she cried. The corner of the case struck the left side of his mouth and drew blood. The case fell to the floor with a tinkling of broken glass. For a fraction of a moment he looked at her, his face set and grim, a tiny worm of blood trickling down into his short beard. Then he wiped away the blood, picked up the case, and put it in his jacket pocket, turned on a heel, flipped the bar crashing to the floor, and left the room, closing the door solidly behind him.

For a moment or two she sat there aghast, then she burst into hot tears. *"Maria Santissima,"* she murmured. "What have I done? *What have I done?*"

★ NINETEEN ★

As the cavalcade of Captain Cooke, James Magoffin, Senor Gonzales, Luke, Quint, and twelve dragoons including a trumpeter reached the rise, they saw in the distance the Royal City of the Holy Faith of St. Francis—Santa Fe, seven thousand feet altitude below the massive backdrop of the Sangre de Cristo Mountains. Santa Fe was the capital of the immense Province of New Mexico. It was the administrative center of many smaller settlements from El Vado de San Miguel near Las Vegas to Jemez. It was like Rome of the ancient world: all roads led to it, the Hub of Trails. The Chihuahua Trail extended from Vera Cruz on the Gulf of Mexico two thousand miles to Santa Fe. The Spanish Trail reached from Santa Fe to Los Angeles on the Pacific Coast nine hundred miles west. The Santa Fe

Trail ran fifteen hundred miles from Missouri to Santa Fe.

The city from a distance looked like a sprawling conglomeration of brick kilns. The box-shaped adobe houses of brown, gold, and white, flat-roofed one-story structures, sat on the rim of a vast plateau sweeping to the west, toward the Valley of the Rio Grande del Norte. West of the river were the blue-hazed Jemez and Sandia Mountains. The plateau was spiked with pointed hills and dotted with green herbage. A peculiar quality of light in the atmosphere gave the impression of looking along the bottom of an immense sea, an unreal and mysterious sensation to the eyes of newcomers.

The morning wind brought the faint, dull sound of ringing bells. A bugle sounded. The road ahead was filled with people hurrying toward the plaza in the center of town.

Santa Fe despite its imposing name and importance in the province was merely a small town huddled haphazardly about a bare sunbaked plaza. The streets were winding, narrow, unpaved, and dirty. Travelers worked their way through a haze of dust, scattering half-naked children, squalling chickens, and countless lean, wolflike dogs barking and baring their fangs. Cats, dogs, pigs, chickens, and burros wandered at large, rooting through piles of garbage in varying stages of decomposition. The pure, clear cold mountain water brought down to the *acequias* or irrigation ditches was fouled with garbage and manure.

The nearer the small band of Americans got to the plaza, the more crowded the narrow streets became with people on foot or riding horses, mules, and burros, all headed in the same direction as the Americans. Their looks were not too friendly, yet at the same time, there were many who smiled or showed no emotion at all.

The *plaza publica,* or public square, La Plaza de la Constitucion—so named in 1821 when the flag of the new Republic of Mexico was raised over the Palace of the Governors—was treeless and shadeless, a huge expanse of sunbaked adobe in dry weather, and in wet a morass of mud thickly mixed with manure. The Palacio, the Governor's Palace, dominated the square along the north side of it. It was about four hundred feet long, forming the southern side of a ten-acre compound surrounded by a high, crumbling wall extending eight hundred feet north. Within the compound, sometimes forming part of the walls, were the palace, quarters for the military garrison, and the fearsome *calabozo*, or prison. There were corrals, a small *campo santo*, or cemetery, a drill ground, or *plaza de armas*, and a military chapel. Other important buildings about the plaza were the Casa Consitorial of the Alcaldes, or mayors, the Castrense, the Capilla de los Soldados, or Chapel of the Soldiers, an *oratorio*, or small chapel, the customhouse, and the Parroquia, or parish church. Houses of affluent citizens and some shops stood wall to wall around the plaza filling in the spaces between the public buildings. They were sheltered by wooden *portales* or *corredores* which provided shelter from sun and rain for the citizenry. The open-air market, the *mercado*, was situated along the outer side of the western wall of the palace extending the full length of the compound to the open fields where horse traders dickered, traded, bought, and sold.

The plaza was thronged almost shoulder to shoulder with soldiers and countrymen obviously called out for the defense of the province. It was almost impossible for the American party to force its way through the masses of people in order to reach the palace, but there seemed to be little outspoken comment against them, and no effort was made to impede them.

"Maybe they ain't sure why we're here," Luke grunted as he kneed his horse to push a way through the crowd.

Quint grinned a little. "For or against?" He looked at Captain Cooke. "Maybe we should give them an idea of the importance of our mission, sir."

Cooke nodded. He tied his white handkerchief to the point of his saber and held it aloft. The people gradually parted to let the Americans pass to the Governor's Palace.

"*Hola*, Don Quintin! Are you a *gringo* soldier too now?" a man called out. It was Jose, Tom Byrne's half-breed Comanche stableman.

Quint smiled. "Tell Doctor Byrne I'm here, eh, Jose? I want to see him after our business here is completed."

Captain Cooke reined in his bay. "Trumpeter," he said over his shoulder. "Sound the Parley."

Trumpeter O'Hearne flourished his brightly polished C trumpet and lipped into the call. The brazen notes echoed between the buildings lining the plaza. The incessant hum of conversation stopped as though everyone had been suddenly struck mute.

Minutes ticked past. No one in an official capacity appeared. Then an officer walked slowly along under the long *portale* and paused beside one of the huge uprights supporting it.

"Are you representing His Excellency Governor Armijo, sir?" Captain Cooke asked Diego in formal Military Academy Spanish.

Captain Diego de las Casas shook his head in response, never taking his eyes from Quint, and jerked a thumb back over his shoulder. "Capitan Ortiz, Mayor de Plaza, is coming," he replied curtly.

"Better not turn your back on that cold-eyed sonofabitch, Big Red," Luke murmured out of the side of his mouth.

Quint nodded. "Aye."

Jim Magoffin grinned. "Anyway, Quint, it's always nice to have your wife's relatives meet you with such warmth and affection."

Captain Ortiz, a large florid man, appeared at last. "Your servant, captain," he said formally. "What may I do for you?"

"I am Captain Philip St. George Cooke, United States Dragoons. I have a message for your governor from Colonel Stephen Watts Kearny, United States Army, commanding officer of the Army of the West, at present in the vicinity of Las Vegas on its way to this city, sir," Captain Cooke replied.

Captain Ortiz bowed. "Have you or your commanding officer, this Colonel Kearny, requested permission to tread the sacred soil of Mexico armed to the teeth?"

Captain Cooke bowed in return. "As you can see, sir, my people and I are under a flag of truce."

Diego de las Casas snorted in disdain. "A rag on a saber tip. Let *me* give them a proper reception, Captain Ortiz."

The *mayor de plaza* shook his head. "We must observe the amenities, captain. We are not barbarians here." He turned on a heel and walked back into the palace.

Quint looked sideways at Cooke. "If I know Armijo he already knows we're here and why we're here."

"And exactly how many soldiers and guns Colonel Kearny has," Jim added.

"Traitor," Diego said clearly, still looking directly at Quint.

Quint looked casually about, at the many soldiers and masses of civilians crowding the plaza, then back at Diego. "Would you like to say that to my face behind the corral, cousin? Or do you feel safer out here in public with the backing of your people and a fast, open line of retreat back into the palace?"

Diego's eyes widened. He flushed. He placed his right hand on the hilt of his sword.

"For God's sake, Kershaw," Cooke hissed out of the side of his mouth. "Can't you settle that damned feud of yours some other time? If he draws that sword there might be hell to pay and no pitch hot."

"Might be interestin'," Luke suggested dryly.

"Thank God," Jim said. "Here comes Ortiz."

Ortiz escorted Captain Cooke, Senor Gonzales, Jim Magoffin, and Quint into the palace. Luke vanished into the crowd on his way to Tom Byrne's *casa*. The dragoon escort waited outside under the hot sun.

Governor Manuel Armijo was seated at a table in a large lofty hall whose earthen floor was carpeted. Eight military and civil officials stood about behind the governor. Manuel Armijo was a large, fine-looking man in his early fifties. His somewhat florid face was dark complexioned. He wore a blue frock coat of fine material with rolling collar and general's shoulder straps. His blue trousers were striped with gold lace. His rather large belly was bound with a red silk sash. He rose to his feet when Captain Cooke was presented to him by Captain Ortiz. He already knew the other three men from long acquaintance. He smiled quickly at Quint. They had been friends since Quint had saved his life during Bartolome de Vasquez's assassination attempt in 1838. Quint still bore the knife scar just below the left of his rib cage when Bartolome had stabbed him. It had come close to killing him. Armijo was also a quarter partner in the Rio Brioso grant, to his great satisfaction, particularly in the way Quint had managed it so profitably. More than governor or soldier, Manuel Armijo was essentially a shrewd trader.

After Captain Cooke had presented the letter entrusted to him for delivery to the governor by Colonel Kearny, Armijo rose to his feet again. "This affair will take some necessary deliberation between myself and my military and civil officials, gentlemen. There are quarters in the palace available to you, Captain Cooke, as well as quarters for your escort. My soldiers will take charge of your mounts and graze them near the city, as there is little corn available at this time. I hope you gentlemen will remain here as long as you are pleased to do so. You will be notified when I come to a decision on this matter."

Later, as Quint worked his way across the still teeming plaza to Tom Byrne's fine, big *casa*, he met Luke just emerging from a *cantina*. "Did yuh see him?" he called out.

"Who?" Quint asked. "The governor? Yes."

Luke shook his head. He looked from one side to the other and spoke in lowered tones, "Your dear brother-in-law, that sonofabitch Bartolome de Vasquez."

"Where did ye see him?"

"Just as I crossed the plaza. He saw me lookin' toward him and faded into the crowd."

"You're sure it was him?"

"Positive, and he wasn't alone."

"What do ye mean?"

"Kiowa was with him."

Quint turned quickly and looked about.

Luke shook his head. "Yuh won't find 'em now. I think they must've seen us enter town with Cooke. Couldn't hardly miss us. I followed them a ways, then lost 'em. Later I *think* I saw Bartolome talkin' to your dear cousin Diego de las Casas, but when I worked my way closer to where they were talkin' both of 'em were gone."

Quint nodded. "You're right. We won't find them now. Take a look-see about town and see what ye can learn. I'd do it myself, but they'd spot me right away. I doubt if Bartolome would try anything against me here in Santa Fe for fear of exposing himself, but as for Kiowa, I think he'd risk anything to get at me, as I would him. Beats me though why Bartolome risks coming back to northern New Mexico. If I know him and his cousin Diego, those two are involved in some kind of plotting to take advantage of this new situation. It might be their chance. With their faults, I'll have to admit both of them are patriots. In that, they're not alone in their family."

"Lupita?"

"Aye, and maybe the most loyal of them at that."

"What about Kiowa?" Luke asked dryly.

Quint looked directly at him. "That is a personal matter between him and me. The man is a murderous pariah who'd side Satan himself if there were profit and women involved."

Tom Byrne greeted Quint at his door with the *abrazo*, gripping him about the shoulders in his strong arms and pounding his back. "Before God, Quintin!" he cried. "Ye get bigger and uglier every time I see ye!"

Quint bent his head modestly. "It's easy, Tom, once ye get the hang of it. At that, ye don't do too badly yourself."

Luz Garcia, Tom's Genizara woman, came to them, holding out her slim lovely hands to grasp Quint's big ones. Whenever she did so, Quint thought of his hands as huge, calloused paws enveloping hers. She had been but fifteen years of age when he had first seen her back in '38, a child-woman of startling and somber beauty with almost a Madonna-like quality about her. Luz Garcia was not her real name. Her mother had been New Mexican from Abiquiu, northwest of Santa Fe on the Chama. She had been captured by Kotsoteka Comanches and taken as wife by one of them, dying in childbirth in their village. New Mexicans had attacked the village and defeated the Kotsotekas, slaying the father of Luz. They had brought the infant female back to Abiquiu with them. Tom had bought her when she was fourteen, naming her Luz, or Light, for she had indeed brought light into his empty, lonely life. They had not married. Tom was said to have left a wife in Ireland years past, but he never spoke of her. He and Luz were devoted to each other despite the great disparity in their ages.

Tom and Quint retired to the library study with brandy and Havana cigars. It contained the best private library north of Chihuahua, if not Mexico City itself, and west of Saint Louis. It had been through Tom that

Quint had grounded himself thoroughly in the history, both secular and sacred, of the Province of New Mexico. It had been partly through Tom's influence that Quint had easily gained Mexican citizenship shortly after his arrival in New Mexico, with the powerful sponsorship of Manuel Armijo, thus avoiding the legal two years' residence required of all applicants. Once Tom had gotten partial possession of the vast de Vasquez grant in the Rio Brioso area, with Armijo and La Tules as his partners, it had been at his instigation that Quint had been offered a quarter interest in exchange for superintending future colonization there, with a long term option to buy half of the El Cerrillo estate on which Tom held the mortgage. Quint disliked intensely being in anyone's debt, even for the smallest amount, but if there was anyone to whom he owed his phenomenal rise to success in New Mexico, it was Tom Byrne.

"Ye took the commission then, eh, Quint?" Tom asked.

Quint nodded. "After some thought," he admitted.

"Why? It's a foregone conclusion New Mexico is now part of the United States. Why did ye have to think about it?"

Quint sipped at the powerful brandy. He looked up at Tom. "Lupita," he said simply.

"She's still adamant about New Mexico remaining Mexican, I know. I'm somewhat surprised. She's an intelligent woman. Further, she's still deeply in love with ye, Quint, although it has often puzzled me. She had everything to gain and nothing to lose by accepting the United States annexation of Mexico. The Rio Grande boundary is an established fact."

"Rather shadowy, is it not?"

Tom relighted his cigar and spoke between puffs. "We'll not go into that now. Kearny is on his way here with the Army of the West. He'll stay here long enough to secure New Mexico, then send Colonel Doniphan and his First Regiment of Missouri Mounted Volunteers south to Chihuahua to meet United States troops marching through northern Mexico from the east. Kearny will then leave a garrison force here in New Mexico and march himself west to secure California for the United States."

"There's still one factor that might change Kearny's plans, at least for a time. Suppose Armijo resists invasion?" Quint asked.

Tom shrugged. "He can very easily do so. He claims to have five or six thousand available troops and seven pieces of artillery, mostly bronze 4-pounders. With such a force he could certainly hold back Kearny, if he selects the right place to do it."

"Apache Canyon. One hundred and fifty well-armed and determined men backed by a few cannon could easily hold back the Army of the West."

Tom nodded. "Leonidas at Thermopylae holding back the Persians."

Quint smiled. "Armijo and his men aren't exactly Spartan-like. Do ye think he'll resist?"

"I think not. He might make a showing, or even a token resistance, but I doubt he'll fight to a finish."

"Ye sound sure of yourself, Tom."

"Haven't ye suspected why Santiago Magoffin came with Captain Cooke?"

"Somewhat. He's well known to Armijo. Perhaps he can talk the governor into accepting the fact that New Mexico is already lost to the United States. Santiago can charm the scales from a snake if he has a mind to."

"Armijo has almost certainly accepted the loss of New Mexico. I happen to know he's been liquidating his holdings in northern New Mexico. Why not? There would be nothing for him here if New Mexico becomes part of the United States. His governorship, general's commission, graft and corruption will no longer serve to fill his money chests."

"What about his quarter share of Rio Brioso?"

"He's already sold it, to La Tules—as well as his partnership in her monte *sala*."

Quint whistled softly. "He *must* be ready to pull foot."

"Santiago evidently has kept his mission secret from everyone. He was approached months ago by Senators Thomas Hart Benton of Missouri and Alexander Jamieson Allan, and through them met President Polk and Secretary of War Marcy. Polk was anxious to secure the northern provinces of Mexico without bloodshed. Santiago seemed to promise the most effectual help in such a situation. What better man could have been found for the job? They supplied him with certain letters for Armijo, hoping to induce, persuade and/or bribe Armijo and his officers to submit peaceably. Perhaps he might accomplish his mission with Armijo, but Colonel Diego Archuleta, Armijo's second-in-command, might be a problem."

"If I know him, he'd rather fight than peaceably surrender the province."

"Perhaps. However, I suggest that Santiago might be able to make a deal with him separate from that which he'll offer Armijo."

"Such as?"

Tom smiled. "Tell Archuleta he can take over control of New Mexico *west* of the Rio Grande."

Quint studied Tom. "But that means . . ." His voice trailed off for a moment. "My God. . . ."

Tom nodded. "Exactly. Once the deal is made and the United States has control of New Mexico to the Rio Grande, Kearny will cross the Rio Grande on his way to conquer California, which, of course, will include all land west of the Rio Grande to the Pacific."

Quint shook his head. "I'd hate to play poker with Polk, Allan, Benton, Marcy, Magoffin, and, I suspect, *you.*"

"Ye'd sure as hell lose your shirt, Big Red," Tom agreed complacently.

"Then it seems as though the occupation might be a foregone conclusion, that is, if Armijo accepts the deal."

"He will. Personally I think he'll be glad to get out of here. The people will be more than glad to see him go. Ye know the New Mexican saying."

Quint nodded. *"Dios en el cielo y Armijo en la tierra."*

"God rules the heavens and Armijo rules the earth."

They raised their glasses to that.

"So, now we are partners in the Rio Brioso with La Tules alone," Quint mused. "She's half owner now. I've always understood she doesn't put faith in anything except gold and silver. I wonder how much she offered Armijo for his share."

"A great deal less than what it is worth. But, gold speaks with a powerful voice, especially if it is offered instead of promises. Armijo had little choice, or he might lose all. She's a shrewd, tough business woman."

Quint eyed Tom closely. "And doesn't think much of land as an investment, particularly during these trying times. Which means she might very well listen to any reasonable offer to dump her share of the Rio Brioso. True, Tom?"

Tom looked up from his glass. "It's possible," he admitted.

"Have you two talked about it?"

Tom nodded.

"And the conclusion?"

"She'll sell her half to me."

"Which means you'll own three-quarters of Rio Brioso." Quint paused for a moment, then leaned forward. "You've no interest in the land, Tom. You're no frontiersman. I project three courses ye might follow concerning the Rio Brioso."

"Go on," Tom urged.

"I can go on managing the grant, with an option to buy ye out when and if I get enough money together. Ye can buy me out and keep the grant for yourself, possibly retaining me as manager with a salary and share of the profits. Or ye can buy me out, then sell the entire grant to an interested party. On that last, I think I know who that party might be."

Tom leaned back in his chair and studied Quint. "You're not a bad businessman for one who's spent a large part of his life trapping beaver in the mountains and running an *estancia* on the frontier."

Quint nodded. "And I'm a man who but for you might not have gotten a chance to gain a quarter share of the Rio Brioso."

Tom waved a hand. "The Rio Brioso would still be a howling wilderness haunted by Comanches if we hadn't picked you for *hacendado*, Quint."

"Then we are even on that score at least."

Tom nodded. "It was a good deal, for all concerned."

"So, which is it to be?"

"I doubt if you'll ever get enough cash money together to buy me out, even with a long-term option. I've no interest in buying ye out and keeping the grant for myself. Yes, I'd be willing to buy ye out and eventually sell the entire grant. However, on that last, it could be arranged so that the new owners would keep ye as manager until they decide the future of the grant. Thus, your third course is the most practical and probable."

"Supposing I refuse to sell my quarter share to ye?"

Tom studied his brandy, swirling it around in the glass. He looked up slowly. "I think ye know as well as I do myself the money with which I originally bought my share of the grant and managed your share as well, and the funds I advanced the de Vasquez family against El Cerrillo, were far more than I could have accumulated alone. Further, whatever assets I had at the time and even at present are frozen in my trading interests."

Quint nodded. "Then it is actually Senator Allan who now owns three-quarters of the Rio Brioso."

"Aye, but it is not for himself. He eventually plans to sell the larger part of it to the United States government for use as a military reservation, retaining some part of it for himself."

"From what I've heard of the senator he has more money and assets than he could ever possibly use. Also, I doubt sincerely he'd ever be interested in ranching on the Rio Brioso, or any other part of New Mexico."

Tom nodded. "Perhaps I might convince him it would be to the great advantage of the Rio Brioso for ye to stay on as manager."

Quint lit another cigar. "The senator has amazing foresight. He can sell a large part of the grant to the government, retaining much of the choice areas to raise cattle, horses, mules, forage, and crops to supply future military establishments, a mighty lucrative business from what I've heard.

"And isn't it a strong possibility that much of his wealth was gained from contracts he established with the government while he was colonel of the First Dragoons and later senator from Kentucky?"

"I hope you're not suggesting chicanery, Quint. The senator is an honest man."

Quint waved a hand. "No question about that, Tom. However, I doubt if I'd care to horse trade with the senator from Kentucky."

Tom smiled. "Nor I."

"Following my line of thought further, if Senator Allan takes full possession of the Rio Brioso, sells part of it to the government for a military establishment, and re-tains part of that property to use in supplying needs for that proposed military establishment, without himself being interested in such an endeavor, nor living in New Mexico, is it possible that he plans the future of the Rio Brioso as an investment for the future of his daughter and son-in-law when Shelby Calhoun retires from the army and establishes himself in this new possession of the United States?"

Tom grinned. "That might be construed as a compound, complex question, Quint."

"Answer it," Quint said dryly.

"We'll need a drink on that," Tom said. He poured, then quickly drained his glass. "In answer to your question: Yes. Ye outlined it precisely."

"And you've got the infernal Irish guts to suggest I remain as manager of the Rio Brioso for Jean and Shelby Calhoun?" Quint shook his head. "Never."

"I didn't think ye would agree to that."

"Which leaves two possible alternatives. I can refuse to part with my share of the grant and fight the senator for it, or let him buy me out and establish myself elsewhere."

"Ye can't win the first. I've already suggested ye sell out to me, for it is his money I'm offering ye. Quint, sell out to me. Use the money to develop El Cerrillo. That's your best bet."

"As a last resort only."

"You're a stubborn mule."

"I may be, but I am also my own man. I don't consider El Cerrillo as being truly mine."

"To the detriment of everything practical and reasonable."

Quint waved a hand. "Be that as it may."

Tom lit a cigar. "There is another alternative. One to which I have given considerable thought. Frankly I only suggest ye stay on as manager of the grant, because in a sense, I feel responsible for ye being there in the first place. However, if ye may have to reestablish yourself, and El Cerrillo is not your choice, I may have something for ye which will more than repay ye for your share of the Rio Brioso and afford a challenge to ye, perhaps as much, or more, than the Rio Brioso. That is, unless I've badly misjudged ye." Tom slanted his keen blue eyes at Quint.

"Tell me about this challenge."

Tom unlocked a desk drawer and withdrew a map from it. He spread it out on the desk top. "See here, Quint. A map of New Mexico."

Quint looked at the map. He whistled softly. "A work of art. This wasn't made by any Mexican."

Tom shook his head. "It was prepared in Washington from data and information supplied by me and Shelby Calhoun after his visit here in '38."

"For the invasion?"

"Aye, and for the establishment of future military posts. See here? Stars show the site of planned posts. Question marks indicate possible sites."

A star had been neatly penciled in overlaying the Rio Brioso and Quint's fortress home. Another was depicted on a low hill overlooking Santa Fe. There were others at strategic points. A question mark stood out plainly at a point west of Socorro, which was about 75 miles south of Albuquerque and 185 miles north of El Paso del Norte. The question mark was about 40 miles west of Socorro at the northerly end of the Plains of San Augustine which extended about 50 miles southwest to northeast from the Tularosa Mountains to the Gallinas and Datil Mountains, and averaged about 15 to 20 miles wide.

Tom placed a finger on the question mark. "In order for our government to control that area there will eventually have to be a military post somewhere within this locale. At one time the Mexican government realized the importance of such a site and attempted to establish a *colonia* there. It failed."

Quint looked sideways at Tom. "It's Mimbreno Apache country, isn't it?"

"Aye, with the Mescaleros to the east and Navajos to the north. Excellent cattle- and horse-raising country. Limitless timber. Plenty of water. Good prospects for minerals of various kinds."

"So?"

"Some years ago Manuel Armijo owed me a considerable sum of money. He didn't know, of course, I was an agent of the U.S. He had the rights to a large grant of land on the San Augustine Plains. The Mexican government, as I said, wanted to establish a *colonia* there. Armijo could not find anyone who was willing to try, not after what happened to the first attempt. It was too remote. Too dangerous. Anyone with half an eye on the future could see the strategic value of having a fortified settlement in that area. The Spanish government had been interested, and later the Mexican, and it's a certainty the United States will also be interested. That is the reason I made a deal with Armijo—undercover of course, as the rights to that grant had come his way in rather a shady manner. Now that Armijo is on his way out and the United States is coming in, the value of that grant has risen immeasurably. I had it in mind to eventually sell it to the United States at a fine profit, for the same reason Senator Allan will sell the major portion of the Rio Brioso. Now, instead of paying ye in cash for your quarter share of the Rio Brioso I offer ye instead the San Augustine grant, free and clear. What say ye?"

Quint drained his glass. "One question—Do Senator Allan and his son-in-law have any part in this deal?"

"Absolutely not! Ye have my word on that," Tom insisted. "Ye'll think about it then?"

Quint nodded.

"Your hand on it?"

They gripped hands. "I'll be getting back to the palace now," Quint said. "As an officer in the Army of the United States I have to become accustomed to taking orders."

"Aye. But ye'll do well. I might warn ye, lieutenant, once the province is occupied I have a feeling the army will see that your work is cut out for ye."

Quint walked to the door.

"Quint!" Tom called out.

Quint turned.

"If there hadn't been the possibility of Shell and Jean Calhoun eventually owning that part of the Rio Brioso not sold to the government, would ye have accepted the proposition of managing it?"

"I'm not sure. I doubt it."

"But certainly not if they gain ownership?"

Quint nodded.

"Because of Jean and Shell together, or separately?"

"I respect Calhoun as a soldier and gentleman. I can't say I particularly like him, or consider him a friend."

"And, bonny Jean?"

Quint studied him for a moment. "Sometimes I think ye know too much, Tom. I'll let ye figure it out." He closed the door behind himself.

Shortly before sunrise August 13 the deafening din of blaring trumpets and beating drums sounding the call to arms resounded throughout Santa Fe, echoing from the nearby hills and awakening the Americans sleeping in the palace.

Quint and Luke made their way across the plaza from Tom's house to the palace. Armed soldiers were forming to the sound of the trumpets and drums.

"Yuh figger we'll get out of here alive, Big Red?" Luke asked.

Quint shrugged. "From the conference last night I got the impression Armijo planned to march to Apache Canyon with six thousand men to hold it against the Americans."

"Yuh think he'll fight?"

"Who knows? I doubt it. I think Santiago Magoffin made some kind of deal with him last night. He's sending a Doctor Henry Connolly back with us to Kearny as his 'commissioner.' Connolly is a Virginian, but raised in your home state Kentucky. He's been a trader in Chihuahua for about twenty years. One of the first persons to make the trip from Chihuahua over the Staked Plains to New Orleans. I have a strong feeling the whole issue is cut and dried, Luke. Within a week the Stars and Stripes might be flying over Santa Fe."

Governor Armijo had his guests served incomparable hot chocolate beaten to a froth, sponge cake and white bread such as only Mexicans can make, all on heavy, solid silver salvers. The room in which breakfast was served had doors covered with buffalo hide painted to look like wood. The walls were covered with many mirrors with festoons of dried Apache ears hung between them, trophies from slain raiders.

Governor Armijo bowed his guests out with a suspiciously good-humored smile, watching them as they rode in a compact group across the crowded plaza.

"Will he fight, Captain Cooke?" Quint asked.

"Hard to say, Lieutenant Kershaw," the officer replied. "He's just been commissioned as general. He's damned uncertain and irresolute, wavering between loyalty to his commission and a desire to escape the dangers of war. He has little or no military experience. An ignorant, avaricious man. I think he's stalling, but why, I can't imagine."

Henry Connolly smiled. "Is there not a large caravan following your army? I suspect he's torn between wanting to flee and being greedy to collect customs on the caravan. I understand that three-fourths of the goods in the caravan are destined for Chihuahua and even beyond. He'd make quite a haul on those taxes, gentlemen."

"Or get a bullet in his fat ass," Luke suggested.

They were still chuckling when they passed beyond the town onto the road for Apache Canyon and the on-coming Army of the West.

★ TWENTY ★

The road to Santa Fe led into Apache Canyon five miles from Pecos. The hills on either side of the canyon were one thousand to two thousand feet above the road. The intermittent daylong rain still slanted down shrouding a clear view of the pass and the heights on either side of it. There was no sign of life in the pass nor on the heights.

Lieutenant Quintin Kershaw, Volunteer Mounted Rifles, dismounted below the pass crest. He turned to Lieutenant Hammond, who led the advance of the Army of the West with a score of dragoons. "Better dismount here, lieutenant," he suggested as he withdrew his Hawken from its saddle sheath. "We're about fifteen miles from Santa Fe. If Armijo plans to resist our advance, this is the last possible place he can do so. The canyon is the gateway to Santa Fe and the northern Rio Grande Valley. If he puts up a stout defense, we'll have one helluva time getting through the pass."

Hammond looked up the rain-shrouded pass. "What's the alternative, Kershaw?"

Quint shrugged. "Backtrack to the Galisteo Road, this side of Pecos. Take the road eighteen miles south to Galisteo. Then westerly another seven miles over the hills to pick up a road going north to Santa Fe, about fifteen miles before the city can be reached. Figure on about forty or more miles over terrible roads in wet weather, with worn-out horses and mules, and tired men."

"After a march of fifteen miles to reach here," Hammond mused. "Which means the general won't reach Santa Fe this day, as he planned."

Luke shifted his chew and spat. "Not less'n he flies over these Gawd-damned hills, lootenant."

"Perhaps the Mexicans are not in there," Hammond suggested.

Quint turned. "Jesus, hold the horses. Luke, Moccasin, and Joshua, follow me." He looked at the officer. "We'll know in a few minutes," he said with a smile.

The four scouts vanished into the thick, wet underbrush bordering the road. They moved phantomlike up the pass, glancing toward the heights, momentarily expecting a deluge of rocks. Quint was in the lead. The only sound was the faint pattering of rain and the soft moaning of wind through the pass. If there were Mexicans in the pass, they were inordinately quiet.

They reached the crest. There was no one there. Luke pointed out a crude abatis of large felled trees with sharpened branches facing outward across the road one hundred yards beyond the gorge. It was undefended. No gun muzzles showed between the branches. No muskets were poised and ready. The heights were unmanned.

The scouts moved forward, still wary of possible ambush. All they found behind the abatis were footprints and hoof marks cut across by the wheel tracks of artillery. The road to Santa Fe was wide open to the conquerors.

Quint shook his head. "My God," he murmured. "A hundred men and a few guns here could have held off our entire army. They could have dropped rocks on us and easily stopped us from reaching their guns. The abatis is in the wrong place. Armijo probably thought he'd let us pass the gorge before he opened fire. But his position instead of being impregnable could have been easily turned."

Luke nodded. "He had no intention of fighting, seems-like." He looked sideways at Quint. "Yuh figger Santiago Magoffin mebbe paid him off to haul tail out'a here?"

"I wouldn't doubt it." Quint turned to Joshua. "Go back and tell Lieutenant Hammond the road is clear. Bring up our horses."

Quint and Luke rode on while Hammond reached the crest. They found a narrow, rutted byroad leading south. It was pitted with many hoof marks and gouged out with wheel tracks.

"There goes Ol' Manuel Armijo," Luke said dryly.

They rode back to the main road. Hoofs thudded on the wet ground. Lieutenant Hammond and his dragoons appeared. Beyond them was the head of the long column of the Army of the West, filling the road, moving slowly but inexorably toward Santa Fe, their goal after less than two months on the trail from the Missouri River to the Rio Grande, a distance of 821 miles. General Kearny—he had just been promoted—was determined to enter the capital before sundown even though his army would have to cover 29 miles that day in order to do so. The road was bad, the horses and mules were worn out, the men were weary, and the army was desperately short of supplies and forage. There was no question of halting. General Kearny, as well as every soldier under his command, knew the psychological advantage of pressing their success before misfortune could intervene.

A little after noon Lieutenant Hammond and his twenty dragoons, with Quint Kershaw and his dozen mounted rifles in the capacity of scouts, met the acting secretary of state of New Mexico and another Mexican bearing a letter to General Kearny from Lieutenant Governor Juan Bautista Vigil y Alarid in Santa Fe. It informed the general of Armijo's flight to the south with his dragoons and artillery, referred to the lieutenant governor's readiness to receive the general, and extended the hospitalities of the city to him.

At three in the afternoon the vanguard caught their first glimpse of the city. General Kearny called a halt in order to allow the remainder of the army to catch up. The rain finally ceased.

At a quarter to five the dragoon C trumpets and the deeper toned infantry G bugles blew for the final advance. The head of the column, now led by the general and his staff followed by the First Dragoons, rounded the last turn in the road and rode down San Miguel Street toward the plaza just as the sun seemed to burst through the clouds massed on a mountain top far to the west. The First Dragoons, despite their somewhat trailworn appearance, had a gallant air about them. The lead company rode black horses, the second white, and the third sorrels. The Laclede Rangers, a spare troop of cavalry from Saint Louis, had been attached to the dragoons and now followed them next in column. Kershaw's polyglot handful of New Mexico Volunteer Mounted Rifles, Anglos, New Mexicans, half-breeds and full-blooded Delawares were behind the dragoons, riding loose and easy in their California saddles. Giant Colonel Alexander William Doniphan led his First Missouri Mounted Volunteer Regiment following the mounted rifles. Two companies of Regular Infantry and a battalion of Missouri Volunteer Infantry marched next in line. They were the long-legged infantry who had outmarched the mounted units on the Santa Fe Trail. Major Meriwether Lewis Clark rode at the head of his battalion of Missouri Light Artillery, nicknamed "The Saint Louis Flying Horse Artillery" composed of two horse artillery batteries, so called because the gunners as well as the drivers were all mounted in order to ride with and support cavalry units. Battery A was commanded by Captain Richard H. Weightman, an exceedingly popular officer who had developed his battery into the "Corps d' Elite" of the expedition. Battery A artillerymen wore flat blue fatigue caps bound with a red band ornamented with brass crossed cannon. Their short blue jackets had red standing collars, and the blue trousers were trimmed with red stripes, one for enlisted men, two for officers. Officers' jackets had gold lace on the collars. Captain Woldemar Fischer, a German Prussian resident of Saint Louis, commanded Battery B. When the horse artillery battalion had been in the process of recruiting, Battery B had suffered for members because of the popularity of Captain Weightman under whom every would-be artilleryman wanted to serve. Captain Fischer had recruited a company of dragoons from among German residents of Saint Louis. There was already a surfeit of mounted units. The army was getting ready to move out. To expedite matters, Fischer's dragoons were converted into Battery B of Clark's battalion. They were handsomely uniformed in gray coats of Kentucky jeans material, gray trousers with a yellow stripe, and forage caps. The long, brass 6-pounder guns and short barreled 12-pounder howitzers, caissons and limbers were each drawn by four-horse teams. A few supply wagons followed, those that had managed to keep up with the army despite their worn-out teams. The remainder of the supply train and the pack mules were strung out on the road all the way back to Apache Canyon.

The Army of the West marched through the dirty, winding streets with every banner, pennant, and guidon flying in the fresh, late afternoon breeze. The men were trailworn, their clothing dirty and tattered, their horses and mules half-starved and worn-out, but their weapons were clean and bright, and the sun glinted on the highly polished brass of bugles, trumpets, ornaments, buttons, and the barrels of guns and howitzers.

Throughout the city among the little houses fear and grief haunted those of the populace who had not fled to the hills. Women covered their faces with *rebozos,* sobbing aloud, cowering in fear, shame, and dread. Armijo and his minions had told them the American soldiers, heretic barbarians to a man, would be turned loose like wild animals from their cages to loot, rape, and kill. The poor and illiterate were sure each of them would be branded U.S. on both cheeks exactly like the big belt buckles the soldiers wore. Churches would be desecrated. Children would be enslaved and sent back east, never to be seen again.

The army marched completely around the plaza then massed in stiff ranks before the Palace of the Governors. General Kearny dismounted and advanced with outstretched hand to the *portale* where he was met by Lieutenant Governor Vigil and a score or more of prominent townspeople and government officials. The lieutenant governor offered Kearny and his officers wine and brandy, but before the general accepted he ordered a temporary flagpole to be erected on the palace roof. As the sun began to sink behind the western mountains, the Stars and Stripes was hoisted and flung to the fresh breeze, accompanied by To The Colors played by the massed bugles, trumpets, and drums of the army. Officers' sabers flashed in salute while the army presented arms. Cannon on one of the hills northeast of the plaza fired a thirteen-gun salute. The heavy thudding reports echoed from the nearby hills while the thick powder-smoke drifted over the city. For the first time in history Americans had conquered a foreign capital. The Army of the West had done exactly what President Polk had instructed them to do: they had taken New Mexico without firing a shot.

The last gun report died away. General Kearny lifted his hand for silence in the plaza. Loudly and deliberately he addressed the populace, "I, Stephen W. Kearny, General of the Army of the United States, have taken possession of the Province of New Mexico in the name of the government of the United States, and in the name of that government do hereby advise and instruct the inhabitants of this country to deliver their arms and to surrender absolutely to the government of the United States in whose name I promise to this country and its people protection to their persons, lives, and property, defending them in their homes and possessions against any savage tribe. For this government is very powerful to protect you in any untoward event, and in this manner I take this Province of New Mexico for the benefit of the United States."

Lieutenant Governor Vigil then stepped forward. "It is not for us to determine the boundaries of nations. The cabinets of Mexico and Washington will arrange these differences. It is for us to obey and respect the established authorities, no matter what may be our private opinions. . . . No one in this world can successfully resist the power of him who is stronger. In the name of the entire department I swear obedience to the Northern Republic and I tender my respect to its laws and authority." There was a note of pathos and humiliation underlying his voice as he spoke.

"Manifest Destiny, Lieutenant Quintin Douglas Kershaw," an unmistakably Irish voice said just behind Quint.

Quint turned. "You've accomplished your mission, Doctor Tomas Byrne," he said quietly.

Tom nodded. "More than a decade of boring from within."

"Any regrets?"

Tom shook his head. "And you?" he asked quietly. "Or is it too early to absorb what has happened?"

Quint reached inside his jacket and touched the bulge in his shirt pocket—the daguerreotype of Jean Calhoun, son Alexander, and niece Catherine. "I know, Tom. I know. . . ." Quint said. In July 1838, at Pecos Ruins, she had prophesied for him, *"The future for you is here in New Mexico, Quintin Ker-Shaw."* A little over eight years to the month.

Tom looked toward Shelby Calhoun, who stood under the palace *portale* with the other staff officers. "There is a man who will make his mark on New Mexico," he said thoughtfully.

"No question about it," Quint agreed. "He has all ace cards—Regular Army commission, powerful political connections, plus a rich wife whose father is one of the most important men in Congress."

"Coupled with intelligence, ambition, and ability."

Quint nodded. "That too."

Tom took out his watch and glanced at it. "It will soon be dark. Have ye been assigned quarters as yet?"

"None that I know of."

"Ye are welcome in my humble home, Quint."

"I have my command to take care of, Tom."

"How many men?"

"One dozen exactly."

Tom shrugged. "Bring them along. We've plenty of room."

"Some of them are half-breed and pure-blood Indians. Ye know they can't stay in the city overnight."

Tom stepped back. "Come here," he suggested. He pointed up at the Stars and Stripes. "Ye see that? When Kearny had that flung to the breeze many of the old laws and taboos were gone forever."

"Ye think it will stay that way in New Mexico?"

They studied each other for a fraction of a minute.

"Well?" Quint asked at last.

Tom snapped shut his watch case. "No," he said quietly. "The laws might be different in content, but they will be just as prohibitory, at least as far as Indians are concerned. I'll pay my respects to General Kearny now." He smiled a little. "It is a day to which I have long been looking forward, Quint." He started toward the palace, then paused, half turned, and looked back over his shoulder. "By the way, Quint, have ye been notified as yet about what duties ye will perform while here in Santa Fe?"

Quint shrugged. "Nothing specific. I'm sure we won't be assigned garrison duty. Probably courier work, scouting, perhaps a little escort duty and such. Why do ye ask?"

"I was just curious as to how long ye'd be quartered with me?"

"I have no idea. Does it make a difference in your plans?"

"Some months ago I received a coded letter from Senator Allan. In it he mentioned the fact that when and if the annexation and occupation of New Mexico took place, he would make it a certainty that Shelby Calhoun would be stationed here in Santa Fe as part of the garrison staff."

"So?"

"He also mentioned that if Shelby were stationed here, Jean Calhoun would likely arrive on the first available caravan to be with her husband. If that happens, naturally both she and her husband will take up quarters in my house. I thought you had better know." He turned and walked on into the palace.

Luke whistled softly. "Salt, pepper, and gravel in the grease," he murmured.

"Perhaps the wheel is turning full circle," Quint said quietly.

"What the hell does that mean?" Luke demanded.

"I'm not at all sure myself, Wandering Wolf."

Long after dark the wagon train straggled into Santa Fe. The heavily loaded wagons were dragged over rough roads to hilltops overlooking the city. The army had pitched its few tents without order in the fields and on nearby hills. There was no feed for the starving horses and mules. Most of the soldiers went supperless. Some of them had no bedding or tents until late at night when

★ 231 ★

the wagon train arrived. Many of the troops soon filled the saloons and hotels in the city until Captain Cooke, acting as provost marshal with a unit of fifty men, drove the reluctant soldiers back to their bivouac. Kearny and his staff slept that night on the floor of the palace.

The next morning the general had the populace assembled in the plaza. He repeated his declaration of annexation, emphasized the peaceful intentions of the occupying force, and stated that all existing officials would retain their offices for the time being, provided they took the oath of allegiance to the United States. A hundred-foot flagpole was erected in the plaza to replace the temporary one on the palace roof.

General Kearny ordered Lieutenant Gilmer of the Topographical Engineers to plan a strong fortification to control and if necessary defend the city. The site selected was the same hill from which the thirteen-gun salute had been fired the evening of the occupation. It was the same eminence where the Pueblo Indian chiefs had established their headquarters during their successful rebellion of 1680. The hill was not more than a third of a mile northeast of the plaza. Guns emplaced in such a fortification could command every part of the city and would be out of gunshot range from nearby hills. The site was mapped by August twenty-second and began on the twenty-fourth by more than one hundred laborers. It was planned as a "Star Fort," to be constructed within a hexagonal polygon, due to the irregular shape of the ground, and surrounded by a deep ditch. It would be a citadel, containing a powder magazine, gun battery, breastworks, two blockhouses, a storehouse and quarters for the garrison. As planned, it would be defended by one thousand soldiers and fourteen cannon.

Pueblo Indians began to slip into Santa Fe from their little villages in the hills. They were a fine, hardy-looking people, generally shy, usually friendly. They wanted to see the great warrior who had come from where the sun rises and overthrown, as if by magic, the Spanish-Mexican rule they had feared and despised for generations. There had been a prophecy of such a great warrior. He would be white and from the east, driving Armijo and oppressors like him from the land. In time they took the oath of allegiance, promising to be among the best and most peaceful inhabitants of American New Mexico, seeking protection against the predatory Apaches and Navajos.

The Navajos came too, the savage raiders and looters dreaded by Mexican and Pueblo alike. They spent their time in the city eating, drinking, and loafing, seemingly noticing little, but certainly sizing up General Kearny's "great medicine." They had heard rumors he planned to enforce strict laws against their ancient and hereditary rights to raid, pillage, and kill Mexicans and Pueblos.

Five days after the occupation Kearny issued another proclamation, not quite as conciliatory as his earlier one. He called on all residents who had not as yet returned to their homes for fear of the Americans, to do so immediately under severe penalty of being considered enemies and confiscation of their possessions. A few days later he announced the confiscation of *all* New Mexico, thus disposing of the weak halfway measure of the Rio Grande del Norte's being the western limit of the Republic of Texas. This was done in order to thwart any claims Colonel Diego Archuleta, former Governor Armijo's second-in-command, might have to governing New Mexico west of the river. Colonel Archuleta, a firebrand patriot, in command of over a thousand troops, might have resisted the Americans at Apache Canyon, if—as Tom Byrne had explained to Quint—Santiago Magoffin had not dissuaded him, promising him the United States was only interested in the Rio Grande boundary. Magoffin had absolutely no authority to make such a promise, but it had worked exceeding well. Further, there was nothing that could be done about it now.

Manuel Armijo had fled south to Albuquerque accompanied by less than one hundred of his dragoons. He had spiked and abandoned his artillery pieces at Galisteo, twenty-seven miles south of Santa Fe. The Americans now used Galisteo Creek for pasturing their horses, mules, and cattle because of the abundance of water and grass in that area. Captain Fischer of the artillery battalion brought Armijo's abandoned guns to Santa Fe. Among the pieces were three bronze 4-pounders cast in Barcelona, Spain dated 1758 and a 4-pounder howitzer dated 1778. One fine brass 6-pounder bore the name of

President Lamar of the Texas Republic. It had been captured by the Mexicans from the Texan "Santa Fe" expedition of 1841. The guns were added to the Star Fort battery, now named in honor of William L. Marcy of New York, United States Secretary of War.

Two weeks after the occupation Lieutenant Quintin Kershaw and Sergeant Luke Connors of the New Mexico Volunteer Mounted Rifles were ordered to proceed to the San Augustine Plains on a reconnaissance mission to determine the feasibility of establishing a military post in that area for the purpose of controlling the Mimbreno Apaches. The day after they left Santa Fe a caravan arrived from Independence, Missouri. One of its mail pouches contained a letter to Captain Shelby Calhoun from his wife Jean, informing him that she would arrive in Santa Fe early October.

★ TWENTY-ONE ★

The chill darkness seemed to have the texture of fine black velvet. The gibbous moon would rise within the hour, but as yet there was no trace of it limned against the eastern sky. A leisurely wind began to blow down from the Gallinas to the vast valley floor. It gently lifted the feathery layer of fine ash covering the bed of embers in the deep firepit. The embers began to glow like fierce predatory eyes.

Luke raised his head. He placed a hand on his Hawken. "Someone comes. One man afoot. Limpin'. I think."

Quint nodded. "You've ears like a wolf."

Luke grinned, drawing his pale thin lips back from his long yellowed teeth, to all appearances like a hunting wolf. "I *am* a wolf, Big Red."

Luke stood up, rifle in hand. He kicked dirt over the fire.

Quint shook his head. "No. It might be Anselmo Campos."

"And if not?"

"Ye said *one* man."

"There might be others. We'll not hear 'Paches."

Quint jerked a thumb toward the tall pines girdling their hidden camp in the shallow rock hollow on the mountainside. "Take a look-see then. Ye'll not be satisfied until ye do. By God, if they are 'Paches, don't let any of them creep up on me, eh, Lukie?"

Luke was gone as silently as the woodsmoke drifting downslope between the trees.

The horses were hobbled and picketed several hundred yards from the camp. It was Mimbreno Apache country, and also well known to their cousins the Mescaleros who haunted the ranges to the east and beyond the Rio Grande. The Navajos occasionally came down from the north to horse-raid the Mimbrenos. They had no love for white men. It was decidedly hostile country.

Quint full-cocked the Hawken lying on the Navajo blanket beside him. He set the trigger. One of his Colts was thrust beneath his belt and its mate hung in a pair of leather loops sewn inside the left breast of his elkskin jacket. He rested his right hand on the butt of the Colt.

He lowered his head a little and raised his eyes to peer from under his shaggy, reddish eyebrows, as though he was really looking down into the smoking firepit. There wasn't much to fear, provided it was just one man. Luke was never wrong on such matters. He had the acute sensitivity of the Indian to the wilderness, with some animallike senses to boot, and beyond that an almost supernatural alertness to danger of any kind.

The shadowy figure came noiselessly through the darkness to stand half-hidden behind a pine, faintly illuminated by the tiny dancing flames that leaped up, windblown from the thick bed of embers. Quint could almost feel the intent gaze of the man upon him.

"You are either a brave man, a damned careless one, or utterly foolhardy to make such a fire whose glow is visible at night in this country, mister," the man said in Spanish.

Quint shrugged. "Perhaps a little bit of each."

"I'll admit I didn't see the fire at first, but the wind carried the woodsmoke odor to me. That's how I found you."

"Good! I wanted to be found, at least by you, if you are the man I seek. Are you Anselmo Campos?"

There was a slight hesitation. "That depends," the man said slowly.

Quint grinned. "Perhaps there are others not so friendly looking for you?"

"That is possible. I know you, however. You are from the north. The Montero Americano called Big Red, or perhaps you prefer Don Quintin?"

Quint casually waved his left hand in deference. He did not release his hold on the butt of his pistol.

"I am Anselmo Campos. You can let go your grip on that hideout pistol now, Don Quintin."

Anselmo limped slightly as he came forward. He stopped on the opposite side of the fire and leaned on his rifle, studying Quint. "What is you want of me?" he asked.

"First there is food and coffee, with a *copita* or more of Pass brandy."

"I am hungry and thirsty, but first tell your companion he can take his rifle sights from between the middle of my shoulder blades and join us."

The New Mexican was not a tall man, and although he was horseman slim of physique, his shoulders were broad, and there was a pumalike quality about his movements despite the limp. He was one of those frontiersmen who seemed to be composed of wagon spring iron and whang leather covered with firm flesh and long flat muscles. Instead of a hat he had bound a band of buckskin about his head to hold back his thick, black mane of hair. His jet black eyes flicked about constantly like those of a wary animal. The nose was proud, jutting out from his broad olive-hued face with its high cheekbones and tiny pockmarks. Although he wore a thin mustache like that of a Chihuahua dandy, the Indian was strong in him. His clothing was of worn leather. His footgear was Apache, the *n'deh b'keh* or thigh-high, pug-nosed, thick-soled desert moccasins folded down and tied just below the knees. Such a man was Anselmo Campos, perhaps twenty-five years old, born and bred, according to hearsay, about seventy-five miles from where he now stood, on the Middle Fork of the Gila River.

Quint placed the coffeepot in the embers. He handed

dried meat and hard biscuit to Anselmo, who squatted and began to gnaw at the dark, tough meat as though he had long fasted.

"Anselmo Campos is your man," Rodrigo Gallegos, the *alcalde* of Socorro, had informed Quint and Luke. "No one knows the Plains of San Augustine and the surrounding mountains as he does, perhaps even as well as the Mimbrenos, although that is hardly possible, you understand, unless one *is* Mimbreno, or at least part Mimbreno. There is no one else, at least here in Socorro, who would be willing to guide you into that country."

"Where can we find this Anselmo Campos?" Quint had asked.

"Who knows? He is a creature of the mountains. Then too, he is not welcome here in Socorro, and further, in the Province of New Mexico and Mexico itself. There is a price on his head. Men who have gone into the mountains west of here have disappeared. Some say the Mimbrenos killed them. Others claim they were murdered by Campos. Perhaps he raids with the Mimbrenos. No one really knows. There is a mountain west of here, beyond the pass between the San Mateos and the Gallinas. It is said to resemble Mary Magdalene, and was so named by the *conquistadores,* although I must confess the resemblance escapes me. Go there and wait. I'll pass the word that you wish to see Anselmo Campos. After that, it will be up to him. It might take days, or perhaps weeks."

"We have the time and the inclination, Don Rodrigo," Quint had assured the *alcalde.*

Don Rodrigo had looked furtively over both his shoulders, as though Anselmo Campos might be within earshot. "He is a dangerous man, Don Quintin, and quite unpredictable."

Quint had smiled. "Why, so are we, Don Rodrigo, so are we."

Don Rodrigo had looked into that lean, scarred face and the icy gray eyes and shivered inwardly. But it was not until the *gringos* were gone that he dared to cross himself, three times.

That was how it had come about. They had waited on the Mountain of Mary Magdalene for twelve days, shifting their hidden camp every night, taking turns at guard, and lying low by day, looking out across the tawny sweep of the great Plains of San Augustine far below them stretching into the hazy horizon of the southwest for seventy miles, and twenty-five to thirty miles east to west.

Anselmo turned quickly as Luke came noiselessly from the shelter of the pines. "Body of God," he murmured, "you walk about at night like the hunting wolf, *hombre.*"

Quint grinned. "He *is* a wolf, Anselmo. Don't turn your back on him unless his belly is full and then be doubly cautious."

"I'd best scout down the mountain, Big Red," Luke said. "Who knows who might have followed him here?"

Anselmo reached for the coffeepot. "No need, wolf who walks like a man. No Mimbrenos followed me here, and if they had, they wouldn't come up on this mountain."

"Why so?" Luke asked. "Why is this mountain different than any others around here?"

Anselmo shrugged. "Who really knows? The *viejos,* the early Franciscan padres, thought this strangely shaped mountain looked like Mary Magdalene. They didn't know it at the time they named it, but this mountain is considered to be enchanted by the Mimbrenos and other Apaches. Many men have been been killed by them from the San Mateos west across the Plains of San Augustine, and from the Datils and Gallinas in the north, south to the Mimbres, but *never* on this mountain of Mary Magdalene."

Luke looked at Quint. "Just the same I'm takin' a look-see. I don't bide much by these superstitions."

Anselmo shook his head. "You can bring my horse back with you, *por favor.*" He watched Luke vanish into the shadows. "You are right, *patron.* He is as suspicious as a wolf; a wolf in human form."

Quint nodded. "The Kotsoteka Comanches called him Isa-Conee, or Wandering Wolf. He lived with them once. Had to leave their company in a hurry. They're still looking for him."

There was a look of respect on Anselmo's face as he dipped a biscuit into his thickly sugared coffee. "To es-

cape from the Kotsotekas and live to tell about it . . ."
His voice trailed off.

Quint laced the coffee with good Pass brandy. "You
traveled far to come here?"

"The Mimbrenos were hunting south of this place. I
had to go the long way around by way of Caballo
Springs. I heard two strangers, *gringos* from the north,
wanted to see me."

"But, you must be suspicious of strangers. There is a
price on your head. Why would you risk coming here?
Perhaps we are bounty hunters."

Anselmo shook his head. "Don Rodrigo would not risk
his life by luring me into a trap. I know he recommended
me as a guide. No one knows this country better than I.
I was born and bred here. I know the land, the wildlife,
and the Mimbrenos better than any other New Mexican.
No Spaniard or Mexican has ever been able to keep a
foothold in this valley although many have tried and
were either driven away or died here." He scraped up a
little of the earth mingled with pine needles and held it
in the cup of his right hand. He hefted it thoughtfully,
then looked at Quint. "It is a good place, but as long as
it is Mimbreno country, no Mexican can take or hold it
for his own. Whoever tries will find that they will make a
desolation of his efforts and take his life and that of his
family." He paused, then slowly took a deep breath.
"Now *you* have come, *patron*," he added quietly.

"You call me *patron*. Why? I've come here as a soldier
to reconnoiter this land for its potential as a military
post for the new government of New Mexico. There is
also a possibility I might eventually settle here on a
grant. But that won't be for some time to come."

Anselmo smiled crookedly. "It is more than a possibility, *patron*, and that you know well. It is the business of
the new government to make sure this land will be under
their control, as the Spaniards and Mexicans wished it to
be, and *failed*. That is why you have come. Your superi-
ors *know* you, Don Quintin. They know you will
eventually come here and make it a good place to live. It
will be dangerous and difficult, but you will succeed. It is
your destiny. There will be much bloodshed. Many men
will die. But you will not be killed or driven away. You
will stick here like a burr under a saddle blanket because

it is well known throughout New Mexico that is your nature." He waved his hand. "Don't ask me how I know these things, but I *know*. You have come here for the help of Anselmo Campos. *Bueno!* I will be your man. *That* is why I call you *patron!*"

It was very quiet except for the Aeolian harping of the wind through the towering pines.

"But why?" Quint asked.

Anselmo poured the dry earth and pine needles from one palm to the other. He looked up. *"Yo tengo raices aqui*—I have roots here," he quietly replied.

Quint gripped the right hand of Anselmo. Some of the earth and pine needles were pressed hard between the calloused palms. It was an unspoken contract between them. They did not know then that it would last through their lifetimes.

A hoof clapped against a stone with a ringing sound. Luke led a tried *grullo* mustang into the firelight. "Poor bastard was ridden too hard," he said. "He's blown."

Anselmo shook his head. "He'll be all right. I was in one hell of a hurry. I rode by night and hid by day. All the Mimbrenos hate me, but none of them as much as their war chief we New Mexicans have nicknamed Cuchillo Roja, Red Knife. The hue of his knife is that of human blood. Old blood has little time to dry before it is refreshed by still more blood. He is a devil in the guise of a human."

Luke squatted beside the fire and shaped a cigarette. He tossed the makings to Quint. "You seem to know a helluva lot about the Mimbrenos from what we've heard," he suggested.

A resinous faggot snapped in the dying fire and sent up a little shower of sparks. The soughing of the wind through the pine tops became more apparent.

Quint shaped two cigarettes and handed one to Anselmo. He lit both cigarettes from a smoldering twig. He filled tin cups with brandy and gave one each to Anselmo and Luke.

Anselmo held up his cup. *"Salud y pesetas,"* he said.

"Health and good wishes," Quint responded.

"You didn't answer my question, Anselmo," Luke said.

Anselmo looked surprised. "Was that a question?" He looked from Luke to Quint. "I see," he said quietly.

"Don Quintin, if we are to work together, there must be no secrets between us."

Quint shrugged as he sipped his brandy. "I have no secrets from you, Anselmo."

Anselmo puffed appreciatively on the cigarette. "I have been out of tobacco for weeks." He sipped at the powerful brandy. "There was once a brave soldier of Mexico, one Eusebio Campos, sergeant major of Provincial Dragoons, who served his country for twenty years and was wounded three times in battle against the Chiricahui Apaches of Sonora and Chihuahua. He was not a *mestizo*, that is to say, one who had some Indian blood in him. He was a Spaniard of good family in Estremadura who had come to the New World to seek his fortune. He rose high as a noncommissioned officer but could not gain the coveted commission of an officer, although he had earned it many times over. His regiment was one of the first in 1810 to declare for independence from Spain.

"At the age of forty, suffering from his wounds and the many years of exposure on the frontier, he was allowed to retire and received a land grant for his services, as the custom was then. That grant was here on the Plains of San Augustine. The year was 1817. Socorro was being resettled. He was warned of the dangers of this fruitful but hostile land. But, Eusebio Campos feared neither man nor devil, and perhaps not even God himself.

"He was forty years old but looked sixty. He limped from an old wound and had only the partial use of his left arm. His family came with him to the plains. His wife, three sons, and a daughter, one of his brothers, and three of his wife's brothers, with their children, and many servants and Indian slaves. The servants were Opata Indians of Mexico, but the slaves were Chiricahuis, a dangerous people to have around. It has always been the custom when capturing such wild people to kill off the adult males, and take only the younger women and children. But, *never* are they allowed to be kept within many hundreds of miles of their homeland, and in large groups. Eusebio Campos laughed at this custom. The settlers were well armed and trained by him. They built a large house of stone and adobe with a *torreon*, or defensive tower at one corner. Fields were plowed. Irrigation ditches were dug. Crops were planted. Sheep and cattle were herded. The settlement began to thrive.

"The Mimbrenos bided their time. One day most of the able-bodied men were away rounding up the cattle. Eusebio was ill in bed. Mimbrenos in great numbers attacked at dawn. Eusebio rose from his bed to take command. He ordered a retreat to the *torreon* hoping to hold out until the men returned. They did not know the men on the roundup had been cut off and slaughtered to a man. When those left at the settlement ran to the *torreon*, they found that the door had been barred from within."

Anselmo stared into the bed of embers. Quint refilled the cups.

"The Chiricahui women had been secretly contacted by the Mimbrenos," Anselmo continued. "The women had gone into the *torreon* before dawn and barred the door. The Mimbrenos slaughtered the men, and the older boys and women. They took the younger women and children as captives. The *rancho* was set afire. The ripening crops were burned. The stock was driven off. The wells were polluted with the corpses of the slain.

"Eusebio had a daughter named Luz. She was fourteen years old at the time of the massacre. The Mimbreno chief took her as one of his wives. She gave birth to his son. When the boy was twelve, many Mexican soldiers came to the *rancheria* of the Mimbrenos to take back any Mexican slaves they had. The chief murdered his wife rather than give her up. The boy was considered an orphan. He was turned over to the Franciscan padres of Chihuahua to be educated and trained as a lay servant of the Church. There was a wild streak in him. After all he was a Genizaro, half Mimbreno. He ran away from the padres and attempted to return to the Mimbrenos. They looked upon him with suspicion. There was a great *tiswin* drunk held in their *rancheria*. A younger son of the chief, a pure-blood, called the older boy a dirty half-breed. They fought with knives. The Mimbreno boy died. His slayer was driven from the band with an *escopeta* ball in his leg. His father, the chief, swore he would kill him on sight." His voice died away. He stared unseeingly into the embers.

"You?" Quint asked quietly. There was really no need to ask.

Anselmo nodded.

"And the Mimbreno chief?"

Anselmo looked up. "Cuchillo Roja," he replied.

The wind shifted, scattering the ashes of the fire. The faint light of the rising moon tinted the eastern sky beyond the mountain ranges east of the Valley of the Rio Grande del Norte.

Somewhere, far down the slopes of the mountain, a coyote howled once.

During the two weeks that followed their meeting with Anselmo, he guided Quint and Luke over a staggering spread of sage-colored plain and blue-hazed mountains under the most cerulean of cloud-dotted skies; a vast loneliness; a pastel landscape of typical New Mexican cast. The San Augustine Plains were an immense expanse of high grassland with the finest of grazing dotted with bands of antelope, wild horses, and burros. This was real plains country to give the word its true meaning. The hazy mountains crouching like colossal hibernating bears bounded the plains on all sides—to the east the San Mateos, with the smaller Magdelenas northeasterly from them. Between them was a wide spreading pass to the east, to Socorro in the Rio Grande del Norte Valley, while to the distant north were the Gallinas Mountains with the Datils west of them. On the west along the towering serrated spine of the Continental Divide were the Gallo Mountains with the Tularosas to the south and still further south the rugged Mogollons. Closing the south gap between the Mogollons to the west and the San Mateos to the east were the Elk Mountains and the Black Range with the Mimbres Mountains further to the south.

The lower slopes and hillsides of the mountains were stippled with spidery cholla cactus, cane cactus, sage with scrub evergreens, piñon and juniper trees, while above them dark evergreens marched in solid phalanxes up the mountainsides. Canyons and arroyos choked with green brush twisted and wormed their way into the stony flanks of the heights. On the highest elevations were millions of board feet of prime sawtimber, mostly western yellow pine with the remainder white fir and spruce. At still higher elevations there appeared stately ponderosa pines towering darkly to the sky. Dashing streams of cold water raced down to lower ground. Clear, cold springs welled up from subterranean depths to pool on the ground surface. In some places hot springs bubbled forth indicating the volcanic origin of much of the terrain. Further proof of this could be seen in the dark outcroppings of volcanic rock. The mountains teemed with wild game—bears, mule and whitetail deer, beaver, and turkeys.

Anselmo Campos had not claimed this vast expanse of virtually virgin country as his own; neither had he allowed Mimbreno or Mexican to drive him from it. In a sense he thought of it like an Indian, owning all of it and yet none of it. He was a nomad, completely in tune with the wilderness, much as Quint and Luke had been in their beaver-trapping days. He took only that which he needed, nothing more, from this great land which he loved with a passion far exceeding the mere fleshly passion of love for a woman. He had everything he needed. There was grazing for his horses, unlimited water and firewood, and the plains and mountains were full of game. It seemed almost uncanny the way he moved unseen through that country inhabited by Apaches, some of the greatest trackers and hunters on the North American continent.

It was late afternoon the end of the second week in the mountains and plains. The sun was almost gone behind the towering heights to the west. Long shadows drifted swiftly down the tree-clad elevations and lower slopes to ink in hollows and depressions. There was still much light on the Plains of San Augustine. The intermittent wind rippled the dry grasses, at times giving the impression of waves marching across a tawny sea while the hazy blue-purple mountains surrounding the plains seemed like mysterious islands on whose shores the sea lapped. In all that vast expanse there was no sign of man or animal. Not a bird soared through the fading sunlight. It was almost like a lunar landscape, so lifeless did it seem. Yet there was one sign of man—a thin, tenuous thread of smoke that rose against a naked peak set amid the heights due south of Caballo Springs.

There was nothing friendly about that smoke. Quint

knew there could only be one source for it, if indeed it had been conjured up by the hand of man. He lay belly-flat behind a fallen pine on a saddleback ridge just above the springs. Anselmo and Luke were watering the tired horses and filling canteens down at the shadowed springs while Quint kept watch. They had moved fast all that day, keeping close to the base of the Tularosas, taking advantage of every scrap of cover, leading the horses over naked rock surfaces or hard ground to avoid making tracks. At intervals one of them would back-trail and erase any possible traces of their passage. Once they had followed a shallow stream for several miles, entering the water from a rock shield that sloped toward the stream and emerging from the water on another impermeable surface. In that dry atmosphere any wet tracks would soon vanish. Until they had reached Caballo Springs, they had the hope they were not being followed. Evidently not so—the smoke signal, if such it was, gave the lie to their hope.

The fire had been cleverly sited so that the smoke rose against the sheer face of the rock peak and was visible only to one who would be expecting to see smoke in that area. Only by the use of his powerful telescope had Quint been able to locate it. He studied the terrain to the south and saw no other smoke. Maybe a chance fire at that. He shook his head. No Apache in his right mind would have given away his position, even in his own bailiwick, by such a fire. It *had* to be a signal.

There were still several hours of daylight. The trail north toward the Gallos would bring them to one of Anselmo's better hideouts long after dark. As long as the smoke was seen only to the south perhaps they were safe enough. It had been Quint who had insisted against the wishes of both Anselmo and Luke that they explore the approaches to the southwest corner of the plains. That area was the rim of Mimbreno heartland. As long as one Mimbreno lived no White-Eye, an American, or Nakai-Yes, a Mexican, could survive in that country. To a Mimbreno it was inviolate. Quint had insisted on seeing it for himself before he made his final decision on accepting the land grant.

Quint looked to the north and east, where he tentatively planned to build his *rancho*. He stiffened and narrowed his eyes. A thin thread of smoke, hardly visible to anyone except the eye of an Indian or a mountain man, rose high into the clear air until the wind at an upper stratum raveled it out like a wisp of cloud. Quint looked quickly to the north. His guts tightened. *Smoke....*

Quint bounded noiselessly down the slope, Hawken rifle at the trail. *"Vamonos!"* he snapped.

There was no need to explain. Luke and Anselmo slung the full gourd canteens over the saddlebows and led the horses into the shelter of the trees. Quint used a leafy branch to erase moccasin and hoof tracks as he backed into the forest.

Luke and Anselmo were tying rawhide boots on the horses when Quint caught up with them. They led the animals at a half trot up the slope toward the shadowed mouth of a canyon. When they had gone several miles from the springs, Anselmo back-trailed to erase any tracks and look for Mimbreno sign.

Luke squatted beside the horses and cut a chew of honeydew tobacco. "Ever figger out if that breed wanted to double-cross us now'd be his best chance to do it?" he asked.

Quint shrugged. "He could have done it almost any time in the past few weeks."

"Mebbe he's waitin' his time, is all."

"Why? Why bother to guide us all over the country first?"

Luke stowed the chew in his mouth and worked it up into juicy pliability. "Might be he's just waitin' for our grub and likker to run out." He slanted his green eyes up at Quint.

Quint leaned back against his horse. "Ye stupid bastard! Ye think he'd risk his life for two weeks' worth of grub and liquor with ye standing suspicious-like behind him with that killing look in your eye?"

They grinned at each other.

Luke shifted his chew. He lifted a flat rock and spat underneath it, then covered it with the rock to hide sign. "Still, I ain't sure, Big Red Badger."

"What does your medicine tell ye?"

Luke shook his head. "Nothing. Mebbe you're right at

that. Well, anyways, we won't have long to wait before we're sure he *ain't* with them."

"Tonight?"

Luke nodded.

Anselmo appeared moving swiftly and noiselessly through the forest shadows like a wisp of drifting smoke. He quickly made the Plains Indian sign language for *Hurry!*

No need to question the half-breed. Apaches had the hearing of animals, and they were now evidently close enough to hear the slightest sound.

There would be a full moon that night. Faint pale traces of its rising showed against the eastern sky not long after the sunlight was gone. Once the moon reached its zenith, the whole landscape would be revealed in light almost as though it was daytime.

Anselmo halted. He turned. He held his closed right hand in front of and a little below his right shoulder then moved the hand downward several inches—*Here remain.*

They were high on a rim just beyond the upper end of a transverse, rough, natural trail that seemed to cling to the canyon side. They had ascended it from the pitch darkness of the canyon bottom into the semidarkness of the rim just before the rising of the moon.

Anselmo led the three horses off into the darkness. The wind was fitful as it always was when darkness cloaked the canyon country. In a little while it would die away altogether, but once the moon rose, the wind would start flowing downslope as it always did when the air cooled.

Anselmo catfooted back to his two companions. They took cover within a shallow declivity rimmed with broken rock. It had about a 270-degree arc for an open field of fire. A company of trained riflemen could not survive an open ground attack against such a position manned as it was by three expert riflemen. Behind the hollow there was another sheer wall of rock rising perhaps eighty feet.

"Is there a way of retreat?" Quint whispered.

Anselmo looked at him as though to say, "What the hell is the matter with you? Of course! Do you think I'd place us in a trap?"

Quint half grinned. He gripped Anselmo's shoulder and nodded his head.

A foreboding silence hung over the canyon. The slightest sound, that of breathing or the rubbing of cloth or leather against rock, seemed inordinately magnified. The mingled odors of stale sweat, unwashed hair and clothing, dusty leather, and the ever-present gun oil seemed stronger than usual.

Minutes ticked past. It was deathly quiet.

Something rustled in the scant brush. A sharp, pitiful squeaking rose and then stopped as suddenly as it had begun. Some tiny nocturnal creature had died suddenly under the claws of a larger predator. The following silence seemed almost to have solidity to it. A moment later an owl rose from the brush with its prey clutched in steely talons and soared noiselessly off into the dimness on velvet wings.

Quint raised his head. He wasn't sure he had *heard* anything, but he was sure he had *sensed* something. Years of living on the razor-edge of imminent danger had honed that sixth sense in him.

They were down in the canyon.

"*Escuche,*" Anselmo whispered.

Listen, hardly necessary to warn his two companions. They already knew.

Apaches. . . .

Apaches—a faint and cloying feeling came over Quint. The thought of dying was bad enough; it was the *way* of dying at their hands if one was caught alive. They had ways of keeping a prisoner alive on the very intimate threshold of death in the most acute and exquisite agony.

The canyon now seemed to hold a brooding menace. The very air seemed to press down on the three men as though to extinguish the life from them.

The eastern sky was washed with pale, silvery gray.

A night bird cheeped sleepily in the canyon depths. A moment later another bird answered the cry of the first. This time it seemed to come from just below the canyon rim where the trail debouched. Quint looked sideways at Anselmo. Anselmo shook his head. Those had not been birds.

A faint thudding sound rose from the canyon, as though rawhide-booted hoofs had struck rock. Three rifle hammers in the hollow clicked faintly to full cock.

The top of the trail was not more than fifty feet from

the hollow. One second there was nothing to be seen there; the next second a rounded object was dimly silhouetted against the faint light of the rising moon. No mistake. It was a hatless head; a thickly maned head bound with a band. Only White-Eyes and Nakai-Yes wore hats in that country. The head rose higher, followed by shoulders and deep chest, along with the tossing head of a horse. Then the mounted warrior stood clearly shaped at the top of the trail. He reined in his mount and turned his head to look directly toward the hollow. The white paint with which he had banded the bridge of his nose and cheekbones stood out ghostlike from the darkness of his face and black mane of hair. He paused for a moment or two then touched his horse with moccasined heels and rode on along the canyon rim and out of view. There had been no sound. It had almost been as though he was unreal, a phantom conjured up out of the brooding darkness of the canyon.

It was deathly quiet.

Luke hissed.

A bead of cold sweat worked loose from under Quint's leather headband. It ran down his left temple and followed the raised course of the scar on his cheek and came to rest in the corner of his mouth. He put out his tongue and tasted the salt of it. Cold sweat began to trickle and itch intolerably down his sides.

One by one, as though manipulated by a master of marionettes, mounted Apache after mounted Apache reached the top of the trail and vanished into the dimness to the north. The heads of the warriors moved constantly from one side to the other, to the rear then ahead, then to the right and left again, only to repeat the process of ceaseless vigilance, the price of survival in that country. Apaches feared surprise more than anything else.

One by one twenty-four mounted warriors passed in front of the three watching men. A double-dozen of sudden, violent death. Then the last of them was gone leaving behind a thin, bitter wraith of astringent-smelling rock dust.

No one moved.

A horse blew on the trail. The head of the horse and rider appeared as though floating up out of a pool of ink.

Anselmo moved. A stone clicked against another.

"Ever figger out that if that breed wanted to double-cross us now'd be his best chance to do it?" Luke had asked Quint.

The Apache had halted his mount. He looked directly toward the three breathless men. It was impossible to see them, they knew that, but yet it seemed as though he did see them.

Quint closed his eyes for a fraction of a second to rest them from the intent strain. *Oh, Jesus, he's scented our damned stink,* he thought. One shot would topple him two hundred feet down to the bottom of the canyon. One shot would bring a quarter of a hundred warriors back thirsty for white man's blood.

The moon had appeared. Its light glistened on the greasy loops of an Apache canteen, a water-swollen horse intestine the buck had slung across his mount's withers. It shone on his deer-grease-polished carbine and white face paint. He sat there for a moment or two, looked back down the trail, then touched his claybank horse with his heels and rode on.

Trigger slacks were eased. Pent up breath gushed out. Aching eyes were closed. It was impossible to move, talk, or think.

Half an hour drifted slowly past. The moon was well up.

Anselmo crawled over the rocks and crouched there listening. Luke shifted. He thrust his Green River knife back into its rawhide sheath. His eyes met those of Quint. There was no need to explain. If Anselmo had made another noise he would have had Luke's knife in him up to Green River. Anselmo did not see the little byplay. He catfooted to the head of the trail, went belly-flat, and wormed his way to peer down into the canyon. He crawled back, rose to his feet, and motioned for Quint and Luke to follow him. They plowed into a wide declivity—it could hardly be termed a branch canyon—choked with vicious acacia, or cat-claw brush that tore at their clothing and sweating flesh with a myriad of tiny hooked needles. They led the horses to the trail. Luke went ahead on foot to scout the trail leading to the canyon bottom. Quint and Anselmo led the horses halfway down the trail, then halted. A night bird cheeped from the trail bottom in exact imitation of the Mimbreno signal heard earlier. Anselmo echoed the signal. The way was clear.

An inches-deep spring-fed stream flowed down the center of the wide shallow valley. Peachleaf willows and scattered cottonwoods bordered the watercourse. The hazy mountains formed a backdrop to the north. To the south the valley widened to where a view could be had of the sweeping, tawny plains. To the east were more mountains lower than those to the north. On both sides of the stream and covering the bottomlands were faint parallel lines in a geometric pattern interspersed with deeper furrows in a wide-spreading grid imposed over the fainter lines. On the far, or eastern, slopes of the valley was a cluster of what at first seemed like a curious cube-shaped rock formation. To one side of the formation rose a rounded pillar of eroded dun-colored material streaked with black.

Anselmo reined in his *grullo*. He pointed. "There," he said quietly. He looked sideways at Quint. "There are ghosts there, *patron*. Their voices can be heard in the night wind."

"Your grandfather's people?"

Anselmo nodded. "No one has lived there except me, and then rarely, for the past twenty-five years. The Mimbrenos shun this place because of the vengeful spirits of those they slew. The Mexicans know it is haunted."

They rode down the long, gentle grassy slope and splashed through the shallow stream. Now the curious rock formation and pillar revealed themselves for what they truly were—the fire-blackened rock and adobe ruins of what had once been a fortresslike ranch house with a tower built near the southwest corner. On a gentle slope beyond the house were many tilted, decaying wooden crosses turned chalk-gray and ebony by the elements over the past twenty-five years.

Anselmo reined in his horse. He rested his crossed forearms on his plate-shaped saddle horn. "The crosses are unnamed," he said, almost as though to himself, "because the bodies were mutilated and badly decomposed by the time the soldiers reached here from Socorro. Then too the coyotes and *zopilotes* had gotten at them. The bodies were buried in a mass grave. The padre had as many crosses made as there were bodies. It was the best he could do."

Anselmo and Luke watered the horses while Quint walked to the ruins. Eusebio Campos had built well in the combined styles of his native Estremadura and Chihuahua. The walls had been built of native rock up to a height of four feet and then finished with adobe bricks. They were almost three feet in thickness. The windows were narrow with the outer opening wider than the inner, like an embrasure in a castle wall. Rusted iron bars still guarded the windows, but the thick wooden shutters had evidently burned off during the conflagration. There were loopholes spaced between the windows. At each corner of the main building were ells with loopholes so that riflemen could cover with enfilade fire an attacker's close approach to the walls. The main structure had been built in the form of a hollow square enclosing a cobbled courtyard in which there was a well. The many rooms were choked with charred debris from the collapsed roof beams and the thick layer of packed earth which had covered them. The upper parts of the outer walls had been extended four feet above the roof to form an embrasured parapet. From the roof riflemen would have a clear field of fire covering all approaches to the house. The *torreon* had been built apart from the house so that, if the house was taken, the attackers could not leap from its roof to the top of the tower, or vice versa if the tower was taken first. The tower roof was also parapeted and embrasured.

There had been many outbuildings to the ranch, but they too had been burned and were now roofless and half filled with debris. The corral was large with a combination rock and adobe wall ten feet high whose troughed top had been filled with earth and thickly planted with spiked cholla to prevent being scaled. The large and heavy double gate had been studded with nails and dozens of heavy, hand-forged bolts to resist bullets, arrows, and fire, but it had been thrown from its hinges by the Mimbrenos and lay now on the ground in front of the gaping opening.

Quint clambered over the debris in the rooms and entered the littered, weed-grown patio. The rubbish could be cleared out. The roof could be replaced. He looked down into the deep well and thought he saw the whitened bones of a skeleton, but he wasn't sure. Likely thrown in there by the Apaches to pollute the well and overlooked by the soldiers. Maybe there should be another unnamed cross on the slope behind the house.

He looked through a window embrasure. There was another well near the outbuildings. The bottomlands still showed traces of the furrows that had been plowed there and the deeper grooves of the *acequias,* or irrigation ditches, run from the stream. The stream, according to Anselmo, rarely went dry in the summer, but if necessary, dams could be thrown across it upstream to form a number of *charcos,* or pools to water the stock.

Quint went to the *torreon.* The door had been torn from its big hand-hewn hinges and lay on the ground before the doorway. It had been fashioned of two thick layers of very hard wood with a sheet of iron between them for protection against bullets and arrows. The outside had been thickly studded with nails.

"Ol' Eusebio thought of everything except one thing," Luke commented dryly from behind Quint.

Quint nodded. "His Chiricahui slaves."

They cooked their food and brewed coffee on the grassy bank of the stream as the sun sank behind the western mountains.

Anselmo shaped a cigarette when he finished eating. "Have you decided yet, *patron?*" he asked.

"Not yet, Anselmo."

"But, if you do, will you accept me with this place?"

"It may take some time. There is a war on. I'm on duty. If I decide, it may take a year or so before I can establish a *rancho* here. I think, with your help, it can be done."

"You do me great honor, *patron.* I'll be in your debt for life," Anselmo said simply.

Quint shook his head. "It is I who will be in your debt."

"Then you accept me?"

Quint nodded.

"But, I am only one man, *patron.*"

Quint smiled. "Why, so am I!"

Their eyes met as they gripped hands across the dying fire.

Quint and Luke saddled up for the night ride to Socorro.

Anselmo slowly shaped a cigarette as he squatted beside the ashes of the fire.

Quint tightened his saddle girth, looking over his shoulder at Anselmo. "Aren't you coming with us? You can't stay hiding in these mountains until I get back. It might be months, perhaps years. But, perhaps you prefer this solitary life you lead?"

Anselmo stared uncomprehendingly at Quint. "You are making fun of me, *patron*. Do you really want me to ride north with you?"

Quint nodded. "I need recruits for my company of New Mexico Mounted Rifle Volunteers. Besides, I will need someone to teach me the tongue of the Mimbrenos. Interested?"

Anselmo threw his saddle on the *grullo*. He turned and studied Quint for a moment. "Why do you want to learn that?" he asked curiously.

Quint shrugged. "It is necessary to know all one can of one's friends and enemies."

"You think to make friends with the Mimbrenos?"

"I can only try. This is their country. I will be the stranger here. Learning their language and offering friendship will make matters much less difficult in the years to come. Is it a deal?"

Anselmo nodded. "Yes, but only if I too can make a deal."

"Such as?"

"Teach me better English in exchange."

"I will that, Anselmo, but you might end up with the accent of the *escoceses*."

"Who are they?"

Luke grinned. "The Scots. The tribe mebbe worse than the 'Paches when it comes to guerrilla warfare."

Anselmo was still puzzled as they rode to the faint weed-grown trail leading to the long disused Soccoro road. Just before the ranch site was lost to view, Quint rode back a few hundred yards. He reined in and studied the lonely-looking valley. The stream was a twisted silver ribbon under the moonlight. Despite the valley's tragic history, there seemed to be a lingering peacefulness about it. Perhaps it was illusion. There had been another valley, almost a decade past, high in the Colorado Rockies, where he had once thought to return and perhaps live out his life. What was the saying? "Man proposes, God disposes."

Quint turned his horse and rode on. He looked back. "This will be the place," he murmured.

He had said the very same thing back in 1837.

★ TWENTY-TWO ★

The population of Santa Fe had tripled since the American occupation with many more Americans on the way. During the day the city was filled with limbered artillery, baggage and ammunition wagons, commissary teams, caravan wagons, pack-mule trains, Mexican *carretas*, flocks of sheep, and herds of beef cattle. Mingled with the native population was a promiscuous throng of American soldiers, traders, visitors, stragglers, trappers, mountaineers, Mexicans from both north and south, and Pueblo Indians with their women and children. Packs of dogs literally possessed the streets, plaza, and suburbs, prowling everywhere, heads down and fangs bared if threatened. The valley resounded with their yelps, howls, and snarling from sundown to sunrise.

Gambling had always been one of the major preoccupations of Santa Feans, even little children and the very old. Now the plaza and its environs had become one vast gambling mart with dozens of monte tables in action within doors, on the side streets, and under the *portales* surrounding the plaza. Anywhere a dealer could place his blanket and deck of cards was his place of business. Dealers for the most part were Mexican men and some women; the bettors were mainly Americans.

While Quint and Luke had been reconnoitering the Plains of San Augustine, much had taken place in Santa Fe. General Kearny had appointed a board consisting of Colonel Alexander William Doniphan, Willard P. Hall and John T. Hughes of the Missouri Volunteers—all lawyers by profession—aided by Francis P. Blair, Jr. to study the existing laws of New Mexico and suggest whatever modifications and additions might be necessary to make them compatible with American institutions and the Constitution of the United States, then codify them to form a basic law for New Mexico. The report was completed by September 22. That same day General Kearny, rising above the mere plane of military command to the stature of statesman, issued a Bill of Rights for New Mexico Territory based on the newly written code. It was clearly derived from the Declaration of Independence and the Bill of Rights, with strong leavenings of the statutes of the State of Missouri. An old Ramage printing press was hauled down from Taos, and the newly christened Kearny Code was printed in both English and Spanish, then widely distributed. Announcement was also made of the appointment of territorial officers of New Mexico: Governor, Charles Bent; United States District Attorney, Francis P. Blair, Jr.; Treasurer, Charles Blumner; Auditor of Public Accounts, Eugene Leitensdorfer; and Judges of the Superior Court, Joab Houghton, Antonio Jose Otero, and Charles Beaubien.

The Navajo, Apache, and Ute decided to test the new conquerors of New Mexico. After all, they had been robbing, enslaving, and murdering New Mexicans for more than two centuries—it was their hereditary right. They redoubled their raids. One wealthy *ranchero* alone lost six thousand sheep to the Navajos. General Kearny's last order to Colonel Doniphan, to whom he had turned over command of Santa Fe and the territory before leaving for California the twenty-fifth of September, was in reference to the Navajo problem. "Put teeth into the pacification," he had ordered firmly. "Invade Navajo country. Release all captives. Reclaim stolen property. Either awe or beat the Indians into submission."

Kearny had marched with three hundred dragoons to conquer California. On the fifth of October he met newly commissioned Lieutenant Kit Carson of the Mounted Rifles in command of sixteen men on his way to Washington, D.C. with mails and official papers. His mission was an express from Commodore Stockton, United States Navy and Lieutenant Colonel Fremont, United States Army reporting that the Californias were already in possession of the Americans under their command and that the country was free from Mexican control. General Kearny ordered Carson to return with him to California as guide along the Gila River Trail. Carson had at first demurred. He had pledged to go to Washington. He had not seen his young wife Josefa in many months. Kearny was persuasive. Carson finally agreed. The general sent back two hundred of his dragoons and marched toward California with the remaining one hundred and Kit Carson. "A leap in the dark of a thousand miles of wild desert and mountain terrain, and into history."

Colonel Sterling Price of Missouri arrived in Santa Fe, relieving Colonel Doniphan of his command. Price's twelve hundred troopers of the Second Regiment of Missouri Mounted Volunteers reached the city shortly thereafter, followed by the long-legged Mormon Battalion, who had marched afoot from Kansas in a record fifty-three days. Regular Army Lieutenant Colonel James Allen, their commander, had died en route. Before Kearny left New Mexico for California, he had detached Captain Philip St. George Cooke, the Virginia martinet, from his command, promoted him to lieutenant colonel, and sent him back to Santa Fe to take command of the Mormon Battalion and lead it on to California.

Guadalupe had written to Quint from Rio Brioso. In the letter she wrote of conditions on the grant, almost as though she was a business manager instead of the wife of the *patron*. She mentioned the twins, of course, but said nothing about David. She made no mention of the unpleasantness between herself and Quint before he had left for Santa Fe. There was no reference to the war and occupation, as though they did not exist. The letter puzzled Quint. There was something underlying Guadalupe's matter-of-fact style of writing. He brought the letter to Tom.

Tom read the letter and looked up. "What is it that bothers ye, Quint?"

Quint shook his head. "I can't put a finger on it, Tom," he confessed. "But it's almost as though she is covering up something with all this prattle about crops and herds at Rio Brioso."

"She may feel badly about what happened between the two of ye and is too proud to admit it."

"It's not that." Quint studied Tom. "Is there something about her physical condition you know and I don't? After all, she spent a great deal of time here with ye last winter. There was no great need for her to do that, as far as I know. Then, before that, in the summer when I returned to El Cerrillo from Rio Brioso she was sorely troubled about something. Padre Martinez hinted at it. At that time I thought it might have been because I had spent so much time away from her and the children."

"A good enough reason, Quint."

Quint shook his head. "Aye, but there was more to it than that. I began to sense it might be her health. Then there was your visit there supposedly to attend the *baile* and dinner she gave in my honor. You gave her a thorough examination at that time, when I was conveniently out of the way."

Tom narrowed his eyes. "Ye knew about that? How?"

"Cristina told me later."

"The young servant girl?"

Quint nodded. He looked into Tom's eyes and was immediately aware that he knew about the past relationship between himself and Cristina. Guadalupe herself must have told him.

"Ye must have the truth then?" Tom asked quietly. "I can't betray a patient's confidence, ye know."

"She's my wife," Quint said simply.

Tom refilled the brandy glasses. "You've had normal intercourse with her these past several years?"

"Aye."

"Ye noticed no manifestations of pain from her. An emission of blood? Anything unusual?"

Quint shook his head. "She's always been small," he admitted.

"Some months before ye returned to El Cerrillo a year ago last summer she came here to see me. At that time I warned her to have no more pregnancies. I told her she'd had all the births she must ever have. It would be dangerous to have another child. It would be too much for her. Dangerous, perhaps even fatal. But, she wanted another child."

"But why?" Quint demanded.

"She thought to hold ye at El Cerrillo, perhaps a kind

★ 258 ★

of insurance if she could not manage to hold you there herself."

"My God! Why didn't ye tell me, Tom?"

"It wasn't for me to tell, much as I would have liked to. I warned her again when I came up to El Cerrillo. No, it was more than just a warning, far more, in fact. I insisted on it. She must not incur another pregnancy. The child might be stillborn, perhaps deformed in body or mind, or both. Further, Guadalupe herself would suffer terribly, possibly ruin her health, or die. . . ."

Quint leaned forward. "Tom, is she pregnant now?" he asked low-voiced.

"I don't know. I haven't seen her since last winter, nor has she asked to see me. If she is pregnant, how is it ye don't know?"

"She might be covering up from the both of us."

"God forbid! If I knew for sure . . ."

Quint shook his head. "She'd never allow abortion." He stood up. "I'll request an emergency leave and return to Rio Brioso as soon as possible."

But within the next hour Quint received peremptory orders to join the rest of his company at Abiquiu on the Chama River forty-five miles northwest of Santa Fe. There Major William Gilpin, First Regiment Missouri Mounted Volunteers, with almost two hundred of his men had been joined by sixty-five Mexican and Pueblo volunteers for duty in Navajo country. Quint immediately sent a letter to Guadalupe at Rio Brioso.

On October 25 Gilpin's command marched for the San Juan River country on a campaign against the incessantly predatory Navajos. Colonel Doniphan with another three hundred men of the First Missouri had already left Santa Fe for Navajo country. Colonel Congreve Jackson with three companies had been in the vicinity of Cubero about 50 miles west of Albuquerque since September. Doniphan's orders to both Gilpin and Jackson were to rendezvous with his command at Ojo del Oso, Bear Spring, approximately 130 miles westerly from Albuquerque. Gilpin's command faced a 150-mile march in winter weather across virtually trackless country infested by hostile Navajos. The Americans were outnumbered by thousands. Lieutenant Quintin Kershaw's company of Volunteer New Mexico Mounted Rifles led the way.

Five days before Gilpin and his command left Abiquiu, the mail courier from Santa Fe was ambushed by bandits at the crossing of Vermejo Creek twenty-five miles south of Rio Brioso. He was shot in the back and stripped of his clothing and weapons. His mule and saddle were taken. The mail pouch was slit open and its contents dumped on the snowy ground in a greedy search for money or valuables. Later the wind blew the discarded letters into the Vermejo which carried them swiftly down to the Canadian River and lost them forever.

★ TWENTY-THREE ★

Kershaw's Volunteer Company of New Mexico Mounted Volunteers returned from the arduous, if rather bloodless, Navajo campaign early on the evening of January 20, almost three months after they had left Abiquiu with Major Gilpin's command to rendezvous with Colonel Doniphan at Ojo del Oso. From Abiquiu to Ojo del Oso and eventually returning to Santa Fe by way of Albuquerque, they had covered over 350 miles of bitter, wintry terrain through trackless country haunted by hostile Navajos. Colonel Doniphan and his command had marched south from Albuquerque early in December for the invasion of Chihuahua. Kershaw's Company was not part of the invasion force. Their six month's enlistment would expire in January, when they would be required to return to Santa Fe for mustering out of the service. During December and early January they had served as wagon train escorts, a duty they thoroughly despised. They considered themselves "fighting men"! Colonel Doniphan and his First Missouri had decisively defeated a large force of Mexicans at Brazito, just north of El Paso del Norte the afternoon of Christmas Day. The Americans occupied El Paso del Norte without a struggle three days later.

Ice-chip stars glittered frostily against the dark blue

blanket of the sky. It was very cold. Hard-packed snow squeaked underfoot. Despite the cold the plaza and *portales* surrounding it, as well as the side streets, were packed with American soldiers and civilians playing monte, or frequenting the many *cantinas*. Reeling, drunken Americans were constantly disgorged from the *cantinas*. Most of the soldiers were from Colonel Sterling Price's Second Regiment of Missouri Mounted Volunteers. A sobering aspect of the scene were the ranked artillery pieces under heavy armed guard placed in position to cover the plaza and the mouths of the streets opening into the plaza, emplaced there as aftermath of the abortive Mexican revolt of Christmas Eve. The artillery guards were cold sober.

Quint left his command in front of the Governor's Palace while he reported in to Lieutenant Boone, the duty officer. "Our six months' tour of duty expires tomorrow, Lieutenant Boone," he said.

Boone nodded. "We'll see to it that you're mustered out tomorrow. That is, unless you'd be interested in another six months' duty. We certainly can use you."

Quint shrugged. "I personally am not against it. It's quite possible most of my men would re-up. But none of us have seen our homes and families for the past six months. The war up here seems to have become a backwater. Things seem quiet enough with the exception of that mob of drunken Americans out in the plaza."

"We're having a hell of a time keeping them under control," Boone admitted. "But, after all, they're only volunteers a thousand miles from home, and there isn't much for them to do here. The gambling, drinking, and brawling goes on day and night. The guardhouse is always full to overflowing. I've been hoping for some kind of action to get the men out of this damned hole of vice and corruption. Besides, the Mexicans are sick of us, Quint. You heard about the Christmas Eve attempt at revolt?"

Quint nodded. "Some."

"It's a miracle they didn't get away with it. Fortunately we were tipped off. I doubt if we'll have any more problems of that sort. Do you have quarters for the night?"

"I've been staying with Doctor Byrne whenever in

town, but I was told Captain Calhoun and his wife were to quarter there."

"They did. However, Captain Calhoun requested duty with Colonel Doniphan for the invasion of Chihuahua and left here in time to fight at Brazito."

"Is Mrs. Calhoun still here in Santa Fe?" Quint asked quietly.

Boone shook his head. "She has been visiting some other army wives in Albuquerque. She left here a few days after Christmas. I assume she didn't want to bother Doctor Byrne."

"Why so?"

"You didn't hear of his woman's death?"

Quint stared at the officer. "Ye mean his Luz died?"

Boone nodded. "She was in San Miguel Church for midnight mass Christmas Eve, the night of the attempted revolt. Her bodyguard was found the next morning, stabbed to death. Her body was not found until two days later, ravished, horribly mutilated, in the quarters of a man said to be one of the conspirators."

"How is Tom taking it?"

"He became very ill at the news. He has not left his house since that day."

"Where can I quarter my men until tomorrow?"

"There is some room in the barracks behind the palace. You can quarter here too, if you like."

Quint shook his head. "I'll go to see Tom Byrne now." He walked to the door and looked back. "Who was the man said to have murdered Luz?" he asked quietly.

"He had only one name. He was a mixed breed of some sort."

"So?"

"The name is Kiowa." Boone was momentarily startled at the icy look that came over Quint's face. "You know him?" he asked.

Quint nodded. "I know him." He closed the door behind himself.

Luke was leaning against his horse when Quint came out of the palace. He was alone. Not one member of the company was to be seen.

"Where are they, Wandering Wolf?" Quint asked. He already knew the answer.

Luke swept out an arm to encompass the plaza, its

cantinas, and gambling *salas.* "What's the orders, Big Red?" he asked.

Quint grinned. "They're supposed to be quartered in the barracks behind the palace. We're to be mustered out tomorrow."

"We'll all be there, Quint. Where yuh bound now?"

"Tom Byrne's."

"I thought your hero Captain Calhoun and his wife were quartered there."

Quint shook his head. "Calhoun went south with Doniphan in pursuit of fickle fame and to further his career. Jean is visiting friends in Albuquerque."

"Then mebbe we can stay with the good doctor until she gets back?"

"Possibly. Tom is very despondent. Luz was murdered last Christmas Eve. They found her mutilated, ravished body a couple of days later. Tom hasn't been the same since. Ye know what they meant to each other."

"Jesus! They know who done it?"

Quint nodded. "A man named Kiowa," he quietly replied.

"They find him?"

Quint shook his head. "Not yet. But *I* will. I'll leave right after muster out to track him down."

"Not without me you don't."

"Are ye coming with me to Tom's?"

"Give him my sympathy. I'll spend the time trying to get a line on Kiowa. *Someone* should know where he is."

Vincente the porter admitted Quint to Doctor Byrne's big cavernous house opening on the plaza. "The *patron* is dozing in the library, Don Quintin."

Quint opened the library door. A fire of piñon logs crackled in the huge fireplace. Tom sat drowsing in his big chair. A bright Navajo blanket covered his legs.

Quint leaned his Hawken in a corner, placing his twin Colts on a table beside it. He stripped off his heavy buffalo robe coat and elkskin jacket, then peeled off his moccasins. He poured himself a glass of *aguardiente* and downed it quickly. The potent spirits exploded silently in his lean gut. "*Wagh!*" he murmured. He sat down in front of the fireplace and held up his big feet in their well-worn socks, wriggling his toes in sensuous pleasure.

"What the hell is that damned smell?" Tom asked.

Quint turned. "Before God, Tom, I thought ye were laid out ready for burial."

Tom shook his head. He extended a hand to grip Quint's. "Not yet, lad." He studied Quint. "Ye just get back from the Navajo country tonight?"

"Aye."

"How was it?"

Quint shrugged. "Ye know about the Norse hell, Tom? Ice and frost instead of hellfire and smoke?"

"I do."

"That's Navajo country in wintertime." Quint studied him. "Are ye all right now, Tom?"

Tom nodded. "I've learned to accept her loss. God help me! She was a treasure and joy to me in my old age."

"Ye know who did it, of course?"

"Aye! That beast named Kiowa. He's still alive after all his crimes. There's no justice in it, Quint."

Quint looked at his Hawken, Colts, and razor-edged bowie knife. "No justice, but vengeance. Luke and I are going after him tomorrow."

"But you're still in service."

"We muster out tomorrow."

"And you're not going first to Rio Brioso?"

Quint shook his head. "Not until after we hunt down Kiowa." He refilled his glass and one for Tom. "This time I'll find him. I promise ye. Come, get drunk with me, Tom. We owe it to ourselves, old friend."

Tom held up his glass. "May the devil not learn ye are dead until half an hour after ye've made it to Heaven, lad."

"What has happened to Kearny's glorious occupation promises, Tom? Seems as though most of the native New Mexicans haven't much faith in them."

"Ye can lay a great part of the blame on the Santa Fe garrison—the Second Missouri. Colonel Doniphan and his First Missouri, with the Regulars, did not antagonize the natives. Doniphan had better control of his men than does Price. Some quality of leadership Price seems to lack. The Second Missouri have turned Santa Fe into a lawless town. They have degenerated into an insubordinate semimilitary mob, constant violators of law and order. Daily they heap insult and injury on the people.

They are overbearing bullies almost to the man. They insult the Mexicans. They are nothing but dirty, rowdy crowds of drunkards, brawling, boasting, but rarely fighting. A most bitter and determined hostility among the Mexicans soon became apparent after Kearny and Doniphan left. Even the officers have turned occupation duty into a vast outing, a day and night pursuit of pleasure and vice. Hardly a night goes by when ye won't find most of them at *fandangos*, gambling *salas*, and in the better *cantinas*. They know not what their men are doing, and worse, seem to care not."

"Who was behind the Christmas Eve plot?"

"The wealthy, the local leaders under the Mexican government. I think the Americans believed the New Mexicans had been sufficiently quelled. They forgot the war was still on and many patriotic Mexicans had not accepted American rule. This, of course, would be incomprehensible to most Americans. Who would not prefer American rule to that of Mexico? That was their big mistake.

"Archuleta led the revolt. He wasn't willing to sit still once he realized Kearny was not going to stop at the Rio Grande.

"There were many important New Mexicans involved in the plot besides Archuleta. Tomas Ortiz was his second-in-command, he who had been chief *alcalde* of Santa Fe under Armijo. Padre Juan Felipe Ortiz went as far north as La Joya at the time of the festival of Nuestra Senora de Guadalupe last December twelfth, ostensibly to perform religious services, but really to arouse the people of Rio Arriba and Taos against the Americans. There were many other important New Mexicans in the plot—Domingo Baca, Miguel Pino, Antonio Trujillo, and Antonio Ortiz of Arroyo Seco, as well as many others. Not one of these important men had favored the abandonment of Apache Canyon by Armijo. Further, they were all interrelated by blood or marriage."

Quint whistled softly. "Sounds like a roll call of the chosen of New Mexico."

Tom nodded. "It was. Ye can add Bartolome de Vasquez and Diego de las Casas. The plot was worked out with utmost secrecy and well organized. The night of December nineteenth they met in the parochial church and remained concealed there. Others were brought in from the surrounding countryside and concealed in nearby houses. The signal was to be the tolling of a single church bell at midnight. They were to sally forth, rendezvous in the plaza, seize the cannon there, and aim them to command the leading approaches. Special detachments were to attack the palace, seizing Colonel Price and all his officers. People throughout the northern territory had already been alerted. As soon as they heard news of the revolt they were to rise as well. Everything seemed favorable. The Americans suspected nothing. But for a postponement at a final meeting their objectives might have been easily attained. But, the timid took over. They felt more time was needed for preparation. The time was changed to Christmas Eve. American discipline would then be relaxed. The soldiers would be celebrating, dispersed in saloons, in the gambling *salas,* and at *fandangos.* Few of them would be on duty, and those off duty would hardly be sober. Thus, they could be easily killed or captured. The postponement turned out to be fatal."

"Someone betrayed them?"

Tom nodded. "Some said a mulatto woman married to one of the plotters. Others claimed it was Augustin Duran, one of the conspirators. Some said it was La Tules."

"I think the fact was really that the secret was kept too long by too many people. It was bound to leak out. They should have struck on the nineteenth. Colonel Price moved swiftly, arresting some of the plotters, but the ringleaders managed to escape. Diego Archuleta and Tomas escaped to the south and Mexico City."

"What about de Vasquez, de las Casas and Kiowa?"

"Who knows? Rumors are that they were seen up north at La Canada and even at Taos. No one knows for certain."

"And all is quiet now?"

"*Quien sabe?* I still think there is a seething undercurrent of rebellion in the Taos area. The Pueblos are dissatisfied with American rule. They had a legend they would be freed from Mexican oppression by fair-haired conquerors from the East. They thought this might mean the Americans. They were disillusioned. Personally, I think if they eliminated the Americans they'd turn on their Mexican allies next and eventually retake their country for themselves."

"For which one could hardly blame them," Quint said quietly.

Tom shook his head. "I'm concerned about Governor Bent. He insisted on going to Taos to see his family. He felt that he might allay some of the discontent there. He was warned repeatedly about going there. It could be dangerous. He even refused an escort of troops. He took only five people with him—Sheriff Steven Lee, Prefect Cornelio Vigil, Circuit Attorney James Leal, and two younger men, Narciso Beaubien, son of Judge Beaubien and Pablo Jaramillo, Charles' brother-in-law."

"Ye think it could be dangerous?" Quint asked.

Tom shrugged. "Charles has lived in Taos for twenty years. He firmly believes the people will not harm him."

"And what do ye think?"

"He's a God-damned fool for going!"

Later, after Tom had passed out, a mental picture came back to Quint out of the past: 1838—the same comfortable library, with Tom in the big chair, as he was now, but with fifteen-year-old Luz Garcia at his feet.

The fire was guttering low. Quint picked Tom up and carried him to his room. He undressed him and put him to bed. He went into the big kitchen and heated water at the huge fireplace. He bathed and dressed in fresh clothing he had left in the house. He returned to the library, replenished the fire, refilled his brandy glass, and lit a Havana cigar. He looked pleasurably at the backs of the many leather-bound volumes lining the shelves which almost completely covered the walls. Tom Byrne knew how to furnish a room.

Vicente had gone to his quarters. The house was empty except for Quint and Tom. The *aguardiente* bottle was empty. Luke might be along soon. Quint went to the *dispensa* and got two more bottles. He passed the room where he had always stayed when he was in Santa Fe. It was the room where he had recuperated from the knife wound he had suffered at the hands of Bartolome de Vasquez in 1838. It was the room where he and Jean Allan had made passionate love, then parted, she to marry Shelby Calhoun and return East, while he rode north to lay suit to Guadalupe de Vasquez.

He opened the door. The faintest of fragrances came to him, that of spring flowers, the perfume Jean had always worn, in contrast to the sensuous and heady French scent always used by Guadalupe. He lit a candle. The first thing that caught his eyes was an exact duplicate of the daguerreotype he had come by during the Comanche fight near Carrizo Creek. He opened one of the wardrobe doors. The fragrance grew ever stronger. Her gowns hung there. Some dragoon officer's uniforms had been crammed in at one end.

The beehive fireplace was ready stacked with piñon logs, ready for the flame when Jean returned from Albuquerque. He opened the top drawer of a chest of drawers. It was filled with perfumed lacy underthings of finest quality and silken hose. Quint quickly closed the drawer. The scent was doing things to him.

He returned to the den, replenished the fire, poured a stiff drink, lit a cigar, blew out the candles, and seated himself in Tom's big chair, enjoying the peace and quiet, the mingled fragrances of good tobacco, fine brandy, and the burning piñon logs. Tomorrow he'd track down and kill Kiowa, then return to the Rio Brioso, Guadalupe, and the children. It was good. He had earned the rest.

The clock struck ten.

Quint opened his eyes at the last chime. A thudding sound came dully through the big *casa* from the front door. Luke likely, Quint thought. He picked up one of his Colts and went to the door. *"Quien es?"* he called out.

"Vicente?" a man replied. "It is Adolpho the coachman! Open up! It's cold out here!"

Quint thrust the Colt under his belt, undid the chains, and lifted off the heavy bar. He took the huge key from its hook beside the door and turned it in the lock. The heavy door creaked open allowing an icy draft to pour into the hallway. A carriage stood at the curb. Adolpho stood at the head of his horses. A hooded figure descended from the carriage interior and walked gracefully toward the door through the tiny, glittering flakes of falling snow.

Quint narrowed his eyes. A woman, somehow vaguely familiar. *"Quien es?"* he called out.

"Don't you know me, Quintin Ker-Shaw?" she asked

musically. She threw back the hood to reveal golden hair upon which the tiny starlike flakes of snow descended to rest like minute, glittering diamonds.

Quint blinked. "Jean," he said softly.

She smiled. "May I come in? It's been a long, cold four days' journey from Albuquerque. At times the road was blocked. Accommodations were most crowded. We lost a wheel near Bernalillo." She turned. "Adolpho! You may leave now!"

She was lovelier even than Quint remembered. How old was she now? Hardly more than twenty-six. Maturity had added to rather than detracted from her girlish beauty of eight years before.

She came into the hallway, close past Quint, looking up into his face with those great male-devastating blue eyes of hers. Quint mechanically closed and locked the door.

"I didn't expect to find you here, Quint," she said.

He turned. "I didn't expect ye back. I'm only here for the night."

"You were on duty in the Navajo country, were you not?"

He nodded. "Just returned today."

She smiled. "To stay awhile?"

He shook his head. "We'll be mustered out tomorrow. Our six months' term of duty is over."

"You'll not re-up?"

Quint shrugged. "Later perhaps. I haven't seen my wife and family for months. But I have a task to perform for Tom Byrne and myself before I return to Rio Brioso. Once that is done, it's home."

She shivered a little. "It's cold standing here."

"Forgive me!" He took her by the arm and walked her into the library. He took her traveling cloak and hung it up. She wore a fine velvet traveling dress of emerald green that set off her hair and creamy complexion. He could not but help noting the taut swelling of her full breasts against the dress material. He looked from there into her eyes. For a fraction of a second he thought he saw a slightly knowing look, but he wasn't sure.

"Are ye hungry?" he asked.

She shook her head. "I had a huge basket of food from Albuquerque. Brandy will suffice."

He filled the glasses.

"I'll have a cigarette too," she added.

He smiled. "Rather daring for an Anglo woman, is it not?"

She shrugged. "When in New Mexico do as the New Mexican women do."

He swiftly rolled a pair of cigarettes, placed one between her lips, and lit it. He looked deep into those glorious blue eyes. To think he had fully possessed that lush body and those ripe lips with a passion and thoroughness he could still vividly remember.

She sat down and warmed her hands at the fire. "You've changed greatly," she observed.

"It's a hard life, this frontier. I've been on it for almost twenty years now."

"But, you like it."

He nodded. "Love is a more accurate word, Jean."

"A woman's greatest rival for the love of Quintin Douglas Ker-Shaw," she suggested knowingly.

"If you're trying to make me uncomfortable, you're succeeding admirably."

"You could have come back East with me, Quint. You would have been a man of importance by now."

"Why mention it now? If the free choice were mine this minute, my reply to you would be the same as it was eight years ago."

"You still love your Lupita that much?"

"Aye, and there are the children too. Do ye still love your Shelby that much?"

She held her lower lip between her teeth and looked quickly away. "You have three children, have you not?" she asked to change the subject. "The older boy David and the twins Francisco and Rafaela."

He nodded. "At Rio Brioso. Ye passed that way last fall. Ye might have seen them."

She shook her head. "I saw your *hacienda* only from a distance. They say you've done wonders with the old de Vasquez grant. The first *patron* to take and hold the land against the hostile Indians."

"Only to lose it all, Jean. To the United States Army, Senator Alexander Jamieson Allan, and, I might add, Captain and Mrs. Shelby Calhoun."

"It was none of my doing, Quint. Still, you could stay

on as *hacendado*. That was to have been part of the original agreement."

Quint shook his head. "Never."

"But, where will you go now? To El Cerrillo?"

"Not if I can help it. Ye must know of the San Augustine Plains. Ye seem to know much more about me than I do of you. In any case, the deal was made between Tom and me. I have been there. It is good country; raw frontier land. First rate for raising cattle, horses, and mules."

"But dangerous. Is that not Mimbreno Apache country?"

"Aye, but I'll make no hostile moves against them. There is one thing I know for certain—that will be *my* land. Kershaw's land! There will be none of the de Vasquez hold on it, nor that of Anglos such as you, your husband, and father, who've come to the frontier to reap the profits earned for ye by the sweat and blood of other men!"

She half smiled. "The Highland way of speech. Direct and to the point. You must have known such a thing would be inevitable. Manifest Destiny! Remember?"

Quint refilled the glasses. "Ye saw none of my family then?" he asked to change the touchy subject.

"Only one small and very lonely little boy. We were passing some miles from the *hacienda* when he rode by to watch us. We spoke. He rode beside my carriage for a time. He said his name was David Kershaw. You know, Quint, there are certain people one meets with whom one has instant rapport. We seemed to sense that in each other." She studied Quint. "Is he the one whose mother was Shoshoni?"

He nodded. "Aye."

"I seemed to know him at once. It was his eyes, Quint. There's no mistaking them."

Quint reached within his shirt pocket and withdrew the daguerreotype he had gotten at Carrizo Creek. He opened it and held it out to her.

She was surprised. "You took this from my room?"

He shook his head and told her of how he had gotten it.

"Shelby said he had lost it on the Trail. Why didn't you return it to him?"

He shrugged. "At first I forgot. Later, when Lupita found it in my clothing and confronted me with it, I took it with me on duty. Somehow, for some obscure reason, I kept it with me."

She searched his face with her eyes. "How obscure? I don't understand."

He looked at the daguerreotype. "The girl is your niece, is she not?"

"Catherine Williston. Shelby and I adopted her."

"And, the boy?"

Her eyes lighted. "Alexander Jamieson Calhoun! Is he not handsome, Quint!" she cried, almost ecstatically.

Their eyes met. She looked away. Immediately he knew.

"He's the apple of his grandfather's eye. The son father always wanted. He will be a soldier like his father and grandfather he says. He thinks of nothing else. His grandfather has had him enrolled in a military academy and will see to it that he enters the Military Academy at West Point as soon as he is of age." She drained her glass quickly and held it out to be refilled. The rich brandy was wet on her lips, warm in the firelight glow.

She turned slowly and looked directly at Quint. "You know, don't you?" It wasn't a question, simply a statement of fact.

"Are *ye* sure yourself?"

There was no hesitation. "I'm positive."

"Does Shelby know?"

She nodded.

"How did he find out?"

"I simply told him."

"Has it made any difference in your relationship?"

She shrugged. "There was never any real love between us. He got what he wanted. The only daughter of one of the richest and most powerful men in Congress. Any situation that might have been created would have cost him his climb up the ladder of success from comparative obscurity to the fame for which he hungers. A woman, as such, means nothing to Shelby. We fashioned an agreement between us. We live as man and wife, our lives still intertwined because of his ambition and hunger for wealth and fame, but there is nothing left between us."

She looked directly at Quint. "*Nothing,* I say. Do you understand?"

The brandy was working well within Quint, creating a pleasurable glow and arousing his senses. It was only a few steps to her room, the room they had shared once to create their son Alexander. They were virtually alone in the house. The night was theirs and theirs alone. . . .

"But, you wouldn't understand," Jean added quietly. "Are things well between you and your Guadalupe?"

"At times," he admitted.

"You love her?"

"Do ye remember of how we talked about love eight years ago? Love? I told ye then and I tell ye now—I've never been sure of the true meaning of the word."

"You were attracted to me then. Are you not attracted to me now?" she asked softly.

He was fully conscious of his attraction to her, this lovely female creature who seemed to need him now, as she had years ago, only to leave as the wife of another man. Now she had been returned into his life by some mad jest of the gods.

She stood up. "Quint?"

The fire was dying out. A faint chill crept into the room. She shivered a little. "I'd best start the fire in my room," she suggested, looking sideways at Quint.

He walked to the door. "I'll do it, lassie," he offered.

"Shall I bring the brandy?" she asked quietly.

He turned. "Will ye need it?" It was a foolish question.

"*We* will," she replied.

He kindled the fire in the old familiar bedroom. The hungry flames licked up the piñon logs and soon a warm comforting glow filled the room.

She stood in the doorway. "Do you remember Pecos Ruins, Quint?"

"Our first real encounter."

"You would have made love to me then."

"Aye, but ye asked time to reconsider."

"You've a fine memory."

He smiled. "It was not easy to forget."

She closed the door behind herself and placed the brandy bottle and two glasses on the bedside table. She filled the glasses. "Then I came to this very room one night and told you I had reconsidered."

"And?"

She quickly drained her glass and turned to face him, resting her hips against the table, and placing her open hands flat on the top, thrusting out her breasts.

He came to her. "That was your answer then."

"I know," she murmured, closing her eyes and raising her mouth to meet his. They came together in a powerful embrace, his hard, winter-cracked lips crushing her soft full mouth. She thrust her tongue against his and pushed her loins hard against him, feeling his growing hardness. There could be no going back now.

"Strip me now, as you did then," she said breathlessly.

He unbuttoned the back of her dress, pulling it down with its warm flannel petticoat about her rounded hips. She unhooked her lacy brassiere and hurled it across the room. They kissed passionately as he worked her dress and petticoat below her hips and let them drop about her ankles. She stepped free of them, still clinging to him, working her mouth against his, tasting of brandy and sweetness. He stepped back at last, eyeing her appreciatively up and down. Her breasts were full, creamy of texture and rose-tipped, warm, luscious, and inviting. He bent and lip-teased the nipples into stiffness, then dropped to his knees kissing the soft warm mound of her belly. He stripped down her fine silk hose. She kicked off her high-heeled shoes and raised her shapely arms high above her head, stripped to the nude. Her features had changed into a sort of avid looseness, as though thirsting for him and his sexual love.

"Before God," he murmured. A quick flash of Lupita crossed his memory, seemingly trying to get between him and Jean, but he drove it from his mind. She had virtually driven him from the Rio Brioso. He hadn't heard from her in months. There had been a time when she had trained Cristina to take her place. What difference did it make now who the woman was that he would bed?

"Quint" Jean whispered huskily.

He stripped, peeled back the bed coverlets, swept her up in his arms and placed her on the bed. He refilled the glass, looking down at her the while. The white body, creamy breasts with rosy nipples, and the soft mat of golden curly hair at her crotch, above those long, slim, beautifully-shaped legs of hers.

He held a glass to her lips. She placed her hands about his and sucked greedily at the potent *aguardiente*, then lay back with half-closed eyes, looking lazily up at him like a sated cat. "Do you remember what you said to me that lovely night of love eight years ago?" she asked.

"I'm not sure."

"You said there would be no going back now."

He nodded. "Ye knew well enough, lassie."

"Do you remember what I said?"

He shook his head.

She reached up for him with one arm, while with the other hand she stroked his hardness. "Do I please you?" she asked. She smiled. "That was what I said."

There were few preliminaries. They had been apart far too long, and there was no need for them. That could come later, during the second time around that night, for sure as hell Quint thought, this was just the beginning. He thrust in savagely to be met just as eagerly. He hadn't had a woman for over six months; perhaps she had not had a man for the same number of years, perhaps longer. They were out to thoroughly satisfy each other that cold winter night. They gave of themselves to the fullest, achieving full orgasm in perfect unison, then fell weakly apart from each other bathed in perspiration.

"My God," she murmured. "I hadn't realized how much I had missed you, and needed that."

He looked at her quizzically. "After eight years?" he asked incredulously.

She laughed gayly. "Couldn't you tell, you great stud of a man?"

He refilled the glasses. They lay side by side now, blotting out the world of reality—Lupita and Shelby, Santa Fe and New Mexico, the war and the future, everything except themselves and the passion between them. It was almost exactly as it had been eight years past, a closeness, mutual understanding and an overpowering physical and sexual attraction.

The fire was dying out. Quint got up and stacked fresh logs vertically in the fireplace, then stood watching the flames attacking the new fuel, licking hungrily up them in the strong draft from the chimney.

Jean raised herself on an elbow. "What are you thinking?" she asked.

He looked back over his shoulder. "Do ye remember
the New Mexican superstition I told ye about the last
time we were together like this in this very room?"

She nodded. "If the piñon fire blazes up when first lit
and the logs stand upright until they are charred, sweet-
hearts will be true."

He turned. "That was what happened to the fire the
night we were first here together."

"Yes. Do you believe it?"

She was lovely, warm, inviting, and all that he had
ever truly desired of any woman.

"Quint?" she asked.

He nodded. God help him! He could not resist her. He
lay down beside her, cradling her, kissing her gently,
murmuring to her.

The fire crackled. The warmth penetrated throughout
the room. It was as though they were in a private world
of their own, apart from everyone and everything except
for their newly awakened consuming passion for each
other. She rolled back and opened out to receive him
again.

Quint raised his head. "What's that?" he asked.

A dull thudding noise reverberated throughout the
house.

He was on his feet instantly, drawing on his trousers,
and shrugging into his shirt. He held his Colt ready as
he padded from the room and into the dark hallway.
Something metallic thudded repeatedly against the front
door.

"*Quien es?*" Quint challenged.

"Quint? It's Luke!" Luke called hoarsely. "For God's
sake open the door. All hell broke loose!"

Quint opened the door. "What the hell is it?" he demanded.

Luke pushed past him and down the hallway, glancing
quickly into the bedroom as he passed, catching a
glimpse of Jean sitting upright in the bed, the warm firelight aglow against her nakedness. Jesus Christ, he
thought, they're back at it again!

Luke walked into the library and grabbed a brandy
bottle. He drank deeply. "I was in Jim Beckwourth's

saloon half an hour ago. Charley Towne from Taos rode into Santa Fe on a dying horse. The Pueblos and some Mexicans have risen in revolt up there. Governor Bent was murdered in his house. Sheriff Steve Lee, Prefect Cornelio Vigil, Circuit Attorney James Leal, young Narciso Beaubien and Pablo Jaramillo have been murdered in the streets. Those Americans and their Mexican friends who haven't been slaughtered have been driven from the town. Turley's Mill at Arroyo Hondo has gone up in flames. Thousands of Pueblos and Mexicans are organizing to march down from Taos to capture Santa Fe and kill every American in sight. It's war, sure enough, Quint!"

"What's being done?" Quint demanded.

"Colonel Price is already organizing a column. He's asked Ceran St. Vrain to form a scouting company of us mountain men and some townies for thirty days' active duty. That's why I'm here. Ceran wants you to be scouting officer."

"Ye told him I'd go?"

"Of course."

"*Bueno!* Round up the rest of the company. I think they'll all sign up. I'll report as soon as I can."

"I figured you would." He looked sideways at Quint. "Remember Jesus Tafoya? He's the rebel leader. Calls himself 'The Santa Ana of the North,' Charley says." Luke grinned. "General Tafoya," he added dryly.

"We'll whip his ass, Lukie. He's no soldier."

"He ain't but he's got some help."

Quint looked quickly at Luke. "Who?"

"Bartolome de Vasquez and Diego de las Casas, according to Charley. Both of them graduated from the Military Academy in Mexico City, didn't they?"

Quint nodded. "Diego stayed in the army. Bartolome resigned, but he's had plenty of experience fighting Apaches and Navajos."

Luke drank again. He lowered the bottle, wiped his mouth, and started for the door taking the bottle with him. He turned. "Forgot to tell you. We've finally located Kiowa. Charley saw him in Taos with de Vasquez and de las Casas." He grinned exactly like a hunting wolf.

Quint returned to the bedroom. "You heard?"

★ 277 ★

She nodded. "He saw me. Does he know about us?"

"He has ever since '38. But he didn't know you'd be here this night."

"You'll be going?" She knew it was a useless question.

"It's my duty."

He refilled their glasses. "There is still a little time," he suggested.

She hastily threw back the covers. This time their lovemaking lacked the burning urgency of the first encounter; instead it had a tenderness and involvement far more enjoyable.

She waited in bed for him while he dressed. He came to her, ready for the trail with belted Colts and bowie knife, Hawken in hand. As he bent down to her she gently caressed the scar on his cheek. He kissed her tenderly then turned on a heel and walked to the door. He looked back at her, perhaps for the last time, feeling that no other man had ever seen her looking quite like she did at that instant.

She pointed. "The logs are charred and still upright," she said quietly.

He studied her, then quickly left the room. *"Vaya,"* he murmured just as he closed the door.

Jean raised the brandy bottle to her lips. She drank deeply, emptying the bottle. Then she hurled it full force into the fireplace. The charred piñon logs collapsed into black, smoking ruin. Her muffled sobbing could not be heard beyond the closed door.

★ TWENTY-FOUR ★

David Kershaw awoke in his bed in the *hacienda* at Rio Brioso. Something had awakened him; the subtlest of warnings. He threw aside the Navajo blankets and grizzly pelt covering him. The room was dark and tomb cold. He shivered uncontrollably while he dressed. He was alone in the *hacienda* except for old Tomas the porter who slept in the servant quarters. David had lived alone since last October. He had not seen or heard from his father in five months since Quint had left for Santa Fe to serve with the Army of the West. He had heard rumors his father was off serving on the Navajo campaign. If Quint had sent him any letters he had not received them. He didn't even know if his stepmother had heard from his father during that long time. If she had, she hadn't mentioned it to David. There had been an estrangement between his father and her since Quint had accepted American citizenship and a commission in the army. By October Guadalupe had had enough of Rio Brioso. She decided to return to El Cerrillo for the winter. She had ordered David to return with her. He had refused. That night he had left the *hacienda* and stayed hidden in the river canyon until he was sure Guadalupe and the twins had left for El Cerrillo. He had then returned to the *hacienda* and stayed there alone except for a few servants. He had hoped every day he'd hear from his father. Perhaps he could join him. But he had heard nothing. If only he had been five or six years older he would have ridden to enlist in his father's company. He was big and strong for his age, a skilled rider and a crack shot.

David draped his buffalo coat about his shoulders and opened the outer door. The cold was intense. Faint gray light streaked the eastern sky. The wind was from the north. A distant popping noise was borne on it. He ran to a ladder and climbed it to the northeast tower. Flashes sparkled through the darkness across the river where the village stood. *Comanches!* That was his first thought. He shook his head. They had an almost superstitious fear of his father, and besides it was the dead of winter. No Indians would attack at that time of the year. *Mexicans!* Yes, that was it! It must be Mexicans! Perhaps the war had come to Rio Brioso.

He plunged down the ladder and ran to his room. He snatched up his Hawken and the small silver-mounted pistol his stepmother had left in the nightstand beside her bed. He returned to the patio and ran to the stable to saddle his pony. The door creaked open behind him. He whirled while cocking his Hawken.

Tomas jumped back and peered around the edge of the door. "For the love of God, Don David," he quavered. "It is only old Tomas. Would you shoot me?"

"There is shooting at the village, Tomas! I'm riding to help them!"

Tomas shook his head. "Come and look," he suggested. He pointed to the north as David left the stable. The sky was lit by soaring flames. The sound of shooting was continuous.

Cautioning advice given David by his father and Luke ran through his mind: "White men usually run to the sound of shooting; Indians stay away from it until they know who's shooting. Heroes are stupid; they die quickly. Cautious men are smart; they survive. Depend on your rifle for your life. Don't make a last stand until you're positive there is no escape, then fight to the death. Don't let yourselves be captured by Indians or bad Mexicans. Above all—*survive!*"

"Escape," Tomas said. "There is yet time."

"I'll saddle a horse for you, Tomas."

The old man shook his head. "No. Where would I go? I could not live outdoors in this weather. You can. Your father and Senor Luke have taught you well."

Something thudded against the east wicket gate. A man shouted.

"Go!" Tomas insisted to David.

David shook his head. "See who it is, Tomas."

Tomas hurried to the gate. *"Quien es?"* he called.

"It's Teodoro Ruiz from Taos. I heard Don David was still here," the man replied.

Tomas looked at David. David nodded. He stepped to one side and held his rifle at hip level pointed at the gate. The porter unbarred and opened the gate. The big Mexican shouldered his way into the patio. "Where is Don David?" he demanded.

David cocked his rifle. "Here," he said. "What do you want?"

Teodoro looked down at the rifle and then at the serious face of the boy. "A fine welcome," he said.

"What's your business here?" David demanded.

"You've heard the shooting and seen the fires by now, Don David. Those are rebels from Taos who've attacked your village."

"But why?" Tomas asked.

The Mexican smiled grimly. "We of the north have risen in revolt against the Americans. We took Taos. The

American governor Bent is dead, as well as many other Americans and Mexican friends of theirs. Our orders are to destroy Rio Brioso and the *hacienda* here. I've come to warn you, Don David. Get out while you still have time. It's only a matter of minutes before they'll be up here to kill, loot, and burn."

"Why are you telling me this?" David asked.

Teodoro shrugged. "Don Quintin has always been fair with me. He gave me money when my mother was very ill. I have no cause against him."

"Then why burn the *hacienda?*"

"Those are the orders."

"Whose orders?"

"Don Bartolome de Vasquez gave those orders. He is one of the leaders of the revolt."

"What of my stepmother and my brother and sister?"

Teodoro smiled. "The orders were that they should not be harmed. After all, is not El Cerrillo rightfully his?"

"*Cabron!*" Tomas shouted.

Teodoro turned. "Watch your mouth, old man," he said coldly. "My offer of salvation does not include you."

"I could kill you right now, Teodoro," David warned.

Teodoro turned to face David. "What good would that do? There are many more rebels in the village. Go! Get out of here now! *Vamonos!*"

He was right. David led his pinto from the stable. He filled a sack with food from the *dispensa* and slung it over the saddle. Tomas gave him the blankets and grizzly hide from David's bed. David bound them into a roll and lashed them behind the saddle. He heard a thudding noise. Teodoro was kicking in a door in his search for loot before the others got there. David led the pony through the corral and out into the open. The sound of rapid hoofbeats thudded on the plank bridge spanning the river.

"*Vaya con Dios,* Don David!" Tomas cried as he closed the rear gate.

"*Vaya!*" David shouted.

He led the pony through the knee-deep snow. Men were riding up to the other side of the sprawling *hacienda*. He heard Tomas shouting angrily at them. There was one rifle shot and Tomas was silent.

By daylight thick smoke stained the clear sky. David

lay hidden on a reverse crest high on the steep slopes overlooking the Valley of the Rio Brioso. The *hacienda* was now a mass of flames, smoke, and soaring sparks. The village and sawmill were burning to the ground. The steady gunfire had ceased, although now and again a single shot punctuated the strange quiet that had enveloped the valley, as some last survivor's hiding place was discovered. Mounted men were rounding up the stock. A few people could be seen fleeing on foot to the south, probably to the Mora. There was little doubt in David's mind about what had happened to the rest of the people in the village. Little would soon remain of the once thriving grant except the eternal land itself.

Where to go? Santa Fe was well over a hundred miles away. Taos was about half that distance over the mountains. His first impulse had been to get to his father as soon as he could. But he wasn't sure where Quint was at this time. He must get to Taos. He had no other choice. He must be extremely wary until he got there, and even then he could not let down his guard. The rebels under the orders of Bartolomé might not harm El Cerrillo and the people there, particularly Guadalupe and the twins. After all, they were blood kin to Bartolomé. Such was not the case for David. His father and Bartolomé were enemies. Bartolomé would feel the same way about David.

David led the pony deeper into the timber. Every lesson taught him by his father and Luke would stand him in good stead now, *if* he remembered them well. "Above all—*survive!*" they had repeatedly admonished him. He would not forget.

<hr>

★ TWENTY-FIVE ★

Quint Kershaw knelt in two feet of snow on a scrub-forested ridge overlooking the valley of the frozen Santa Cruz. La Villa Nueva de Santa Cruz de los Espanoles Mexicanos del Rey Nuestro Senor Don Carlos Segundo lay huddled on the north side of the river, a cluster of drab adobe houses around a plaza dominated by the Spanish Mission. Quint adjusted the focus on his telescope. "The New Town of the Holy Cross of the Spanish Mexicans of the King Our Master Carlos Second," he said.

Jim Beckwourth wiped the frozen drip from his nose. "Damned name is longer than the damned village, Quint."

Quint shrugged. "Never heard anyone ever call it that, Jim. All I ever heard it called was La Canada, meaning a gulch, ravine, or simply The Land Between."

Jim grunted. "Fits it better, anyway. Wasn't there a fracas hereabouts in '37?"

Quint nodded. "Between the insurrectionists and federal troops in the Chimayo Rebellion. Federals got the shit kicked out of them."

The mission was a massive cruciform church surrounded by a high, strong-looking adobe wall. The Franciscan padres had built it over a hundred years ago. Its stark and simple exterior lines, lack of any windows, flat roof, and twin square-buttressed corner towers gave it the look of a fortress more than a place of worship. The padres had planned it as a place of defense in the days when the valley had been at the mercy of constant Navajo and Apache raids.

Quint studied the town. "If the rebels hole up in the town and mission, we'll have a hell of a time rooting them out."

"How much longer do yuh plan stayin' up here sightseein', Big Red?" Jim asked.

Quint shrugged. "Until I get an idea of how many rebels are in and around the town. Why?"

Jim pointed. "Look," he suggested.

Dark figures distinct against the snow moved about on the heights above the town. The faint sound of their voices carried on the north wind. There were hundreds of them.

"There are a lot more of them workin' around the foot of this ridge. Won't take long for them to get in behind us," Jim warned.

Quint grinned. "Ye worried, Jim lad?"

Jim shook his head. "I can cut my way through a hundred of them greasers and yellowskin Pueblos. It's you, Luke, and Jesus got me a mite worried, in case yuh can't protect yourselves. Well, Ol' Jim will take care of yuh." He cocked and capped his rifle.

Luke crawled up the slope through the deep snow, cursing softly as it worked its icy way up his sleeves and down his collar. "I figger mebbe four or five hunnert of them forted up in the village houses and the church, Big Red. Them church walls must be at least three feet thick."

Quint stood up close to a tree to get a better look down the steep slopes to his left. A complex of several adobe houses and outbuildings down there was surrounded by a strong corral, and an adobe wall enclosing a dense fruit orchard buried in drifted snow was on the level ground beside the road. Men moved about in the area. The flat sound of axe blows carried on the wind as loopholes were cut in the thick wooden shutters. Rifle fire from the position could cover the road from Santa Fe along which the troops were advancing.

The dry cracking sound like a splitting shingle came to Quint. Something struck the tree. Bits of bark stung his right cheek. Jim's rifle "Old Bullthrower" echoed the shot. A man stood up among some scrub trees far down the slope, whirled about, and pitched forward face down in the snow. He did not move.

Quint dropped to the ground. "Sonofabitch," he said as he wiped the blood from his cheek.

Jim grinned widely as he reloaded. "Anyway, yuh won't have a scar on that side like the one yuh got on the left. How'd yuh like that shot of mine?"

Quint shrugged. "Not bad."

"Three hundred yards," bragged the mulatto.

"Shit, Jim, yuh can't even *see* that far," Luke scoffed.

"Gawd dammit! Yuh want to bet?"

"Sure thing, but, yuh got to pace it off, sonny, afore I accept three hundred yards, and with witnesses to boot."

Jim looked at Quint. "Well?" he asked expectantly.

Quint yawned. "Ye figure that Pueblo, or Mexican, whatever the hell he was, God rest his murderous soul, damned near got *me*?"

Jim nodded. "That's so."

"Ye ever see any Pueblo or Mexican who could shoot

★ 284 ★

three hundred yards uphill in this light and *that* close to hitting a man's head?"

Jim looked at Luke, then at Quint, then back at Luke. "You damned whites are all against me. How far *would* yuh say it was, Big Red?"

Quint closed his telescope with a snap and started down the ridge to where Jesús Martinez held the horses. "About two hundred and ninety plus, Jim boy!" he shouted back.

"Yuh Scotch sonofabitch!" Jim yelled.

Quint looked back. "Scots," he corrected, then grinned and plunged through a drift toward his horse.

Luke and Jim slipped and floundered down the snowy slope. "Is he always like that, Luke?" Jim asked.

Luke nodded. "Usually when yuh least expect it."

Quint pulled the cork out of a black bottle of *aguardiente* with his teeth and handed the bottle to Jim. "What's your rebel count, Luke?" he asked.

"Mebbe a thousand in the hills. Might be four or five hundred in the town and the church, like I said."

Quint nodded. "Something like twelve hundred to fifteen hundred Mexicans and Pueblos combined. The rumors were not exaggerated."

Jim handed the bottle to Luke. "Odds of better than five to one."

Luke drank, wiped his mouth, and passed the bottle to Jesus. "And them holding the town and hills."

"Aye," Quint agreed quietly. "We've got no way of bypassing them, and anyway, we've got to take that town for shelter this night. We've got to beat them to get on to Taos. We can't leave them in our rear. Poor tactics. Could be disastrous. So, we've got to attack."

"Supposing *we* get beat?" Jim asked.

Quint drank and recorked the bottle. "Damned few of us, if any, will ever get back to Santa Fe," he replied.

They looked at each other out of the corners of their eyes.

A rifle cracked up on the ridge they had just vacated. The bottle was shattered, leaving just the neck in Quint's hand. "*Vamonos!*" he shouted.

Quint knelt in front of Colonel Price and his assembled officers sketching the enemy positions on the snow.

"They command the road into La Canada," he explained. "They've fortified three strong farm buildings across the river covering the road. They've occupied the hills overlooking that position and the town itself. I'd estimate about twelve hundred of them in the buildings and on the nearby hills. Maybe another thousand on the heights above the town. About four or five hundred in the town occupying the houses and the church. It will be one hell of a job rooting them out of the town, and even if we do, the riflemen in the hills can still cover the road north and fire down into La Canada like shooting fish in a barrel."

Colonel Price shrugged. "It's getting on in the day. We've got to get possession of the road north. It will be dusk most likely by the time we can get control of the town. By that time the rebels in the hills won't be able to see anything to shoot at. And we'll need shelter for the night in this bitter weather. I say we attack at once, carry the buildings across the river, and advance on the town to take it by assault." He looked about at his officers. "Any objections?" No one spoke. "Good," the colonel said, well pleased. "We'll advance infantry and the artillery by the left flank, cross the river on the ice, and take up artillery position within range of the fortified farm. If we can rout the enemy by artillery fire alone, we'll follow up with a determined infantry charge to drive them back on the town. Now, return to your commands, and God be with us this day!"

Company B, Missouri Light Artillery, crossed the river and went into battery. Captain Angney's Missouri Infantry battalion took cover along the riverbank behind the battery. The four stubby howitzers roared into action, driving back on their trails, blasting out flame and smoke. The hollow, booming reports echoed from the hills. During the short intervals between firing the pict-pict-pict of enemy bullets could be heard. The shells exploded over the hills or dug up showers of powder-blackened snow and frozen clods. Others smashed into the thick, absorbent adobe walls of the farm buildings with little effect. The rebels on the hills could see the smoking shells approaching and scattered out of harm's way. The artillery bombardment was a waste of ammunition.

Colonel Price lowered his binoculars. "It's no use. We'll have to take them by storm." He began shouting out his orders. The infantry units took up position for the attack.

"Colonel Price, sir," Ceran St. Vrain said. "You've forgotten my company."

The colonel nodded. "Get to the rear and escort the ammunition wagons up here as quick as you can. We're going to need that reserve ammunition before too long."

"Dammit, sir!" Ceran snapped. "We're *fighting* men!"

"Dammit, sir! I am in command here! Do as you're told!" Price roared.

Ceran turned his horse away from the angry colonel. "Follow me, boys!" he shouted. "We're to escort the baggage train!"

The rebels had begun working their way down the hillsides toward the slowly moving baggage train. They plowed on foot through drifted arroyos or slid down the slopes. A knot of horsemen appeared from around the base of a hill led by a sword-waving officer mounted on a magnificent bay.

"By God! They're after our wagons! Forward, men! Charge, damn you! *Charge!*" Ceran bellowed. He led the way pounding along the rutted road with snow flying up from under his horse's hoofs.

The teamsters halted their wagons, snatched up their rifles, and dropped to the ground to face the oncoming attack. Rifles cracked flatly. Little puffs of smoke drifted on the wind. Here and there rebels went down. The mounted men reached the last ammunition wagon. They killed the driver and began to lead the mules from the road toward the hill base. The mounted rebel officer knew his business. He ordered some of his men to dismount and take cover in a gully beside the road to hold back the charge of the mountain men. They immediately opened fire.

A bullet plucked at Quint's left sleeve. He fired his Hawken, thrust it into the saddle sheath, took the reins in his teeth, then drew out both Colts. He spurred directly toward the gully heedless of the gunfire from it. He fired the revolvers. A bullet flipped off his hat. Then he was in among the rebels, Colts crackling and flaming until they ran dry. Ten rounds left seven rebels dead or wounded. The mountaineers drove the enemy back up the hillside, shooting from the saddle while whooping and yelling like Comanches.

The attack was broken. The enemy clawed their way up the slippery slopes looking fearfully back over their shoulders at the shouting madmen who had defeated them, especially the giant *rubio,* the readhead who had been the heart and soul of the attack.

One rebel did not retreat. He was the mounted officer. He gripped his blood-wet sword and spurred toward Quint intent on running him through the back.

"Behind you, Quint!" Ceran yelled.

Quint turned his mount. He parried the sword with one of his smoking pistols. The blade rang on the gun barrel. Sparks flew. The horses crashed together. Quint forced back the sword, ducked low under a sweeping slash, and raised his Colt to smash it into the contorted face of the rebel. It was then he recognized him. "You!" he shouted.

The bay was drawn up into a hoof-pawing rear, then turned. The officer bent low in the saddle and looked back over his shoulder as he spurred away from certain death. "We'll meet again, Quintin Kershaw!" he cried.

Luke reined in his mount beside Quint. He raised his Hawken and aimed at the fleeing officer. He couldn't miss. Quint struck up the rifle just as Luke fired.

"Damn yuh!" Luke cursed. "I had him certain wolf bait!"

Quint shook his head. "Did ye see who it was?"

Luke shook his head. "They all look alike to me. Targets are all they mean to me. Weren't no Pueblo. Who was he?"

"Bartolome de Vasquez," Quint said quietly.

"Then why'd yuh make me miss?"

Bartolome was just disappearing around the base of the hill.

Quint shrugged. "He's brother to my wife," he said simply.

The infantry carried the fortified farm, then advanced up over the hills, dragging the howitzers with them. Ceran St. Vrain left some of his townies to guard the baggage train, then led the mountain men to flank the hill and get in behind the enemy being driven toward La Canada and the Valley of the Santa Cruz.

An enemy officer mounted on a white horse tried to rally his dispirited command. He lashed at them with his whip aided by Bartolome de Vasquez swinging his sword flat-bladed against the backs of the men. Slowly a line formed. Gunfire began to flash and smoke along it.

Ceran peered through Quint's telescope. "That's 'General' Jesus Tafoya on the white horse. The Santa Ana of the North, as he calls himself. Seems to be succeeding making his men stand." He looked sideways at Quint. "Can you hit him from here?"

The pale watery-looking sun was slanting low to the west. Long shadows darkened the slopes. It was that time of day when light was most deceptive. Quint lit a cigarette and threw it on the ground to check wind drift. Anselmo held Quint's horse steady. Quint rested "Auld Clootie" across the saddle. He had a 200-grain powder charge in it almost equal in grain weight to the ball. The rifle should fire flat or nearly level at 250 yards.

"As soon as he fires the rest of you open fire on his men. Don't matter if you don't get hits. The sound of hot Galena pills whining about their ears should make up their minds to skedaddle once Tafoya falls," Ceran said as he capped his rifle nipple.

Quint cocked the hammer, set the trigger, drew in a deep breath, let out about half of it, sighted fine and barely touched the trigger. Auld Clootie bellowed hoarsely and kicked backward solidly. Tafoya went over backward from the saddle, dead before he hit the ground. The mountaineers fired simultaneously. Rebels went down to lie still or thrashed on the ground. The remainder bolted at the second volley and retreated north up the Valley of the Santa Cruz with Bartolome de Vasquez galloping ahead of them.

The victory at La Canada was a cheap one. One officer and six enlisted men had been wounded. Two men had been killed. Forty-five rebel prisoners, both Pueblos and Mexicans, had been taken. The number of their wounded was unknown. Thirty-six of them, including their general, lay dead freezing solid on the field of battle.

The Americans marched north the morning of the twenty-fifth of January. The weather was freezing cold.

A road had to be broken open through the deep snow filling the arroyos and canyons. The farther north the march pushed the narrower the canyons became. A road was cut through trees, and boulders had to be pried from the frozen ground in order for the artillery and baggage train to go forward.

The force was augmented by a company of dragoons and one of Missouri Mounted Volunteers. They brought a 6-pounder field gun capable of firing solid shot with them. The command now consisted of 479 effectives and an artillery battery of four howitzers and the new field gun.

On February second the exhausted command struggled into the tiny mountain village of Rio Chiquito at the entrance to the Valley of Taos. That night Lieutenant Quint Kershaw was ordered to reconnoiter Taos preparatory to the advance of the army.

★ TWENTY-SIX ★

Taos was cold and silent. The streets were deserted. The stars sparkled like reflected crystal against the dark blue dome of the sky. Seven dark noiseless figures crept in from the outskirts separated at intervals and close to the walls. The air was so cold it hurt to breathe. Mustaches and beards were frozen. The metal of weapons could not be touched with bare hands.

Quint led the way, pausing at each intersection, then waving his men on as the way was clear. It was so deathly quiet he wondered if the town had been abandoned. Something dark like a man in ambush lay close beside a wall. Quint thrust up an arm to halt his patrol. He covered the dark object with his rifle as he moved closer. It was a corpse. Frozen blood darkened the snow about the body. It was naked, scalped, castrated, and horribly mutilated, and the eyes had been gouged out. Broken arrows remained stuck in the frozen flesh. The pigs and dogs had been at it, the final indignity.

Luke and Jim Beckwourth closed up behind Quint. "Anyone we know?" Luke asked dryly.

Moccasin came around a nearby corner. "There's another in a shed down the next street."

Jim spat to one side. "Blood thirsty bastards."

"No quarter," Luke said.

"What now?" Jim asked.

"Information. We'll go to Francois Charbonne's," Quint replied.

"If he's still alive," Jim said.

"Maybe he'll be all right," Quint suggested. "Everyone likes Boudins. Even the Pueblos."

Francois' restaurant and house seemed unharmed. A faint thread of smoke rose from the chimney. Quint tapped his rifle butt against the rear door. He waited, then tapped again.

"*Quien es?*" the hoarse voice said through the door.

Quint replied in Shoshoni. "Boudins! It's Quint Kershaw! Let us in before we freeze off our man-parts!" Who else in Taos but Francois, Luke, and Quint had any knowledge of Shoshoni?

The door creaked open. Francois let down the hammers of his double-barreled shotgun. "Were you followed?" he asked tensely. Quint shook his head as he entered the warm kitchen followed by his patrol, shivering, stamping their numbed feet, and rubbing chapped hands together.

Francois closed and barred the door. He placed a small oval keg of *aguardiente* on the chopping block. "You're safe enough here. At least until daylight. Ain't many rebels left in town, if any. When they got beat at La Canada and El Embudo they came back here. Most of the Mexicans skedaddled when they knew the war might be lost. Now they run around town telling everybody they don't fight against Americans, or else them Pueblos *made* them fight. Bullshit!"

Quint emptied his cup. He blinked hard as the high proof *aguardiente* hit him a low blow. "What about the Pueblos?" he asked hoarsely.

"They won't quit. They been fortifyin' their pueblo ever since they got back. They got a couple of Mex *ricos* advising them. Bartolome de Vasquez and Diego de las Casas."

Quint nodded. "They were at Santa Fe stirring up

revolt. De Vasquez fought at La Canada. I didn't see de las Casas though."

"He was there all right."

"Yuh seen that sonofabitch Kiowa around?" Luke asked.

"He came here with de Vasquez," Francois said.

"Where is he now?" Quint asked quickly.

Francois shrugged. "Who knows? Maybe at the pueblo. He ain't in Taos as far as I know. How soon will the American soldiers get here?"

Quint drank again. "As soon as the way is clear. We'll have to scout the pueblo tonight. I'll send a courier back to Colonel Price before we leave." He turned to Joshua. "Get some traveling grub. Head back to the army. Tell Colonel Price it's safe to enter Taos. I'm going to scout the pueblo tonight, but we should be back here when the soldiers arrive." He looked at Jesus. "Take a look-see up at El Cerrillo to see if everything is all right. I don't want the enemy to see you up there. Report back here as soon as you can."

The huge Taos Pueblo was three miles to the north. The moon was rising when Quint's patrol concealed themselves on a rise overlooking the community. It consisted of two massive, irregular, truncated pyramids, multistoried communal living blocks located on either side of the frozen Taos River. The brownish-red adobe structures were very old, made of the red earth of the valley tempered with straw and pebbles. They had existed long before the coming of the Spaniards. Rising above the base structures were terraced stories. For security purposes there were doors or windows on the ground floor. Ladders were used for ascending to upper floors. They could be drawn up to deny the use of them to anyone not wanted. The tall-towered seventeenth-century church was at the extreme northwest corner of the community. Its walls were five to six feet thick. A bridge of enormous logs spanned the river between the two communal blocks. The blocks were connected by stout timber and adobe walls except where the river intercepted them. At those two places defensive towers had been built. To reduce the stronghold by siege would have been a painfully slow process, costly in casualties. The place was always well stocked with food and there was plenty of water from the river.

The moonlight was almost as bright as day. It etched sharp shadows on the snow-covered ground as though they had been cut from black paper. Thin smoke rose from the many chimney pots and formed a layered haze in the windless air. Blanketed figures bearing rifles stood guard on the towers and stockade walks. New loopholes could be seen dotting the outer walls of the church.

"Someone comes," Moccasin hissed.

They scattered into cover. Rifle hammers clicked back.

"Jesus, he's a big one," Luke whispered.

The lone figure moved ponderously but comparatively noiselessly toward the hidden scouts.

"He's wearin' a hat," Luke said. "Mebbe a white man or Mexkin."

The big man stopped and looked about. "Gawd dammit, Big Red," he drawled. "I seen yuh come up here. Where the hell are yuh? It's Ol' Dick Wooton, come here from Pueblo."

"I'll be damned," Quint said, low-voiced. "Get into cover, Dick. Ye make a wonderful target in this moonlight."

"Hellsfire," Dick whispered hoarsely. "I knew you'd never mistake this sizeable chile for no Pueblo or Mexkin. Say, I run into one of your lads who told me yuh was headin' to this pueblo."

"Jesus?"

"That war his name. He was goin' to El Cerrillo."

"What are you doing here, Dick?" Jim asked.

"Heard about the revolt. Come from Pueblo with a few mountain men to help out if we could. We been hidin' in the hills waitin' for the soldiers to come. They comin'?"

Quint nodded. "Should be here tomorrow."

Richens Lacey Wooton was a Virginia giant two hundred and fifty pounds on the hoof. He was an expert rifleman, trailer, remarkable horseman, and a pathbreaker of the first rank. Eight years past he and a party of trappers had traveled from Bent's Fort on the Arkansas following the river to its source, thence north to the Yellowstone. After that they had traced the Snake and Salmon Rivers to the Columbia, thence down the Pacific

Coast to California. They had returned to the Arkansas by way of Arizona, Utah, and Colorado.

"Can I sign up for the fightin' now?" Dick asked.

Quint nodded. "You're in."

Dick raised his eyebrows. "That a fact? How so?"

Luke grinned. "You're addressin' Lootenant Kershaw, Dick, commandin' officer of Kershaw's Company of New Mexico Volunteer Mounted Rifles."

Dick looked about at the five of them. "This the *company?*" he asked thoughtfully.

Luke nodded. "Waal, actually we're temporarily part of Captain St. Vrain's Santa Fe Company of mountain men and some townies. Big Red here is scoutin' officer."

Dick slowly shook his head. "I've seen the elephant now," he said slowly. He grinned. "When do I get my uniform?"

"You're wearing it," Quint said dryly. "Hold up your right hand and I'll swear ye in."

Moccasin moved off through the brush, then came quickly back. "Pueblo patrol headin' this way," he warned.

By the time the patrol reached the foot of the rise, there was no sign of the scouts. Dick had returned to his hideout to get his companions. Quint and his men returned to Francois' house and a good meal laced with plenty of *aguardiente.* Jesus had not yet returned from El Cerrillo.

★ TWENTY-SEVEN ★

FEBRUARY 1847. TAOS PUEBLO.

The American forces entered Taos at midday. Captain St. Vrain's mountaineers led the way riding loose and easy in their saddles, frost on beards and mustaches, rifles across saddlebows or butts resting on hips, looking coldly at the few Mexicans along the march route. The foot troops slogged wearily along muffled in heavy clothing showing signs of the wear and tear of a winter campaign. One thing was quite obvious to the onlookers—the weapons of the Americans were clean and bright, ready for instant use.

Colonel Price wasted no time. A way was broken through the drifted snow for the artillery to be double-teamed and drawn into position threatening the pueblo three miles north of town. The colonel selected the church at the northwest corner of the complex as the point of attack. Originally the church walls facing outward had been devoid of windows, but now irregularly shaped loopholes dotted the thick adobe. The guns opened fire. The two-and-a-half-hour bombardment had little effect on the church. The ammunition wagons did not come up. The troops were almost exhausted from their long march and suffering from the intense cold. The attack was called off and the command returned to Taos for shelter. Snow fell heavily that bitter night.

At dawn the next day a way was cleared through the fresh snow. St Vrain's company stood easy at the heads of their horses waiting for orders. Gunfire was flashing and smoking from the stockade and church loopholes. Spent bullets hissed past or plopped into the snow.

Ceran turned to look at Quint. "Any sign yet of Martinez?"

Quint shook his head. He looked easterly toward the hill slopes where El Cerrillo stood some miles off. Its brownish-red adobe walls showed in irregular patches through the somber green and black of the surrounding trees.

"I'd be willing to let you scout over that way, Quint," Ceran said, "but we'll be needing you here. Colonel Price has asked for you to serve as an aide. Take Luke along as your orderly."

Quint nodded. He looked again toward El Cerrillo as he mounted. It wasn't like Jesus to be derelict in his duty.

The artillery roared into action. The bombardment like the day before had little effect. The firing ceased after two hours. Colonel Price ordered in the infantry. Captain Burgwin's Company G of the First Dragoons and Company D of the Second Missouri were to charge the west flank church wall. Angney's infantry battalion and two companies of the Second Missouri were to charge the north wall. Sharp orders rang out. The infantry fixed bayonets and extended into attack formation.

"Colonel Price, sir," Quint said. "I'd like to volunteer to go with Captain Burgwin's company."

Price nodded. "He'll need all the fighting men he can get. Take command of the support party. They've fabricated a storming ladder with which to reach the church roof. I want the roof set ablaze. Good luck."

The bugles blew The Charge. The hoarse sound of cheering rose from the infantry as they surged forward. Bullets sleeted over the heads of Burgwin's storming party, but they made it to the west wall. They crouched closed to the wall. Rifles flashed from the loopholes just above their heads, but they could not be depressed enough to sight on them. Quint led the support party to the wall. They raised the ladder and planted it against the church. Captain Burgwin led his men to the front of the church. Fire from the west side loopholes slackened as the defenders rushed to the front door of the church to hold it against attack.

"Light your torch," Quint ordered a dragoon.

Quint slung his Hawken and started up the shaky ladder followed closely by the dragoon with the flaming torch and Luke. Quint was almost to the top when a rifle was fired from the nearby defensive tower. The dragoon fell backward. Luke swung to one side to let him fall but managed to wrest the torch from his hand. The falling dragoon carried the rest of the men on the ladder to the ground with him. Luke passed the torch up to Quint. Quint rolled over the parapet with the torch in one hand and a cocked Colt in the other. There was no one on the roof.

There was a pile of snow-covered lumber close by. Quint kicked it apart to get at the dry wood underneath. He poured powder from his horn on the drier wood then applied the torch to it just as a burly Pueblo rose up from a trapdoor at the north end of the roof. Luke's Hawken cracked. The Pueblo went back down like a jack-in-the-box. The powder flashed and flared. The fire began to lick at the wood. Quint poked the torch in between two boards and poured more powder over it. He snatched the torch back as the fire started and ran to a roof vent covered by slats. Luke clubbed another Pueblo down inside the trap opening. Quint smashed in the slats and dropped the torch through the opening. He snatched up a burning board and ran to the trapdoor. He dropped the board down the hole. Luke slammed the door down and stood on it. Smoke began to swirl up from the vent. Smoke began to seep around the edges of the trapdoor.

"*Vamonos!*" Quint yelled. He slung his Hawken and sprinted after Luke to the ladder. Luke started down. Someone yelled behind Quint. He turned. The trapdoor had been flung up emitting a gush of smoke. A Pueblo came through the smoke aiming a double-barreled shotgun at Quint. Quint fired one of his Colts twice. The Pueblo dropped half in and out of the trapdoor.

Quint followed Luke down the swaying, creaking ladder. They hit the ground running with bullets hissing past and overhead. They rounded the front of the church. Some of the attackers were in the corral giving covering fire to the group led by Captain Burgwin and Lieutenant McIlvaine who were battering at the thick door of the church with a heavy timber.

The front of the church was thickly shrouded in powdersmoke. Guns flashed and cracked without pause. The ram thudded against the ponderous bolt-studded doors echoing thunderously within the church. Captain Burgwin was shot twice. He staggered back into Quint's arms. "I'm done for, Kershaw," he gasped. "This is hopeless. Get my men out of here while they still live." Quint raised him across his shoulders and ran crouched away from the church. The storming party gave him cover as they retreated.

The church roof was aflame. A towering cloud of dense smoke mingled with flickering flames and huge soaring sparks rose high in the air. There was no cessation of gunfire. The dragoons hacked at the adobe walls with axes. They thrust 12-pounder shells with three-second fuses into the church. They exploded with muffled roars among the closely packed defenders creating bloody havoc.

The 6-pounder gun opened up fire at two hundred yards raking the interior of the pueblo compound with grapeshot. The Pueblos fought back furiously. The soldiers were driven back time after time. At last they fell back, powder-blackened and sweating profusely despite the cold.

Quint and Luke prowled about the smoke-shrouded battlefield hunting for Kiowa, Bartolome, and Diego. They were nowhere to be found. "They've hauled tail, Big Red," Luke insisted. "They know the Pueblos can't win."

Quint nodded. "Go join Ceran. I'll have to report back to Colonel Price. Get moving!"

Luke trotted off through the smoke.

"Wandering Wolf!" Quint shouted.

Luke turned.

"Watch out for that skinny ass of yours!" Quint yelled.

They grinned at each other.

At half-past three the 6-pounder gun was run up within sixty yards of the church. Careful aim was taken at one of the axe holes. Ten rounds of solid shot followed by three rounds of grape slammed in through the hole. Dick Green, Charles Bent's devoted black servant of many years, was first in through the gap laying about himself with his clubbed rifle.

Quint entered the church. The burning roof was sagging. Bodies littered the interior. The reek of blood, burning wood, and acrid powdersmoke hung thickly throughout the building. The shrieks and screams of the dying and wounded mingled with the hoarse shouts of the dragoons and still defiant Pueblos, the crackling of gunfire, and roaring flames.

Quint could not find his enemies within the church. He began to drag wounded out of it. Just as the last of the wounded were removed by some of the dragoons, the north end of the roof collapsed sending up a huge cloud of gas, smoke, and sparks that soared high into the air. The surviving Pueblos took shelter within the two communal buildings. Others fled panic-stricken over the east wall in an attempt to reach the mountains. They didn't know Colonel Price had sent St. Vrain's mountaineers and Slack's company of Missourians there to cut off any retreat.

Quint mounted his horse, and leading Luke's horse he galloped across the compound through fleeing Pueblos who made no effort to shoot at him or stop him. He rode through the east gateway. A big warrior limped out from behind a shed and raised his rifle. Quint reined in and thrust out one of his cocked Colts. Neither man fired. Rifle and pistol were lowered.

"Big Red," the warrior said quietly.

Quint nodded. "Black Beaver."

Blood from a scalp wound trickled down the Delaware's powder-grimed face. His right legging was stained dark red. He deliberately turned his back and limped off.

"Ye haven't a chance!" Quint called.

Beaver looked back over his shoulder. "I have if I reach mountain. They never catch me there."

Quint shook his head. "Listen!"

Rifle fire crackled to the north and east.

"There's a company of mountain men waiting for ye," Quint said.

Beaver turned slowly. "I'll die fightin' before I let them take me, Big Red. They'll try to kill me on sight."

Quint held out the reins of Luke's sorrel. "Take him! Get the hell out of here! *Vamonos!*"

The Delaware mounted. "I won't forget," he promised.

"Get moving, damn ye!" Quint shouted.

Beaver rode fast to the north.

"Never come back!" Quint warned.

The mountaineers were intent on grim vengeance for the death of Charles Bent and other slain Americans and friendly Mexicans. This was their type of warfare; Indian-fighting where no mercy was ever shown or quarter given. They rode down the fleeing Pueblos, shooting, clubbing, and scalping.

Quint found Luke pulling a bloody scalp through his belt. "Where the hell is my sorrel, Big Red?" Luke asked.

Quint was leading a stray bay he had found. He held out the reins to Luke. " A Pueblo gave me fifty pesos for him. Here, take the bay."

Luke mounted. "Yuh sure he wasn't a Delaware?"

"Come to think of it he was."

Luke nodded. "I thought that was him on my sorrel. Think he'll make it?"

Quint shrugged. "He's got a good chance."

They rode toward Ceran and Dick Wooton.

Luke looked sideways. "Where's the fifty pesos?"

"He said he'd mail it."

They grinned at each other.

Those Pueblos who had not been killed in the fields had escaped to the shelter of the mountains and the shadows of late afternoon. No prisoners had been taken.

"How many casualties, Ceran?" Quint asked.

Ceran finished knotting a bandage about his left wrist. He tightened it with his teeth. "None, Big Red."

"The enemy?"

"I counted an even fifty a little while ago," Dick said. A rifle flatted off in the shadows. "Fifty-one," he corrected himself. He grinned.

The shooting had died away at the pueblo.

"I'll report to the colonel," Quint said.

They rode back to where Colonel Price was listening to the butcher's bill report of one of his aides.

"Is the battle over, sir?" Quint asked.

Price shook his head. "For today, at any rate. It's getting too dark. The remaining Pueblos are holed up in their buildings. They've been badly beaten. The spirit is out of them. I'll attack by daylight if they don't surrender. However, I believe they will give up. They haven't a chance of stopping our attack."

The muffled and eerie sound of wailing came from the darkened buildings.

"Counting their dead," Luke said quietly.

"What are our losses, sir?" Quint asked.

"Seven killed and about forty-five wounded. Captain Burgwin has been mortally wounded, I fear. Some of the other wounded will probably die. We've bagged quite a few prisoners. One of them is their Chief Tomasito. He was wearing one of Governor Bent's shirts when we captured him."

"What are my orders, colonel?" Quint asked.

"We've found no trace of two Mexicans said to have been leaders in this revolt. Bartolome de Vasquez and Captain Diego de las Casas. De Vasquez is your brother-in-law, is he not?"

Quint nodded. "And de las Casas is his cousin."

"I *want* those men," Price said grimly. "Hunt them down, lieutenant."

Luke checked the caps on his pistol. "Dead or alive, sir?"

"Either way. Alive if possible, but alive or dead I *want* them!"

Price watched them ride off into the thickening shadows. "God help de Vasquez and de las Casas," he said quietly to himself.

Darkness enveloped the land.

★ TWENTY-EIGHT ★

El Cerrillo de Vasquez was in darkness. Not a light showed. Quint and Luke tethered their horses in a draw north of the *hacienda* and then moved across the frozen fields to the outer limits of the thick *bosque* mantling the north slope of the flat-topped hill upon which El Cerrillo had been built. The premoon darkness was windless. The only sound was that of moccasin soles squeaking faintly on the crisp snow.

A man lay face down beside the frozen *acequia madre*. Quint hooked a foot under him and threw him over on his back, stiffened arms outflung. The corpse was frozen solid. Quint looked closely at the contorted blue face. "Jesus Martinez," he said. "Throat cut from ear to ear. He's been dead a couple of days, before the Pueblo fight."

They circled around the *hacienda* to the farthest outbuildings on the south side. Another body lay face down beside a big shed used to store hay. The haft of a knife stuck out between his shoulder blades. Luke rolled him over. "Yuh know this one?" he whispered.

"Tomas Valdez, one of the field workers. A born rebel."

The moon was rising. Luke pulled open the shed door to get under cover. The faint and ominous click of a rifle hammer being full cocked came from the dark interior. Quint and Luke darted sideways to opposite sides of the door.

"Is that you, father?" a small boy's voice quavered.

"Davie, lad!" Quint cried. "Is it ye indeed?"

David came to the door, Hawken at the alert. When he

saw his father he gripped him about his waist, but still clung to his rifle. His body shook uncontrollably.

"Yuh alone, Davie?" Luke asked.

The boy shook his head. "Rafaela and Francisco are hidden behind the hay."

Quint picked up Davie and carried him into the shed. Luke came in and closed the door behind himself. "Rafaela? Francisco?" Quint called. "Ye can come out. It's your father."

Two little figures clambered over the hay and raced to Quint. He stood there smiling uncomfortably, not at all sure he was in his right senses. He set the three of them on hay bales. "Now," he said firmly, "just what the hell are ye all doing here? Why are ye not at Rio Brioso? Davie?"

David looked up. "There *is* no Rio Brioso settlement or Kershaw's Fort anymore," he said quietly.

"You mean *hacienda*," Francisco corrected.

"I mean Kershaw's Fort," David insisted. "The Goddamned greaser rebels came there and killed a lot of our people and set fire to the settlement, the sawmill, and the fort."

"What of your mother?" Quint asked, fearful of the answer.

David looked strangely at his father. He slowly shook his head. "Mother took Rafaela and Francisco from there last October. Didn't you know?"

"David refused to come here with us," Francisco said. "He stayed at the Rio Brioso."

It was very quiet in the shed. Faint rays of moonlight probed through cracks in the east wall.

Quint found his voice at last. "Where is your mother?" he asked quietly. An awful realization had begun to creep through his mind.

"She's still in the *hacienda*," Rafaela piped.

Francisco nodded. "We didn't want to leave her, but Cristina made us go with David. We just got out of there before Uncle Bartolome and Cousin Diego came there this afternoon with some other men."

"But why? Why?" Quint asked, almost as though to himself. "I wrote to your mother last September before I left for the Navajo country. Were you still at Rio Brioso then?"

Rafalea nodded. "Yes, but she never got a letter from you."

Luke looked down at David. "And you came across the mountains to El Cerrillo after the rebels attacked Rio Brioso?"

David nodded solemnly. "There was nothing I could do there to help. I just got here a couple of days ago. I found the body of Jesus Martinez fresh killed near the *acequia madre*. I was afraid to go near the house. I hid in the outbuildings. The servants and field hands killed Federico Casias and ran away. Cristina came out to get some stores. She found me. Bartolome, Diego, and their men were coming up the hill then. She got the twins out of the house and put me in charge of them."

"I wanted to stay and fight the rebels," Francisco said bravely.

"I wanted Cristina to come with us," David continued. "She said mother was all alone and she couldn't leave her."

"Why?" Quint asked quietly.

Rafaela spoke up, "Because mother has been very ill, father. She has been since we came back to El Cerrillo."

Quint looked from one to the other of them. "Why wasn't I told?" he demanded.

Rafaela shrugged. "Because we didn't know where you were."

Quint could say nothing to that.

"Who killed Tomas Valdez?" Luke asked.

Rafaela looked at David. "He did."

David looked up. "Tomas found us here. He took my pistol and Hawken. He was drunk. He said he was going to rape mother and Cristina, loot the *hacienda*, then join the rebels, taking Cristina with him as his woman."

"Tomas turned his back on David when he left with the rifle," Rafaela said proudly. "Tomas forgot David still had his Green River knife."

David quickly wiped his nose both ways. "I should have pulled it out of him when I killed him. It was stuck between his ribs and he was beginning to freeze."

Quint and Luke looked at each other over the boy's head.

"I remembered everything you and Uncle Luke taught me, father," David said gravely.

"Are Uncle Bartolome, Cousin Diego, and those other men still in the *hacienda?*" Quint asked.

David nodded. "I watched them saddle fresh horses in the big stable and load them with filled saddlebags. They also were going to take an extra horse each. They figured on riding over Palo Flechado Pass, then across the mountains to Rio Brioso to head south toward the Pecos River and avoid the American soldiers, then to Chihuahua to join the Mexican army."

"How do you know that?" Quint asked.

David shrugged. "I sneaked up on the stable and listened. I thought first of running off the horses, but then I figured it might be better to let them get the hell out of here for good."

"How many of them are there?" Luke asked.

"Counting Uncle Bartolome and Cousin Diego, maybe eight or nine," David replied.

"Ye see a mixed breed with them? A dark-complected man, a sure-enough rough-face, with but one good eye?" Quint asked.

"I'm not sure, father. I wasn't that close to any of them."

Quint rubbed his jaw. "They were probably waiting for moonrise to see their way clear to the pass. If so, they won't be long in setting out. David, stay here and guard the twins. Luke, let's see what we can do about those nice fresh horses."

They moved through the shadows to the stable. Eight saddled and saddlebagged horses were in the stalls, and eight others had been fitted with long lead ropes.

They untethered the saddled horses. Luke led four of them toward the stable door. A gun spat flame and smoke. Luke spun about, released the horses, and went down on one knee. "Broke my God-damned right arm, Big Red," he grunted.

The released horses stampeded through the door bowling aside a man who stood there with smoking pistol in hand. Quint fired a Colt over Luke's head. Boots thudded on the frozen ground. Quint ran to the door in time to see several men round the *hacienda* near its rear entrance. A door banged shut.

David came running, rifle at the ready. "Get Luke out

of here, Davie," Quint ordered. "Bandage his wound. Ye all right, Lukie?"

Luke gripped his right arm. His lean face was taut with pain. "Bullet broke the bone and then passed on out. I'll be all right. Tie me up, Big Red, and I'll still go with yuh."

Quint shook his head. He handed one of his Colts to David. "Luke can use this if he has to. Get out of here! *Vamonos!*"

When Luke and David were gone, Quint released the rest of the horses and drove them from the stable. They stampeded toward the open fields to join the others. Quint rounded the stable on the far side from the *hacienda*. He bent low and darted across to another outbuilding. A rifle cracked from the *hacienda*. The slug smacked into the outbuilding. Quint hit the dirt and bellied under a *carreta*. He peered around one of the big, thick wheels. A gun flashed from a loophole. The bullet hummed past the *carreta*. They were shooting blind. Quint grinned. Evidently they didn't know only one man was besieging them.

Quint crawled to a nearby *acequia* and rolled down into it, lying flat on the frozen surface. It led past the rear of the *hacienda*. He worked his way there toward the east wall which was the rear of the original old corral, long since converted into domestic servants' quarters and storerooms. Quint darted across the intervening space, leaped upward to catch hold of one of the projecting roof drains, swung a long leg up and over the parapet, reached up to hook an arm, then pulled himself over onto the snow-covered roof.

Wispy smoke drifted up from some of the chimney pots studding the big complex of interjoined rooms and hallways broken up by half a dozen inner courtyards from which protruded tall, leafless trees. A door banged in the servants' courtyard. A man came staggering out of a storeroom with a bottle in his hand. He stopped in the center of the courtyard and raised the bottle to his lips. All he heard an instant before he died was a thudding noise just behind him as Quint's feet struck the ground, followed by the powerful thrust of a bowie knife between his ribs and into his heart. Quint caught the dead man before he hit the ground. He dragged him into the storeroom and dumped him into a half-empty corn bin. Quint drank from the bottle, then replaced it on a shelf.

A half-drunken Pueblo sat at the kitchen table by the light of one flickering candle, greedily stuffing food into his mouth. His mouth was still full when he died where he sat. He ended up in another storeroom bin.

Quint passed like a ghost through one of the long passageways between two patios. The door at the far end suddenly banged open. Quint saw the dark silhouette of a man. *"Quien es?"* the man challenged. That was his mistake. He should have shot first and challenged later. Quint fired his Colt at hip level a fraction of a second before his opponent's pistol cracked. The passageway filled with powdersmoke. The man went down. His pistol bullet smashed into the cylinder of the Colt, driving it from Quint's stinging hand. Men shouted in the patio beyond the dead man. Quint snatched up his Colt, retreated through the passageway, and ascended a courtyard ladder leading to the roof. He had just rolled over the parapet when two men plunged into the courtyard.

Diego de las Casas shouted, "How the hell did he get in?"

Bartolome de Vasquez shook his head. "Damned if I know! We'll have to find him. Where's Kiowa?"

Diego shrugged. "Prowling around trying to find that servant girl, I suppose. That's all that breed bastard ever has on his mind."

Quint peered quickly over the parapet. Diego was in his full uniform of captain commanding the Santa Fe Company of Active Militia Cavalry, long brass-hilted sword and all. The sonofabitch probably figured the uniform would save him from the hangman's noose if he was captured by the Americans.

"We'd better make a break for it, Bartolome," Diego said.

"The horses have been stampeded! There may be more Americans out there waiting for us to make our break!"

"Better that we try to reach the horses than to get caught in here like rats in a trap! It's only a matter of time before more Americans will get here!"

Bartolome passed a hand across his eyes. "Perhaps you're right, Diego. But I must see Guadalupe once more."

"Forget her! It's our lives that are at stake! If we don't get over Palo Flechado Pass before moonset, we might never be able to make it!"

Bartolome shook his head. "I can't leave her like that, Diego. Before God, cousin, do you think I want that on my soul?"

Diego shrugged. "I'll round up the men and send some of them out to draw the American fire. If there is too much of it, you and I can leave through the rear of the house. But, for God's sake, cousin, don't be too long in your leave-taking!"

They hurried from the courtyard, Diego shouting for his men.

Quint checked his Colt. It was useless. The big, soft lead slug had firmly implanted itself where the axis of the cylinder turned within the frame. There was no time to free it. He ran across the rooftops to the main patio adjacent to the main *sala* and the master bedroom. The fountain did not play. The pool was frozen over. Dead leaves and packed snow covered the flagstones. Quint hung by the eaves of a *portale* and dropped lightly into the patio. He ran toward the door to the master bedroom. Two men burst into the patio. Quint looked back.

"Yanqui bastard!" Diego cried dramatically. He whipped out his saber, glittering in the moonlight. Quint cast the heavy bowie knife. It struck the throat of the man with Diego. He fell in front of Diego. Diego stumbled over the body. It gave Quint just enough time to kick open the *sala* door, whirl, and slam it shut. The door bar was missing. Quint ran to the front door and removed the bar from it. He turned just as Diego came through the patio doorway, saber in one hand, single-shot pistol in the other. Quint hurled the bar at him. He fended it off with his saber, giving Quint just enough time to reach the wall where Don Rodrigo's ledendary Toledo sword hung. He ripped it from the suspension hooks and whirled to face Diego.

Diego smiled slowly. "Before God! I've prayed for a chance like this!" He was a skilled swordsman, well taught by Orlando Esquivel, master-at-arms of the Military Academy in Mexico City. Esquivel had rated him one of his best pupils.

Diego closed, tapping Quint's blade with his, feeling

for weakness or an insecure grip. He was disappointed. He withdrew a little to try a new tactic. That was a mistake. Quint closed impetuously, striking, slashing, thrusting like a Viking berserker heedless of his own life. Diego retreated, parrying desperately, his right hand stinging from the powerful blows against his blade.

They circled, Diego working his way to the other side of the table in the center of the *sala*. Quint risked snatching up the patio door bar and dropping it into the supports to hold back Diego's men. It was almost a fatal mistake. Diego closed. His blade flicked out a little too soon and nicked Quint's left shoulder, hardly penetrating the thick elkskin jacket and wool shirt, but drawing blood. Quint felt it running hotly down his chest and belly to his crotch.

They met each other beyond the table battering away without science in their lust to kill quickly. The *sala* rang with the clashing of the metal. At last Diego staggered back clasping the left side of his face with his hand. Blood leaked between his fingers.

Quint grinned. "Now you've a scar to match mine, *cobarde!*"

Diego threw caution aside. He leaped into the attack, driving Quint back, ever back with the sheer ferocity of his skilled swordsmanship. Quint circled behind the heavy table. He couldn't stand much more of this. Diego was too good for him. There wasn't much time left. Diego would have to die soon. Diego lunged and thrust across the table. Quint sidestepped and slammed his sword down atop Diego's pinning it to the tabletop. He leaned far across the table and slammed a big freckled fist against Diego's finely chiseled patrician nose just as the Mexican pulled his single-shot pistol from his belt. Diego staggered back in agony, blood pouring from his smashed nose.

"*Loch Moy! Loch Moy! A MacIntosh! A MacIntosh!*" Quint shouted as he came around the side of the table. He smashed Diego's sword from his grip, slashed sideways to strike the pistol from his hand, then lunged with all his power, driving the tip of his sword through Diego's taut throat, pinning him back against the outer door. Diego rolled his eyes upwards and died, hanging limply from the sword. Quint withdrew his blade. Diego collapsed to the floor.

Quint stepped back. He wiped the sweat from his face. "Ye damned fool," he said softly. "Ye should have shot me when ye had the chance."

A man shouted from the patio. Quint picked up Diego's pistol, blew out the candles, slid the patio door bar off its supports, and then flattened his back against the wall.

The door was pushed open. A man thrust in his head. "Don Diego?" he said. He waited, then cautiously entered the *sala*. He died with six inches of steel in his back.

Quint walked into the moonlit patio. Faint light showed under the master bedroom door and that of the chapel. He eased open the bedroom door. A single candle guttered on a table beside the bed. A small figure lay under the heavy bed coverlets. The door to the chapel was closed, showing only a faint line of light under it. Quint catfooted to the door. He placed an ear against it. Someone was praying loudly within the chapel.

Quint walked to the bed. "Lupita," he said softly. "It's Quint." He hardly recognized her, so white of face and emaciated was she.

She opened her eyes. "Somehow I knew I would see you before I died, my heart," she murmured weakly. "Take care of the child as you always did the others. It is all I can leave you now, husband—the children and my great love for you."

He dropped the blood reddened sword on the floor and cupped his hands about her face. "Before God!" he cried. "Why didn't you let me know?"

She smiled a little and reached out a thin, cold hand to touch his scarred face. "You were doing that which you always loved best, my soul. I never could hold you. For that I am sorry." She closed her eyes.

The chapel door opened. Quint turned, pistol in hand. Bartolome held up his empty hands and shook his head. "She hasn't long to live, Quintin," he said quietly. "I think she would like to know we are no longer enemies."

Quint looked down at her. "But why?" he asked brokenly.

"Has she told you of the child?"

"I was not sure what she meant."

"She gave birth to a premature daughter several days ago. It was too much for her."

"Where is the child now?" Quint asked quickly.

"Cristina has her hidden," Guadalupe said weakly. "I didn't want anything to happen to her."

A man called out from the patio. "Don Diego? Don Bartolome? There are no Americans outside the *hacienda!* The moon is up! The way is clear, but we must leave now!"

Bartolome looked at the bloodstained sword. "Diego?" he asked quietly.

Quint nodded.

Bartolome studied Quint. "You know of the legend about that sword?"

"Yes. It is said that as long as it hangs on the wall of the *sala* in the great *hacienda* of de Vasquez the family and *hacienda* will survive. But if it is taken down to fight for the family, the direct line of de Vasquez will die out eventually as a girdled tree must surely die out in time, and El Cerrillo de Vasquez will no longer exist."

"Do you believe it?"

Quint shrugged. "Who knows?"

"I do," Bartolome said simply. "I am the last of the direct line." He bent over his sister. "Forgive me," he murmured. He kissed her then turned to Quint and held out his hand.

There was a deathly coldness within Quint. The burning killing urge had been replaced by an implacable desire to thrust the blade hard and sure into the body of this man he hated.

Guadalupe raised her head a little. "Forgive him, beloved," she whispered.

Quint turned his back on Bartolome and threw the sword into the fireplace. A moment later the door closed behind Bartolome.

"Quint, my husband," Guadalupe murmured.

He turned. "Yes?"

"Name her Guadalupe after me."

"I will," he promised.

Minutes ticked past. He sat down on the bed and drew her close, barely feeling her irregular breathing. Then she was gone forever. He kissed her cold lips, tasting the salt from his tears. He wiped them from his eyes and gently drew the coverlet up over her drawn face.

Kiowa! The hated name drove through Quint's mind like the thrust of a Comanche lance. He snatched up the sword and ran to the patio door, pulling it open. A strong, cold draft poured into the room. He glanced at the shrouded form on the bed then closed the door behind himself. The draft overturned the single candle onto Guadalupe's sewing materials covering the tabletop. Thread and yarn caught fire first, spreading quickly to bits and pieces of material. Flaming pieces fell to the floor atop the thick woolen carpeting. Others landed within a basket of sewing materials beside a tall chest of drawers. The basket soon flared up. A thin tongue of flame licked greedily up the oiled surface of the highly polished wood. The fire began to burn through the carpeting. A flicker of flame touched the corner of a thin coverlet hanging down from the bed.

Quint looked quickly about the patio.

"Drop the sword, Kershaw," Kiowa ordered from under the *portale* on the opposite side of the patio. Moonlight glistened on the barrel of his pistol. He gripped Cristina's wrist with his other hand.

"Run, Don Quintin!" Cristina screamed.

Kiowa struck his pistol barrel alongside her head, driving her down on her knees. He kicked her to one side. "Drop the God-damned sword!" he roared.

The sword rang on the snow-covered flagstones.

"Throw me that belt pistol! Careful now!" Kiowa ordered.

Quint tossed the pistol. Kiowa caught it deftly. He covered Quint with it. "Before yuh die, you sonofabitch," he said low-voiced, "I'm going to put out your eyes in payment for what you did to me at Cañon Chacuaco."

Quint nodded. "*Bueno!* But you'll have to come closer, ye breed bastard. Ye can't put out an eye with a pistol bullet without killing me as well."

Kiowa moved out into the moonlight. "Yuh always been huntin' me, Kershaw. Now yuh found me." He grinned. "Not quite the way yuh expected." He moved a little closer, while raising one of the pistols. "Mebbe I can bark your skull from here so's I can get at them eyes of yourn."

Cristina, forgotten, rose to her feet clutching a heavy dirt-filled pot in both strong hands. She raised it high overhead and brought it crashing down on top of Kiowa's head. Quint hurdled the frozen pond, slapped the pistols from Kiowa's hands as the breed inadvertently bent forward, then locked his hands together and smashed them down on the nape of his neck. Kiowa went down, smashing his face against the flagstones. Quint kicked him behind the ear. Kiowa rolled over sideways striving for one of the pistols. Cristina kicked it spinning across the patio. Quint dragged the breed to his feet. Kiowa had enough strength left to lock his powerful hands in a vise-like grip about Quint's throat. Quint clasped his throat in turn. They struggled and swayed back and forth striving to get a foothold on the slippery flagstones. They each stared into the other's contorted face, ruled by nothing but sheer savage hatred dating back over eight years.

Cristina snatched up the sword. She catfooted about just beyond the two struggling men, waiting her chance for a telling stroke or thrust. But there was no need. At last Quint swung Kiowa off his feet and forced him back. His calves struck the raised rim of the pond. He fell backward with Quint on top of him. His head broke through the ice and Quint forced it beneath the surface. Quint saw nothing but a red mist between him and the dimly contorted face beneath the moonlit water.

"Don Quintin!" Cristina cried. "He's dead! For the love of God! He's dead, I tell you!"

Quint looked up. Slowly the mist cleared. He released his hold and stood up. "Where's the baby?" he asked calmly.

Cristina smiled with relief. "I hid her in one of the *dispensas*," she replied happily. "Such a little thing is not difficult to hide. Come, Don Quintin."

They did not see the smoke seeping from under the bedroom and chapel doors nor hear the subdued roaring of the flames.

The tiny baby was all great dark eyes, swaddled in Navajo blankets, resting comfortably on top of the shelled corn in a bin.

"The one-eyed man found me," Cristina related, "I went with him to lead him away from the baby. I knew I would have to kill him, or the baby might not be found and would die here all alone in the darkness." She looked up at Quint, her dark eyes aswim with tears. "You've seen Doña Guadalupe?"

Quint nodded. "She died, Cristina."

The girl sobbed. *"Maria Santissima!* We lose her, Don Quintin, but Heaven gains an angel."

"You loved her very much."

"Yes! Yes!"

"Who delivered the baby?"

She smiled through her tears. "I did. Is she not beautiful?"

Aye, Quint thought, but at what a terrible price. He turned his head a little. He could hardly bear to look at her.

"Have the Americans retaken Taos?" Cristina asked.

"Yes. And the children are safe."

Quint suddenly turned toward the open door. "Smoke!" He ran back to the patio and to the bedroom door. He pushed it open. Smoke and flames gushed toward him. He jumped back, coughing and shielding his face with his hands. The room was a roaring inferno. He ran to the *dispensa* and snatched up the baby. They fled from the doomed *hacienda*.

They stood in the bright moonlight watching the smoke and flames soaring upward against the moonlit sky, a dense funeral pall for Guadalupe de Vasquez Kershaw—*Lupita. . . .*

"There will be nothing left but blackened ruins by dawn," Luke said quietly.

Quint nodded. "The end of an era."

They rode down the Little Hill of the de Vasquezes; none of them looked back.

★ EPILOGUE ★

OCTOBER, 1847 - PLAINS OF SAN AUGUSTINE

The war was not over, but the fighting had ended. Kershaw's Company of New Mexico Mounted Rifles had been mustered out of their second six months' enlistment. Most of them elected to follow their commanding officer to his new grant of land on the Plains of San Augustine. Those who once had called Rio Brioso their home had not gone back to it. After all, what was there to go back to? Three-quarters of the old de Vasquez grant was now the property of the United States, and a strong military post had already been established there. The remaining quarter, where once Kershaw's Fort had stood, had been taken over by Major Shelby Calhoun and his wife Jean, although the major remained in the service. El Cerrillo de Vasquez had not been rebuilt. The land had been leased out by Don Quintin, the profits to be equally divided among his three younger children, the sturdy twins Francisco and Rafaela, and the tiny, frail Guadalupe.

The old *hacienda* and its guardian *torreon* on the plains had been solidly rebuilt. The outbuildings had been reconstructed and others had been newly built. Cattle, sheep, horses, and mules had been driven to the ranch and herded on the plains and the mountain slopes. There were familiar faces among the people of the ranch—Luke Connors, Black Moccasin and Joshua, the fighting Delawares, Anselmo Campos, of course, home again to the land he loved, and many others, tough fighting men of the Rio Brioso and the Mora. Cristina was there, sturdy, efficient, and always smiling. She had become a foster mother to the children despite her years. She loved the place.

It was Cristina who christened the place one moonlit night, when the moon was like a great Japanese lantern in the fall sky. Quint had asked her opinion. She thought for a while, and then turned to look up into Quint's scarred face. "*Querencia,*" she murmured at last.

Querencia—a place for which one has affection, longing; a favorite spot.

So it would be.